IMPOSSIBLE THINGS

In "Even the Queen," liberated women try to come to terms with *the* women's issue.

Political correctness and religious vigilance run amok on campus in "Ado."

In "Time-Out," an incredible experiment turns a small town upside down.

An illiterate woman uncovers the ultimate Shakespeare conspiracy in "Winter's Tale."

In "In the Late Cretaceous," it becomes clear what killed the academic dinosaurs of a university paleontology department: relevance.

Hollywood becomes the proving ground for the theories of quantum physics in "At the Rialto."

IMPOSSIBLE THINGS

Connie Willis

BANTAM BOOKS
NEW YORK LONDON TORONTO AUCKLAND SYDNEY

IMPOSSIBLE THINGS
A Bantam Spectra Book / January 1994
PUBLISHING HISTORY
"The Last of the Winnebagos" first appeared in *Asimov's Science Fiction* © 1988.
"Even the Queen" first appeared in *Asimov's Science Fiction* © 1992.
"Schwarzschild Radius" first appeared in *The Universe*, ed. by Byron Preiss, Bantam Books, © 1987.
"Ado" first appeared in *Asimov's Science Fiction* © 1988.
"Spice Pogrom" first appeared in *Asimov's Science Fiction* © 1986.
"Winter's Tale" first appeared in *Asimov's Science Fiction* © 1988.
"Chance" first appeared in *Asimov's Science Fiction* © 1986.
"In the Late Cretaceous" first appeared in *Asimov's Science Fiction* © 1991.
"Time Out" first appeared in *Asimov's Science Fiction* © 1989.
"Jack" first appeared in *Asimov's Science Fiction* © 1991.
"At the Rialto" first appeared in *Omni* © 1989.

ISBN 0-553-56436-6
Published simultaneously in the United States and Canada

Bantam Books are published by Bantam Books, a division of Bantam Doubleday Dell Publishing Group, Inc. Its trademark, consisting of the words "Bantam Books" and the portrayal of a rooster, is Registered in U.S. Patent and Trademark Office and in other countries. Marca Registrada. Bantam Books, 1540 Broadway, New York, New York 10036.

PRINTED IN THE UNITED STATES OF AMERICA
RAD 0 9 8 7 6 5 4 3 2 1

Dedicated with love and gratitude
to Mrs. Jones
and Lenora Mattingly Weber

Contents

Foreword

by Gardner Dozois
Editor, *Asimov's Science Fiction Magazine*

Connie Willis's first published story, "The Secret of Santa Titicaca," was ferreted out of a magazine slush pile by an eager, bright-eyed young slush reader named Gardner Dozois, and was published in the winter 1970 issue of *Worlds of Fantasy* magazine. Although the story embarrasses Connie tremendously (I doubt you'll ever see it in one of her collections), and indeed shows only a few flashes of her later wit and style, it is a decent enough light fantasy, unexceptional but solid novice work, nothing to be ashamed of, and certainly much better than, say, my first published story. As it turns out, though, I did Connie no favor by fishing her story out of the slush pile, since its appearance in 1970 disqualified her for consideration for the John W. Campbell Award for Best New Writer later in the decade when she began making a stir with more mature work, and in fact may well have cost her the award, for which she was a heavy favorite. So it goes. We never know all the consequences of our actions, and the intentions behind them sometimes matter little—a very Connie Willis–like moral.

Ever since then, however, I've felt a proprietary interest in Connie's career and have kept a careful eye on it.

It's been quite a career to watch, too.

"The Secret of Santa Titicaca" sank out of public consciousness without arousing a single ripple (something for which Connie was probably grateful later on), and Connie was subsequently not heard of again until the late seventies, when she started attracting attention with a number of striking and unusual stories in the now defunct magazine *Galileo*—one of those stories, "Daisy, in the Sun," marked her first appearance on major award ballots, and was her first story to be selected for a Best of the Year anthology; it was far from her last such story to have such honors bestowed upon it, however.

Connie first attracted really serious attention with her first major story, "Fire Watch," which won both the Hugo Award and the Nebula Award in 1982. Her story "A Letter from the Clearys" also won a Nebula Award in 1982, and suddenly a lot of other people were watching Connie's career as well. They were going to have a lot to look at.

In the eighties Connie became one of the mainstays of *Isaac Asimov's Science Fiction Magazine* and also appeared regularly in markets such as *Omni, The Magazine of Fantasy and Science Fiction, The Twilight Zone Magazine, Whispers,* and elsewhere. She was becoming one of the most prolific and popular short-story writers of the day. Her first collection, *Fire Watch*, appeared in 1985. She published two entertaining but relatively minor collaborative novels with Cynthia Felice, *Water Witch* and *Light Raid*, and then, in 1987, published an outstanding first solo novel, the quietly moving *Lincoln's Dreams*, which I regard as one of the best novels of the decade. She again won both the Hugo and the Nebula awards in 1989 for her novella "The Last of the Winnebagos," and won another Nebula Award in 1990 for her story "At the Rialto." Then, in 1992, she published a major new solo novel, *Doomsday Book*, one of the most successful and critically acclaimed novels of the year, and a good indication that Connie will probably be as prominent in the decade of the nineties as she was in the decade just past.

Which brings us to the book you hold in your hands at this moment, Connie Willis's second collection of short fiction—Connie Willis's long-overdue second collection of short fiction, one might even fairly say, considering that she may well have been the most consistently honored short-story writer of the eighties, and certainly one of the most influential.

It might have been less long in coming if Connie had bothered to learn the art of perpetual hype and constant self-promotion mastered by several of her peers—but that's not Connie's style. Not that she couldn't master it if she wanted to; very little is beyond her.

Because she wears Peter Pan collars, and looks relentlessly cheerful and normal, and talks openly about going to Tupperware parties and choir practice, and has a deadpan and ferociously sardonic sense of humor, and is after all a suburban housewife and mother, people tend to underestimate Connie. This is a serious mistake. Connie is as tough-minded and smart as anyone in the business. One is tempted to trot out an old cliché and say that Connie has a mind like a steel trap—except that in Connie's case it would be some much rarer and more subtle device, something with mirrors and lasers perhaps, that would somehow give the mice such a good laugh that they'd never even notice that their throats were being cut.

Connie's work is like that, too. Deceptive and deadly, and ruthlessly effective.

It also tends to be underestimated, especially by bored sophisticates. I have heard Connie's work dismissed as "sentimental," but that's a dangerously superficial reading. Connie is not afraid of honest emotion, and certainly there's a good deal of it in her work—but it is never all that is going on there, just as even the fastest and funniest of her comic stories (and Connie at her best may be one of the funniest modern writers since Thurber, in any genre) are never just funny. One is always ill-advised to take one of Connie's stories at face value. No matter how quiet and simple they appear, there is often a delayed kick to them, a hidden edge; even the ostensibly most "sentimental" of her stories have that hidden edge to them—like a paper cut, you may not feel the wound when you receive it, you may finish the story and think you've been untouched, but then you move and your hand falls off. Or your arm. Or your head.

Thus a story like "Ado" is one of the funniest stories I've ever read, one of the few ever to make me laugh out loud—but it is also a dead-on-target and lethally accurate warning about the dangers of censorship and well-meaning Political Correctness, a classic If-This-Goes-On cautionary tale that seems more likely every day to come true, and which sticks in the mind long after it's read (it was also one of Isaac Asimov's favorite stories of all the stories published in the magazine that bears his name). Thus "Even the Queen" is as bright and fast and clever as the best of the old-fashioned screwball comedies, such as *Bringing up Baby*, that Connie loves—but, by God, it also contains an ingenious and totally valid science-fictional idea, worked out with uncompromising rigor, the implications of which would change human society forever. Thus "The Last of the Winnebagos," which I've heard self-consciously Cool People sneer at for being too sentimental ("Everybody mopes around because there aren't any dogs left, for Gawd's sake! Who cares!"), contains a relentlessly grim and decidedly unsentimental message that we would do well to listen to before it's too late (if it isn't already), and in fact is as unsettling or more so than many a well-known apocalyptic story that features more dramatic and wider-screen catastrophes. Thus "Chance" is ostensibly a simple and simply told story of a housewife who becomes dissatisfied with her housewifely life, the stuff of a million soap operas and sitcoms—and yet, in Connie's hands, it is as powerful and profoundly tragic a story as I know, a story that I think will eventually come to be recognized as one of the best pieces of short fiction to appear in any genre during the decade of the eighties.

Nor are even the "simplest" of Connie's stories ever as "simple" as they appear. Connie almost never uses the stylistic tricks or nonlinear story lines or pretentiously opaque language that is often taken as the hallmark of High Art. Line by line, her work is clear and vivid and supple. Connie's art is more devious than that, and the work she puts in to achieve the effects she wants is buried well under the surface; like Fred Astaire, who rehearsed relentlessly to make his performances look effortless and elegant, Connie somehow makes it all look easy, as natural and "simple" as someone talking to you over a casual cup of coffee. Look closer, though, and you'll realize that most of Connie's plot lines are far from "simple"—in fact, Connie is a master of plotting, perhaps the best in science fiction today. Some of her stories, especially the baroque comic extravaganzas such as "Spice Pogrom," "Blued Moon," and "At the Rialto," are as intricate and complexly intermeshing of plot as one of those Victorian designs for perpetual-motion machines that feature a sequence of weights endlessly tumbling over one another. And yet, somehow the pieces all tumble into place at the end, no matter how recomplicatedly they whirl, in what rococo patterns.

I think that part of the reason why they work is that Connie's stories are always peopled with real human beings, no matter where or when they take place, recognizably real people whom we immediately believe in and accept—and this is true whether she is writing about the courtiers and peasants of Shakespeare's day in "Winter's Tale" or the embattled civil-defense workers of World War II London in "Jack" or the ordinary small-town Americans of "Time Out" and "In the Late Cretaceous."

In one of her story introductions here, Connie says that Shakespeare wrote about Human Issues, as opposed to narrow sectarian concerns: "fear and ambition and guilt and regret and love—the issues that trouble and delight all of us." Connie writes about those Human Issues too, as you will see—and writes about them well enough to make this book, the one you're holding in your hands right now, very probably the best short-story collection of the year, and certainly one of the best of the last two decades.

So now turn the page, and enjoy. . . .

—Gardner Dozois

Alice laughed. "There's no use trying," she said: "One *can't* believe impossible things."

"I daresay you haven't had much practice," said the Queen. "When I was your age, I always did it for half-an-hour a day. Why, sometimes I've believed as many as six impossible things before breakfast."

—Lewis Carroll,
Through the Looking Glass

Nothing can save us that is possible.

—*W. H. Auden,*
For the Time Being

LATELY I HAVE BEEN THINKING A LOT ABOUT THE end of the world. Science fiction is full of disasters that destroy the World As We Know It by blowing it up or turning it into a wasteland of one kind or another. Or by having Martians or viruses or asteroids kill everyone except for a handful of survivors.

Oddly, though, the stories almost never address the effect the end of the world would have on those survivors. They're always too busy looking for a can opener, or building a portable generator, or fending off mutants or walking plants or their fellow survivors to think about what they've lost.

There are exceptions. Nevil Shute's On the Beach *seems to me to be less about fallout than about sorrow, and J. G. Ballard's "The Drowned Giant" is an essay in wonder and regret. But on the whole, the end of the world in science fiction is more* The Adventures of Robinson Crusoe *than Armageddon, which I suppose is why it's so popular.*

But the end of the world as we know it is never an adventure, and it isn't necessarily catastrophically sudden or cataclysmically large. "Do not wait for the last judgment," Camus says. "It happens every day."

So it does, a piece at a time, and our problem is not so much survival as living through it, a different thing altogether.

The Last of the Winnebagos

On the way out to Tempe I saw a dead jackal in the road. I was in the far left lane of Van Buren, ten lanes away from it, and its long legs were facing away from me, the squarish muzzle flat against the pavement so it looked narrower than it really was, and for a minute I thought it was a dog.

I had not seen an animal in the road like that for fifteen years. They can't get onto the divideds, of course, and most of the multiways are fenced. And people are more careful of their animals.

The jackal was probably somebody's pet. This part of Phoenix was mostly residential, and after all this time, people still think they can turn the nasty, carrion-loving creatures into pets. Which was no reason to have hit it and, worse, left it there. It's a felony to strike an animal and another one to not report it, but whoever had hit it was long gone.

I pulled the Hitori over onto the center shoulder and sat there awhile, staring at the empty multiway. I wondered who had hit it and whether they had stopped to see if it was dead.

Katie had stopped. She had hit the brakes so hard,

she sent the car into a skid that brought it up against the ditch, and jumped out of the Jeep. I was still running toward him, floundering in the snow. We made it to him almost at the same time. I knelt beside him, the camera dangling from my neck, its broken case hanging half-open.

"I hit him," Katie had said. "I hit him with the Jeep."

I looked in the rearview mirror. I couldn't even see over the pile of camera equipment in the backseat with the eisenstadt balanced on top. I got out. I had come nearly a mile, and looking back, I couldn't see the jackal, though I knew now that's what it was.

"McCombe! David! Are you there yet?" Ramirez's voice said from inside the car.

I leaned in. "No," I shouted in the general direction of the phone's mike. "I'm still on the multiway."

"Mother of God, what's taking you so long? The governor's conference is at twelve, and I want you to go out to Scottsdale and do a layout on the closing of Taliessin West. The appointment's for ten. Listen, McCombe, I got the poop on the Amblers for you. They bill themselves as 'One Hundred Percent Authentic,' but they're not. Their RV isn't really a Winnebago, it's an Open Road. It *is* the last RV on the road, though, according to Highway Patrol. A man named Eldridge was touring with one, also *not* a Winnebago, a Shasta, until March, but he lost his license in Oklahoma for using a tanker lane, so this is it. Recreation vehicles are banned in all but four states. Texas has legislation in committee, and Utah has a full-divided bill coming up next month. Arizona will be next, so take lots of pictures, Davey boy. This may be your last chance. And get some of the zoo."

"What about the Amblers?" I said.

"Their name *is* Ambler, believe it or not. I ran a lifeline on them. He was a welder. She was a bank teller. No kids. They've been doing this since eighty-nine when he retired. Nineteen years. David, are you using the eisenstadt?"

We had been through this the last three times I'd been on a shoot. "I'm not *there* yet," I said.

"Well, I want you to use it at the governor's conference. Set it on his desk if you can."

I intended to set it on a desk, all right. One of the desks at the back, and let it get some nice shots of the rear ends of reporters as they reached wildly for a little clear airspace to shoot their pictures in, some of them holding their vidcams in their upstretched arms and aiming them in what they hope is the right direction because they can't see the governor at all, let it get a nice shot of one of the reporter's arms as he knocked it facedown on the desk.

"This one's a new model. It's got a trigger. It's set for faces, full-lengths, and vehicles."

So great. I come home with a hundred-frame cartridge full of passersby and tricycles. How the hell did it know when to click the shutter or which one the governor was in a press conference of eight hundred people, full-length *or* face? It was supposed to have all kinds of fancy light-metrics and computer-composition features, but all it could really do was mindlessly snap whatever passed in front of its idiot lens, just like the highway speed cameras.

It had probably been designed by the same government types who'd put the highway cameras along the road instead of overhead so that all it takes is a little speed to reduce the new side-license plates to a blur, and people go faster than ever. A great camera, the eisenstadt. I could hardly wait to use it.

"Sun-Co's very interested in the eisenstadt," Ramirez said. She didn't say good-bye. She never does. She just stops talking and then starts up again later. I looked back in the direction of the jackal.

The multiway was completely deserted. New cars and singles don't use the undivided multiways much, even during rush hours. Too many of the little cars have been squashed by tankers. Usually there are at least a few obsoletes and renegade semis taking advantage of the Patrol's being on the divideds, but there wasn't anybody at all.

I got back in the car and backed up even with the jackal. I turned off the ignition but didn't get out. I could see the trickle of blood from its mouth from here. A tanker went roaring past out of nowhere, trying to beat the cameras, straddling the three middle lanes and crushing the jackal's rear half to a bloody mush. It was a good thing I hadn't been trying to cross the road. He never would have even seen me.

I started the car and drove to the nearest off-ramp to find a phone. There was one at an old 7-Eleven on McDowell.

"I'm calling to report a dead animal on the road," I told the woman who answered the Society's phone.

"Name and number?"

"It's a jackal," I said. "It's between Thirtieth and Thirty-second on Van Buren. It's in the far right lane."

"Did you render emergency assistance?"

"There was no assistance to be rendered. It was dead."

"Did you move the animal to the side of the road?"

"No."

"Why not?" she said, her tone suddenly sharper, more alert.

Because I thought it was a dog. "I didn't have a shovel," I said, and hung up.

I got out to Tempe by eight-thirty, in spite of the fact that every tanker in the state suddenly decided to take Van Buren. I got pushed out onto the shoulder and drove on that most of the way.

The Winnebago was set up in the fairgrounds between Phoenix and Tempe, next to the old zoo. The flyer had said they would be open from nine to nine, and I had wanted to get most of my pictures before they opened, but it was already a quarter to nine, and even if there were no cars in the dusty parking lot, I was probably too late.

It's a tough job being a photographer. The minute most people see a camera, their real faces close like a shutter in too much light, and all that's left is their camera face, their public face. It's a smiling face, except in the case of Saudi terrorists or senators, but, smiling or not, it shows no real emotion. Actors, politicians, people who have their pictures taken all the time are the worst. The longer the person's been in the public eye, the easier it is for me to get great vidcam footage and the harder it is to get anything approaching a real photograph, and the Amblers had been at this for nearly twenty years. By a quarter to nine they would already have their camera faces on.

I parked down at the foot of the hill next to the clump of ocotillos and yucca where the zoo sign had been, pulled my Nikon longshot out of the mess in the backseat, and took some shots of the sign they'd set up by the multiway: "See a Genuine Winnebago. One Hundred Percent Authentic."

The Genuine Winnebago was parked longways against the stone banks of cacti and palms at the front of the zoo. Ramirez had said it wasn't a real Winnebago, but it had the identifying *W* with its extending stripes running the length of the RV, and it seemed to me to be the right shape, though I hadn't seen one in at least ten years.

I was probably the wrong person for this story. I had never had any great love for RVs, and my first thought when Ramirez called with the assignment was that there are some things that should be extinct, like mosquitoes and lane dividers, and RVs are right at the top of the list. They had been everywhere in the mountains when I'd lived in Colorado, crawling along in the left-hand lane, taking up two lanes even in the days when a lane was fifteen feet wide, with a train of cursing cars behind them.

I'd been behind one on Independence Pass that had stopped cold while a ten-year-old got out to snap pictures of the scenery with an Instamatic, and one of them had tried to take the curve in front of my house and ended up in my ditch, looking like a beached whale. But that was always a bad curve.

An old man in an ironed short-sleeved shirt came out the side door and around to the front end and began washing the Winnebago with a sponge and a bucket. I wondered where he had gotten the water. According to Ramirez's advance work, which she'd sent me over the modem about the Winnebago, it had maybe a fifty-gallon water tank, tops, which is barely enough for drinking water, a shower, and maybe washing a dish or two, and there certainly weren't any hookups here at the zoo, but he was swilling water onto the front bumper and even over the tires as if he had more than enough.

I took a few shots of the RV standing in the huge expanse of parking lot and then hit the longshot to full for a picture of the old man working on the bumper. He had large reddish-brown freckles on his arms and the top of his bald head, and he scrubbed away at the bumper with a vengeance. After a minute he stopped and stepped back, and then called to his wife. He looked worried, or maybe just crabby. I was too far away to tell if he had snapped out her name impatiently or simply called her to come and look, and I couldn't see his face. She opened the metal side door, with its narrow louvered window, and stepped down onto the metal step.

The old man asked her something, and she, still standing on the step, looked out toward the multiway and shook her head, and then came around to the front, wiping her hands on a dishtowel, and they both stood there looking at his handiwork.

They were One Hundred Percent Authentic, even if the Winnebago wasn't, down to her flowered blouse and polyester slacks, probably also one hundred percent, and the cross-stitched rooster on the dishtowel. She had on brown leather slip-ons like I remembered my grandmother wearing, and I was willing to bet she had set her thinning white hair on bobby pins. Their bio said they were in their eighties, but I would have put them in their nineties, although I wondered if they were too perfect and therefore fake, like the Winnebago. But she went on wiping her hands on the dishtowel the way my grandmother had when she was upset, even though I couldn't see if her face was showing any emotion, and that action at least was authentic.

She apparently told him the bumper looked fine because he dropped the dripping sponge into the bucket and went around behind the Winnebago. She went back inside, shutting the metal door behind her even though it had to be already at least 110 out, and they hadn't even bothered to park under what scanty shade the palms provided.

I put the longshot back in the car. The old man came around the front with a big plywood sign. He propped it against the vehicle's side. "The Last of the Winnebagos," the sign read in somebody's idea of what Indian writing should look like. "See a vanishing breed. Admission—Adults—$8.00, Children under twelve—$5.00. Open 9 A.M. to Sunset." He strung up a row of red and yellow flags and then picked up the bucket and started toward the door, but halfway there he stopped and took a few steps down the parking lot to where I thought he probably had a good view of the road, and then went back, walking like an old man, and took another swipe at the bumper with the sponge.

"Are you done with the RV yet, McCombe?" Ramirez said on the car phone.

I slung the camera into the back. "I just got here. Every tanker in Arizona was on Van Buren this morning. Why the hell don't you have me do a piece on abuses of the multiway system by water-haulers?"

"Because I want you to get to Tempe alive. The governor's press conference has been moved to one, so you're okay. Have you used the eisenstadt yet?"

"I told you, I just got here. I haven't even turned the damned thing on."

"You don't turn it on. It self-activates when you set it bottom down on a level surface."

Great. It had probably already shot its hundred-frame cartridge on the way here.

"Well, if you don't use it on the Winnebago, make sure you use it at the governor's conference," she said. "By the way, have you thought any more about moving to investigative?"

That was why Sun-Co was really so interested in the eisenstadt. It had been easier to send a photographer who could write stories than it had to send a photographer and a reporter, especially in the little one-seater Hitoris they were ordering now, which was how I got to be a photojournalist. And since that had worked out so well, why send either? Send an eisenstadt and a DAT deck and you won't need an Hitori and way-mile credits to get them there. You can send them through the mail. They can sit unnoticed on the old governor's desk, and after a while somebody in a one-seater who wouldn't have to be either a photographer *or* a reporter can sneak in to retrieve them and a dozen others.

"No," I said, glancing back up the hill. The old man gave one last swipe to the front bumper and then walked over to one of the zoo's old stone-edged planters and dumped the bucket in on a tangle of prickly pear, which would probably think it was a spring shower and bloom before I made it up the hill. "Look, if I'm going to get any pictures before the touristas arrive, I'd better go."

"I wish you'd think about it. And use the eisenstadt this time. You'll like it once you try it. Even *you'll* forget it's a camera."

"I'll bet," I said. I looked back down the multiway.

Nobody at all was coming now. Maybe that was what all the Amblers' anxiety was about—I should have asked Ramirez what their average daily attendance was and what sort of people used up credits to come this far out and see an old beat-up RV. The curve into Tempe alone was 3.2 miles. Maybe nobody came at all. If that was the case, I might have a chance of getting some decent pictures. I got in the Hitori and drove up the steep drive.

"Howdy," the old man said, all smiles, holding out his reddish-brown freckled hand to shake mine. "Name's Jake Ambler. And this here's Winnie," he said, patting the metal side of the RV. "Last of the Winnebagos. Is there just the one of you?"

"David McCombe," I said, holding out my press pass. "I'm a photographer. Sun-Co. Phoenix *Sun*, Tempe-Mesa *Tribune*, Glendale *Star*, and affiliated stations. I was wondering if I could take some pictures of your vehicle?" I touched my pocket and turned the taper on.

"You bet. We've always cooperated with the media, Mrs. Ambler and me. I was just cleaning old Winnie up," he said. "She got pretty dusty on the way down from Globe." He didn't make any attempt to tell his wife I was there, even though she could hardly avoid hearing us, and she didn't open the metal door again. "We been on the road now with Winnie for almost twenty years. Bought her in 1992 in Forest City, Iowa, where they were made. The wife didn't want to buy her, didn't know if she'd like traveling, but now she's the one wouldn't part with it."

He was well into his spiel now, an open, friendly, I-have-nothing-to-hide expression on his face that hid everything. There was no point in taking any stills, so I got out the vidcam and shot the TV footage while he led me around the RV.

"This up here," he said, standing with one foot on the flimsy metal ladder and patting the metal bar around the top, "is the luggage rack, and this is the holding tank. It'll hold thirty gallons and has an automatic electric pump that hooks up to any waste hookup. Empties in five minutes, and you don't even get your hands dirty." He held up his fat pink hands palms forward as if to show me. "Water tank," he said, slapping a silver metal tank next to it. "Holds forty gallons, which is plenty for just the two of us. Interior space is a hundred fifty cubic feet with six feet four of headroom. That's plenty even for a tall guy like yourself."

He gave me the whole tour. His manner was easy, just short of slap-on-the-back hearty, but he looked relieved when an ancient VW bug came chugging catty-cornered up through the parking lot. He must have thought they wouldn't have any customers either.

A family piled out, Japanese tourists, a woman with short black hair, a man in shorts, two kids. One of the kids had a ferret on a leash.

"I'll just look around while you tend to the paying customers," I told him.

I locked the vidcam in the car, took the longshot, and went up toward the zoo. I took a wide-angle of the zoo sign for Ramirez. I could see it now—she'd run a caption like, "The old zoo stands empty today. No sound of lion's roar, of elephant's trumpeting, of children's laughter, can be heard here. The old Phoenix Zoo, last of its kind—while just outside its gates stands yet another last of its kind. Story on page 10." Maybe it would be a good idea to let the eisenstadts and the computers take over.

I went inside. I hadn't been out here in years. In the late eighties there had been a big flap over zoo policy. I had taken the pictures, but I hadn't covered the story since there were still such things as reporters back then. I had photographed the cages in question and the new zoo director, who had caused all the flap by stopping the zoo's renovation project cold and giving the money to a wildlife protection group.

"I refuse to spend money on cages when in a few years we'll have nothing to put in them. The timber wolf, the California condor, the grizzly bear, are in imminent danger of becoming extinct, and it's our responsibility to save them, not make a comfortable prison for the last survivors."

The Society had called him an alarmist, which just goes to show you how much things can change. Well, he was an alarmist, wasn't he? The grizzly bear isn't extinct in the wild—it's Colorado's biggest tourist draw, and there are so many whooping cranes Texas is talking about limited hunting.

In all the uproar, the zoo had ceased to exist, and the animals all went to an even more comfortable prison in Sun City—sixteen acres of savanna land for the zebras and lions, and snow manufactured daily for the polar bears.

They hadn't really been cages, in spite of what the zoo director said. The old capybara enclosure, which was the first thing inside the gate, was a nice little meadow with a low stone wall around it. A family of prairie dogs had taken up residence in the middle of it.

I went back to the gate and looked down at the Winnebago. The family circled the Winnebago, the man bending down to look underneath the body. One of the kids was hanging off the ladder at the back of the RV. The ferret was nosing around the front wheel Jake Ambler had so carefully scrubbed down, looking like it was about ready to lift its leg, if ferrets do that. The kid yanked on its leash and then picked it up in his arms. The mother said something to him. Her nose was sunburned.

Katie's nose had been sunburned. She had had that white cream on it that skiers used to use. She was wearing a parka and jeans and bulky pink-and-white moonboots that she couldn't run in, but she still made it to Aberfan before I did. I pushed past her and knelt over him.

"I hit him," she said bewilderedly. "I hit a dog."

"Get back in the jeep, damn it!" I shouted at her. I

stripped off my sweater and tried to wrap him in it. "We've got to get him to the vet."

"Is he dead?" Katie said, her face as pale as the cream on her nose.

"No!" I had shouted. "No, he isn't dead."

The mother turned and looked up toward the zoo, her hand shading her face. She caught sight of the camera, dropped her hand, and smiled, a toothy, impossible smile. People in the public eye are the worst, but even people having a snapshot taken close down somehow, and it isn't just the phony smile. It's as if that old superstition is true, and cameras do really steal the soul.

I pretended to take her picture and then lowered the camera. The zoo director had put up a row of tombstone-shaped signs in front of the gate, one for each endangered species. They were covered with plastic, which hadn't helped much. I wiped the streaky dust off the one in front of me. "Canis latrans," it said, with two green stars after it. "Coyote. North American wild dog. Due to large-scale poisoning by ranchers, who saw it as a threat to cattle and sheep, the coyote is nearly extinct in the wild." Underneath there was a photograph of a ragged coyote sitting on its haunches and an explanation of the stars. Blue—endangered species. Yellow—endangered habitat. Red—extinct in the wild.

After Misha died, I had come out here to photograph the dingo and the coyotes and the wolves, but they were already in the process of moving the zoo, so I couldn't get any pictures, and it probably wouldn't have done any good. The coyote in the picture had faded to a greenish-yellow, and its yellow eyes were almost white, but it stared out of the picture looking as hearty and unconcerned as Jake Ambler, wearing its camera face.

The mother had gone back to the bug and was herding the kids inside. Mr. Ambler walked the father back to the car, shaking his shining bald head, and the man talked some more, leaning on the open door, and then got in and drove off. I walked back down.

If he was bothered by the fact that they had only stayed ten minutes and that, as far as I had been able to see, no money had changed hands, it didn't show in his face. He led me around to the side of the RV and pointed to a chipped and faded collection of decals along the painted bar of the *W*. "These here are the states we've been in." He pointed to the one nearest the front. "Every state in the Union, plus Canada and Mexico. Last state we were in was Nevada."

Up this close it was easy to see where he had painted out the name of the original RV and covered it with the bar of red. The paint had the dull look of unauthenticity. He had covered up the "Open Road" with a burnt-wood plaque that read "The Amblin' Amblers."

He pointed at a bumper sticker next to the door that said, "I got lucky in Vegas at Caesar's Palace," and had a picture of a naked showgirl. "We couldn't find a decal for Nevada. I don't think they make them anymore. And you know something else you can't find? Steering-wheel covers. You know the kind. That keep the wheel from burning your hands when it gets hot?"

"Do you do all the driving? I asked.

He hesitated before answering, and I wondered if one of them didn't have a license. I'd have to look it up in the lifeline. "Mrs. Ambler spells me sometimes, but I do most of it. Mrs. Ambler reads the map. Damn maps nowadays are so hard to read. Half the time you can't tell what kind of road it is. They don't make them like they used to."

We talked for a while more about all the things you couldn't find a decent one of anymore and the sad state things had gotten in generally, and then I announced I wanted to talk to Mrs. Ambler, got the vidcam and the eisenstadt out of the car, and went inside the Winnebago.

She still had the dishtowel in her hand, even though there couldn't possibly be space for that many dishes in the tiny RV. The inside was even smaller than I had thought it would be, low enough that I had to duck and so narrow I had to hold the Nikon close to my body to keep from hitting the lens on the passenger seat. It felt like an oven inside, and it was only nine o'clock in the morning.

I set the eisenstadt down on the kitchen counter, making sure its concealed lens was facing out. If it would work anywhere, it would be here. There was basically nowhere for Mrs. Ambler to go that she could get out of range. There was nowhere I could go either, and sorry, Ramirez, there are just some things a live photographer can do better than a preprogrammed one, like stay out of the picture.

"This is the galley," Mrs. Ambler said, folding her dishtowel and hanging it from a plastic ring on the cupboard below the sink with the cross-stitch design showing. It wasn't a rooster after all. It was a poodle wearing a sunbonnet and carrying a basket. "Shop on Wednesday," the motto underneath said.

"As you can see, we have a double sink with a hand-pump faucet. The refrigerator is LP-electric and holds four cubic feet. Back here is the dinette area. The table folds up into the rear wall, and we have our bed. And this is our bathroom."

She was as bad as her husband. "How long have you had the Winnebago?" I said to stop the spiel. Sometimes, if you can get people talking about something besides what they intended to talk about, you can disarm them into something like a natural expression.

"Nineteen years," she said, lifting up the lid of the chemical toilet. "We bought it in 1992. I didn't want to buy it—I didn't like the idea of selling our house and going gallivanting off like a couple of hippies, but Jake went ahead and bought it, and now I wouldn't trade it for anything. The shower operates on a forty-gallon pressurized water system." She stood back so I could get a picture of the shower stall, so narrow you wouldn't have to worry about dropping the soap. I dutifully took some vidcam footage.

"You live here full-time then?" I said, trying not to let my voice convey how impossible that prospect sounded. Ramirez had said they were from Minnesota. I had assumed they had a house there and only went on the road for part of the year.

"Jake says the great outdoors is our home," she said. I gave up trying to get a picture of her and snapped a few high-quality detail stills for the papers: the "Pilot" sign taped on the dashboard in front of the driver's seat, the crocheted granny-square afghan on the uncomfortable-looking couch, a row of salt and pepper shakers in the back windows—Indian children, black Scottie dogs, ears of corn.

"Sometimes we live on the open prairies and sometimes on the seashore," she said. She went over to the sink and hand-pumped a scant two cups of water into a little pan and set it on the two-burner stove. She took down two turquoise Melmac cups and flowered saucers and a jar of freeze-dried and spooned a little into the cups. "Last year we were in the Colorado Rockies. We can have a house on a lake or in the desert, and when we get tired of it, we just move on. Oh, my, the things we've seen."

I didn't believe her. Colorado had been one of the first states to ban recreational vehicles, even before the gas crunch and the multiways. It had banned them on the passes first and then shut them out of the national forests, and by the time I left, they weren't even allowed on the interstates.

Ramirez had said RVs were banned outright in forty-seven states. New Mexico was one, Utah had heavy restricks, and daytime travel was forbidden in all the western states. Whatever they'd seen, and it sure wasn't Colorado, they had seen it in the dark or on some unpatrolled multiway, going like sixty to outrun the cameras.

Not exactly the footloose and fancy-free life they tried to paint.

The water boiled. Mrs. Ambler poured it into the cups, spilling a little on the turquoise saucers. She blotted it up with the dishtowel. "We came down here because of the snow. They get winter so early in Colorado."

"I know," I said. It had snowed two feet, and it was only the middle of September. Nobody even had their snow tires on. The aspens hadn't turned yet, and some of the branches broke under the weight of the snow. Katie's nose was still sunburned from the summer.

"Where did you come from just now?" I asked her.

"Globe," she said, and opened the door to yell to her husband. "Jake! Coffee!" She carried the cups to the table-that-converts-into-a-bed. "It has leaves that you can put in it so it seats six," she said.

I sat down at the table so she was on the side where the eisenstadt could catch her. The sun was coming in through the cranked-open back windows, already hot. Mrs. Ambler got onto her knees on the plaid cushions and let down a woven cloth shade, carefully, so it wouldn't knock the salt and pepper shakers off.

There were some snapshots stuck up between the ceramic ears of corn. I picked one up. It was a square Polaroid from the days when you had to peel off the print and glue it to a stiff card: The two of them, looking exactly the way they did now, with that friendly, impenetrable camera smile, were standing in front of a blur of orange rock—the Grand Canyon? Zion? Monument Valley? Polaroid had always chosen color over definition. Mrs. Ambler was holding a little blur in her arms that could have been a cat but wasn't. It was a dog.

"That's Jake and me at Devil's Tower," she said, taking the picture away from me. "And Taco. You can't tell from this picture, but she was the cutest little thing. A chihuahua." She handed it back to me and rummaged behind the salt and pepper shakers. "Sweetest little dog you ever saw. This will give you a better idea."

The picture she handed me was considerably better, a matte print done with a decent camera. Mrs. Ambler was holding the chihuahua in this one, too, standing in front of the Winnebago.

"She used to sit on the arm of Jake's chair while he drove, and when we came to a red light she'd look at it, and when it turned green she'd bark to tell him to go. She was the smartest little thing."

I looked at the dog's flaring, pointed ears, its bulging eyes and rat's snout. The dogs never come through. I took dozens of pictures, there at the end, and they might as well have been calendar shots. Nothing of the real dog at all. I decided it was the lack of muscles in their faces—they could not smile, in spite of what their owners claimed. It is the muscles in the face that make people leap across the years in pictures. The expressions on dogs' faces were what breeding had fastened on them—the gloomy bloodhound, the alert collie, the rakish mutt—and anything else was wishful thinking on the part of the doting master, who would also swear that a color-blind chihuahua with a brain pan the size of a Mexican jumping bean could tell when the light changed.

My theory of the facial muscles doesn't really hold water, of course. Cats can't smile either, and they come through. Smugness, slyness, disdain—all of those expressions come through beautifully, and they don't have any muscles in their faces either, so maybe it's love that you can't capture in a picture because love was the only expression dogs were capable of.

I was still looking at the picture. "She is a cute little thing," I said, and handed it back to her. "She wasn't very big, was she?"

"I could carry Taco in my jacket pocket. We didn't name her Taco. We got her from a man in California that named her that," she said, as if she could see herself that the dog didn't come through in the picture. As if, had she named the dog herself, it would have been different. Then the name would have been a more real name, and Taco would have, by default, become more real as well. As if a name could convey what the picture didn't—all the things the little dog did and was and meant to her.

Names don't do it either, of course. I had named Aberfan myself. The vet's assistant, when he heard it, typed it in as Abraham.

"Age?" he had said calmly, even though he had no business typing all this into a computer—he should have been in the operating room with the vet.

"You've got that in there, damn it," I shouted.

He looked calmly puzzled. "I don't know any Abraham. . . ."

"Aberfan, damn it. Aberfan!"

"Here it is," the assistant said imperturbably.

Katie, standing across the desk, looked up from the screen. "He had the newparvo and lived through it?" she said bleakly.

"He had the newparvo and lived through it," I said, "until you came along."

"I had an Australian shepherd," I told Mrs. Ambler.

Jake came into the Winnebago, carrying the plastic bucket. "Well, it's about time," Mrs. Ambler said. "Your coffee's getting cold."

"I was just going to finish washing off Winnie," he said. He wedged the bucket into the tiny sink and began pumping vigorously with the heel of his hand. "She got mighty dusty coming down through all that sand."

"I was telling Mr. McCombe here about Taco," she said, getting up and taking him the cup and saucer. "Here, drink your coffee before it gets cold."

"I'll be in in a minute," he said. He stopped pumping and tugged the bucket out of the sink.

"Mr. McCombe had a dog," she said, still holding

the cup out to him. "He had an Australian shepherd. I was telling him about Taco."

"He's not interested in that," Jake said. They exchanged one of those warning looks that married couples are so good at. "Tell him about the Winnebago. That's what he's here for."

Jake went back outside. I screwed the longshot's lens cap on and put the vidcam back in its case. She took the little pan off the miniature stove and poured the coffee back into it. "I think I've got all the pictures I need," I said to her back.

She didn't turn around. "He never liked Taco. He wouldn't even let her sleep on the bed with us. Said it made his legs cramp. A little dog like that that didn't weigh anything."

I took the longshot's lens cap back off.

"You know what we were doing the day she died? We were out shopping. I didn't want to leave her alone, but Jake said she'd be fine. It was ninety degrees that day, and he just kept on going from store to store, and when we got back she was dead." She set the pan on the stove and turned on the burner. "The vet said it was the newparvo, but it wasn't. She died from the heat, poor little thing."

I set the Nikon down gently on the Formica table and estimated the settings.

"When did Taco die?" I asked her, to make her turn around.

"Ninety-six," she said. She turned back to me, and I let my hand come down on the button in an almost soundless click, but her public face was still in place: apologetic now, smiling, a little sheepish. "My, that was a long time ago."

I stood up and collected my cameras. "I think I've got all the pictures I need," I said again. "If I don't, I'll come back out."

"Don't forget your briefcase," she said, handing me the eisenstadt. "Did your dog die of the newparvo, too?"

"He died fifteen years ago," I said. "In ninety-eight."

She nodded understandingly. "The third wave," she said.

I went outside. Jake was standing behind the Winnebago, under the back window, holding the bucket. He shifted it to his left hand and held out his right hand to me. "You get all the pictures you needed?" he asked.

"Yeah," I said. "I think your wife showed me about everything." I shook his hand.

"You come on back out if you need any more pictures," he said, and sounded, if possible, even more jovial, openhanded, friendly than he had before. "Mrs. Ambler and me, we always cooperate with the media."

"Your wife was telling me about your chihuahua," I said, more to see the effect on him than anything else.

"Yeah, the wife still misses that little dog after all these years," he said, and he looked the way she had, mildly apologetic, still smiling. "It died of the newparvo. I told her she ought to get it vaccinated, but she kept putting it off." He shook his head. "Of course, it wasn't really her fault. You know whose fault the newparvo really was, don't you?"

Yeah, I knew. It was the communists' fault, and it didn't matter that all their dogs had died, too, because he would say their chemical warfare had gotten out of hand or that everybody knows commies hate dogs. Or maybe it was the fault of the Japanese, though I doubted that. He was, after all, in a tourist business. Or the Democrats or the atheists or all of them put together, and even that was One Hundred Percent Authentic—portrait of the kind of man who drives a Winnebago—but I didn't want to hear it. I walked over to the Hitori and slung the eisenstadt in the back.

"You know who really killed your dog, don't you?" he called after me.

"Yes," I said, and got in the car.

I went home, fighting my way through a fleet of red-painted water tankers who weren't even bothering to try to outrun the cameras and thinking about Taco. My grandmother had had a chihuahua. Perdita. Meanest dog that ever lived. Used to lurk behind the door waiting to take Labrador-sized chunks out of my leg. And my grandmother's. It developed some lingering chihauhua ailment that made it incontinent and even more ill-tempered, if that was possible.

Toward the end, it wouldn't even let my grandmother near it, but she refused to have it put to sleep and was unfailingly kind to it, even though I never saw any indication that the dog felt anything but unrelieved spite toward her. If the newparvo hadn't come along, it probably would still have been around making her life miserable.

I wondered what Taco, the wonder dog, able to distinguish red and green at a single intersection, had really been like, and if it had died of heat prostration. And what it had been like for the Amblers, living all that time in 150 cubic feet together and blaming each other for their own guilt.

I called Ramirez as soon as I got home, breaking in without announcing myself, the way she always did. "I need a lifeline," I said.

"I'm glad you called," she said. "You got a call from the Society. And how's this as a slant for your story? 'The Winnebago and the Winnebagos.' They're an Indian tribe. In Minnesota, I think—why the hell aren't you at the governor's conference?"

"I came home," I said. "What did the Society want?"

"They didn't say. They asked for your schedule. I told them you were with the governor in Tempe. Is this about a story?"

"Yeah."

"Well, you run a proposal past me before you write

it. The last thing the paper needs is to get in trouble with the Society."

"The lifeline's for Katherine Powell." I spelled it.

She spelled it back to me. "Is she connected with the Society story?"

"No."

"Then what is she connected with? I've got to put something on the request-for-info."

"Put down background."

"For the Winnebago story?"

"Yes," I said. "For the Winnebago story. How long will it take?"

"That depends. When do you plan to tell me why you ditched the governor's conference? *And* Taliessin West. Jesus Maria, I'll have to call the *Republic* and see if they'll trade footage. I'm sure they'll be thrilled to have shots of an extinct RV. That is, assuming you got any shots. You did make it out to the zoo, didn't you?"

"Yes. I got vidcam footage, stills, the works. I even used the eisenstadt."

"Mind sending your pictures in while I look up your old flame, or is that too much to ask? I don't know how long this will take. It took me two days to get clearance on the Amblers. Do you want the whole thing—pictures, documentation?"

"No. Just a résumé. And a phone number."

She cut out, still not saying good-bye. If phones still had receivers, Ramirez would be a great one for hanging up on people. I highwired the vidcam footage and the eisenstadts in to the paper and then fed the eisenstadt cartridge into the developer. I was more than a little curious about what kind of pictures it would take, in spite of the fact that it was trying to do me out of a job. At least it used high-res film and not some damn two-hundred-thousand-pixel TV substitute. I didn't believe it could compose, and I doubted if the eisenstadt would be able to do foreground-background either, but it might, under certain circumstances, get a picture I couldn't.

The doorbell rang. I answered the door. A lanky young man in a Hawaiian shirt and baggies was standing on the front step, and there was another man in a Society uniform out in the driveway.

"Mr. McCombe?" he said, extending a hand. "Jim Hunter. Humane Society."

I don't know what I'd expected—that they wouldn't bother to trace the call? That they'd let somebody get away with leaving a dead animal on the road?

"I just wanted to stop by and thank you on behalf of the Society for phoning in that report on the jackal. Can I come in?"

He smiled, an open, friendly, smug smile, as if he expected me to be stupid enough to say, "I don't know what you're talking about," and slam the screen door on his hand.

"Just doing my duty," I said, smiling back at him.

"Well, we really appreciate responsible citizens like you. It makes our job a whole lot easier." He pulled a folded readout from his shirt pocket. "I just need to double-check a couple of things. You're a reporter for Sun-Co, is that right?"

"Photojournalist," I said.

"And the Hitori you were driving belongs to the paper?"

I nodded.

"It has a phone. Why didn't you use it to make the call?"

The uniform was bending over the Hitori.

"I didn't realize it had a phone. The paper just bought the Hitoris. This is only the second time I've had one out."

Since they knew the paper had had phones put in, they also knew what I'd just told them. I wondered where they'd gotten the info. Public phones were supposed to be tap free, and if they'd read the license number off one of the cameras, they wouldn't know who'd had the car unless they'd talked to Ramirez, and if they'd talked to her, she wouldn't have been talking blithely about the last thing she needed being trouble with the Society.

"You didn't know the car had a phone," he said, "so you drove to—" He consulted the readout, somehow giving the impression he was taking notes. I'd have bet there was a taper in the pocket of that shirt. "—the 7-Eleven at McDowell and Fortieth Street, and made the call from there. Why didn't you give the Society rep your name and address?"

"I was in a hurry," I said. "I had two assignments to cover before noon, the second out in Scottsdale."

"Which is why you didn't render assistance to the animal either. Because you were in a hurry."

You bastard, I thought. "No," I said. " I didn't render assistance because there wasn't any assistance to be rendered. The—it was dead."

"And how did you know that, Mr. McCombe?"

"There was blood coming out of its mouth," I said.

I had thought that that was a good sign, that he wasn't bleeding anywhere else. The blood had come out of Aberfan's mouth when he tried to lift his head, just a little trickle, sinking into the hard-packed snow. It had stopped before we even got him into the car. "It's all right, boy," I told him. "We'll be there in a minute."

Katie started the Jeep, killed it, started it again, backed it up to where she could turn around.

Aberfan lay limply across my lap, his tail against the gear shift. "Just lie still, boy," I said. I patted his neck. It was wet, and I raised my hand and looked at the palm, afraid it was blood. It was only water from the melted snow. I dried his neck and the top of his head with the sleeve of my sweater.

"How far is it?" Katie said. She was clutching the steering wheel with both hands and sitting stiffly forward in the seat. The windshield wipers flipped back and forth, trying to keep up with the snow.

"About five miles," I said, and she stepped on the gas pedal and then let up on it again as we began to skid. "On the right side of the highway."

Aberfan raised his head off my lap and looked at me. His gums were gray, and he was panting, but I couldn't see any more blood. He tried to lick my hand. "You'll make it, Aberfan," I said. "You made it before, remember?"

"But you didn't get out of the car and go check, to make sure it was dead?" Hunter said.

"No."

"And you don't have any idea who hit the jackal?" he said, and made it sound like the accusation it was.

"No."

He glanced back at the uniform, who had moved around the car to the other side. "Whew," Hunter said, shaking his Hawaiian collar, "it's like an oven out here. Mind if I come in?" which meant the uniform needed more privacy. Well, then, by all means, give him more privacy. The sooner he sprayed print-fix on the bumper and tires and peeled off the incriminating traces of jackal blood that weren't there and stuck them in the evidence bags he was carrying in the pockets of that uniform, the sooner they'd leave. I opened the screen door wider.

"Oh, this is great," Hunter said, still trying to generate a breeze with his collar. "These old adobe houses stay so cool." He glanced around the room at the developer and the enlarger, the couch, the dry-mounted photographs on the wall. "You don't have any idea who might have hit the jackal?"

"I figure it was a tanker," I said. "What else would be on Van Buren that time of morning?"

I was almost sure it had been a car or a small truck. A tanker would have left the jackal a spot on the pavement. But a tanker would get a license suspension and two weeks of having to run water into Santa Fe instead of Phoenix, and probably not that. Rumor at the paper had it the Society was in the water board's pocket. If it was a car, on the other hand, the Society would take away the car and stick its driver with a prison sentence.

"They're all trying to beat the cameras," I said. "The tanker probably didn't even know it'd hit it."

"What?" he said.

"I said, it had to be a tanker. There isn't anything else on Van Buren during rush hour."

I expected him to say, "Except for you," but he didn't. He wasn't even listening. "Is this your dog?" he said.

He was looking at the photograph of Perdita. "No," I said. "That was my grandmother's dog."

"What is it?"

A nasty little beast. And when it died of the newparvo, my grandmother had cried like a baby. "A chihuahua."

He looked around at the other walls. "Did you take all these pictures of dogs?" His whole manner had changed, taking on a politeness that made me realize just how insolent he had intended to be before. The one on the road wasn't the only jackal around.

"Some of them," I said. He was looking at the photograph next to it. "I didn't take that one."

"I know what this one is," he said, pointing at it. "It's a boxer, right?"

"An English bulldog," I said.

"Oh, right. Weren't those the ones that were exterminated? For being vicious?"

"No," I said.

He moved on to the picture over the developer, like a tourist in a museum. "I bet you didn't take this one either," he said, pointing at the high shoes, the old-fashioned hat on the stout old woman holding the dogs in her arms.

"That's a photograph of Beatrix Potter, the English children's author," I said. "She wrote *Peter Rabbit.*"

He wasn't interested. "What kind of dogs are those?"

"Pekingese."

"It's a great picture of them."

It is, in fact, a terrible picture of them. One of them has wrenched his face away from the camera, and the other sits grimly in her owner's hand, waiting for its chance. Obviously neither of them liked having its picture taken, though you can't tell that from their expressions. They reveal nothing in their little flat-nosed faces, in their black little eyes.

Beatrix Potter, on the other hand, comes through beautifully, in spite of the attempt to smile for the camera and the fact that she must have had to hold on to the Pekes for dear life, or maybe because of that. The fierce, humorous love she felt for her fierce, humorous little dogs is all there in her face. She must never, in spite of *Peter Rabbit* and its attendant fame, have developed a public face. Everything she felt was right there, unprotected, unshuttered. Like Katie.

"Are any of these your dog?" Hunter asked. He was standing looking at the picture of Misha that hung above the couch.

"No." I said.

"How come you don't have any pictures of your dog?" he asked, and I wondered how he knew I had had a dog and what else he knew.

"He didn't like having his picture taken."

He folded up the readout, stuck it in his pocket, and turned around to look at the photo of Perdita again. "He looks like he was a real nice little dog," he said.

The uniform was waiting on the front step, obviously finished with whatever he had done to the car.

"We'll let you know if we find out who's responsible," Hunter said, and they left. On the way out to the street the uniform tried to tell him what he'd found, but

Hunter cut him off. The suspect has a house full of photographs of dogs, therefore he didn't run over a poor facsimile of one on Van Buren this morning. Case closed.

I went back over to the developer and fed the eisenstadt film in. "Positives, one two three order, five seconds," I said, and watched as the pictures came up on the developer's screen. Ramirez had said the eisenstadt automatically turned on whenever it was set upright on a level surface. She was right. It had taken a half-dozen shots on the way out to Tempe. Two shots of the Hitori it must have taken when I set it down to load the car, open door of same with prickly pear in the foreground, a blurred shot of palm trees and buildings with a minuscule, sharp-focused glimpse of the traffic on the expressway. Vehicles and people. There was a great shot of the red tanker that had clipped the jackal and ten or so of the yucca I had parked next to at the foot of the hill.

It had gotten two nice shots of my forearm as I set it down on the kitchen counter of the Winnebago and some beautifully composed still lifes of Melmac with Spoons. Vehicles and people. The rest of the pictures were dead losses: my back, the open bathroom door, Jake's back, and Mrs. Ambler's public face.

Except the last one. She had been standing right in front of the eisenstadt, looking almost directly into the lens. "When I think of that poor thing, all alone," she had said, and by the time she turned around, she had her public face back on, but for a minute there, looking at what she thought was a briefcase and remembering, there she was, the person I had tried all morning to get a picture of.

I took it into the living room and sat down and looked at it awhile.

"So you knew this Katherine Powell in Colorado," Ramirez said, breaking in without preamble, and the highwire slid silently forward and began to print out the lifeline. "I always suspected you of having some deep dark secret in your past. Is she the reason you moved to Phoenix?"

I was watching the highwire advance the paper. Katherine Powell, 4628 Dutchman Drive, Apache Junction. Forty miles away.

"Holy Mother, you were really cradle-robbing. According to my calculations, she was seventeen when you lived there."

Sixteen.

"Are you the owner of the dog?" the vet had asked her, his face slackening into pity when he saw how young she was.

"No." she said. "I'm the one who hit him."

"My God," he said. "How old are you?"

"Sixteen," she said, and her face was wide open. "I just got my license."

"Aren't you even going to tell me what she has to do with this Winnebago thing?" Ramirez said.

"I moved down here to get away from the snow," I said, and cut out without saying good-bye.

The lifeline was still rolling silently forward. Hacker at Hewlett-Packard. Fired in 2008, probably during the unionization. Divorced. Two kids. She had moved to Arizona five years after I did. Management programmer for Toshiba. Arizona driver's license.

I went back to the developer and looked at the picture of Mrs. Ambler. I had said dogs never came through. That wasn't true. Taco wasn't in the blurry snapshots Mrs. Ambler had been so anxious to show me, in the stories she had been so anxious to tell. But she was in this picture, reflected in the pain and love and loss on Mrs. Ambler's face. I could see her plain as day, perched on the arm of the driver's seat, barking impatiently when the light turned green.

I put a new cartridge in the eisenstadt and went out to see Katie.

• • •

I had to take Van Buren—it was almost four o'clock, and the rush hour would have started on the divideds—but the jackal was gone anyway. The Society is efficient. Like Hitler and his Nazis.

"Why don't you have any pictures of your dog?" Hunter had asked. The question could have been based on the assumption that anyone who would fill his living room with photographs of dogs must have had one of his own, but it wasn't. He had known about Aberfan, which meant he'd had access to my lifeline, which meant all kinds of things. My lifeline was privacy coded, so I had to be notified before anybody could get access, except, it appeared, the Society. A reporter I knew at the paper, Dolores Chiwere, had tried to do a story awhile back claiming that the Society had an illegal link to the lifeline banks, but she hadn't been able to come up with enough evidence to convince her editor. I wondered if this counted.

The lifeline would have told them about Aberfan but not about how he died. Killing a dog wasn't a crime in those days, and I hadn't pressed charges against Katie for reckless driving or even called the police.

"I think you should," the vet's assistant had said. "There are less than a hundred dogs left. People can't just go around killing them."

"My God, man, it was snowing and slick," the vet had said angrily, "and she's just a kid."

"She's old enough to have a license," I said, looking at Katie. She was fumbling in her purse for her driver's license. "She's old enough to have been on the roads."

Katie found her license and gave it to me. It was so new it was still shiny. Katherine Powell. She had turned sixteen two weeks ago.

"This won't bring him back," the vet had said, and taken the license out of my hand and given it back to her. "You go on home now."

"I need her name for the records," the vet's assistant had said.

She had stepped forward. "Katie Powell," she had said.

"We'll do the paperwork later," the vet had said firmly.

They never did do the paperwork, though. The next week the third wave hit, and I suppose there hadn't seemed any point.

I slowed down at the zoo entrance and looked up into the parking lot as I went past. The Amblers were doing a booming business. There were at least five cars and twice as many kids clustered around the Winnebago.

"Where the hell are you?" Ramirez said. "And where the hell are your pictures? I talked the *Republic* into a trade, but they insisted on scoop rights. I need your stills now!"

"I'll send them in as soon as I get home," I said. "I'm on a story."

"The hell you are! You're on your way out to see your old girlfriend. Well, not on the paper's credits, you're not."

"Did you get the stuff on the Winnebago Indians?" I asked her.

"Yes. They were in Wisconsin, but they're not anymore. In the mid-seventies there were sixteen hundred of them on the reservation and about forty-five hundred altogether, but by 2000 the number was down to five hundred, and now they don't think there are any left, and nobody knows what happened to them."

I'll tell you what happened to them, I thought. Almost all of them were killed in the first wave, and people blamed the government and the Japanese and the ozone layer, and after the second wave hit, the Society passed all kinds of laws to protect the survivors, but it was too late, they were already below the minimum-survival population limit, and then the third wave polished off the rest of them, and the last of the Winnebagos sat in a cage somewhere, and if I had been there, I would probably have taken his picture.

"I called the Bureau of Indian Affairs," Ramirez said, "and they're supposed to call me back, and you don't give a damn about the Winnebagos. You just wanted to get me off the subject. What's this story you're on?"

I looked around the dashboard for an exclusion button.

"What the hell is going on, David? First you ditch two big stories, now you can't even get your pictures in. Jesus, if something's wrong, you can tell me. I want to help. It has something to do with Colorado, doesn't it?"

I found the exclusion button and cut her off.

Van Buren got crowded as the afternoon rush spilled over off the divideds. Out past the curve, where Van Buren turns into Apache Boulevard, they were putting in new lanes. The cement forms were already up on the eastbound side, and they were building the wooden forms up in two of the six lanes on my side.

The Amblers must have just beaten the workmen, though at the rate the men were working right now, leaning on their shovels in the hot afternoon sun and smoking stew, it had probably taken them six weeks to do this stretch.

Mesa was still open multiway, but as soon as I was through downtown, the construction started again, and this stretch was nearly done—forms up on both sides and most of the cement poured. The Amblers couldn't have come in from Globe on this road. The lanes were barely wide enough for the Hitori, and the tanker lanes were gated. Superstition Mountain is full-divided, and the old highway down from Roosevelt is, too, which meant they hadn't come in from Globe at all. I wondered how they had come in—probably in some tanker lane on a multiway.

"Oh, my, the things we've seen," Mrs. Ambler had

said. I wondered how much they'd been able to see skittering across the dark desert like a couple of kangaroo mice, trying to beat the cameras.

The roadworkers didn't have the new exit signs up yet, and I missed the exit for Apache Junction and had to go halfway to Superior, trapped in my narrow, cement-sided lane, till I hit a change-lanes and could get turned around.

Katie's address was in Superstition Estates, a development pushed up as close to the base of Superstition Mountain as it could get. I thought about what I would say to Katie when I got there. I had said maybe ten sentences altogether to her, most of them shouted directions, in the two hours we had been together. In the Jeep on the way to the vet's I had talked to Aberfan, and after we got there, sitting in the waiting room, we hadn't talked at all.

It occurred to me that I might not recognize her. I didn't really remember what she looked like—only the sunburned nose and that terrible openness, and now, fifteen years later, it seemed unlikely that she would have either of them. The Arizona sun would have taken care of the first, and she had gotten married and divorced, been fired, had who knows what else happen to her in fifteen years to close her face. In which case, there had been no point in my driving all the way out here. But Mrs. Ambler had had an almost impenetrable public face, and you could still catch her off guard. If you got her talking about the dogs. If she didn't know she was being photographed.

Katie's house was an old-style passive solar, with flat black panels on the roof. It looked presentable, but not compulsively neat. There wasn't any grass—tankers won't waste their credits coming this far out, and Apache Junction isn't big enough to match the bribes and incentives of Phoenix or Tempe—but the front yard was laid out with alternating patches of black lava chips and prickly pear. The side yard had a parched-looking palo verde tree, and there was a cat tied to it. A little girl was playing under the tree with toy cars.

I took the eisenstadt out of the back and went up to the front door and rang the bell. At the last moment, when it was too late to change my mind, walk away, because she was already opening the screen door, it occurred to me that she might not recognize me, that I might have to tell her who I was.

Her nose wasn't sunburned, and she had put on the weight a sixteen-year-old puts on to get to be thirty, but otherwise she looked the same as she had that day in front of my house. And her face hadn't completely closed. I could tell, looking at her, that she recognized me and that she had known I was coming. She must have put a notify on her lifeline to have them warn her if I asked her whereabouts. I thought about what that meant.

She opened the screen door a little, the way I had to the Humane Society. "What do you want?" she said.

I had never seen her angry, not even when I turned on her at the vet's. "I wanted to see you," I said.

I had thought I might tell her I had run across her name while I was working on a story and wondered if it was the same person or that I was doing a piece on the last of the passive solars. "I saw a dead jackal on the road this morning," I said.

"And you thought I killed it?" she said. She tried to shut the screen door.

I put out my hand without thinking, to stop her. "No," I said. I took my hand off the door. "No, of course I don't think that. Can I come in? I just want to talk to you."

The little girl had come over, clutching her toy cars to her pink T-shirt, and was standing off to the side, watching curiously.

"Come on inside, Jana," Katie said, and opened the screen door a fraction wider. The little girl scooted through. "Go on in the kitchen," she said. "I'll fix you some Kool-Aid." She looked up at me. "I used to have nightmares about your coming. I'd dream that I'd go to the door and there you'd be."

"It's really hot out here," I said, and knew I sounded like Hunter. "Can I come in?"

She opened the screen door all the way. "I've got to make my daughter something to drink," she said, and led the way into the kitchen, the little girl dancing in front of her.

"What kind of Kool-Aid do you want?" Katie asked her, and she shouted, "Red!"

The kitchen counter faced the stove, refrigerator, and water cooler across a narrow aisle that opened out into an alcove with a table and chairs. I put the eisenstadt down on the table and then sat down myself so she wouldn't suggest moving into another room.

Katie reached a plastic pitcher down from one of the shelves and stuck it under the water tank to fill it. Jana dumped her cars on the counter, clambered up beside them, and began opening the cupboard doors.

"How old's your little girl?" I asked.

Katie got a wooden spoon out of the drawer next to the stove and brought it and the pitcher over to the table. "She's four," she said. "Did you find the Kool-Aid?" she asked the little girl.

"Yes," the little girl said, but it wasn't Kool-Aid. It was a pinkish cube she peeled a plastic wrapping off of. It fizzed and turned a thinnish red when she dropped it into the pitcher. Kool-Aid must have become extinct, too, along with Winnebagos and passive solar. Or else changed beyond recognition. Like the Humane Society.

Katie poured the red stuff into a glass with a cartoon whale on it.

"Is she your only one?" I asked.

"No, I have a little boy," she said, but warily, as if she wasn't sure she wanted to tell me, even though if I'd requested the lifeline, I already had access to all this information. Jana asked if she could have a cookie and then took it and her Kool-Aid back down the hall and outside. I could hear the screen door slam.

Katie put the pitcher in the refrigerator and leaned against the kitchen counter, her arms folded across her chest. "What do you want?"

She was just out of range of the eisenstadt, her face in the shadow of the narrow aisle.

"There was a dead jackal on the road this morning," I said. I kept my voice low so she would lean forward into the light to try and hear me. "It'd been hit by a car, and it was lying funny, at an angle. It looked like a dog. I wanted to talk to somebody who remembered Aberfan, somebody who knew him."

"I didn't know him," she said. "I only killed him, remember? That's why you did this, isn't it, because I killed Aberfan?"

She didn't look at the eisenstadt, hadn't even glanced at it when I set it on the table, but I wondered suddenly if she knew what I was up to. She was still carefully out of range. And what if I said to her, "That's right. That's why I did this, because you killed him, and I didn't have any pictures of him. You owe me. If I can't have a picture of Aberfan, you at least owe me a picture of you remembering him."

Only she didn't remember him, didn't know anything about him except what she had seen on the way to the vet's, Aberfan lying on my lap and looking up at me, already dying. I had had no business coming here, dredging all this up again. No business.

"At first I thought you were going to have me arrested," Katie said, "and then after all the dogs died, I thought you were going to kill me."

The screen door banged. "Forgot my cars," the little girl said, and scooped them into the tail of her T-shirt. Katie tousled her hair as she went past and then folded her arms again.

" 'It wasn't my fault,' I was going to tell you when you came to kill me," she said. " 'It was snowy. He ran right in front of me. I didn't even see him.' I looked up everything I could find about newparvo. Preparing for the defense. How it mutated from parvovirus and from cat distemper before that and then kept on mutating, so they couldn't come up with a vaccine. How even before the third wave they were below the minimum survival population. How it was the fault of the people who owned the last survivors because they wouldn't risk their dogs to breed them. How the scientists didn't come up with a vaccine until only the jackals were left. 'You're wrong,' I was going to tell you. 'It was the puppy-mill owners' fault that all the dogs died. If they hadn't kept their dogs in such unsanitary conditions, it never would have gotten out of control in the first place.' I had my defense all ready. But you'd moved away."

Jana banged in again, carrying the empty whale glass. She had a red smear across the whole lower half of her face. "I need some more," she said, making "some more" into one word. She held the glass in both hands while Katie opened the refrigerator and poured her another glassful.

"Wait a minute, honey," she said. "You've got Kool-Aid all over you," and bent to wipe Jana's face with a paper towel.

Katie hadn't said a word in her defense while we waited at the vet's, not, "It was snowy," or, "He ran right out in front of me," or, "I didn't even see him." She had sat silently beside me, twisting her mittens in her lap, until the vet came out and told me Aberfan was dead, and then she had said, "I didn't know there were any left in Colorado. I thought they were all dead."

And I had turned to her, to a sixteen-year-old not even old enough to know how to shut her face, and said, "Now they all are. Thanks to you."

"That kind of talk isn't necessary," the vet had said warningly.

I had wrenched away from the hand he tried to put on my shoulder. "How does it feel to have killed one of the last dogs in the world?" I shouted at her. "How does it feel to be responsible for the extinction of an entire species?"

The screen door banged again. Katie was looking at me, still holding the reddened paper towel.

"You moved away," she said, "and I thought maybe that meant you'd forgiven me, but it didn't, did it?" She came over to the table and wiped at the red circle the glass had left. "Why did you do it? To punish me? Or did you think that's what I'd been doing the last fifteen years, roaring around the roads murdering animals?"

"What?" I said.

"The Society's already been here."

"The Society?" I said, not understanding.

"Yes," she said, still looking at the red-stained towel. "They said you had reported a dead animal on Van Buren. They wanted to know where I was this morning between eight and nine A.M."

I nearly ran down a roadworker on the way back into Phoenix. He leaped for the still-wet cement barrier, dropping the shovel he'd been leaning on all day, and I ran right over it.

The Society had already been there. They had left my house and gone straight to hers. Only that wasn't possible, because I hadn't even called Katie then. I hadn't even seen the picture of Mrs. Ambler yet. Which meant they had gone to see Ramirez after they left me, and the last thing Ramirez and the paper needed was trouble with the Society.

"I thought it was suspicious when he didn't go to the governor's conference," she had told them, "and just now he called and asked for a lifeline on this person here.

Katherine Powell, 4628 Dutchman Drive. He knew her in Colorado."

"Ramirez!" I shouted at the car phone. "I want to talk to you!" There wasn't any answer.

I swore at her for a good ten miles before I remembered I had the exclusion button on. I punched it off. "Ramirez, where the hell are you?"

"I could ask you the same question," she said. She sounded even angrier than Katie, but not as angry as I was. "You cut me off, you won't tell me what's going on."

"So you decided you had it figured out for yourself, and you told your little theory to the Society."

"What?" she said, and I recognized that tone, too. I had heard it in my own voice when Katie told me the Society had been there. Ramirez hadn't told anybody anything, she didn't even know what I was talking about, but I was going too fast to stop.

"You told the Society I'd asked for Katie's lifeline, didn't you?" I shouted.

"No," she said. "I didn't. Don't you think it's time you told me what's going on?"

"Did the Society come see you this afternoon?"

"No. I told you. They called this morning and wanted to talk to you. I told them you were at the governor's conference."

"And they didn't call back later?"

"No. Are you in trouble?"

I hit the exclusion button. "Yes," I said. "Yes, I'm in trouble."

Ramirez hadn't told them. Maybe somebody else at the paper had, but I didn't think so. There had after all been Dolores Chiwere's story about their having illegal access to the lifelines. "How come you don't have any pictures of your dog?" Hunter had asked me, which meant they'd read my lifeline, too. So they knew we had both lived in Colorado, in the same town, when Aberfan died.

"What did you tell them?" I had demanded of Katie. She had been standing there in the kitchen still messing with the Kool-Aid-stained towel, and I had wanted to yank it out of her hands and make her look at me. "What did you tell the Society?"

She looked up at me. "I told them I was on Indian School Road, picking up the month's programming assignments from my company. Unfortunately, I could just as easily have driven in on Van Buren."

"About Aberfan!" I shouted. "What did you tell them about Aberfan?"

She looked steadily at me. "I didn't tell them anything. I assumed you'd already told them."

I had taken hold of her shoulders. "If they come back, don't tell them anything. Not even if they arrest you. I'll take care of this. I'll . . ."

But I hadn't told her what I'd do because I didn't know. I had run out of her house, colliding with Jana in the hall on her way in for another refill, and roared off for home, even though I didn't have any idea what I would do when I got there.

Call the Society and tell them to leave Katie alone, that she had nothing to do with this? That would be even more suspicious than everything else I'd done so far, and you couldn't get much more suspicious than that.

I had seen a dead jackal on the road (or so I said), and instead of reporting it immediately on the phone right there in my car, I'd driven to a convenience store two miles away. I'd called the Society, but I'd refused to give them my name and number. And then I'd canceled two shoots without telling my boss and asked for the lifeline of one Katherine Powell, whom I had known fifteen years ago and who could have been on Van Buren at the time of the accident.

The connection was obvious, and how long would it take them to make the connection that fifteen years ago was when Aberfan had died?

Apache was beginning to fill up with rush-hour overflow and a whole fleet of tankers. The overflow obviously spent all their time driving divideds—nobody bothered to signal that they were changing lanes. Nobody even gave an indication that they knew what a lane was. Going around the curve from Tempe and onto Van Buren, they were all over the road. I moved over into the tanker lane.

My lifeline didn't have the vet's name on it. They were just getting started in those days, and there was a lot of nervousness about invasion of privacy. Nothing went on-line without the person's permission, especially not medical and bank records, and the lifelines were little more than puff bios: family, occupation, hobbies, pets. The only things on the lifeline besides Aberfan's name was the date of his death and my address at the time, but that was probably enough. There were only two vets in town.

The vet hadn't written Katie's name down on Aberfan's record. He had handed her driver's license back to her without even looking at it, but Katie had told her name to the vet's assistant. He might have written it down. There was no way I could find out. I couldn't ask for the vet's lifeline because the Society had access to the lifelines. They'd get to him before I could. I could maybe have the paper get the vet's records for me, but I'd have to tell Ramirez what was going on, and the phone was probably tapped, too. And if I showed up at the paper, Ramirez would confiscate the car. I couldn't go there.

Wherever the hell I was going, I was driving too fast to get there. When the tanker ahead of me slowed down to ninety, I practically climbed up his back bumper. I had gone past the place where the jackal had been hit without ever seeing it. Even without the traffic, there probably hadn't been anything to see. What the Society hadn't taken care of, the overflow probably had, and anyway, there hadn't been any evidence to begin with. If there had been, if the cameras had seen the car that hit it, they wouldn't have come after me. And Katie.

The Society couldn't charge her with Aberfan's death—killing an animal hadn't been a crime back then—but if they found out about Aberfan they would charge her with the jackal's death, and it wouldn't matter if a hundred witnesses, a hundred highway cameras had seen her on Indian School Road. It wouldn't matter if the print-fix on her car was clean. She had killed one of the last dogs, hadn't she? They would crucify her.

I should never have left Katie. "Don't tell them anything," I had told her, but she had never been afraid of admitting guilt. When the receptionist had asked her what had happened, she had said, "I hit him," just like that, no attempt to make excuses, to run off, to lay the blame on someone else.

I had run off to try to stop the Society from finding out that Katie had hit Aberfan, and meanwhile the Society was probably back at Katie's, asking her how she'd happened to know me in Colorado, asking her how Aberfan died.

I was wrong about the Society. They weren't at Katie's house. They were at mine, standing on the porch, waiting for me to let them in.

"You're a hard man to track down," Hunter said.

The uniform grinned. "Where you been?"

"Sorry," I said, fishing my keys out of my pocket. "I thought you were all done with me. I've already told you everything I know about the incident."

Hunter stepped back just far enough for me to get the screen door open and the key in the lock. "Officer Segura and I just need to ask you a couple more questions."

"Where'd you go this afternoon?" Segura asked.

"I went to see an old friend of mine."

"Who?"

"Come on, come on," Hunter said. "Let the guy get

in his own front door before you start badgering him with a lot of questions."

I opened the door. "Did the cameras get a picture of the tanker that hit the jackal?" I asked.

"Tanker?" Segura said.

"I told you," I said, "I figure it had to be a tanker. The jackal was lying in the tanker lane." I led the way into the living room, depositing my keys on the computer and switching the phone to exclusion while I talked. The last thing I needed was Ramirez bursting in with, "What's going on? Are you in trouble?"

"It was probably a renegade that hit it, which would explain why he didn't stop." I gestured at them to sit down.

Hunter did. Segura started for the couch and then stopped, staring at the photos on the wall above it. "Jesus, will you look at all the dogs!" he said. "Did you take all these pictures?"

"I took some of them. That one in the middle is Misha."

"The last dog, right?"

"Yes," I said.

"No kidding. The very last one."

No kidding. She was being kept in isolation at the Society's research facility in St. Louis when I saw her. I had talked them into letting me shoot her, but it had to be from outside the quarantine area. The picture had an unfocused look that came from shooting it through a wire-mesh-reinforced window in the door, but I wouldn't have done any better if they'd let me inside. Misha was past having any expression to photograph. She hadn't eaten in a week at that point. She lay with her head on her paws, staring at the door, the whole time I was there.

"You wouldn't consider selling this picture to the Society, would you?"

"No, I wouldn't."

He nodded understandingly. "I guess people were pretty upset when she died."

Pretty upset. They had turned on anyone who had anything to do with it—the puppy-mill owners, the scientists who hadn't come up with a vaccine, Misha's vet—and a lot of others who hadn't. And they had handed over their civil rights to a bunch of jackals who were able to grab them because everybody felt so guilty. Pretty upset.

"What's this one?" Segura asked. He had already moved on to the picture next to it.

"It's General Patton's bull terrier Willie."

They fed and cleaned up after Misha with those robot arms they used to use in the nuclear plants. Her owner, a tired-looking woman, was allowed to watch her through the wire-mesh window but had to stay off to the side because Misha flung herself barking against the door whenever she saw her.

"You should make them let you in," I had told her. "It's cruel to keep her locked up like that. You should make them let you take her back home."

"And let her get the newparvo?" she said.

There was nobody left for Misha to get the newparvo from, but I didn't say that. I set the light readings on the camera, trying not to lean into Misha's line of vision.

"You know what killed them, don't you?" she said. "The ozone layer. All those holes. The radiation got in and caused it."

It was the communists, it was the Mexicans, it was the government. And the only people who acknowledged their guilt weren't guilty at all.

"This one here looks kind of like a jackal," Segura said. He was looking at a picture I had taken of a German shepherd after Aberfan died. "Dogs were a lot like jackals, weren't they?"

"No," I said, and sat down on the shelf in front of the developer's screen, across from Hunter. "I already told you everything I know about the jackal. I saw it lying in the road, and I called you."

"You said when you saw the jackal it was in the far right lane," Hunter said.

"That's right."

"And you were in the far left lane?"

"I was in the far left lane."

They were going to take me over my story, point by point, and when I couldn't remember what I'd said before, they were going to say, "Are you sure that's what you saw, Mr. McCombe? Are you sure you didn't see the jackal get hit? Katherine Powell hit it, didn't she?"

"You told us this morning you stopped, but the jackal was already dead. Is that right?" Hunter asked.

"No," I said.

Segura looked up. Hunter touched his hand casually to his pocket and then brought it back to his knee, turning on the taper.

"I didn't stop for about a mile. Then I backed up and looked at it, but it was dead. There was blood coming out of its mouth."

Hunter didn't say anything. He kept his hands on his knees and waited—an old journalist's trick: If you wait long enough, they'll say something they didn't intend to, just to fill the silence.

"The jackal's body was at a peculiar angle," I said, right on cue. "The way it was lying, it didn't look like a jackal. I thought it was a dog." I waited till the silence got uncomfortable again. "It brought back a lot of terrible memories," I said. "I wasn't even thinking. I just wanted to get away from it. After a few minutes I realized I should have called the Society, and I stopped at the 7-Eleven."

I waited again, till Segura began to shoot uncomfortable glances at Hunter, and then started in again. "I thought I'd be okay, that I could go ahead and work, but after I got to my first shoot, I knew I wasn't going to make it, so I came home." Candor. Openness. If the Amblers can do it, so can you. "I guess I was still in shock or something. I didn't even call my boss and have her get somebody to cover the governor's conference. All I could think about was—" I stopped and rubbed my hand across my face. "I needed to talk to somebody. I had the paper look up an old friend of mine, Katherine Powell."

I stopped, I hoped this time for good. I had admitted lying to them and confessed to two crimes: leaving the scene of the accident and using press access to get a lifeline for personal use, and maybe that would be enough to satisfy them. I didn't want to say anything about going to see Katie. They would know she would have told me about their visit and decide this confession was an attempt to get her off, and maybe they'd been watching the house and knew it anyway, and this was all wasted effort.

The silence dragged on. Hunter's hands tapped his knees twice and then subsided. The story didn't explain why I'd picked Katie, who I hadn't seen in fifteen years, who I knew in Colorado, to go see, but maybe, maybe they wouldn't make the connection.

"This Katherine Powell," Hunter said, "you knew her in Colorado, is that right?"

"We lived in the same little town."

We waited.

"Isn't that when your dog died?" Segura said suddenly. Hunter shot him a glance of pure rage, and I thought, it isn't a taper he's got in that shirt pocket. It's the vet's records, and Katie's name is on them.

"Yes," I said. "He died in September of ninety-eight."

Segura opened his mouth.

"In the third wave?" Hunter asked before he could say anything.

"No," I said. "He was hit by a car."

They both looked genuinely shocked. The Amblers could have taken lessons from them. "Who hit it?" Segura asked, and Hunter leaned forward, his hand moving reflexively toward his pocket.

"I don't know," I said. "It was a hit and run. Whoever it was just left him lying there in the road. That's why when I saw the jackal, it . . . that was how I met Katherine Powell. She stopped and helped me. She helped me get him into her car, and we took him to the vet's, but it was too late."

Hunter's public face was pretty indestructible, but Segura's wasn't. He looked surprised and enlightened and disappointed all at once.

"That's why I wanted to see her," I said unnecessarily.

"Your dog was hit on what day?" Hunter asked.

"September thirtieth."

"What was the vet's name?"

He hadn't changed his way of asking the questions, but he no longer cared what the answers were. He had thought he'd found a connection, a cover-up, but here we were, a couple of dog lovers, a couple of Good Samaritans, and his theory had collapsed. He was done with the interview, he was just finishing up, and all I had to do was be careful not to relax too soon.

I frowned. "I don't remember his name. Cooper, I think."

"What kind of car did you say hit your dog?"

"I don't know," I said, thinking, not a Jeep. Make it something besides a Jeep. "I didn't see him get hit. The vet said it was something big, a pickup maybe. Or a Winnebago."

And I knew who had hit the jackal. It had all been right there in front of me—the old man using up their forty-gallon water supply to wash the bumper, the lies about their coming in from Globe—only I had been too intent on keeping them from finding out about Katie, on getting the picture of Aberfan, to see it. It was like the damned parvo. When you had it licked in one place, it broke out somewhere else.

"Were there any identifying tire tracks?" Hunter said.

"What?" I said. "No. It was snowing that day." It had to show in my face, and he hadn't missed anything yet. I passed my hand over my eyes. "I'm sorry. These questions are bringing it all back."

"Sorry," Hunter said.

"Can't we get this stuff from the police report?" Segura asked.

"There wasn't a police report," I said. "It wasn't a crime to kill a dog when Aberfan died."

It was the right thing to say. The look of shock on their faces was the real thing this time, and they looked at each other in disbelief instead of at me. They asked a few more questions and then stood up to leave. I walked them to the door.

"Thank you for your cooperation, Mr. McCombe," Hunter said. "We appreciate what a difficult experience this has been for you."

I shut the screen door between us. The Amblers would have been going too fast, trying to beat the cameras because they weren't even supposed to be on Van Buren. It was almost rush hour, and they were in the tanker lane, and they hadn't even seen the jackal till they hit it, and then it was too late. They had to know the penalty for hitting an animal was jail and confiscation of the vehicle, and there wasn't anybody else on the road.

"Oh, one more question," Hunter said from halfway down the walk. "You said you went to your first assignment this morning. What was it?"

Candid. Open. "It was out at the old zoo. A sideshow kind of thing."

I watched them all the way out to their car and down the street. Then I latched the screen, pulled the inside door shut, and locked it, too. It had been right there in front of me—the ferret sniffing the wheel, the bumper, Jake anxiously watching the road. I had thought he was looking for customers, but he wasn't. He was expecting to see the Society drive up. "He's not interested in that," he had said when Mrs. Ambler said she had been telling me about Taco. He had listened to our whole conversation, standing under the back window with his guilty bucket, ready to come back in and cut her off if she said too much, and I hadn't tumbled to any of it. I had been so intent on Aberfan I hadn't even seen it when I looked right through the lens at it. And what kind of an excuse was that? Katie hadn't even tried to use it, and she was learning to drive.

I went and got the Nikon and pulled the film out of it. It was too late to do anything about the eisenstadt pictures or the vidcam footage, but I didn't think there was anything in them. Jake had already washed the bumper by the time I'd taken those pictures.

I fed the longshot film into the developer. "Positives, one two three order, fifteen seconds," I said, and waited for the image to come on the screen.

I wondered who had been driving. Jake, probably. "He never liked Taco," she had said, and there was no mistaking the bitterness in her voice. "I didn't want to buy the Winnebago."

They would both lose their licenses, no matter who was driving, and the Society would confiscate the Winnebago. They would probably not send two octogenarian specimens of Americana like the Amblers to prison. They wouldn't have to. The trial would take six months, and Texas already had legislation in committee.

The first picture came up. A light-setting shot of an ocotillo.

Even if they got off, even if they didn't end up taking away the Winnebago for unauthorized use of a tanker lane or failure to purchase a sales-tax permit, the Amblers had six months left at the outside. Utah was all ready to pass a full-divided bill, and Arizona would be next. In spite of the road crews' stew-slowed pace, Phoenix would be all-divided by the time the investigation was over, and they'd be completely boxed in. Permanent residents of the zoo. Like the coyote.

A shot of the zoo sign, half-hidden in the cactus. A close-up of the Amblers' balloon-trailing sign. The Winnebago in the parking lot.

"Hold," I said. "Crop." I indicated the areas with my finger. "Enlarge to full screen."

The longshot takes great pictures, sharp contrast, excellent detail. The developer only had a five-hundred-thousand-pixel screen, but the dark smear on the bumper was easy to see, and the developed picture would be much clearer. You'd be able to see every splatter, every grayish-yellow hair. The Society's computers would probably be able to type the blood from it.

"Continue," I said, and the next picture came on the screen. Artsy shot of the Winnebago and the zoo entrance. Jake washing the bumper. Red-handed.

Maybe Hunter had bought my story, but he didn't have any other suspects, and how long would it be before he decided to ask Katie a few more questions? If he thought it was the Amblers, he'd leave her alone.

The Japanese family clustered around the waste-disposal tank. Close-up of the decals on the side. Interiors—Mrs. Ambler in the galley, the upright-coffin shower stall, Mrs. Ambler making coffee.

No wonder she had looked that way in the eisenstadt shot, her face full of memory and grief and loss. Maybe in the instant before they hit it, it had looked like a dog to her, too.

All I had to do was tell Hunter about the Amblers, and Katie was off the hook. It should be easy. I had done it before.

"Stop," I said to a shot of the salt-and-pepper collection. The black-and-white Scottie dogs had painted red-plaid bows and red tongues. "Expose," I said. "One through twenty-four."

The screen went to question marks and started beeping. I should have known better. The developer could handle a lot of orders, but asking it to expose perfectly good film went against its whole memory, and I didn't have time to give it the step-by-steps that would convince it I meant what I said.

"Eject," I said. The Scotties blinked out. The developer spat out the film, rerolled into its protective case.

The doorbell rang. I switched on the overhead and pulled the film out to full length and held it directly under the light. I had told Hunter an RV hit Aberfan, and he had said on the way out, almost an afterthought, "That first shoot you went to, what was it?" And after he left, what had he done, gone out to check on the sideshow kind of thing, gotten Mrs. Ambler to spill her guts? There hadn't been time to do that and get back. He must have called Ramirez. I was glad I had locked the door.

I turned off the overhead. I rerolled the film, fed it back into the developer, and gave it a direction it could handle. "Permanganate bath, full strength, one through twenty-four. Remove one hundred percent emulsion. No notify."

The screen went dark. It would take the developer at least fifteen minutes to run the film through the bleach bath, and the Society's computers could probably enhance a picture out of two crystals of silver and thin air, but at least the detail wouldn't be there. I unlocked the door.

It was Katie.

She held up the eisenstadt. "You forgot your briefcase," she said.

I stared blankly at it. I hadn't even realized I didn't have it. I must have left it on the kitchen table when I went tearing out, running down little girls and stewed roadworkers in my rush to keep Katie from getting involved. And here she was, and Hunter would be back any minute, saying, "That shoot you went on this morning, did you take any pictures?"

"It isn't a briefcase," I said.

"I wanted to tell you," she said, and stopped. "I shouldn't have accused you of telling the Society I'd killed the jackal. I don't know why you came to see me today, but I know you're not capable of—"

"You have no idea what I'm capable of," I said. I opened the door enough to reach for the eisenstadt. "Thanks for bringing it back. I'll get the paper to reimburse your way-mile credits."

Go home. Go home. If you're here when the Society comes back, they'll ask you how you met me, and I just destroyed the evidence that could shift the blame to the Amblers. I took hold of the eisenstadt's handle and started to shut the door.

She put her hand on the door. The screen door and the fading light made her look unfocused, like Misha. "Are you in trouble?"

"No," I said. "Look, I'm very busy."

"Why did you come to see me?" she asked. "Did you kill the jackal?"

"No," I said, but I opened the door and let her in.

I went over to the developer and asked for a visual status. It was only on the sixth frame. "I'm destroying evidence," I said to Katie. "I took a picture this morning of the vehicle that hit it, only I didn't know it was the guilty party until a half an hour ago." I motioned for her to sit down on the couch. "They're in their eighties. They were driving on a road they weren't supposed to be on, in an obsolete recreation vehicle, worrying about the cameras and the tankers. There's no way they could have seen it in time to stop. The Society won't see it that way, though. They're determined to blame somebody, anybody, even though it won't bring them back."

She set her canvas carryit and the eisenstadt down on the table next to the couch.

"The Society was here when I got home," I said. "They'd figured out we were both in Colorado when Aberfan died. I told them it was a hit and run, and you'd stopped to help me. They had the vet's records, and your name was on them."

I couldn't read her face. "If they come back, you tell them that you gave me a ride to the vet's." I went back to the developer. The longshot film was done. "Eject," I said, and the developer spit it into my hand. I fed it into the recycler.

"McCombe! Where the hell are you?" Ramirez's voice exploded into the room, and I jumped and started for the door, but she wasn't there. The phone was flashing. "McCombe! This is important!"

Ramirez was on the phone and using some override I didn't even know existed. I went over and pushed it back to access. The lights went out. "I'm here," I said.

"You won't believe what just happened!" She sounded outraged. "A couple of terrorist types from the Society just stormed in here and confiscated the stuff you sent me!"

All I'd sent her was the vidcam footage and the shots from the eisenstadt, and there shouldn't have been anything on those. Jake had already washed the bumper. "What stuff?" I said.

"The prints from the eisenstadt!" she said, still shouting. "Which I didn't have a chance to look at when they came in because I was too busy trying to work a trade on your governor's conference, not to mention trying to track you down! I had hardcopies made and sent the originals straight down to composing with your vidcam footage. I finally got to them half an hour ago, and while I'm sorting through them, this Society creep just grabs them away from me. No warrants, no 'would you mind?'—nothing. Right out of my hand. Like a bunch of—"

"Jackals," I said. "You're sure it wasn't the vidcam footage?" There wasn't anything in the eisenstadt shots except Mrs. Ambler and Taco, and even Hunter couldn't have put that together, could he?

"Of course I'm sure," Ramirez said, her voice bouncing off the walls. "It was one of the prints from the eisenstadt. I never even saw the vidcam stuff. I sent it straight to composing. I told you."

I went over to the developer and fed the cartridge in. The first dozen shots were nothing, stuff the eisenstadt had taken from the backseat of the car. "Start with frame ten," I said. "Positives. One two three order. Five seconds."

"What did you say?" Ramirez demanded.

"I said, did they say what they were looking for?"

"Are you kidding? I wasn't even there as far as they were concerned. They split up the pile and started through them on *my* desk."

The yucca at the foot of the hill. More yucca. My forearm as I set the eisenstadt down on the counter. My back.

"Whatever it was they were looking for, they found it," Ramirez said.

I glanced at Katie. She met my gaze steadily, unafraid. She had never been afraid, not even when I told her she had killed all the dogs, not even when I showed up on her doorstep after fifteen years.

"The one in the uniform showed it to the other one," Ramirez was saying, "and said, 'You were wrong about the woman doing it. Look at this.' "

"Did you get a look at the picture?"

Still life of cups and spoons. Mrs. Ambler's arm. Mrs. Ambler's back.

"I tried. It was a truck of some kind."

"A truck? Are you sure? Not a Winnebago?"

"A truck. What the hell is going on over there?"

I didn't answer. Jake's back. Open shower door. Still life with Sanka. Mrs. Ambler remembering Taco.

"What woman are they talking about?" Ramirez said. "The one you wanted the lifeline on?"

"No," I said. The picture of Mrs. Ambler was the last one on the cartridge. The developer went back to the beginning. Bottom half of the Hitori. Open car door. Prickly pear. "Did they say anything else?"

"The one in uniform pointed to something on the hardcopy and said, 'See. There's his number on the side. Can you make it out?' "

Blurred palm trees and the expressway. The tanker hitting the jackal.

"Stop," I said. The image froze.

"What?" Ramirez said.

It was a great action shot, the back wheels passing right over the mess that been the jackal's hind legs. The jackal was already dead, of course, but you couldn't see that or the already drying blood coming out of its mouth because of the angle. You couldn't see the truck's license number either because of the speed the tanker was going, but the number was there, waiting for the Society's computers. It looked like the tanker had just hit it.

"What did they do with the picture?" I asked.

"They took it into the chief's office. I tried to call up the originals from composing, but the chief had already sent for them *and* your vidcam footage. Then I tried to get you, but I couldn't get past your damned exclusion."

"Are they still in there with the chief?"

"They just left. They're on their way over to your house. The chief told me to tell you he wants 'full cooperation,' which means hand over the negatives and any other film you just took this morning. He told *me* to keep my hands off. No story. Case closed."

"How long ago did they leave?"

"Five minutes. You've got plenty of time to make me a print. Don't highwire it. I'll come pick it up."

"What happened to, 'The last thing I need is trouble with the Society'?"

"It'll take them at least twenty minutes to get to your place. Hide it somewhere the Society won't find it."

"I can't," I said, and listened to her furious silence. "My developer's broken. It just ate my longshot film," I said, and hit the exclusion button again.

"You want to see who hit the jackal?" I said to Katie, and motioned her over to the developer. "One of Phoenix's finest."

She came and stood in front of the screen, looking at the picture. If the Society's computers were really good, they could probably prove the jackal was already dead, but the Society wouldn't keep the film long enough for that. Hunter and Segura had probably already destroyed the highwire copies. Maybe I should offer to run the cartridge sheet through the permanganate bath for them when they got here, just to save time.

I looked at Katie. "It looks guilty as hell, doesn't it?" I said. "Only it isn't." She didn't say anything, didn't move. "It would have killed the jackal if it had hit it. It was going at least ninety. But the jackal was already dead."

She looked across at me.

"The Society would have sent the Amblers to jail. It would have confiscated the house they've lived in for fifteen years for an accident that was nobody's fault. They didn't even see it coming. It just ran right out in front of them."

Katie put her hand up to the screen and touched the jackal's image.

"They've suffered enough," I said, looking at her. It was getting dark. I hadn't turned on any lights, and the red image of the tanker made her nose look sunburned.

"All these years she's blamed him for her dog's death, and he didn't do it," I said. "A Winnebago's a hundred square feet on the inside. That's about as big as this developer, and they've lived inside it for fifteen years, while the lanes got narrower and the highways shut down, hardly enough room to breathe, let alone live, and her blaming him for something he didn't do."

In the ruddy light from the screen she looked sixteen.

"They won't do anything to the driver, not with the tankers hauling thousands of gallons of water into Phoenix every day. Even the Society won't run the risk of a boycott. They'll destroy the negatives and call the case closed. And the Society won't go after the Amblers," I said. "Or you."

I turned back to the developer. "Go," I said, and the image changed. Yucca. Yucca. My forearm. My back. Cups and spoons.

"Besides," I said. "I'm an old hand at shifting the blame." Mrs. Ambler's arm. Mrs. Ambler's back. Open shower door. "Did I ever tell you about Aberfan?"

Katie was still watching the screen, her face pale now from the light-blue 100 percent Formica shower stall.

"The Society already thinks the tanker did it. The only one I've got to convince is my editor." I reached across to the phone and took the exclusion off. "Ramirez," I said, "wanta go after the Society?"

Jake's back. Cups, spoons, and Sanka.

"I did," Ramirez said in a voice that could have frozen the Salt River, "but your developer was broken, and you couldn't get me a picture."

Mrs. Ambler and Taco.

I hit the exclusion button again and left my hand on it. "Stop," I said. "Print." The screen went dark, and the print slid out into the tray. "Reduce frame. Permanganate bath by one percent. Follow on screen." I took my hand off. "What's Dolores Chiwere doing these days, Ramirez?"

"She's working investigative. Why?"

I didn't answer. The picture of Mrs. Ambler faded a little, a little more.

The Society *does* have a link to the lifelines!" Ramirez said, not quite as fast as Hunter, but almost.

"That's why you requested your old girlfriend's line, isn't it? You're running a sting."

I had been wondering how to get Ramirez off Katie's trail, and she had done it herself, jumping to conclusions just like the Society. With a little effort, I could convince Katie, too: Do you know why I really came to see you today? To catch the Society. I had to pick somebody the Society couldn't possibly know about from my lifeline, somebody I didn't have any known connection with.

Katie watched the screen, looking like she already half believed it. The picture of Mrs. Ambler faded some more. Any known connection.

"Stop," I said.

"What about the truck?" Ramirez demanded. "What does it have to do with this sting of yours?"

"Nothing," I said. "And neither does the water board, which is an even bigger bully than the Society. So do what the chief says. Full cooperation. Case closed. We'll get them on lifeline tapping."

She digested that, or maybe she'd already hung up and was calling Dolores Chiwere. I looked at the image of Mrs. Ambler on the screen. It had faded enough to look slightly overexposed but not enough to look tampered with. And Taco was gone.

I looked at Katie. "The Society will be here in another fifteen minutes," I said, "which gives me just enough time to tell you about Aberfan." I gestured at the couch. "Sit down."

She came and sat down. "He was a great dog," I said. "He loved the snow. He'd dig through it and toss it up with his muzzle and snap at the snowflakes, trying to catch them."

Ramirez had obviously hung up, but she would call back if she couldn't track down Chiwere. I put the exclusion back on and went over to the developer. The image of Mrs. Ambler was still on the screen. The bath hadn't affected the detail that much. You could still see the wrinkles, the thin white hair, but the guilt, or blame, the look of loss and love, was gone. She looked serene, almost happy.

"There are hardly any good pictures of dogs," I said. "They lack the necessary muscles to take good pictures, and Aberfan lunged at you as soon as he saw the camera."

I turned the developer off. Without the light from the screen, it was almost dark in the room. I turned on the overhead.

"There were less than a hundred dogs left in the United States, and he'd already had the newparvo once and nearly died. The only pictures I had of him had been taken when he was asleep. I wanted a picture of Aberfan playing in the snow."

I leaned against the narrow shelf in front of the developer's screen. Katie looked the way she had at the vet's, sitting there with her hands clenched, waiting for me to tell her something terrible.

"I wanted a picture of him playing in the snow, but he always lunged at the camera," I said, "so I let him out in the front yard, and then I sneaked out the side door and went across the road to some pine trees where he wouldn't be able to see me. But he did."

"And he ran across the road," Katie said. "And I hit him."

She was looking down at her hands. I waited for her to look up, dreading what I would see in her face. Or not see.

"It took me a long time to find out where you'd gone," she said to her hands. "I was afraid you'd refuse me access to your lifeline. I finally saw one of your pictures in a newspaper, and I moved to Phoenix, but after I got here, I was afraid to call you for fear you'd hang up on me."

She twisted her hands the way she had twisted her mittens at the vet's. "My husband said I was obsessed with it, that I should have gotten over it by now, everybody else had, that they were only dogs anyway." She looked up, and I braced my hands against the developer. "He said forgiveness wasn't something somebody else could give you, but I didn't want you to forgive me exactly. I just wanted to tell you I was sorry."

There hadn't been any reproach, any accusation in her face when I told her she was responsible for the extinction of a species that day at the vet's, and there wasn't now. Maybe she didn't have the facial muscles for it, I thought bitterly.

"Do you know why I came to see you today?" I said angrily. "My camera broke when I tried to catch Aberfan. I didn't get any pictures." I grabbed the picture of Mrs. Ambler out of the developer's tray and flung it at her. "Her dog died of newparvo. They left it in the Winnebago, and when they came back, it was dead."

"Poor thing," she said, but she wasn't looking at the picture. She was looking at me.

"She didn't know she was having her picture taken. I thought if I got you talking about Aberfan, I could get a picture like that of you."

And surely now I would see it, the look I had really wanted when I set the eisenstadt down on Katie's kitchen table, the look I still wanted, even though the eisenstadt was facing the wrong way, the look of betrayal the dogs had never given us. Not even Misha. Not even Aberfan. How does it feel to be responsible for the extinction of an entire species?

I pointed at the eisenstadt. "It's not a briefcase. It's a camera. I was going to take your picture without your even knowing it."

She had never known Aberfan. She had never known Mrs. Ambler either, but in that instant before she started to cry, she looked like both of them. She put her hand up to her mouth. "Oh," she said, and the love, the loss was there in her voice, too. "If you'd had it then, it wouldn't have happened."

I looked at the eisenstadt. If I had had it, I could have set it on the porch and Aberfan would never have even noticed it. He would have burrowed through the snow and tossed it up with his nose, and I could have thrown snow up in big glittering sprays that he would have leapt at, and it never would have happened. Katie Powell would have driven past, and I would have stopped to wave at her, and she, sixteen years old and just learning to drive, would maybe even have risked taking a mittened hand off the steering wheel to wave back, and Aberfan would have wagged his tail into a blizzard and then barked at the snow he'd churned up.

He wouldn't have caught the third wave. He would have lived to be an old dog, fourteen or fifteen, too old to play in the snow anymore, and even if he had been the last dog in the world, I would not have let them lock him up in a cage, I would not have let them take him away. If I had had the eisenstadt.

No wonder I hated it.

It had been at least fifteen minutes since Ramirez called. The Society would be here any minute. "You shouldn't be here when the Society comes," I said, and Katie nodded and smudged the tears off her cheeks and stood up, reaching for her carryit.

"Do you ever take pictures?" she said, shouldering the carryit. "I mean, besides for the papers?"

"I don't know if I'll be taking pictures for them much longer. Photojournalists are becoming an extinct breed."

"Maybe you could come take some pictures of Jana and Kevin. Kids grow up so fast, they're gone before you know it."

"I'd like that," I said. I opened the screen door for her and looked both ways down the street at the darkness. "All clear," I said, and she went out. I shut the screen door between us.

She turned and looked at me one last time with her dear, open face that even I hadn't been able to close. "I miss them," she said.

I put my hand up to the screen. "I miss them, too."

I watched her to make sure she turned the corner and then went back in the living room and took down the picture of Misha. I propped it against the developer so Segura would be able to see it from the door. In a month or so, when the Amblers were safely in Texas and the Society had forgotten about Katie, I'd call Segura and tell him I might be willing to sell it to the Society, and then in a day or so I'd tell him I'd changed my mind. When he came out to try to talk me into it, I'd tell him about Perdita and Beatrix Potter, and he would tell me about the Society.

Chiwere and Ramirez would have to take the credit for the story—I didn't want Hunter putting anything else together—and it would take more than one story to break them, but it was a start.

Katie had left the print of Mrs. Ambler on the couch. I picked it up and looked at it a minute and then fed it into the developer. "Recyle," I said.

I picked up the eisenstadt from the table by the couch and took the film cartridge out. I started to pull the film out to expose it, and then shoved it into the developer instead and turned it on. "Positives, one two three order, five seconds."

I had apparently set the camera on its activator again—there were ten shots or so of the back seat of the Hitori. Vehicles and people. The pictures of Katie were all in shadow. There was a Still Life of Kool-Aid Pitcher with Whale Glass and another one of Jana's toy cars, and some near-black frames that meant Katie had laid the eisenstadt facedown when she brought it to me.

"Two seconds," I said, and waited for the developer to flash the last shots so I could make sure there wasn't anything else on the cartridge and then expose it before the Society got here. All but the last frame was of the darkness that was all the eisenstadt could see lying on its face. The last one was of me.

The trick in getting good pictures is to make people forget they're being photographed. Distract them. Get them talking about something they care about.

"Stop," I said, and the image froze.

Aberfan was a great dog. He loved to play in the snow, and after I had murdered him, he lifted his head off my lap and tried to lick my hand.

The Society would be here any minute to take the longshot film and destroy it, and this one would have to go, too, along with the rest of the cartridge. I couldn't risk Hunter's being reminded of Katie. Or Segura taking a notion to do a print-fix and peel on Jana's toy cars.

It was too bad. The eisenstadt takes great pictures. "Even you'll forget it's a camera," Ramirez had said in her spiel, and that was certainly true. I was looking straight into the lens.

And it was all there, Misha and Taco and Perdita and the look he gave me on the way to the vet's while I stroked his poor head and told him it would be all right, that look of love and pity I had been trying to capture all these years. The picture of Aberfan.

The Society would be here any minute. "Eject," I said, and cracked the cartridge open, and exposed it to the light.

I'VE GOTTEN A BUNCH OF FLACK RECENTLY FOR NOT writing about Women's Issues. You hear a lot of this kind of talk these days—as if we were dogs and cats and parakeets instead of people, and had not only different things on our minds but different mental processes altogether.

Shakespeare also gets flack, in his case for being a Dead White Elizabethan Male, which apparently limits him to addressing only Dead White Elizabethan Male Issues. (Are there any? What on earth are they?)

I hate this kind of literary demagoguery. Anyone who's ever read Shakespeare knows he had bigger fish to fry than Elizabethan Issues. He wrote about Human Issues—fear and ambition and guilt and regret and love—the issues that trouble and delight all of us, women included. And the only ones I want to write about.

But, as I say, I've been getting all this flack, and I thought to myself, "Fine. They want me to write about Women's Issues. I'll write about Women's Issues. I'll write about The Women's Issue.*" So I did. I hope they're happy.*

Even the Queen

The phone sang as I was looking over the defense's motion to dismiss. "It's the universal ring," my law clerk Bysshe said, reaching for it. "It's probably the defendant. They don't let you use signatures from jail."

"No, it's not," I said. "It's my mother."

"Oh." Bysshe reached for the receiver. "Why isn't she using her signature?"

"Because she knows I don't want to talk to her. She must have found out what Perdita's done."

"Your daughter Perdita?" he asked, holding the receiver against his chest. "The one with the little girl?"

"No, that's Viola. Perdita's my younger daughter. The one with no sense."

"What's she done?"

"She's joined the Cyclists."

Bysshe looked inquiringly blank, but I was not in the mood to enlighten him. Or in the mood to talk to Mother. "I know exactly what Mother will say. She'll ask me why I didn't tell her, and then she'll demand to know what I'm going to do about it, and there is nothing I *can* do about it, or I obviously would have done it already."

Bysshe looked bewildered. "Do you want me to tell her you're in court?"

"No." I reached for the receiver. "I'll have to talk to her sooner or later." I took it from him. "Hello, Mother," I said.

"Traci," Mother said dramatically, "Perdita has become a Cyclist."

"I know."

"Why didn't you tell me?"

"I thought Perdita should tell you herself."

"Perdita!" She snorted. "She wouldn't tell me. She knows what I'd have to say about it. I suppose you told Karen."

"Karen's not here. She's in Iraq." The only good thing about this whole debacle was that thanks to Iraq's eagerness to show it was a responsible world-community member and its previous penchant for self-destruction, my mother-in-law was in the one place on the planet where the phone service was bad enough that I could claim I'd tried to call her but couldn't get through, and she'd have to believe me.

The Liberation has freed us from all sorts of indignities and scourges, including Iraq's Saddams, but mothers-in-law aren't one of them, and I was almost happy with Perdita for her excellent timing. When I didn't want to kill her.

"What's Karen doing in Iraq?"' Mother asked.

"Negotiating a Palestinian homeland."

"And meanwhile her granddaughter is ruining her life," she said irrelevantly. "Did you tell Viola?"

"I *told* you, Mother. I thought Perdita should tell all of you herself."

"Well, she didn't. And this morning one of my patients, Carol Chen, called me and demanded to know what I was keeping from her. I had no idea what she was talking about."

"How did Carol Chen find out?"

"From her daughter, who almost joined the Cyclists last year. *Her* family talked her out of it," she said accusingly. "Carol was convinced the medical community had discovered some terrible side effect of ammenerol and were covering it up. I cannot believe you didn't tell me, Traci."

And I cannot believe I didn't have Bysshe tell her I was in court, I thought. "I told you, Mother. I thought it was Perdita's place to tell you. After all, it's her decision."

"Oh, *Tra*ci!" Mother said. "You cannot mean that!"

In the first fine flush of freedom after the Liberation, I had entertained hopes that it would change everything—that it would somehow do away with inequality and matriarchal dominance and those humorless women determined to eliminate the word "manhole" and third-person singular pronouns from the language.

Of course it didn't. Men still make more money, "herstory" is still a blight on the semantic landscape, and my mother can still say, "Oh, *Tra*ci!" in a tone that reduces me to preadolescence.

"Her decision!" Mother said. "Do you mean to tell me you plan to stand idly by and allow your daughter to make the mistake of her life?"

"What can I do? She's twenty-two years old and of sound mind."

"If she were of sound mind, she wouldn't be doing this. Didn't you try to talk her out of it?"

"Of course I did, Mother."

"And?"

"And I didn't succeed. She's determined to become a Cyclist."

"Well, there must be something we can do. Get an injunction or hire a deprogrammer or sue the Cyclists for brainwashing. You're a judge, there must be some law you can invoke—"

"The law is called personal sovereignty, Mother, and since it was what made the Liberation possible in the first place, it can hardly be used against Perdita. Her decision meets all the criteria for a case of personal sovereignty: It's a personal decision, it was made by a sovereign adult, it affects no one else—"

"What about my practice? Carol Chen is convinced shunts cause cancer."

"Any effect on your practice is considered an indirect effect. Like secondary smoke. It doesn't apply. Mother, whether we like it or not, Perdita has a perfect right to do this, and we don't have any right to interfere. A free society has to be based on respecting others' opinions and leaving each other alone. We have to respect Perdita's right to make her own decisions."

All of which was true. It was too bad I hadn't said any of it to Perdita when she called. What I had said, in a tone that sounded exactly like my mother's, was "Oh, Per*di*ta!"

"This is all your fault, you know," Mother said. "I *told* you you shouldn't have let her get that tattoo over her shunt. And don't tell me it's a free society. What good is a free society when it allows my granddaughter to ruin her life?" She hung up.

I handed the receiver back to Bysshe.

"I really liked what you said about respecting your daughter's right to make her own decisions," he said. He held out my robe. "And about not interfering in her life."

"I want you to research the precedents on deprogramming for me," I said, sliding my arms into the sleeves. "And find out if the Cyclists have been charged with any free-choice violations—brainwashing, intimidation, coercion."

The phone sang, another universal. "Hello, who's calling?" Bysshe said cautiously. His voice became suddenly friendlier. "Just a minute." He put his hand over the receiver. "It's your daughter Viola."

"I took the receiver. "Hello, Viola."

"I just talked to Grandma," she said. "You will not

believe what Perdita's done now. She's joined the Cyclists."

"I know," I said.

"You *know*? And you didn't tell me? I can't believe this. You never tell me anything."

"I thought Perdita should tell you herself," I said tiredly.

"Are you kidding? She never tells me anything either. That time she had eyebrow implants, she didn't tell me for three weeks, and when she got the laser tattoo, she didn't tell me at all. *Twidge* told me. You should have called me. Did you tell Grandma Karen?"

"She's in Baghdad," I said.

"I know," Viola said. "I called her."

"Oh, Viola, you didn't!"

"Unlike you, Mom, I believe in telling members of our family about matters that concern them."

"What did she say?" I asked, a kind of numbness settling over me now that the shock had worn off.

"I couldn't get through to her. The phone service over there is terrible. I got somebody who didn't speak English, and then I got cut off, and when I tried again, they said the whole city was down."

Thank you, I breathed silently. Thank you, thank you, thank you.

"Grandma Karen has a right to know, Mother. Think of the effect this could have on Twidge. She thinks Perdita's wonderful. When Perdita got the eyebrow implants, Twidge glued LEDs to hers, and I almost never got them off. What if Twidge decides to join the Cyclists, too?"

"Twidge is only nine. By the time she's supposed to get her shunt, Perdita will have long since quit." I hope, I added silently. Perdita had had the tattoo for a year and a half now and showed no signs of tiring of it. "Besides, Twidge has more sense."

"It's true. Oh, Mother, how *could* Perdita do this? Didn't you tell her about how awful it was?"

"Yes," I said. "And inconvenient. And unpleasant and unbalancing and painful. None of it made the slightest impact on her. She told me she thought it would be fun."

Bysshe was pointing to his watch and mouthing, "Time for court."

"Fun!" Viola said. "When she saw what I went through that time? Honestly, Mother, sometimes I think she's completely brain dead. Can't you have her declared incompetent and locked up or something?"

"No," I said, trying to zip up my robe with one hand. "Viola, I have to go. I'm late for court. I'm afraid there's nothing we can do to stop her. She's a rational adult."

"Rational!" Viola said. "Her eyebrows light up, Mother. She has Custer's Last Stand lased on her arm."

I handed the phone to Bysshe. "Tell Viola I'll talk to her tomorrow." I zipped up my robe. "And then call Baghdad and see how long they expect the phones to be out." I started into the courtroom. "And if there are any more universal calls, make sure they're local before you answer."

Bysshe couldn't get through to Baghdad, which I took as a good sign, and my mother-in-law didn't call. Mother did, in the afternoon, to ask if lobotomies were legal.

She called again the next day. I was in the middle of my Personal Sovereignty class, explaining the inherent right of citizens in a free society to make complete jackasses of themselves. They weren't buying it.

"I think it's your mother," Bysshe whispered to me as he handed me the phone. "She's still using the universal. But it's local. I checked."

"Hello, Mother," I said.

"It's all arranged," Mother said. "We're having lunch with Perdita at McGregor's. It's on the corner of Twelfth Street and Larimer."

"I'm in the middle of class," I said.

"I know. I won't keep you. I just wanted to tell you not to worry. I've taken care of everything."

I didn't like the sound of that. "What have you done?"

"Invited Perdita to lunch with us. I told you. At McGregor's."

"Who is 'us,' Mother?"

"Just the family," she said innocently. "You and Viola."

Well, at least she hadn't brought in the deprogrammer. Yet. "What are you up to, Mother?"

"Perdita said the same thing. Can't a grandmother ask her granddaughters to lunch? Be there at twelve-thirty."

"Bysshe and I have a court-calendar meeting at three."

"Oh, we'll be done by then. And bring Bysshe with you. He can provide a man's point of view."

She hung up.

"You'll have to go to lunch with me, Bysshe," I said. "Sorry."

"Why? What's going to happen at lunch?"

"I have no idea."

On the way over to McGregor's, Bysshe told me what he'd found out about the Cyclists. "They're not a cult. There's no religious connection. They seem to have grown out of a pre-Liberation women's group," he said, looking at his notes, "although there are also links to the pro-choice movement, the University of Wisconsin, and the Museum of Modern Art."

"What?"

"They call their group leaders 'docents.' Their philosophy seems to be a mix of pre-Liberation radical feminism and the environmental primitivism of the eighties. They're floratarians and they don't wear shoes."

"Or shunts," I said. We pulled up in front of McGregor's and got out of the car. "Any mind-control convictions?" I asked hopefully.

"No. A bunch of suits against individual members, all of which they won."

"On grounds of personal sovereignty."

"Yeah. And a criminal one by a member whose family tried to deprogram her. The deprogrammer was sentenced to twenty years, and the family got twelve."

"Be sure to tell Mother about that one," I said, and opened the door to McGregor's.

It was one of those restaurants with a morning-glory vine twining around the maître d's desk and garden plots between the tables.

"Perdita suggested it," Mother said, guiding Bysshe and me past the onions to our table. "She told me a lot of the Cyclists are floratarians."

"Is she here?" I asked, sidestepping a cucumber frame.

"Not yet." She pointed past a rose arbor. "There's our table."

Our table was a wicker affair under a mulberry tree. Viola and Twidge were seated on the far side next to a trellis of runner beans, looking at menus.

"What are you doing here, Twidge?" I asked. "Why aren't you in school?"

"I am," she said, holding up her LCD slate. "I'm remoting today."

"I thought she should be part of this discussion," Viola said. "After all, she'll be getting her shunt soon."

"My friend Kensy says she isn't going to get one. Like Perdita," Twidge said.

"I'm sure Kensy will change her mind when the time

comes," Mother said. "Perdita will change hers, too. Bysshe, why don't you sit next to Viola?"

Bysshe slid obediently past the trellis and sat down in the wicker chair at the far end of the table. Twidge reached across Viola and handed him a menu. "This is a great restaurant," she said. "You don't have to wear shoes." She held up a bare foot to illustrate. "And if you get hungry while you're waiting, you can just pick something." She twisted around in her chair, picked two of the green beans, gave one to Bysshe, and bit into the other one. "I bet Kensy doesn't. Kensy says a shunt hurts worse than braces."

"It doesn't hurt as much as not having one," Viola said, shooting me a Now-Do-You-See-What-My-Sister's-Caused? look.

"Traci, why don't you sit across from Viola?" Mother said to me. "And we'll put Perdita next to you when she comes."

"If she comes," Viola said.

"I told her one o'clock," Mother said, sitting down at the near end. "So we'd have a chance to plan our strategy before she gets here. I talked to Carol Chen—"

"Her daughter nearly joined the Cyclists last year," I explained to Bysshe and Viola.

"*She* said they had a family gathering, like this, and simply talked to her daughter, and she decided she didn't want to be a Cyclist after all." She looked around the table. "So I thought we'd do the same thing with Perdita. I think we should start by explaining the significance of the Liberation and the days of dark oppression that preceded it—"

"*I* think," Viola interrupted, "we should try to talk her into just going off the ammenerol for a few months instead of having the shunt removed. If she comes. Which she won't."'

"Why not?"

"Would you? I mean, it's like the Inquisition. Her sitting here while all of us 'explain' at her. Perdita may be crazy, but she's not stupid."

"It's hardly the Inquisition," Mother said. She looked anxiously past me toward the door. "I'm sure Perdita—" She stopped, stood up, and plunged off suddenly through the asparagus.

I turned around, half expecting Perdita with light-up lips or a full-body tattoo, but I couldn't see through the leaves. I pushed at the branches.

"Is it Perdita?" Viola said, leaning forward.

I peered around the mulberry bush. "Oh, my God," I said.

It was my mother-in-law, wearing a black abayah and a silk yarmulke. She swept toward us through a pumpkin patch, robes billowing and eyes flashing. Mother hurried in her wake of trampled radishes, looking daggers at me.

I turned them on Viola. "It's your Grandmother Karen," I said accusingly. "You told me you didn't get through to her."

"I didn't," she said. "Twidge, sit up straight. And put your slate down."

There was an ominous rustling in the rose arbor, as of leaves shrinking back in terror, and my mother-in-law arrived.

"Karen!" I said, trying to sound pleased. "What on earth are you doing here? I thought you were in Baghdad."

"I came back as soon as I got Viola's message," she said, glaring at everyone in turn. "Who's this?" she demanded, pointing at Bysshe. "Viola's new live-in?"

"No!" Bysshe said, looking horrified.

"This is my law clerk, Mother," I said. "Bysshe Adams-Hardy."

"Twidge, why aren't you in school?"

"I *am*," Twidge said. "I'm remoting." She held up her slate. "See? Math."

"I see," she said, turning to glower at me. "It's a serious enough matter to require my great-grandchild's being pulled out of school *and* the hiring of legal assistance, and yet you didn't deem it important enough to notify *me*. Of course, you *never* tell me anything, Traci."

She swirled herself into the end chair, sending leaves and sweet-pea blossoms flying and decapitating the broccoli centerpiece. "I didn't get Viola's cry for help until yesterday. Viola, you should never leave messages with Hassim. His English is virtually nonexistent. I had to get him to hum me your ring. I recognized your signature, but the phones were out, so I flew home. In the middle of negotiations, I might add."

"How *are* negotiations going, Grandma Karen?" Viola asked.

"They *were* going extremely well. The Israelis have given the Palestinians half of Jerusalem, and they've agreed to time-share the Golan Heights." She turned to glare momentarily at me. "*They* know the importance of communication." She turned back to Viola. "So why are they picking on you, Viola? Don't they like your new live-in?"

"I am *not* her live-in," Bysshe protested.

I have often wondered how on earth my mother-in-law became a mediator and what she does in all those negotiation sessions with Serbs and Catholics and North and South Koreans and Protestants and Croats. She takes sides, jumps to conclusions, misinterprets everything you say, refuses to listen. And yet she talked South Africa into a Mandelan government and would probably get the Palestinians to observe Yom Kippur. Maybe she just bullies everyone into submission. Or maybe they have to band together to protect themselves against her.

Bysshe was still protesting. "I never even met Viola till today. I've only talked to her on the phone a couple of times."

"You must have done *something*," Karen said to Viola. "They're obviously out for your blood."

"Not mine," Viola said. "Perdita's. She's joined the Cyclists."

"The Cyclists? I left the West Bank negotiations because you don't approve of Perdita joining a biking club? How am I supposed to explain this to the president of Iraq? She will *not* understand, and neither do I. A biking club!"

"The Cyclists do not ride bicycles," Mother said.

"They menstruate," Twidge said.

There was a dead silence of at least a minute, and I thought, it's finally happened. My mother-in-law and I are actually going to be on the same side of a family argument.

"All this fuss is over Perdita's having her shunt removed?" Karen said finally. "She's of age, isn't she? And this is obviously a case where personal sovereignty applies. You should know that, Traci. After all, you're a judge."

I should have know it was too good to be true.

"You mean you approve of her setting back the Liberation twenty years?" Mother said.

"I hardly think it's that serious," Karen said. "There are antishunt groups in the Middle East, too, you know, but no one takes them seriously. Not even the Iraqis, and they still wear the veil."

"Perdita is taking them seriously."

Karen dismissed Perdita with a wave of her black sleeve. "They're a trend, a fad. Like microskirts. Or those dreadful electronic eyebrows. A few women wear silly fashions like that for a little while, but you don't see women as a whole giving up pants or going back to wearing hats."

"But Perdita . . ." Viola said.

"If Perdita wants to have her period, I say let her. Women functioned perfectly well without shunts for thousands of years."

Mother brought her fist down on the table. "Women

also functioned *perfectly well* with concubinage, cholera, and corsets," she said, emphasizing each word with her fist. "But that is no reason to take them on voluntarily, and I have no intention of allowing Perdita—"

"Speaking of Perdita, where is the poor child?" Karen said.

"She'll be here any minute," Mother said. "I invited her to lunch so we could discuss this with her."

"Ha!" Karen said. "So you could browbeat her into changing her mind, you mean. Well, I have no intention of collaborating with you. *I* intend to listen to the poor thing's point of view with interest and an open mind. 'Respect,' that's the key word, and one you all seem to have forgotten. Respect and common courtesy."

A barefoot young woman wearing a flowered smock and a red scarf tied around her left arm came up to the table with a sheaf of pink folders.

"It's about time," Karen said, snatching one of the folders away from her. "Your service here is dreadful. I've been sitting here for ten minutes. She snapped the folder open. "I don't suppose you have Scotch."

"My name is Evangeline," the young woman said. "I'm Perdita's docent." She took the folder away from Karen. "She wasn't able to join you for lunch, but she asked me to come in her place and explain the Cyclist philosophy to you."

She sat down in the wicker chair next to me.

"The Cyclists are dedicated to freedom," she said. "Freedom from artificiality, freedom from body-controlling drugs and hormones, freedom from the male patriarchy that attempts to impose them on us. As you probably already know, we do not wear shunts."

She pointed to the red scarf around her arm. "Instead, we wear this as a badge of our freedom and our femaleness. I'm wearing it today to announce that my time of fertility has come."

"We had that, too," Mother said, "only we wore it on the back of our skirts."

I laughed.

The docent glared at me. "Male domination of women's bodies began long before the so-called 'Liberation,' with government regulation of abortion and fetal rights, scientific control of fertility, and finally the development of ammenerol, which eliminated the reproductive cycle altogether. This was all part of a carefully planned takeover of women's bodies, and by extension, their identities, by the male patriarchal regime."

"What an interesting point of view!" Karen said enthusiastically.

It certainly was. In point of fact, ammenerol hadn't been invented to eliminate menstruation at all. It had been developed for shrinking malignant tumors, and its uterine lining-absorbing properties had only been discovered by accident.

"Are you trying to tell us," Mother said, "that men *forced* shunts on women? We had to *fight* everyone to get ammenero approved by the FDA!"

It was true. What surrogate mothers and antiabortionists and the fetal-rights issue had failed to do in uniting women, the prospect of not having to menstruate did. Women had organized rallies, petitioned, elected senators, passed amendments, been excommunicated, and gone to jail, all in the name of Liberation.

"Men were *against* it," Mother said, getting rather red in the face. "And the religious right, and the maxipad manufacturers, and the Catholic Church—"

"They knew they'd have to allow women priests," Viola said.

"Which they did," I said.

"The Liberation hasn't freed you," the docent said loudly. "Except from the natural rhythms of your life, the very wellspring of your femaleness."

She leaned over and picked a daisy that was growing

under the table. "We in the Cyclists celebrate the onset of our menses and rejoice in our bodies," she said, holding the daisy up. "Whenever a Cyclist comes into blossom, as we call it, she is honored with flowers and poems and songs. Then we join hands and tell what we like best about our menses."

"Water retention," I said.

"Or lying in bed with a heating pad for three days a month," Mother said.

"*I* think I like the anxiety attacks best," Viola said. "When I went off the ammenerol, so I could have Twidge, I'd have these days where I was convinced the space station was going to fall on me."

A middle-aged woman in overalls and a straw hat had come over while Viola was talking and was standing next to Mother's chair. "I had these mood swings," she said. "One minute I'd feel cheerful and the next like Lizzie Borden."

"Who's Lizzie Borden?" Twidge asked.

"She killed her parents," Bysshe said. "With an ax."

Karen and the docent glared at both of them. "Aren't you supposed to be working on your math, Twidge?" Karen said.

"I've always wondered if Lizzie Borden had PMS," Viola said, "and that was why—"

"No," Mother said. "It was having to live before tampons and ibuprofen. An obvious case of justifiable homicide."

"I hardly think this sort of levity is helpful," Karen said, glowering at everyone.

"Are you our waitress?" I asked the straw-hatted woman hastily.

"Yes," she said, producing a slate from her overalls pocket.

"Do you serve wine?" I asked.

"Yes. Dandelion, cowslip, and primrose."

"We'll take them all."

"A bottle of each?"

"For now," I said. "Unless you have them in kegs."

"Our specials for today are watermelon salad and *choufleur gratinée,*" she said, smiling at everyone. Karen and the docent did not smile back. "You handpick your own cauliflower from the patch up front. The floratarian special is sautéed lily buds with marigold butter."

There was a temporary truce while everyone ordered. "I'll have the sweet peas," the docent said, "and a glass of rose water."

Bysshe leaned over to Viola. "I'm sorry I sounded so horrified when your grandmother asked if I was your live-in," he said.

"That's okay," Viola said. "Grandma Karen can be pretty scary."

"I just didn't want you to think I didn't like you. I do. Like you, I mean."

"Don't they have soyburgers?" Twidge asked.

As soon as the waitress left, the docent began passing out the pink folders she'd brought with her. "These will explain the working philosophy of the Cyclists," she said, handing me one, "along with practical information on the menstrual cycle." She handed Twidge one.

"It looks just like those books we used to get in junior high," Mother said, looking at hers. " 'A Special Gift,' they were called, and they had all these pictures of girls with pink ribbons in their hair, playing tennis and smiling. Blatant misrepresentation."

She was right. There was even the same drawing of the fallopian tubes I remembered from my middle-school movie, a drawing that had always reminded me of *Alien* in the early stages.

"Oh, yuck," Twidge said. "This is disgusting."

"Do your math," Karen said.

Bysshe looked sick. "Did women really *do* this stuff?"

The wine arrived, and I poured everyone a large

glass. The docent pursed her lips disapprovingly and shook her head. "The Cyclists do not use the artificial stimulants or hormones that the male patriarchy has forced on women to render them docile and subservient."

"How long do you menstruate?" Twidge asked.

"Forever," Mother said.

"Four to six days," the docent said. "It's there in the booklet."

"No, I mean, your whole life or what?"

"A woman has her menarche at twelve years old on the average and ceases menstruating at age fifty-five."

"I had my first period at eleven," the waitress said, setting a bouquet down in front of me. "At school."

"I had my last one on the day the FDA approved ammenerol," Mother said.

"Three hundred and sixty-five divided by twenty-eight," Twidge said, writing on her slate. "Times forty-three years." She looked up. "That's five hundred and fifty-nine periods."

"That can't be right," Mother said, taking the slate away from her. "It's at least five thousand."

"And they all start on the day you leave on a trip," Viola said.

"Or get married," the waitress said. Mother began writing on the slate.

I took advantage of the cease-fire to pour everyone some more dandelion wine.

Mother looked up from the slate. "Do you realize with a period of five days, you'd be menstruating for nearly three thousand days? That's over eight solid years."

"And in between there's PMS," the waitress said, delivering flowers.

"What's PMS?" Twidge asked.

"Premenstrual syndrome was the name the male medical establishment fabricated for the natural variation in hormonal levels that signal the onset of menstruation," the docent said. "This mild and entirely normal fluctuation was exaggerated by men into a debility." She looked at Karen for confirmation.

"I used to cut my hair," Karen said.

The docent looked uneasy.

"Once I chopped off one whole side," Karen went on. "Bob had to hide the scissors every month. And the car keys. I'd start to cry every time I hit a red light."

"Did you swell up?" Mother asked, pouring Karen another glass of dandelion wine.

"I looked just like Orson Welles."

"Who's Orson Welles?" Twidge asked.

"Your comments reflect the self-loathing thrust on you by the patriarchy," the docent said. "Men have brainwashed women into thinking menstruation is evil and unclean. Women even called their menses 'the curse' because they accepted men's judgment."

"I called it the curse because I thought a witch must have laid a curse on me," Viola said. "Like in 'Sleeping Beauty.' "

Everyone looked at her.

"Well, I did," she said. "It was the only reason I could think of for such an awful thing happening to me." She handed the folder back to the docent. "It still is."

"I think you were awfully brave," Bysshe said to Viola, "going off the ammenerol to have Twidge."

"It was awful," Viola said. "You can't imagine."

Mother sighed. "When I got my period, I asked my mother if Annette had it, too."

"Who's Annette?" Twidge said.

"A Mouseketeer," Mother said, and added, at Twidge's uncomprehending look, "On TV."

"High-rez," Viola said.

"The Mickey Mouse Club," Mother said.

"There was a high-rezzer called the Mickey Mouse Club?" Twidge said incredulously.

"They were days of dark oppression in many ways," I said.

Mother glared at me. "Annette was every young girl's ideal," she said to Twidge. "Her hair was curly, she had actual breasts, her pleated skirt was always pressed, and I could not imagine that she could have anything so *messy* and undignified. Mr. Disney would never have allowed it. And if Annette didn't have one, I wasn't going to have one either. So I asked my mother—"

"What did she say?" Twidge cut in.

"She said every woman had periods," Mother said. "So I asked her, 'Even the Queen of England?' And she said, 'Even the Queen.' "

"Really?" Twidge said. "But she's so *old*!"

"She isn't having it now," the docent said irritatedly. "I told you, menopause occurs at age fifty-five."

"And then you have hot flashes," Karen said, "and osteoporosis and so much hair on your upper lip, you look like Mark Twain."

"Who's—" Twidge said.

"You are simply reiterating negative male propaganda," the docent interrupted, looking very red in the face.

"You know what I've always wondered?" Karen said, leaning conspiratorially close to Mother. "If Maggie Thatcher's menopause was responsible for the Falklands War."

"Who's Maggie Thatcher?" Twidge said.

The docent, who was now as red in the face as her scarf, stood up. "It is clear there is no point in trying to talk to you. You've all been completely brainwashed by the male patriarchy." She began grabbing up her folders. "You're blind, all of you! You don't even see that you're victims of a male conspiracy to deprive you of your biological identity, of your very womanhood. The Liberation wasn't a liberation at all. It was only another kind of slavery."

"Even if that were true," I said, "even if it had been

a conspiracy to bring us under male domination, it would have been worth it."

"She's right, you know," Karen said to Mother. "Traci's absolutely right. There are some things worth giving up anything for, even your freedom, and getting rid of your period is definitely one of them."

"Victims!" the docent shouted. "You've been stripped of your femininity, and you don't even care!" She stomped out, destroying several squash and a row of gladiolas in the process.

"You know what I hated most before the Liberation?" Karen said, pouring the last of the dandelion wine into her glass. "Sanitary belts."

"And those cardboard tampon applicators," Mother said.

"I'm never going to join the Cyclists," Twidge said.

"Good," I said.

"Can I have dessert?"

I called the waitress over, and Twidge ordered sugared violets. "Anyone else want dessert?" I asked. "Or more primrose wine?"

"I think it's wonderful the way you're trying to help your sister," Bysshe said, leaning closer to Viola.

"And those Modess ads," Mother said. "You remember, with those glamorous women in satin-brocade evening dresses and long white gloves, and below the picture was written, 'Modess, because . . .' I thought Modess was a perfume."

Karen giggled. "I thought it was a brand of *champagne*!"

"I don't think we'd better have any more wine," I said.

The phone started singing the minute I got to my chambers the next morning, the universal ring.

"Karen went back to Iraq, didn't she?" I asked Bysshe.

"Yeah," he said. "Viola said there was some snag over whether to put Disneyland on the West Bank or not."

"When did Viola call?"

Bysshe looked sheepish. "I had breakfast with her and Twidge this morning."

"Oh." I picked up the phone. "It's probably Mother with a plan to kidnap Perdita. Hello?"

"This is Evangeline, Perdita's docent," the voice on the phone said. "I hope you're happy. You've bullied Perdita into surrendering to the enslaving male patriarchy."

"I have?" I said.

"You obviously employed mind control, and I want you to know we intend to file charges." She hung up. The phone rang again immediately, another universal.

"What is the good of signatures when no one ever uses them?" I said, and picked up the phone.

"Hi, Mom," Perdita said. "I thought you'd want to know I've changed my mind about joining the Cyclists."

"Really?" I said, trying not to sound jubilant.

"I found out they wear this red scarf thing on their arm. It covers up Sitting Bull's horse."

"That is a problem," I said.

"Well, that's not all. My docent told me about your lunch. Did Grandma Karen really tell you you were right?"

"Yes."

"Gosh! I didn't believe that part. Well, anyway, my docent said you wouldn't listen to her about how great menstruating is, that you all kept talking about the negative aspects of it, like bloating and cramps and crabbiness, and I said, 'What are cramps?' and she said, 'Menstrual bleeding frequently causes headaches and discomfort,' and I said, 'Bleeding? Nobody ever said anything about bleeding!' Why didn't you tell me there was blood involved, Mother?"

I had, but I felt it wiser to keep silent.

"And you didn't say a word about its being painful. And all the hormone fluctuations! Anybody'd have to be crazy to want to go through that when they didn't have to! How did you stand it before the Liberation?"

"They were days of dark oppression," I said.

"I *guess*! Well, anyway, I quit, and so my docent is really mad. But I told her it was a case of personal sovereignty, and she has to respect my decision. I'm still going to become a floratarian, though, and I *don't* want you to try to talk me out of it."

"I wouldn't dream of it," I said.

"You know, this whole thing is really your fault, Mom! If you'd told me about the pain part in the first place, none of this would have happened. Viola's right! You never tell us *anything*!"

WHEN YOU'RE A WRITER, THE QUESTION PEOPLE ALways *ask you is, "Where do you get your ideas?" Writers hate this question. It's like asking Humphrey Bogart in* The African Queen, *"Where do you get your leeches?" You don't get ideas. Ideas get you.*

You see something or hear something or read something, and unlike the hundreds of other things you've seen and heard and read, this one triggers something—some connection nobody else sees—and you know you'll never be able to explain it. So you write a story about it.

"Idea" is even the wrong word. It implies something rational, a concept, a thought, and there's usually nothing rational about it. It's not a light bulb going on over your head. It's a tightening of the throat, a shiver down the middle of the back, a stab to the chest. Or the sudden impulse to shout, "Get out! Before it's too late! Run!"

Schwarzschild Radius

"When a star collapses, it sort of falls in on itself." Travers curved his hand into a semicircle and then brought the fingers in. "And sometimes it reaches a kind of point of no return where the gravity pulling in on it is stronger than the nuclear and electric forces, and when it reaches that point, nothing can stop it from collapsing and it becomes a black hole." He closed his hand into a fist. "And that critical diameter, that point where there's no turning back, is called the Schwarzschild radius." Travers paused, waiting for me to say something.

He had come to see me every day for a week, sitting stiffly on one of my chairs in an unaccustomed shirt and tie, and talked to me about black holes and relativity, even though I taught biology at the university before my retirement, not physics. Someone had told him I knew Schwarzschild, of course.

"The Schwarzschild radius?" I said in my quavery, old man's voice, as if I could not remember ever hearing the phrase before, and Travers looked disgusted. He wanted me to say, "The Schwarzschild radius! Ah, yes, I served with Karl Schwarzschild on the Russian front in World War I!" and tell him all about how he had formulated his theory of black holes while serving with the artillery, but I had not decided yet what to tell him. "The event horizon," I said.

"Yeah. It was named after Schwarzschild because he was the one who worked out the theory," Travers said. He reminded me of Muller with his talk of theories. He was the same age as Muller, with the same shock of stiff yellow hair and the same insatiable curiosity, and perhaps that was why I let him come every day to talk to me, though it was dangerous to let him get so close.

"I have drawn up a theory of the stars," Muller says while we warm our hands over the Primus stove so that they will get enough feeling in them to be able to hold the liquid barretter without dropping it. "They are not balls of fire, as the scientists say. They are frozen."

"How can we see them if they are frozen?" I say. Muller is insulted if I do not argue with him. The arguing is part of the theory.

"Look at the wireless!" he says, pointing to it sitting disemboweled on the table. We have the back off the wireless again, and in the barretter's glass tube is a red reflection of the stove's flame. "The light is a reflection off the ice of the star."

"A reflection of what?"

"Of the shells, of course."

I do not say that there were stars before there was this war, because Muller will not have an answer to this, and I have no desire to destroy his theory, and besides, I do not really believe there was a time when this war did not exist. The star shells have always exploded over the snow-covered craters of No Man's Land, shattering in a spray of white and red, and perhaps Muller's theory is true.

"At that point," Travers said, "at the event horizon, no more information can be transmitted out of the black hole because gravity has become so strong, and so the collapse appears frozen at the Schwarzschild radius."

"Frozen," I said, thinking of Muller.

"Yeah. As a matter of fact, the Russians call black holes 'frozen stars.' You were at the Russian front, weren't you?"

"What?"

"In World War I."

"But the star doesn't really freeze," I said. "It goes on collapsing."

"Yeah, sure," Travers said. "It keeps collapsing in on itself until even the atoms are stripped of their electrons and there's nothing left except what they call a naked singularity, but we can't see past the Schwarzschild radius, and nobody inside a black hole can tell us what it's like in there because they can't get messages out, so nobody can ever know what it's like inside a black hole."

"I know," I said, but he didn't hear me.

He leaned forward. "What was it like at the front?"

It is so cold we can only work on the wireless a few minutes at a time before our hands stiffen and grow clumsy, and we are afraid of dropping the liquid barretter. Muller holds his gloves over the Primus stove and then puts them on. I jam my hands into my ice-stiff pockets.

We are fixing the wireless set. Eisner, who had been delivering messages between the sectors, got sent up to the front when he could not fix his motorcycle. If we cannot fix the wireless, we will cease to be telegraphists and become soldiers, and we will be sent to the front lines.

We are already nearly there. If it were not snowing, we could see the barbed wire and pitted snow of No Man's Land, and the big Russian coal boxes sometimes land in the communication trenches. A shell hit our wireless hut two weeks ago. We are ahead of our own artillery lines, and some of the shells from our guns fall on us, too, because the muzzles are worn out. But it is not the front, and we guard the liquid barretter with our lives.

"Eisner's unit was sent up on wiring fatigue last night," Muller says, "and they have not come back. I have a theory about what happened to them."

"Has the mail come?" I say, rubbing my sore eyes and then putting my cold hands immediately back in my pockets. I must get some new gloves, but the quartermaster has none to issue. I have written my mother three times to knit me a pair, but she has not sent them yet.

"I have a theory about Eisner's unit," he says doggedly. "The Russians have a magnet that has pulled them into the front."

"Magnets pull iron, not people," I say.

I have a theory about Muller's theories. Littering the communications trenches are things that the soldiers going up to the front have discarded: water bottles and haversacks and bayonets. Hans and I sometimes tried to puzzle out why they would discard such important things.

"Perhaps they were too heavy," I would say, though that did not explain the bayonets or the boots.

"Perhaps they know they are going to die," Hans would say, picking up a helmet.

I would try to cheer him up. "My gloves fell out of my pocket yesterday when I went to the quartermaster's. I never found them. They are in this trench somewhere."

"Yes," he would say, turning the helmet round and round in his hands, "perhaps as they near the front, these things simply drop away from them."

My theory is that what happens to the water bottles and helmets and bayonets is what has happened to Muller. He was a student in university before the war, but his knowledge of science and his intelligence have fallen away from him, and now we are so close to the front, all he has left are his theories. And his curiosity, which is a dangerous thing to have kept.

"Exactly. Magnets pull iron, and *they* were carrying

barbed wire!" he says triumphantly. "And so they were pulled in to the magnet."

I put my hands practically into the Primus flame and rub them together, trying to get rid of the numbness. "We had better get the barretter in the wireless again or this magnet of yours will suck it to the front, too."

I go back to the wireless. Muller stays by the stove, thinking about his magnet. The door bangs open. It is not a real door, only an iron humpie tied to the beam that reinforces the dugout and held with a wedge, and when someone pushes against it, it flies inward, bringing the snow with it.

Snow swirls in, and light, and the sound from the front, a low rumble like a dog growling. I clutch the liquid barretter to my chest, and Muller flings himself over the wireless as if it were a wounded comrade. Someone bundled in a wool coat and mittens, with a wool cap pulled over his ears, stands silhouetted against the reddish light in the doorway, blinking at us.

"Is Private Rottschieben here? I have come to see him about his eyes," he says, and I see it is Dr. Funkenheld.

"Come in and shut the door," I say, still carefully protecting the liquid barretter, but Muller has already jammed the metal back against the beam.

"Do you have news?" Muller says to the doctor, eager for new facts to spin his theories from. "Has the wiring fatigue come back? Is there going to be a bombardment tonight?"

Dr. Funkenheld takes off his mittens. "I have come to examine your eyes," he says to me. His voice frightens me. All through the war he has kept his quiet bedside voice, speaking to the wounded in the dressing station and at the stretcher bearer's posts as if they were in his surgery in Stuttgart, but now he sounds agitated, and I am afraid it means a bombardment is coming and he will need me at the front.

When I went to the dressing station for medicine for

my eyes, I foolishly told him I had studied medicine with Dr. Zuschauer in Jena. Now I am afraid he will ask me to assist him, which will mean going up to the front. "Do your eyes still hurt?" he says.

I hand the barretter to Muller and go over to stand by the lantern that hangs from a nail in the beam.

"I think he should be invalided home, Herr Doktor," Muller says. He knows it is impossible, of course. He was at the wireless the day the message came through that no one was to be invalided out for frostbite or "other non-contagious diseases."

"Can you find me a better light?" the doctor says to him.

Muller's curiosity is so strong that he cannot bear to leave any place where something interesting is happening. If he went up to the front, I do not think he would be able to pull himself away, and now I expect him to make some excuse to stay, but I have forgotten that he is even more curious about the wiring fatigue. "I will go see what has happened to Eisner's unit," he says, and opens the door. Snow flies in, as if it had been beating against the door to get in, and the doctor and I have to push against the door to get it shut again.

"My eyes have been hurting," I say, while we are still pushing the metal into place, so that he cannot ask me to assist him. "They feel like sand has gotten into them."

"I have a patient with a disease I do not recognize," he says. I am relieved, though disease can kill us as easily as a trench mortar. Soldiers die of pneumonia and dysentery and blood poisoning every day in the dressing station, but we do not fear it the way we fear the front.

"The patient has fever, excoriated lesions, and suppurating bullae," Dr. Funkenheld says.

"Could it be boils?" I say, though of course he would recognize something so simple as boils, but he is not listening to me, and I realize that it is not a diagnosis from me that he has come for.

"The man is a scientist, a Jew named Schwarzschild, attached to the artillery," he says, and because the artillery are even farther back from the front lines than we are, I volunteer to go and look at the patient, but he does not want that either.

"I must talk to the medical headquarters in Bialystok," he says.

"Our wireless is broken," I say, because I do not want to have to tell him why it is impossible for me to send a message for him. We are allowed to send only military messages, and they must be sent in code, tapped out on the telegraph key. It would take hours to send his message, even if it were possible. I hold up the dangling wire. "At any rate, you must clear it with the commandant," but he is already writing out the name and address on a piece of paper, as if this were a telegraph office.

"You can send the message when you get the wireless fixed. I have written out the symptoms."

I put the back on the wireless. Muller comes in, kicking the door open, and snow flies everywhere, picking up Dr. Funkenheld's message and sending it circling around the dugout. I catch it before it spirals into the flame of the Primus stove.

"The wiring fatigue was pinned down all night," Muller says, setting down a hand lamp. He must have gotten it from the dressing station. "Five of them froze to death, the other eight have frostbite. The commandant thinks there may be a bombardment tonight." He does not mention Eisner, and he does not say what has happened to the rest of the thirty men in Eisner's unit, though I know. The front has gotten them. I wait, holding the message in my stiff fingers, hoping Dr. Funkenheld will say, "I must go attend to their frostbite."

"Let me examine your eyes," the doctor says, and shows Muller how to hold the hand lamp. Both of them peer into my eyes. "I have an ointment for you to use twice daily," he says, getting a flat jar out of his bag. "It will burn a little."

"I will rub it on my hands then. It will warm them," I say, thinking of Eisner frozen at the front, still holding the roll of barbed wire, perhaps.

He pulls my bottom eyelid down and rubs the ointment on with his little finger. It does not sting, but when I have blinked it into my eye, everything has a reddish tinge. "Will you have the wireless fixed by tomorrow?" he says.

"I don't know. Perhaps."

Muller has not put down the hand lamp. I can see by its light that he has forgotten all about the wiring fatigue and the Russian magnet and is wondering what the doctor wants with the wireless.

The doctor puts on his mittens and picks up his bag. I realize too late I should have told him I would send the message in exchange for them. "I will come check your eyes tomorrow," he says, and opens the door to the snow. The sound of the front is very close.

As soon as he is gone, I tell Muller about Schwarzschild and the message the doctor wants to send. He will not let me rest until I have told him, and we do not have time for his curiosity. We must fix the wireless.

"If you were on the wireless, you must have sent messages for Schwarzschild," Travers said eagerly. "Did you ever send a message to Einstein? They've got the letter Einstein sent to him after he wrote him his theory, but if Schwarzschild sent him some kind of message, too, that would be great. It would make my paper."

"You said that no message can escape a black hole?" I said. "But they could escape a collapsing star. Is that not so?"

"Okay," Travers said impatiently, and made his fingers into a semicircle again. "Suppose you have a fixed observer over here." He pulled his curved hand back and held the forefinger of his other hand up to represent the fixed observer. "And you have somebody in the star. Say when the star starts to collapse, the person in it shines a light at the fixed observer. If the star hasn't reached the Schwarzschild radius, the fixed observer will be able to see the light, but it will take longer to reach him because the gravity of the black hole is pulling on the light, so it will seem as if time on the star has slowed down, and the wavelengths will have been lengthened, so the light will be redder. Of course that's just a thought problem. There couldn't really be anybody in a collapsing star to send the messages."

"We sent messages," I said. "I wrote my mother asking her to knit me a pair of gloves."

There is still something wrong with the wireless. We have received only one message in two weeks. It said, "Russian opposition collapsing," and there was so much static we could not make out the rest of it. We have taken the wireless apart twice. The first time we found a loose wire, but the second time we could not find anything. If Hans were here, he would be able to find the trouble immediately.

"I have a theory about the wireless," Muller says. He has had ten theories in as many days: The magnet of the Russians is pulling our signals in to it; the northern lights, which have been shifting uneasily on the horizon, make a curtain the wireless signals cannot get through; the Russian opposition is not collapsing at all. They are drawing us deeper and deeper into a trap.

I say,- "I am going to try again. Perhaps the trouble has cleared up," and put the headphones on so I do not have to listen to his new theory. I can hear nothing but a rumbling roar that sounds like the front.

I take out the folded piece of paper Dr. Funkenheld gave me and lay it on the wireless. He comes nearly every night to see if I have gotten an answer to his message, and

I take off the headphones and let him listen to the static. I tell him that we cannot get through, but even though that is true, it is not the real reason I have not sent the message. I am afraid of the commandant finding out. I am afraid of being sent to the front.

I have compromised by writing a letter to the professor that I studied medicine with in Jena, but I have not gotten an answer from him yet, and so I must go on pretending to the doctor.

"You don't have to do that," Muller says. He sits on the wireless, swinging his leg. He picks up the paper with the symptoms on it and holds it to the flame of the Primus stove. I grab for it, but it is already burning redly. "I have sent the message for you."

"I don't believe you. Nothing has been getting out."

"Didn't you notice the northern lights did not appear last night?"

I have not noticed. The ointment the doctor gave to me makes everything look red at night, and I do not believe in Muller's theories. "Nothing is getting out now," I say, and hold the headphones out to him so he can hear the static. He listens, still swinging his leg. "You will get us both in trouble. Why did you do it?"

"I was curious about it." If we are sent up to the front, his curiosity will kill us. He will take apart a land mine to see how it works. "We cannot get in trouble for sending military messages. I said the commandant was afraid it was a poisonous gas the Russians were using." He swings his leg and grins because now I am the curious one.

"Well, did you get an answer?"

"Yes," he says maddeningly, and puts the headphones on. "It is not a poisonous gas."

I shrug as if I do not care whether I get an answer or not. I put on my cap and the muffler my mother knitted for me and open the door. "I am going out to see if the mail has come. Perhaps there will be a letter there from my professor."

"Nature of disease unknown," Muller shouts against the sudden force of he snow. "Possibly impetigo or glandular disorder."

I grin back at him and say, "If there is a package from my mother, I will give you half of what is in it."

"Even if it is your gloves?"

"No, not if it is my gloves," I say, and go to find the doctor.

At the dressing station they tell me he has gone to see Schwarzschild and give me directions to the artillery staff's headquarters. It is not very far, but it is snowing and my hands are already cold. I go to the quartermaster's and ask him if the mail has come in.

There is a new recruit there, trying to fix Eisner's motorcycle. He has parts spread out on the ground all around him in a circle. He points to a burlap sack and says, "That is all the mail there is. Look through it yourself."

Snow has gotten into the sack and melted. The ink on the envelopes has run, and I squint at them, trying to make out the names. My eyes begin to hurt. There is not a package from my mother or a letter from my professor, but there is a letter for Lieutenant Schwarzschild. The return address says "Doctor." Perhaps he has written to a doctor himself.

"I am delivering a message to the artillery headquarter," I say, showing the letter to the recruit. "I will take this up, too." The recruit nods and goes on working.

It has gotten dark while I was inside, and it is snowing harder. I jam my hands in the ice-stiff pockets of my coat and start to the artillery headquarters in the rear. It is pitch-dark in the communication trenches, and the wind twists the snow and funnels it howling along them. I take off my muffler and wrap it around my hands like a girl's muff.

A band of red shifts uneasily all along the horizon, but I do not know if it is the front or Muller's northern lights, and there is no shelling to guide me. We are running out of shells, so we do not usually begin shelling until nine o'clock. The Russians start even later. Sometimes I hear machine-gun fire, but it is distorted by the wind and the snow, and I cannot tell what direction it is coming from.

The communication trench seems narrower and deeper than I remember it from when Hans and I first brought the wireless up. It takes me longer than I think it should to get to the branching that will lead north to the headquarters. The front has been contracting, the ammunition dumps and officer's billets and clearing stations moving up closer and closer behind us. The artillery headquarters has been moved up from the village to a dugout near the artillery line, not half a mile behind us. The nightly firing is starting. I hear a low rumble, like thunder.

The roar seems to be ahead of me, and I stop and look around, wondering if I can have gotten somehow turned around, though I have not left the trenches. I start again, and almost immediately I see the branching and the headquarters.

It has no door, only a blanket across the opening, and I pull my hands free of the muffler and duck through it into a tiny space like a rabbit hole, the timber balks of the earthen ceiling so low I have to stoop. Now that I am out of the roar of the snow, the sound of the front separates itself into the individual crack of a four-pounder, the whine of a star shell, and under it the almost continuous rattle of machine guns. The trenches must not be as deep here. Muller and I can hardly hear the front at all in our wireless hut.

A man is sitting at an uneven table spread with papers and books. There is a candle on the table with a red glass chimney, or perhaps it only looks that way to me. Everything in the dugout, even the man, looks faintly red.

He is wearing a uniform but no coat, and gloves with the finger ends cut off, even though there is no stove here. My hands are already cold.

A trench mortar roars, and clods of frozen dirt clatter from the roof onto the table. The man brushes the dirt from the papers and looks up.

"I am looking for Dr. Funkenheld," I say.

"He is not here." He stands up and comes around the table, moving stiffly, like an old man, though he does not look older than forty. He has a mustache, and his face looks dirty in the red light.

"I have a message for him."

An eight-pounder roars, and more dirt falls on us. The man raises his arm to brush the dirt off his shoulder. The sleeve of his uniform has been slit into ribbons. All along the back of his raised hand and the side of his arm are red sores running with pus. I look back at his face. The sores in his mustache and around his nose and mouth have dried and are covered with a crust. Excoriated lesions. Suppurating bullae. The gun roars again, and dirt rains down on his raw hands.

"I have a message for him," I say, backing away from him. I reach in the pocket of my coat to show him the message, but I pull out the letter instead. "There was a letter for you, Lieutenant Schwarzschild." I hold it out to him by one corner so he will not touch me when he takes it.

He comes toward me to take the letter, the muscles in his jaw tightening, and I think in horror that the sores must be on his legs as well. "Who is it from?" he says. "Ah, Herr Professor Einstein. Good," and turns it over. He puts his fingers on the flap to open the letter and cries out in pain. He drops the letter.

"Would you read it to me?" he says, and sinks down into the chair, cradling his hand against his chest. I can see there are sores in his fingernails.

I do not have any feeling in my hands. I pick the envelope up by its corners and turn it over. The skin of his finger is still on the flap. I back away from the table. "I must find the doctor. It is an emergency."

"You would not be able to find him," he says. Blood oozes out of the tip of his finger and down over the blister in his fingernail. "He has gone up to the front."

"What?" I say, backing and backing until I run into the blanket. "I cannot understand you."

"He has gone up to the front," he says, more slowly, and this time I can puzzle out the words, but they make no sense. How can the doctor be at the front? This is the front.

He pushes the candle toward me. "I order you to read me the letter."

I do not have any feeling in my fingers. I open it from the top, tearing the letter almost in two. It is a long letter, full of equations and numbers, but the words are warped and blurred. " 'My Esteemed Colleague! I have read your paper with the greatest interest. I had not expected that one could formulate the exact solution of the problem so simply. The analytical treatment of the problem appears to me splendid. Next Thursday I will present the work with several explanatory words, to the Academy!' "

"Formulated so simply," Schwarzschild says, as if he is in pain. "That is enough. Put the letter down. I will read the rest of it."

I lay the letter on the table in front of him, and then I am running down the trench in the dark with the sound of the front all around me, roaring and shaking the ground. At the first turning, Muller grabs my arm and stops me. "What are you doing here?" I shout. "Go back! Go back!"

"Go back?" he says. "The front's that way." He points in the direction he came from. But the front is not that way. It is behind me, in the artillery headquarters. "I told you there would be a bombardment tonight. Did you see the doctor? Did you give him the message? What did he say?"

"So you actually held the letter from Einstein?" Travers said. "How exciting that must have been! Only two months after Einstein had published his theory of general relativity. And years before they realized black holes really existed. When was this exactly?" He took out a notebook and began to scribble notes. "My esteemed colleague . . . ," he muttered to himself. "Formulated so simply. This is great stuff. I mean, I've been trying to find out stuff on Schwarzschild for my paper for months, but there's hardly any information on him. I guess because of the war."

"No information can get out of a black hole once the Schwarzschild radius has been passed," I said.

"Hey, that's great!" he said, scribbling. "Can I use that in my paper?"

Now I am the one who sits endlessly in front of the wireless sending out messages to the Red Cross, to my professor in Jena, to Dr. Einstein. I have frostbitten the forefinger and thumb of my right hand and have to tap out the letters with my left. But nothing is getting out, and I must get a message out. I must find someone to tell me the name of Schwarzschild's disease.

"I have a theory," Muller says. "The Jews have seized power and have signed a treaty with the Russians. We are completely cut off."

"I am going to see if the mail has come," I say, so that I do not have to listen to any more of his theories, but the doctor stops me on my way out of the hut.

I tell him what the message said. "Impetigo!" the doctor shouts. "You saw him! Did that look like impetigo to you?"

I shake my head, unable to tell him what I think it looks like.

"What are his symptoms?" Muller asks, burning with curiosity. I have not told him about Schwarzschild. I am afraid that if I tell him, he will only become more curious and will insist on going up to the front to see Schwarzschild himself.

"Let me see your eyes," the doctor says in his beautiful calm voice. I wish he would ask Muller to go for a hand lamp again so that I could ask him how Schwarzschild is, but he has brought a candle with him. He holds it so close to my face that I cannot see anything but the red flame.

"Is Lieutenant Schwarzschild worse? What are his symptoms?" Muller says, leaning forward.

His symptoms are craters and shell holes, I think. I am sorry I have not told Muller, for it has only made him more curious. Until now I have told him everything, even how Hans died when the wireless hut was hit, how he laid the liquid barretter carefully down on top of the wireless before he tried to cough up what was left of his chest and catch it in his hands. But I cannot tell him this.

"What symptoms does he have?" Muller says again, his nose almost in the candle's flame, but the doctor turns from him as if he cannot hear him and blows the candle out. The doctor unwraps the dressing and looks at my fingers. They are swollen and red. Muller leans over the doctor's shoulder. "I have a theory about Lieutenant Schwarzschild's disease," he says.

"Shut up," I say. "I don't want to hear any more of your stupid theories," and do not even care about the wounded look on Muller's face or the way he goes and sits by the wireless. For now I have a theory, and it is more horrible than anything Muller could have dreamed of.

We are all of us—Muller, and the recruit who is trying to put together Eisner's motorcycle, and perhaps even the doctor with his steady bedside voice—afraid of the front. But our fear is not complete, because unspoken in it is our belief that the front is something separate from us, something we can keep away from by keeping the wireless or the motorcycle fixed, something we can survive by flattening our faces into the frozen earth, something we can escape altogether by being invalided out.

But the front is not separate. It is inside Schwarzschild, and the symptoms I have been sending out, suppurative bullae and excoriated lesions, are not what is wrong with him at all. The lesions on his skin are only the barbed wire and shell holes and connecting trenches of a front that is somewhere farther in.

The doctor puts a new dressing of crepe paper on my hand. "I have tried to invalid Schwarzschild out," the doctor says, and Muller looks at him, astounded. "The supply lines are blocked with snow."

"Schwarzschild cannot be invalided out," I say. "The front is inside him."

The doctor puts the roll of crepe paper back in his kit and closes it. "When the roads open again, I will invalid you out for frostbite. And Muller, too."

Muller is so surprised, he blurts, "I do not have frostbite."

But the doctor is no longer listening. "You must both escape," he says—and I am not sure he is even listening to himself—"while you can."

"I have a theory about why you have not told me what is wrong with Schwarzschild," Muller says as soon as the doctor is gone.

"I am going for the mail."

"There will not be any mail," Muller shouts after me. "The supply lines are blocked." But the mail is there, scattered among the motorcycle parts. There are only a few parts left. As soon as the roads are cleared, the recruit will be able to climb on the motorcycle and ride away.

I gather up the letters and take them over to the lantern to try to read them, but my eyes are so bad, I cannot see anything but a red blur. "I am taking them back to the wireless hut," I say, and the recruit nods without looking up.

It is starting to snow. Muller meets me at the door, but I brush past him and turn the flame of the Primus stove up as high as it will go and hold the letters up behind it.

"I will read them for you," Muller says eagerly, looking through the envelopes I have discarded. "Look, here is a letter from your mother. Perhaps she has sent your gloves."

I squint at the letters one by one while he tears open my mother's letter to me. Even though I hold them so close to the flame that the paper scorches, I cannot make out the names.

" 'Dear son,' " Muller reads, " 'I have not heard from you in three months. Are you hurt? Are you ill? Do you need anything?' "

The last letter is from Professor Zuschauer in Jena. I can see his name quite clearly in the corner of the envelope, though mine is blurred beyond recognition. I tear it open. There is nothing written on the red paper.

I thrust it at Muller. "Read this," I say.

"I have not finished with your mother's letter yet," Muller says, but he takes the letter and reads: " 'Dear Herr Rottschieben, I received your letter yesterday. I could hardly decipher your writing. Do you not have decent pens at the front? The disease you describe is called Neumann's disease or pemphigus—' "

I snatch the letter out of Muller's hands and run out the door. "Let me come with you!" Muller shouts.

"You must stay and watch the wireless!" I say joyously, running along the communication trench. Schwarzschild does not have the front inside him. He has pemphigus, he has Neumann's disease, and now he can be invalided home to hospital.

I go down and think I have tripped over a discarded helmet or a tin of beef, but there is a crash, and dirt and revetting fall all around me. I hear the low buzz of a daisy cutter and flatten myself into the trench, but the buzz does not become a whine. It stops, and there is another crash and the trench caves in.

I scramble out of the trench before it can suffocate me and crawl along the edge toward Schwarzschild's dug-out, but the trench has caved in all along its length, and when I crawl up and over the loose dirt, I lose it in the swirling snow.

I cannot tell which way the front lies, but I know it is very close. The sound comes at me from all directions, a deafening roar in which no individual sounds can be distinguished. The snow is so thick, I cannot see the burst of flame from the muzzles as the guns fire, and no part of the horizon looks redder than any other. It is all red, even the snow.

I crawl in what I think is the direction of the trench, but as soon as I do, I am in barbed wire. I stop, breathing hard, my face and hands pressed into the snow. I have come the wrong way. I am at the front. I hear a sound out of the barrage of sound, the sound of tires on the snow, and I think it is a tank and cannot breathe at all. The sound comes closer, and in spite of myself I look up and it is the recruit who was at the quartermaster's.

He is a long way away, behind a coiled line of barbed wire, but I can see him quite clearly in spite of the snow. He has the motorcycle fixed, and as I watch, he flings his leg over it and presses his foot down. "Go!" I shout. "Get out!" The motorcycle jumps forward. "Go!"

The motorcycle comes toward me, picking up speed. It rears up, and I think it is going to jump the barbed wire, but it falls instead, the motorcycle first and then the recruit, spiraling slowly down into the iron spikes. The ground heaves, and I fall, too.

I have fallen into Schwarzchild's dugout. Half of it has caved in, the timber balks sticking out at angles from the heap of dirt and snow, but the blanket is still over the door, and Schwarzschild is propped in a chair. The doctor is bending over him. Schwarzschild has his shirt off. His chest looks like Hans's did.

The front roars and more of the roof crumbles. "It's all right! It's a disease!" I shout over it. "I have brought you a letter to prove it," and hand him the letter which I have been clutching in my unfeeling hand.

The doctor grabs the letter from me. Snow whirls down through the ruined roof, but Schwarzschild does not put on his shirt. He watches uninterestedly as the doctor reads the letter.

" 'The symptoms you describe are almost certainly those of Neumann's disease, or pemphigus vulgaris. I have treated two patients with the disease, both Jews. It is a disease of the mucous membranes and is not contagious. Its cause is unknown. It always ends in death.' " Dr. Funkenheld crumples up the paper. "You came all this way in the middle of a bombardment to tell me there is no hope?" he shouts in a voice I do not even recognize, it is so unlike his steady doctor's voice. "You should have tried to get away. You should have—" and then he is gone under a crashing of dirt and splintered timbers.

I struggle toward Schwarzschild through the maelstrom of red dust and snow. "Put your shirt on!" I shout at him. "We must get out of here!" I crawl to the door to see if we can get out through the communication trench.

Muller bursts through the blanket. He is carrying, impossibly, the wireless. The headphones trail behind him in the snow. "I came to see what had happened to you. I thought you were dead. The communication trenches are shot to pieces."

It is as I had feared. His curiosity has got the best of him, and now he is trapped, too, though he seems not to know it. He hoists the wireless onto the table without looking at it. His eyes are on Schwarzschild, who leans against the remaining wall of the dugout, his shirt in his hands.

"Your shirt!" I shout, and come around to help Schwarzschild put it on over the craters and shell holes of his blasted skin. The air screams and the mouth of the dugout blows in. I grab at Schwarzschild's arm, and the skin of it comes off in my hands. He falls against the table, and the wireless goes over. I can hear the splintering tinkle of the liquid barretter breaking, and then the whole dugout is caving in and we are under the table. I cannot see anything.

"Muller!" I shout. "Where are you?"

"I'm hit," he says.

I try to find him in the darkness, but I am crushed against Schwarzschild. I cannot move. "Where are you hit?"

"In the arm," he says, and I hear him try to move it. The movement dislodges more dirt, and it falls around us, shutting out all sound of the front. I can hear the creak of wood as the table legs give way.

"Schwarzschild?" I say. He doesn't answer, but I know he is not dead. His body is as hot as the Primus stove flame. My hand is underneath his body, and I try to shift it, but I cannot. The dirt falls like snow, piling up around us. The darkness is red for a while, and then I cannot see even that.

"I have a theory," Muller says in a voice so close and so devoid of curiosity it might be mine. "It is the end of the world."

"Was that when Schwarzschild was sent home on sick leave?" Travers said. "Or validated, or whatever you Germans call it? Well, yeah, it had to be, because he died in March. What happened to Muller?"

I had hoped he would go away as soon as I had told him what had happened to Schwarzschild, but he made no move to get up. "Muller was invalided out with a broken arm. He became a scientist."

"The way you did." He opened his notebook again. "Did you see Schwarzschild after that?"

The question makes no sense.

"After you got out? Before he died?"

It seems to take a long time for his words to get to me. The message bends and curves, shifting into the red, and I can hardly make it out. "No," I say, though that is a lie.

Travers scribbles. "I really do appreciate this, Dr. Rottschieben. I've always been curious about Schwarzschild, and now that you've told me all this stuff, I'm even more interested," Travers says, or seems to say. Messages coming in are warped by the gravitational blizzard into something that no longer resembles speech. "If you'd be willing to help me, I'd like to write my thesis on him."

Go. Get out. "It was a lie," I say. "I never knew Schwarzschild. I saw him once, from a distance—your fixed observer."

Travers looks up expectantly from his notes as if he is still waiting for me to answer him.

"Schwarzschild was never even in Russia," I lie. "He spent the whole winter in hospital in Göttingen. I lied to you. It was nothing but a thought problem."

He waits, pencil ready.

"You can't stay here!" I shout. "You have to get away. There is no safe distance from which a fixed observer can watch without being drawn in, and once you are inside the Schwarzschild radius, you can't get out. Don't you understand? We are still there!"

We are still there, trapped in the trenches of the Russian front, while the dying star burns itself out, spiraling down into that center where time ceases to exist, where everything ceases to exist except the naked singularity that is somehow Schwarzschild.

Muller tries to dig the wireless out with his crushed arm so he can send a message that nobody can hear—

"Help us! Help us!"—and I struggle to free the hands that in spite of Schwarzschild's warmth are now so cold I cannot feel them, and in the very center Schwarzschild burns himself out, the black hole at his center imploding him cell by cell, carrying him down into darkness, and us with him.

"It is a trap!" I shout at Travers from the center, and the message struggles to escape and then falls back.

"I wonder how he figured it out," Travers says, and now I can hear him clearly. "I mean, can you imagine trying to figure out something like the theory of black holes in the middle of a war and while you were suffering from a fatal disease? And just think, when he came up with the theory, he didn't have any idea that black holes even existed."

*THE "IF THIS GOES ON . . ." STORY HAS LONG BEEN A staple of science fiction, probably because it's a naturally occurring train of thought. The writer looks at current trends and tendencies and thinks, "If nobody does anything about overpopulation . . ." ("Make Room, Make Room" by Harry Harrison) or "If computer incompetence continues to proliferate . . ." ("Computers Don't Argue" by Gordon Dickson) or "If urban violence gets any worse . . ." (*A Clockwork Orange *by Anthony Burgess) and carries them to their logical (or illogical) extreme.*

Luckily, most of these extrapolated bitter ends never come true. Overpopulation is stopped in its tracks by our old pals Famine, War, and Pestilence, and countertrends and unpredictable variables like rehabilitation programs and Bernard Goetz keep the original trend from going off the charts—at least partly.

I wrote "Ado" when political correctness was still just a gleam in some activist's eye, and the only thing the Fundamentalists were trying to do was keep The Catcher in the Rye *from being taught in high school. In the years since, productions of* The Taming of the Shrew *have been picketed by feminists, a federal judge has upheld the banning of* The Wizard of Oz *and "Cinderella" from Tennessee public schools, and the Nancy Drew books have been removed from the Boulder Public Library on the grounds that they are sexist and racist.*

Last year Culver City took "Little Red Riding Hood"

off its shelves because of their school substance-abuse program—Red's basket of wine and bread "sent the wrong message." And a few months ago Penn State ruled that a print of Goya's The Naked Maja *constituted sexual harassment in the classroom.*

I hope those countertrends and unpredictable variables I talked about get here pretty soon. At this point I'd even settle for Bernard Goetz. Or Pestilence.

Ado

The Monday before spring break I told my English lit class we were going to do Shakespeare. The weather in Colorado is usually wretched this time of year. We get all the snow the ski resorts needed in December, use up our scheduled snow days, and end up going an extra week in June. The forecast on the *Today* show hadn't predicted any snow till Saturday, but with luck it would arrive sooner.

My announcement generated a lot of excitement. Paula dived for her corder and rewound it to make sure she'd gotten my every word, Edwin Sumner looked smug, and Delilah snatched up her books and stomped out, slamming the door so hard it woke Rick up. I passed out the release/refusal slips and told them they had to have them back in by Wednesday. I gave one to Sharon to give Delilah.

"Shakespeare is considered one of our greatest writers, possibly *the* greatest," I said for the benefit of Paula's corder. "On Wednesday I will be talking about Shakespeare's life, and on Thursday and Friday we will be reading his work."

Wendy raised her hand. "Are we going to read all the plays?"

I sometimes wonder where Wendy has been the last few years—certainly not in this school, possibly not in this universe. "What we're studying hasn't been decided yet," I said. "The principal and I are meeting tomorrow."

"It had better be one of the tragedies," Edwin said darkly.

By lunch the news was all over the school. "Good luck," Greg Jefferson, the biology teacher, said in the teachers' lounge. "I just got done doing evolution."

"Is it really that time of year again?" Karen Miller said. She teaches American lit across the hall. "I'm not even up to the Civil War yet."

"It's that time of year again," I said. "Can you take my class during your free period tomorrow? I've got to meet with Harrows."

"I can take them all morning. Just have your kids come into my room tomorrow. We're doing 'Thanatopsis.' Another thirty kids won't matter."

" 'Thanatopsis'?" I said, impressed. "The whole thing?"

"All but lines ten and sixty-eight. It's a terrible poem, you know. I don't think anybody understands it well enough to protest. And I'm not telling anybody what the title means."

"Cheer up," Greg said. "Maybe we'll have a blizzard."

Tuesday was clear, with a forecast of temps in the sixties. Delilah was outside the school when I got there, wearing a red "Seniors Against Devil Worship in the Schools" T-shirt and shorts. She was carrying a picket sign that said, "Shakespeare is Satan's Spokesman." "Shakespeare" and "Satan" were both misspelled.

"We're not starting Shakespeare till tomorrow," I

told her. "There's no reason for you not to be in class. Ms. Miller is teaching 'Thanatopsis.' "

"Not lines ten and sixty-eight, she's not. Besides, Bryant was a Theist, which is the same thing as a Satanist." She handed me her refusal slip and a fat manila envelope. "Our protests are in there." She lowered her voice. "What does the word 'thanatopsis' really mean?"

"It's an Indian word. It means, 'One who uses her religion to ditch class and get a tan.' "

I went inside, got Shakespeare out of the vault in the library, and went into the office. Ms. Harrows already had the Shakespeare file and her box of Kleenex out. "Do you have to do this?" she said, blowing her nose.

"As long as Edwin Sumner's in my class, I do. His mother's head of the President's Task Force on Lack of Familiarity with the Classics." I added Delilah's list of protests to the stack and sat down at the computer.

"Well, it may be easier than we think," she said. "There have been a lot of suits since last year, which takes care of *Macbeth*, *The Tempest*, *Midsummer Night's Dream*, *The Winter's Tale*, and *Richard III*."

"Delilah's been a busy girl," I said. I fed in the unexpurgated disk and the excise and reformat programs. "I don't remember there being any witchcraft in *Richard III*."

She sneezed and grabbed for another Kleenex. "There's not. That was a slander suit. Filed by his great-great-grand-something. He claims there's no conclusive proof that Richard III killed the little princes. It doesn't matter anyway. The Royal Society for the Restoration of Divine Right of Kings has an injunction against all the history plays. What's the weather supposed to be like?"

"Terrible," I said. "Warm and sunny." I called up the catalog and deleted *Henry IV, Parts I* and *II*, and the rest of her list. "*The Taming of the Shrew?*"

"Angry Women's Alliance. Also *Merry Wives of Windsor*, *Romeo and Juliet*, and *Love's Labour's Lost*."

"*Othello?* Never mind. I know that one. *The Merchant of Venice?* The Anti-Defamation League?"

"No. American Bar Association. And Morticians International. They object to the use of the word 'casket' in Act III." She blew her nose.

It took us first and second period to deal with the plays and most of the third to finish the sonnets. "I've got a class fourth period and then lunch duty," I said. "We'll have to finish up the rest of them this afternoon."

"Is there anything left for this afternoon?" Ms. Harrows asked.

"*As You Like It* and *Hamlet*," I said. "Good heavens, how did they miss *Hamlet*?"

"Are you sure about *As You Like It*?" Ms. Harrows said, leafing through her stack. "I thought somebody'd filed a restraining order against it."

"Probably the Mothers Against Transvestites," I said. "Rosalind dresses up like a man in Act II."

"No, here it is. The Sierra Club. 'Destructive attitudes toward the environment.' " She looked up. "What destructive attitudes?"

"Orlando carves Rosalind's name on a tree." I leaned back in my chair so I could see out the window. The sun was still shining maliciously down. "I guess we go with *Hamlet*. This should make Edwin and his mother happy."

"We've still got the line-by-lines to go," Ms. Harrows said. "I think my throat is getting sore."

I got Karen to take my afternoon classes. It was sophomore lit and we'd been doing Beatrix Potter—all she had to do was pass out a worksheet on *Squirrel Nutkin*. I had outside lunch duty. It was so hot I had to take my jacket off. The College Students for Christ were marching around the school carrying picket signs that said, "Shakespeare was a Secular Humanist."

Delilah was lying on the front steps, reeking of suntan oil. She waved her "Shakespeare is Satan's Spokesman" sign languidly at me. " 'Ye have sinned a great sin,' " she quoted. " 'Blot me, I pray thee, out of thy book which thou has written.' Exodus Chapter 32, Verse 30."

"First Corinthians 13:3," I said. " 'Though I give my body to be burned and have not charity, it profiteth me nothing.' "

"I called the doctor," Ms. Harrows said. She was standing by the window looking out at the blazing sun. "He thinks I might have pneumonia."

I sat down at the computer and fed in *Hamlet*. "Look on the bright side. At least we've got the E and R programs. We don't have to do it by hand the way we used to."

She sat down behind the stack. "How shall we do this? By group or by line?"

"We might as well take it from the top."

"Line one. 'Who's there?' The National Coalition Against Contractions."

"Let's do it by group," I said.

"All right. We'll get the big ones out of the way first. The Commission on Poison Prevention feels the 'graphic depiction of poisoning in the murder of Hamlet's father may lead to copycat crimes.' They cite a case in New Jersey where a sixteen-year-old poured Drano in his father's ear after reading the play. Just a minute. Let me get a Kleenex. The Literature Liberation Front objects to the phrases, 'Frailty, thy name is woman,' and 'O, most pernicious woman,' the 'What a piece of work is man' speech, and the queen."

"The whole queen?"

She checked her notes. "Yes. All lines, references, and allusions." She felt under her jaw, first one side, then the other. "I think my glands are swollen. Would that go along with pneumonia?"

Greg Jefferson came in, carrying a grocery sack. "I

thought you could use some combat rations. How's it going?"

"We lost the queen," I said. "Next?"

"The National Cutlery Council objects to the depiction of swords as deadly weapons. 'Swords don't kill people. People kill people.' The Copenhagen Chamber of Commerce objects to the line, 'Something is rotten in the state of Denmark.' Students Against Suicide, the International Federation of Florists, and the Red Cross object to Ophelia's drowning."

Greg was setting out the bottles of cough syrup and cold tablets on the desk. He handed me a bottle of Valium. "The International Federation of Florists?" he said.

"She fell in picking flowers," I said. "What was the weather like out there?"

"Just like summer," he said. "Delilah's using an aluminum sun reflector."

"Ass," Ms. Harrows said.

"Beg pardon?" Greg said.

"ASS, the Association of Summer Sunbathers, objects to the line, 'I am too much i' the sun,' " Ms. Harrows said, and took a swig from the bottle of cough syrup.

We were only half-finished by the time school let out. The Nuns' Network objected to the line "Get thee to a nunnery," Fat and Proud of It wanted the passage beginning "Oh, that this too too solid flesh should melt" removed, and we didn't even get to Delilah's list, which was eight pages long.

"What play are we going to do?" Wendy asked me on my way out.

"*Hamlet,*" I said.

"*Hamlet*?" she said. "Is that the one about the guy whose uncle murders the king and then the queen marries the uncle?"

"Not anymore," I said.

Delilah was waiting for me outside. " 'Many of them brought their books together and burned them,' " she quoted. "Acts 19:19."

" 'Look not upon me, because I am black, because the sun hath looked upon me,' " I said.

It was overcast Wednesday but still warm. The Veterans for a Clean America and the Subliminal Seduction Sentinels were picnicking on the lawn. Delilah had on a halter top. "That thing you said yesterday about the sun turning people black, what was that from?"

"The Bible," I said. "Song of Solomon. Chapter 1, Verse 6."

"Oh," she said, relieved. "That's not in the Bible anymore. We threw it out."

Ms. Harrows had left a note for me. She was at the doctor's. I was supposed to meet with her third period.

"Do we get to start today?" Wendy asked.

"If everybody remembered to bring in their slips. I'm going to lecture on Shakespeare's life," I said. "You don't know what the forecast for today is, do you?"

"Yeah, it's supposed to be great."

I had her collect the refusal slips while I went over my notes. Last year Delilah's sister Jezebel had filed a grievance halfway through the lecture for "trying to preach promiscuity, birth control, and abortion by saying Anne Hathaway got pregnant before she got married." "Promiscuity," "abortion," "pregnant," and "before" had all been misspelled.

Everybody had remembered their slips. I sent the refusals to the library and started to lecture.

"Shakespeare—" I said. Paula's corder clicked on. "William Shakespeare was born on April twenty-third, 1564, in Stratford-on-Avon."

Rick, who hadn't raised his hand all year or even given an indication that he was sentient, raised his hand. "Do you intend to give equal time to the Baconian theory?" he said. "Bacon was not born on April twenty-third, 1564. He was born on January twenty-second, 1561."

Ms. Harrows wasn't back from the doctor's by third period, so I started on Delilah's list. She objected to forty-three references to spirits, ghosts, and related matters, twenty-one obscene words, ("obscene" misspelled), and seventy-eight others that she thought might be obscene, such as pajock and cockles.

Ms. Harrows came in as I was finishing the list and threw her briefcase down. "Stress induced!" she said. "I have pneumonia, and he says my symptoms are stress induced!"

"Is it still cloudy out?"

"It is seventy-two degrees out. Where are we?"

"Morticians International," I said. "Again. 'Death presented as universal and inevitable.' " I peered at the paper. "That doesn't sound right."

Ms. Harrows took the paper away from me. "That's their 'Thanatopsis' protest. They had their national convention last week. They filed a whole set at once, and I haven't had a chance to sort through them." She rummaged around in her stack. "Here's the one on *Hamlet.* 'Negative portrayal of interment-preparation personnel—' "

"The gravedigger."

" '—And inaccurate representation of burial regulations. Neither a hermetically sealed coffin nor a vault appear in the scene.' "

We worked until five o'clock. The Society for the Advancement of Philosophy considered the line "There are more things in heaven and earth, Horatio, than are dreamt of in your philosophy" a slur on their profession. The Actors' Guild challenged Hamlet's hiring of nonunion employees, and the Drapery Defense League objected to Polonius being stabbed while hiding behind a curtain.

"The clear implication of the scene is that the arras is dangerous," they had written in their brief. "Draperies don't kill people. People kill people."

Ms. Harrows put the paper down on top of the stack and took a swig of cough syrup. "And that's it. Anything left?"

"I think so," I said, punching *reformat* and scanning the screen. "Yes, a couple of things. How about, 'There is a willow grows aslant a brook / That shows his hoar leaves in the glassy stream.' "

"You'll never get away with 'hoar,' " Ms. Harrows said.

Thursday I got to school at seven-thirty to print out thirty copies of *Hamlet* for my class. It had turned colder and even cloudier in the night. Delilah was wearing a parka and mittens. Her face was a deep scarlet, and her nose had begun to peel.

" 'Hath the Lord as great delight in burnt offerings as in obeying the voice of the Lord?' " I asked. "First Samuel 15:22." I patted her on the shoulder.

"Yeow," she said.

I passed out *Hamlet* and assigned Wendy and Rick to read the parts of Hamlet and Horatio.

" 'The air bites shrewdly; it is very cold,' " Wendy read.

"Where are we?" Rick said. I pointed out the place to him. "Oh. 'It is a nipping and an eager air.' "

" 'What hour now?' " Wendy read.

" 'I think it lacks of twelve.' "

Wendy turned her paper over and looked at the back. "That's it?" she said. "That's all there is to *Hamlet*? I thought his uncle killed his father and then the ghost told him his mother was in on it and he said 'To be or not to be' and Ophelia killed herself and stuff." She turned the paper back over. "This can't be the whole play."

"It better not be the whole play," Delilah said. She came in, carrying her picket sign. "There'd better not be any ghosts in it. Or cockles."

"Did you need some Solarcaine, Delilah?" I asked her.

"I *need* a Magic Marker," she said with dignity.

I got her one out of the desk. She left, walking a little stiffly, as if it hurt to move.

"You can't just take parts of the play out because somebody doesn't like them," Wendy said. "If you do, the play doesn't make any sense. I bet if Shakespeare were here, he wouldn't let you just take things out—"

"Assuming Shakespeare wrote it," Rick said. "If you take every other letter in line two except the first three and the last six, they spell 'pig,' which is obviously a code word for Bacon."

"Snow day!" Ms. Harrow said over the intercom. Everybody raced to the windows. "We will have early dismissal today at nine-thirty."

I looked at the clock. It was 9:28.

"The Overprotective Parents Organization has filed the following protest: 'It is now snowing, and as the forecast predicts more snow, and as snow can result in slippery streets, poor visibility, bus accidents, frostbite, and avalanches, we demand that school be closed today and tomorrow so as not to endanger our children.' Buses will leave at nine thirty-five. Have a nice spring break!"

"The snow isn't even sticking on the ground," Wendy said. "Now we'll never get to do Shakespeare."

Delilah was out in the hall, on her knees next to her picket sign, crossing out the word "man" in "Spokesman."

"The Feminists for a Fair Language are here," she said disgustedly. "They've got a court order," She wrote "person" above the crossed-out "man." "A court order! Can you believe that? I mean, what's happening to our right to freedom of speech?"

"You misspelled 'person,' " I said.

I'VE BEEN IN LOVE WITH SCREWBALL COMEDIES since I first watched Bringing up Baby *and* Shall We Dance *on Academy Matinee. They're wonderful. They always have a heroine (Jean Arthur) who's engaged to the wrong person (Ray Milland), and a hero (Cary Grant) who isn't what he seems to be, and all sorts of smart-aleck or daffy or obnoxious supporting characters. The plot makes almost no sense (usually the hero and heroine have to get married at some point to keep his job or save her reputation or win a bet), but it doesn't matter because there are all these complications and chases and bantering conversations and sometimes singing and dancing, and you know they're not going to get it annulled.*

"Spice Pogrom" is my heartfelt homage to The More the Merrier, *and to* It Happened One Night *and* How to Steal a Million *and* Little Miss Marker. *It's a tribute to everything I love best about movie comedies: meeting cute and good-hearted chorus girls, and marriages-in-name-only, and traveling incognito, and all those revoltingly adorable little girls. And most of all to the view of the world that says good sense may be in short supply and goodness in even shorter, but sanity (sort of) and true love are still possible.*

SPICE POGROM

"You've got to talk to him," Chris said. "I've told him there isn't enough space, but he keeps bringing things home anyway."

"Things?" Stewart said absently. He had his head half-turned as if he were listening to someone out of the holographic image.

"Things. A six-foot high Buddha, two dozen baseball caps, and a Persian rug!" Chris shouted at him. "Things I didn't even know they had on Sony. Today he brought home a piano! How did they even get a piano up here with the weight restrictions?"

"What?" Stewart said. The person who had been talking to him moved into the holo-image, focusing as he entered, put a piece of paper in front of Stewart, and then stood there, obviously waiting for some kind of response. "Listen, Chris, darling, can I put you on hold? Or would you rather call me back?"

It had taken her almost an hour to get him in the first place. "I'll hold," she said, and watched the screen grimly as it went back to a two-dimensional wall image on the phone's screen and froze with Stewart still smiling placatingly at her. Chris sighed and leaned back against the piano. There was hardly room to stand in the narrow hall, but she knew that if she wasn't right in view when Stewart came back on the line, he'd use it as an excuse to hang up. He'd been avoiding her for the last two days.

Stewart's image jerked into a nonsmiling one and grew to a full holo-image again. With the piano in here, there wasn't really enough room for the phone. Stewart's desk blurred and dissolved on the keyboard, but Chris wanted Stewart to see how crowded the piano made the hall. "Chris, I really don't have time to worry about a few souvenirs," he said. "We've got real communications difficulties over here with the aliens. The Japanese translation team's been negotiating with them for a space program for over a week, but the Eahrohhs apparently don't understand what it is we want."

"I'm having communications difficulties over here, too," Chris said. "I tell Mr. Ohghhi . . ." She stopped and looked at the alien's name she had written on her hand so she could pronounce it. "Mr. Ohghhifoehnnahigrheeh that there isn't room in my apartment and that he's got to stop buying things, and he seems to understand what I'm saying, but he goes right on buying. I've only got a two-room apartment, Stewart."

"You could move your couch out of the living room," he said.

"Then where would I sleep? On top of the piano? You said you'd try to find him someplace else to stay."

"I'm giving the matter top priority, darling, but you don't know how impossible it is to find any kind of space at all, let alone space with the kinds of specifications Mr. Ohghhifoehnnahigrheeh requires." A blond young woman moved into the image and put a computer printout down in front of Stewart. Chris braced herself against being put on hold again. "We were already full over here at NASA, and today Houston sent a dozen linguistic specialists up on the shuttle, and I don't know where we're going to put them." He shook his head. "With all these reporters and tourists coming up, there isn't a spare room on Sony."

"Can't you send some of these people back down to earth?" Chris said. "I've got two little girls living on my stairs who're here because they think Spielberg's bound to make a movie about the aliens so they came up here to try to get a part in it, which is ridiculous. I'm not even sure Spielberg's still alive, but if he is, he's got to be at least eighty. Isn't there some way to send people like that home?"

"You know Sony's got an automatic thirty-day travel permission wait. It's been in effect since Sony was first built so that immigrants couldn't change their minds before they got over shuttle-lag. NASA's trying to get the Japanese to limit the earth-to-Sony traffic, but so far they've refused because they like all the business it's bringing up."

"Can't NASA put on its own limits? They own the shuttle."

"We don't want to jeopardize relations with the Japanese. We've got too many of our own people who need to come up to see the aliens."

"And they're all using my bathroom," Chris said. "How long will it take you to find another apartment for him?"

"Chris, darling, I don't think you understand the overcrowding problem we've got over here. . . . Hold on a second, will you?" he said, and flattened and froze.

"We've got an overcrowding problem over here, too, Stewart," Chris said. Someone rang the bell. "Come in," Chris shouted, and then was sorry.

Molly came in. "My mother thaid to tell you to get off the phone," she said, lisping the word "said."

"I'm really six," Molly had told her without a trace of a lisp the day she and her mother moved onto the landing outside Chris's apartment, "but six is box-office poison, because your teeth are going to fall out pretty soon, so my screen age is four and a half." She was certainly dressed to look four and a half today, in a short yellow smock with ducks embroidered on it and a giant yellow bow in her shingled brown bob.

"My mother thayth to tell you we're eckthpecting a call from my agent," she said, with her dimpled hands on her hips.

"Your mother does not have phone privileges in this apartment. Your agent can call you on the pay phone in the hall."

"It'th a holo-call," Molly said, and strolled over to the piano. "He thaid he'd call at thickthteen-thirty. Did you know thum new people moved in on the thtairs today?"

"A slut and an old guy," Bets said, coming into the hall. She was wearing a pink dress with a sash, pink ribbon bows, and black patent-leather shoes, "My mother says to ask you how we're supposed to get the lead in Spielberg's movie if we can't talk to our agent."

"How could new people move in?" Chris said. Molly's mother had sublet half of the landing to Bets (who was also six according to Molly, even though she swore she was five) and her mother last week, and Chris had thought at the time that the only good thing about it was that nobody else could move in because Mr. Nagisha's cousins were renting the hall outside Chris's apartment, and Mr. Nagisha himself was living in the downstairs hall.

"Mr. Nagithha rented them the thtairth," Molly said, plunking the piano keys, "for twenty thouthand yen apiethe."

"The slut says she's in show business," Bets said archly, patting her golden curls, "but I think she's a hooker."

"The old guy came up to thee the alienth," Molly said, banging out "Chopsticks." "He thayth he'th alwayth wanted to meet one. My mother thayth he'th thenile."

"Chris," Stewart said, his face expanding out from

the screen. Molly stopped banging on the piano. Bets tossed her yellow curls. They both turned and flashed Stewart a dimpled smile.

"They were just leaving," Chris said hastily, and pushed them out of the hall.

"What adorable little girls!" Stewart said. "Do they live in your apartment building?"

"They live on the stairs, Stewart. At last count, so do four other people, not counting Mr. Nagisha's cousins, who are living in the hall outside my apartment. They use my bathroom and make earthside calls on my phone, and I don't have room for them or for Mr. Ogyfen . . . whatever his name is."

"Ohghhifoehnnahigrheeh," Stewart said disapprovingly. "You're going to have to learn how to pronounce his name properly. You don't want to make him angry. I've told you before how important it is we don't do anything that might offend the Eahrohhs."

"He can't stay here, Stewart."

He looked aghast. Chris thought about putting him on hold that way. It was better than his frozen smile. "You can't mean that, Chris. The negotiations are at an incredibly delicate stage. We can't risk having anything upset them. It's a matter of national security. Besides, NASA intends to make generous compensation to people whose apartments have been requisitioned."

"You work for NASA. Why can't he stay with you?"

"Chris, darling, we've been through all this before. You know Mother's xenophobic. Just the thought of the Eahrrohhs being on Sony has given her terrible migraines. And you know Mr. Oghhifoehnnahigrheeh has to have ceilings at least twelve feet high for his vertical claustrophobia, and you were the only other person I knew who had ceilings that high. The Japanese didn't design Sony for Americans. It's hard enough to find buildings with even normal American ceilings, let alone twelve-foot ones.

And with the Eahrohhs' privacy fetish, we can't ask them to double up with people."

"I know, Stewart," Chris said, "but . . ."

"The only twelve-foot ceilings on Sony are in the apartment buildings Misawa designed. Like your building."

And your mother's, Chris thought.

"It'll only be for a few more days. We're currently negotiating with the Japanese to transfer the Eahrohhs down to Houston. When that happens, you'll have your apartment all to yourself again." He pressed some buttons on his desk. "Darling, I've got a call coming in. Can't we . . ."

The door to her apartment slid open, and someone said, "Hey, this is great!"

She looked back at Stewart. He had flattened out again, this time with a decidedly impatient look on his face.

"My room in here," Ohghhifoehnnahigrheeh said, and squeezed past Chris carrying two shopping bags, a bouquet of cherry blossoms, and what looked like a tent. The pockets of his long orange coat looked lumpy, too, but Chris hadn't figured out yet which of the bulges and lumps were part of Mr. Ohghhifoennahigrheeh's peculiar shape and which weren't.

He looked a little like a sack of potatoes with short, wide legs and arms. His legs and arms were lumpy, too, and so was his head, except for the top, which was round and bald and surrounded by a fringe of fine pinkish-orange hair that extended down the sides of his face in wispy sideburns. "Except for he's an alien, he'd never make it in the movies," Bets had said the first time she'd seen him.

"Mr. Ohghhifoeh . . ." She stopped and looked down at her hand to get the name right. "Mr. Ohghhifoehnnahigrheeh, I have to talk to you. You've got to stop buying things. There simply isn't any more room for . . ."

Ohghhifoehnnahigrheeh smiled at her, his wide mouth curving upward toward the two pinkish-orange lumps that were his cheeks. He put down the two shopping bags and the thing that looked like a tent and handed Chris the bouquet of cherry blossoms. "*Hana*," he said. "Buy you."

Chris had no idea what *hana* meant. "Thank you for the cherry blossoms, but . . ."

He shook his head vigorously, the wisps of cotton-candy hair flying out in all directions. "Hutchins buy *hana*."

"Hutchins?" Chris said, wishing she had the Japanese translation team here.

"Pete Hutchins," a tall young man said. He was wearing jeans and a satin bomber jacket and was trying to maneuver a duffel bag and a bicycle into the narrow hall. He held out a hand for her to shake. "He means I bought you the cherry blossoms. *Hana* means cherry blossoms in Japanese. You must be Chris. Okee's told me all about you."

"I'm very busy right now," Stewart said from the phone. "Can't this wait till tomorrow?"

"Hutchins stay here," Ohghhifoehnnahigrheeh said. He slid open his door and ducked inside with the shopping bags and the tent before Chris could even get a glimpse of what was inside.

"Just a minute, Stewart," Chris said, and pushed the hold button. "Mr. Hutchins, what is it you want with Mr. Ohghhifoehnn . . ." She had to stop and read from her hand. "Mr. Ohghhifoehnnahigrheeh?"

He twisted around to get a look at her hand. "Had to write it on there, huh?" he said. "I can't pronounce it either, so I just call him Okeefenokee. And you can call me Pete."

She closed her hand. "I don't know what Mr. . . . he told you, but he doesn't speak English very well, and . . ."

"I really appreciate Okee doing this. I just came up

on the shuttle today, and I'm shot. So if you could just show me to my room . . ."

"Excuse me. Is this where the john is?" a woman with an elaborate topknot of brass-colored hair said. She was holding a skimpy hapi coat closed with one hand and carrying a makeup case. "The little kids said it was in here. I'm Charmaine. I just moved in. Top half of the stairs, but I don't mind. The seventy percent gravity's great for me in my job. And I've never seen so many cute guys in my life. Do you live here?" she said to Hutchins.

"Yes," Hutchins said.

"No," Chris said. "There's been some misunderstanding."

"About the john?" Charmaine said nervously. "Mr. Nagisha told me I had bathroom privileges."

"No, I mean, you can use the bathroom, Charmaine. There isn't anybody in there." She turned back to Hutchins. "Mr. Hutchins, I don't know what Mr. Ohghhifoehnn . . ."—she resisted the temptation to look at her hand—". . . ackafee told you, but he sometimes has trouble understanding. . . ."

" 'Scuse me," Charmaine said, and slithered past Hutchins, making no effort at all to stay away from him. "I gotto go do my makeup for my show. I'm a specialty dancer down at Luigi's. You oughta come see me." She waggled her fingers at him as she slid the bathroom door shut.

"Aren't you off the phone yet?" Molly said from the doorway. She had her dimpled arms folded across her yellow-ducked middle and was tapping a black-patented foot. "My mother thayth to tell you that my agent hath very important newth. He'th thyure Thpielberg ith on Thony and . . ."

While she was talking, Bets was sidling past Molly and behind Hutchins, holding something behind her pink-sashed back. Chris reached around Hutchins and made a grab for it. She got hold of the curling iron by the cord and took it away from Bets.

"Electrical appliances are not allowed in the bathroom," Chris said. She wrapped the cord around the curling iron and put it on top of the piano. "I told you last time I was going to take it away from you if it happened again. You're supposed to use the outlets in Mr. Nagisha's apartment."

"We can't use the ones in Mr. Nagisha's apartment. He blew a fuse, and our agent's calling us at eighteen o'clock!"

"Not on my phone he isn't," Chris said. "The phone! I forgot all about Stewart." She punched the *reinstate* button, wondering if he'd already hung up. Hutchins and the little girls backed up as the holo-image spread, but they were still in the way. Hutchins seemed to be standing in the middle of Stewart's desk. Molly and Bets's face were covered with blurry brown. Chris hit the flat-image button, and Stewart retreated to the screen. "I'm sorry, Stewart," she said.

He was writing busily. "Can this wait till tomorrow, Chris?" he said without looking up. "We'll have lunch and you can tell me all about it. The Garden of Meditation. In the ginza. Thirteen-thirty."

Hutchins was watching the screen. "All right, Stewart, but . . . ," Chris said.

"Till then just go along with whatever Ohghhifoehnnahigrheeh says. The negotiations are at a very delicate stage. Anything could break them off. Let him do anything he wants. I love you, darling. See you tomorrow," he said, still without looking up, and blanked the screen before Chris had a chance to say anything.

Hutchins was looking at her curiously. "Who is that guy?" he said.

"He's my fiancé," Chris said. Molly had climbed up on the piano bench and was kneeling on the keyboard, trying to reach the curling iron. Chris grabbed it away from her and put it behind her back.

"You better give my curling iron back!" Bets said. "I'm going to tell my mother you stole it."

"Out," she said. She escorted both of them out of her apartment, slid the door shut, and went into the living room. She lifted up the pile of folded blankets on the end of the couch and stuck the curling iron under it.

"You're really engaged to that guy on the phone?" Hutchins said, leaning against the door, his hands in his jeans pockets.

"Yes," she said, straightening back up. "Why?"

"Because 'let him do anything he wants,' covers a lot of territory. What if Okee decided he wanted to carry you off with him to Eahrohhsani, or wherever it is they came from, and make you his bride?"

"Mr. Ohghhifoehnn . . . he is a very nice man. Alien. Eahrohh. And he would not . . ."

"Earrose. They drop an *e* and add some *h*'s to make it plural."

"Earrose. Mr. Hutchins, I don't care what Mr. . . . he told you. You can't stay here. There isn't any space. The landlord has people living on the stairs."

"Hutchins stay here," Ohghhifoehnnahigrheeh said. He peeked around Hutchins and then disappeared back into the hall.

Chris went after him.

"Tall," he said, smiling and nodding. "High ceilings. Stay here."

"But there isn't any space. Mr. Ohghhifoehnnah . . . where will he sleep?"

"My room." He took hold of the handlebars of the bike and started pulling it toward his door. Chris backed up against the piano to get out of the way of the handlebars. "I keep in here. Lots of space."

" 'Scuse me," Charmaine said brightly. She had put

on her makeup, but not where Chris had expected it. She had the hapi coat draped over her arm.

"Where exactly do you work?" Chris said.

"Luigi's Tempura Pizzeria and Sutorippu. That means strip show. I'm in the Fan Tan Fannie number," she said. She turned around.

"I can see that," Chris said.

"Cute idea, huh?" she said. "I just love my fans."

"So do I," Hutchins said.

Charmaine started edging out of the hall, this time trying hard not to touch Hutchins for fear of smearing her makeup. Ohghhifoehnnahigrheeh went on tugging at the bicycle. Chris tried to turn around to get out from the piano so Charmaine could get past and found herself nose to nose with Hutchins. She backed into the piano. The keys made a crash of noise as her open hands hit them.

"Listen," Hutchins said, taking a step toward her, and towering over her. He really was tall. "In all seriousness, there's obviously been a mix-up. I met Okee on the bullet, and he said he'd sublet half of his room to me, and I said okay. I'd just gotten in on the shuttle, and I guess I wasn't thinking clearly. I felt like hell."

He rubbed his hand across his forehead. He did look tired. Chris remembered what she had felt like when she came up on the shuttle. Everyone had kept telling her how lucky she was not to be nauseated, but she hadn't felt lucky. She'd felt bone-tired, so weary she had burst into tears at the thought of getting through customs, even in the zero gravity of Sony's axis.

"As a matter of fact, I still feel like hell," he said.

"It's shuttle-lag," Chris said. "Aspirin helps. And vitamin A." She didn't say he should be glad he wasn't the kind to get nauseated. "And you should get some sleep."

"Sleep," he said, leaning against the piano. "You wouldn't know of any good hotels, would you?"

She shook her head. "There's only one hotel on Sony,

and it's full of Eahrohhs. So's everything else. There are over four hundred of them, you know."

"Four hundred," he said, looking at Ohghhifoehnnahigrheeh, who had gotten the handlebars and the front wheel turned around so the bike wouldn't budge. Hutchins helped him straighten it out. "Where are they putting them all?"

"All over. The officials, the headmen or chiefs or whatever you call them, and all the translators are staying at NASA. They're negotiating a treaty. They're going to give us a space program."

"Are they?" Hutchins said with an odd note in his voice. "What about the rest of them?"

"They put them anyplace there was room. Vacant apartments, extra rooms. It wasn't so bad when it was just the aliens, but now that all these sightseers have come up . . ."

"They're living on the stairs," Hutchins said. "What about that? Do you think your landlord would rent me a step or two?"

She bit her lip. "No. He lets as many extra people sleep on the stairs at night as the fire regulations will permit—he sells them 'overnight leases'—but he'd already sold out by nine this morning."

Mr. Ohghhifoehnnahigrheeh had gotten the handlebars of the bike wedged in the screen of his bedroom door and was struggling with it. "Want Hutchins stay," he said.

If she threw Hutchins out and then Mr. Ohghhi . . . he got angry or refused to cooperate, Stewart would be furious. He had told her explicitly to do whatever he wanted, and what he wanted was for Mr. Hutchins to stay. While she was on the phone, she had decided to insist that Stewart come home with her after lunch and talk to him about all these things he was buying. She could ask Stewart what to do then, and he could find Mr. Hutchins an apartment.

"All right," she said. Ohghhifoehnnahigrheeh got the

handlebars unstuck and disappeared into his room with the bicycle.

"All right, what?" Hutchins said.

"You can stay here tonight and look for a room tomorrow."

"I love you," he said.

"Mr. Nagisha said you're violating your lease by taking my curling iron away from me," Bets said.

"It's in the living room. On the couch. But if I catch you with it in the bathroom one more time, I'm flushing it down the o-benjo," Chris said. Bets flounced off, stamping her feet so the ruffles on her petticoat showed.

"I'm only letting you stay because Mr. Ohghhi . . . he wants you to, and I don't want to upset him. Negotiations are at a very delicate stage. Tomorrow when I have lunch with my fiancé, I'll ask him about it, but I'm sure he'll want you to find another place to stay."

"Do you have any vitamin A?" Hutchins said.

"In the bathroom." Chris pointed at the door. It was shut. "Bets, you come out of there. You are not allowed to have electrical appliances in there."

Bets slid the door open. "I was brushing my teeth," she said indignantly, holding up a pink toothbrush shaped like a bunny.

"I'll bet." She got Hutchins aspirin and vitamin-A packets and herded Bets out of her apartment. "I'll get you a bathroom schedule and the apartment rules," she said.

Mr. Nagisha's cousins were squatting around a hibachi in the middle of the landing, cooking something vile smelling. Chris stepped over them and started down the steps. She wondered how Mr. Nagisha would take the news that Mr. Ohghhi . . . her alien had sublet half of his room to Mr. Hutchins. Probably not very well, unless he could think of a way to make money off the deal. Mr. Nagisha had welcomed him with open arms since NASA had agreed to pay the equivalent of a six months' lease.

Even at that, he had insisted on rent based on changing property values, which were soaring with the sudden influx of people. He was going to make a killing.

Molly was sitting on the steps above the landing reading *Variety*. "Have you seen Mr. Nagisha?" Chris said.

"My mother'th talking to him about how you took the curling iron away from Betth. She thayth . . ."

"Are they in the apartment? I need a copy of the bathroom schedule." She pushed down past their trunks and almost stepped on the old man who had just moved in. He had a baseball cap that read "Blue Harvest" pulled down over his eyes and was snoring loudly. She took hold of the banister to make the last jump over Mr. Nagisha's file drawers and lap terminal and knocked on his apartment door.

Mr. Nagisha had rented his own apartment out to as many people as it would hold and taken up residence on the bottom steps, but he wasn't in the apartment, even though half of Sony's population appeared to be. He'd better not say anything to me about my alien subletting half of his room, Chris thought. She went back out to Mr. Nagisha's terminal, entered Mr. Hutchins's name under Ohghhifoehnnahigrheeh and asked for a revised schedule.

" 'Scuse me," Charmaine said, putting down one high-heeled shoe next to the printer. "I gotta leave for work. My shift doesn't start till nineteen, but I gotta walk on account of my makeup gets smeared on the bullet."

"I can imagine," Chris said. She tore off the printout and stood up. Charmaine was wearing a pink smock that stood out stiffly from her body and made her look much younger than she had in the hall. She had her hair done in an elaborate topknot. "You'd better take an umbrella. It might rain."

"I thought on the L-5's it was only supposed to rain at night after everybody'd gone to bed."

"It is, but the sprinklers are set to come on when a given area gets overheated, and with all these people, they've been coming on at funny times. Mr. Ohghhi . . . ," she said, and glanced guiltily at her hand as if Hutchins were watching her, "foehnnahigrheeh and I got caught in the ginza yesterday." He hadn't been the least bit dismayed. He had gone into the nearest department store and bought five dozen oiled-paper umbrellas. "Why don't you ask Mr. . . . my alien to loan you an umbrella? He's got more than enough."

"Gee, thanks," Charmaine said, and started up the stairs.

"He doesn't speak English very well. Just say 'umbrella' and act it out." She went through the motions of opening an umbrella and holding it above her head. "Better yet, ask Mr. Hutchins to ask him. He doesn't seem to have any trouble communicating with him."

"I bet he wouldn't have trouble communicating with anybody," Charmaine said, and clattered on up the stairs in her spike heels.

Chris printed out copies of the bathroom schedules and the apartment rules, tore them off, and started back up the stairs.

"He loaned me a red one to go with my fans," Charmaine said, twirling it as she came down the stairs. "I love it. I might use it in my single. Can I ask you something about this guy Hutchins? Is he your boyfriend?"

"No," Chris said. "I'm engaged."

"I knew it," Charmaine said. "The cute ones are always already taken. Even when the ratio of guys to women is as good as it is right now on Sony. Especially the tall cute ones."

"I'm not engaged to Mr. Hutchins. I don't even know him. NASA requisitioned half of my apartment for Mr. Ohghhi . . . my alien, and he sublet half of it to Mr. Hutchins."

"Oh," she said, opening and closing the umbrella.

"The little kids told me he was moving in with you, so I figured he was your boyfriend."

"He is not my boyfriend. He is not my anything."

"So you wouldn't be mad if I put the moves on him, then? I mean, I'm here to try to find a husband, but I wouldn't want to steal your boyfriend or anything." She snapped the umbrella open and put it over her shoulder. "Is he a lawyer?"

"I don't know," Chris said, and frowned. Come to think of it, he hadn't said a word about what he did for a living or why he was on Sony.

"I hope not. They always try to make marriage into a real-estate deal or something." She sighed. "My old boyfriend down on earth was a lawyer, and gee, you woulda thought I was a condo or something. Well, I gotta go. See you at the show." She flounced out, twirling the umbrella.

Chris started back up the stairs, maneuvering between rolled-up bedding and a stack of dishes from the deli next door. The old man was sitting up, watching Charmaine's exit with a dazed expression. Mr. Nagisha's cousins were watching, too, and eating fried fish. Molly and Bets were leaning over the landing railing, their chins resting on their arms.

"I told you thyee was a thlut," Molly said. "Did you thee those fanth on her ath?"

"At least she's really in show business," Chris said. "Unlike some people I could name."

She went back into the apartment. Hutchins was in the hall, leaning against the door of her room with the aspirin packet still in his hand as if he were too tired to take it.

"Mr. Hutchins," she said, "I'm afraid this isn't going to work. I know Mr. Ohghhi . . . he told you you could stay, but . . ."

"But you've been talking to Hedda and Louella, and they've been busily spreading the news that you have a live-in lover. Are you sure they're not forty-year-old circus midgets?"

"No," Chris said, feeling sorry for him all over again. He had leaned his head against the wall as if it hurt, and even though he was smiling at her, it looked like it took an effort.

"Am I supposed to ache all over?"

"Yes. Did you take the vitamin A?"

"Yes."

"Good." She handed him the printouts. "These are the bathroom schedules. Everyone gets an initial two minutes in the morning using this schedule, which begins at five o'clock. At six-fifteen the second rotation begins, which allows you an additional five minutes. If you miss your turn, you automatically go to the end of the schedule. There's soap, and water for brushing your teeth in the bathroom. You get your shower water from the tank in the basement. You're allowed sixteen ounces."

"No electrical appliances in the bathroom," he said wearily.

"The apartment rules are on the other sheet. You'll feel better as soon as the aspirin starts working. I'll make you a cup of tea and you can lie down." She started past him into the living room, but he put his arm up with surprising speed.

"It's a great idea, but it won't work," he said.

"Why not? Did Mr. Ohghhi . . . my alien buy another piano while I was downstairs?"

"Worse," he said. "He wants us all to go out on the town. 'I want to drink sake and see a *sutorippu*,' was the way he put it." He handed Chris a card that said, "Luigi's Tempura Pizzeria and Sutorippu. Topless. Bottomless. Continuous shows."

She looked at him suspiciously. "Are you sure you're not the one who wants to see the *sutorippu*?" she said. "Mr. Ohghhifoehnn . . ." She stopped and read from her hand, determined not to let him intimidate her.

". . . ahigrheeh doesn't know enough English to say a sentence that long."

"How do you know?" he said. "You're so busy worrying about how to pronounce his name that you don't even listen to him."

"Well, you definitely shouldn't go," she said to change the subject. "This Luigi's place is down in Shitamachi, on the equator. You're shuttlelagged enough as it is. The last thing you need is full gravity."

"I'm doing okay. Your vitamin A must be working. And anyway, we don't have any choice in the matter. Your boyfriend said we had to do whatever Okee wanted, and what he wants is to watch a strip show."

Ohghhifoehnnahigrheeh slid open the door to his room. He had combed down his wispy hair and put a pink tie on over his long orange coat. "Topless," he said happily. "Bottomless. Continuous shows."

They took the bullet. It was jammed. Chris spent the trip wedged between a large bearded man and a middle-aged woman who looked like she was the kind who *did* get nauseated on the shuttle. Ohghhifoehnnahigrheeh had bought a large paper kite on the platform when Chris wasn't looking, and he and Hutchins were holding it above their heads so it wouldn't get crushed.

The bullet got progressively more crowded as they got closer to the ginza and Shitamachi. In the crush to get off at their stop, Ohghhifoehnnahigrheeh's kite got torn and Chris lost her shoe. Hutchins dived into the tangle of legs as the doors were closing and rescued it.

"Thank you, Mr. Hutchins," Chris said, leaning against a pillar to put it back on.

"Now you're mispronouncing my name," he said, with a grin that looked like he was feeling better. "It's Pete."

Luigi's Tempura Pizzeria was about the size of Chris's hall, if you took out the piano, only with such low ceilings that Hutchins had to duck. It was nearly as crowded as the bullet had been. There was no sign of a stage that Chris could see, and the tables were too small to dance on.

The waiter led them through the mob to a tiny table, pulled it out from the wall so Chris could sit down, and then shoved it back in place, pinning her firmly between Hutchins and Ohghhifoehnnahigrheeh. The waiter handed them menus that were bigger than the table and then stood there, holding a hand terminal and a stylus and looking impatient.

"In the tempura pizza, is it just the tomato sauce that's deep-fried in batter?" Hutchins asked. "Or do you dip in the whole pizza?"

"Have eat?" Chris asked Ohghhifoehnnahigrheeh, pointing to the pictures on the menu. "Fish? Rice?" Ohghhifoehnnahigrheeh smiled blankly at her and nodded. "Eat?" She picked up a pair of chopsticks and pantomimed eating. "Have eat?"

"What are you going to have, Okee?" Hutchins interrupted. "The sashimi lasagna looks good. I don't know about the linguini with eel sauce."

"Why do you talk to him like that?" Chris whispered. "You know Mr. Ohghhi . . ."—she consulted her hand,—"foehnnahigrheeh only speaks a few words of English."

Hutchins took hold of her hand and looked at the palm. "Why do you have his name written on your hand?" he whispered back.

She tried to pull her hand away. "Stewart says the Eahrohhs are very sensitive about how their names are pronounced."

"Is Stewart the guy on the phone, the one you're engaged to?"

"Yes."

"Did he tell you to talk to Okee like he's deaf and feebleminded, too? 'Have eat? Fish? Rice?' "

"Mr. Ohghhi . . ." She tried to look at her hand, but Hutchins folded it firmly shut.

"Okee speaks better English than Charmaine. He's only talking that ridiculous pidgin to you because you've got him intimidated with all this correct pronunciation stuff. He's afraid if he talks to you, he'll mispronounce something, so he doesn't say anything. If you'd quit worrying about how to pronounce his name, and just talk to him . . ."

"Your order, signor?" the waiter said.

"Go ahead," Hutchins said. "Ask him what he'd like to have for dinner." His hand was still firmly closed over hers. The waiter tapped the stylus on his hand terminal.

"Mr Ohghhi . . . ," she said.

"Okeefenokee," Hutchins said. "Like the swamp."

"Okeefenokee," she said timidly, "what would you like to have for dinner?"

Mr. Ohghhifoehnnahigrheeh's smile straightened out into an expression Chris hadn't seen before. His cheek knobs seemed to grow more orange, and two lines formed above his nose. "I'll have the sushi and spaghetti," he said. "And you do have any sake? *Majori?* Good. I'd like a bottle. And three cups."

Chris stared at him.

"And you, signorina?" the waiter said.

"She'll have the sushi and spaghetti," Hutchins said.

" 'Scuse me," Charmaine said, brushing past the waiter. She was wearing another hapi coat, made of a glittery fabric you could see through. "They told me you guys were here," she said, "and I would've come right over only on the way down here some guy pinched me. I had to do one of my fans all over again."

"We'll all have the sushi and spaghetti," Hutchins said, "and bring another sake cup."

"Oh, gee, no, not for me," she said, bending over the table to talk to Hutchins. "I'm on at nineteen o'clock.

Right after Omiko and Her Orbiting Colonies." She leaned over farther.

"Great," Hutchins said.

"Would you like to sit down?" Chris said.

"I can't. On account of my fans." She looked around the room. "This is a great place to work. Three guys have proposed to me already."

"Charmaine came up here to find a husband," Chris told Hutchins.

"Yeah," Charmaine said. She leaned over Hutchins. "I wanted to go someplace romantic, someplace where guys wouldn't treat me like I was a piece of real estate. I guess you think that's kind of a crazy reason, huh? But I've met some people whose reasons are even crazier. Did you know that sweet old guy who lives above me on the steps came up because he'd always wanted to meet an alien? And this weird guy I met tonight told me he came up because he figures these arrows guys are going to kill us all, and he wants to get it over with. No offense, Mr. Fenokee," she said, turning to lean over Okee. His face twisted up in an unfathomable expression.

"Why did you come up to Sony, Mr. Hutchins?" Chris said hastily.

"Not to get married. So you thought Sony was a romantic place to come?" he said, watching Charmaine lean over the table.

"Gee, yeah," she said, leaning over even farther. "I mean, the stars and the moon are right outside and everything. It's bound to have a romantic effect on a guy. It might even have a romantic effect on my old boyfriend, but I doubt it. I mean, he acted like he was a prospective buyer and I was a two-bedroom split-level. He kept calling our wedding a closing, and instead of going on a honeymoon, he wanted to 'establish occupancy.' Can you believe that?" She sighed an impressive sigh. "But I don't know if Sony's going to be any better. Omiko says the marriage contracts up here are really real-estate deals, with property clauses and everything, and that people get married all the time just to get their hands on a place to live."

"Does your fiancé have his own apartment?" Hutchins asked.

"He lives with his mother," Chris said stiffly. "Stewart says the lack of space on Sony makes property very valuable, and the marriage laws are bound to reflect that, but it doesn't mean . . ."

"Gee, your fiancé sounds just like my old boyfriend," Charmaine said, leaning over about as far as she could go. "I mean, there's gotta be a romantic guy around somewhere."

The waiter came back with the bottle of sake and four porcelain cups the size of soup bowls.

" 'Scuse me, I gotta go get ready for my number." She wriggled away between the tables.

"Now there's a woman whose property value is in the high forties," Hutchins said, pouring out the sake.

"My wife has large cups, too," Okee said.

Hutchins poured sake on the table. Chris bit her lip.

"They are not painted and made of . . ." Okee stopped and searched for a word. His face was screwed up into that odd expression again. He looked like a newborn baby about to cry.

"Porcelain?" Chris said calmly, picking up the empty sake cup and handing it to Okee. "These cups are made of a kind of glazed clay called porcelain."

"Porcelain," he said, the two lines above his nose deepening. "My wife would like these cups."

Chris passed the empty cup to Hutchins so he could fill it. Now he was the one with the odd expression, and she didn't seem to be any better at interpreting his than Okee's.

"Cups," he said thoughtfully, and poured some more sake on the table.

"I didn't know you were married, Mr. Okeefenokee," Chris said, mopping up sake with her napkin.

"Yes," he said, and his face screwed up again. He drank down his bowlful of sake in one swallowless gulp and set it in front of Hutchins. "My wife and I drink . . ."—he said an unpronounceable word with enough *s*'s in it to defeat Molly's lisp—"out of cups like these. It is better than sake."

" 'Scuse me," Charmaine said. She had put on her headdress, which consisted of giant red-lacquered chopsticks stuck at various angles into her brass-colored topknot. If she bent over Hutchins like she'd been doing before, she would do herself an injury. "Can I borrow Mr. Fenokee for a minute? The girls in the show all want to meet him."

Okee took another incredibly large swallow of sake and followed her through the crowd.

"Don't you think we should go with him?" Chris said, watching the bobbing red headdress work its way through the crowd.

"He'll be all right. How did you know he was talking about the sake cups and not Charmaine's, um, selling points?"

She reached for her cup of sake. "Just because they were the first thing that sprang to your mind. . . ."

He put his hand over hers. "I'm serious. How did you know for sure he was talking about the sake cups?"

"Because he asked me at breakfast what the coffee cups were called, and I told him they were cups, so I knew he knew the word, and he doesn't seem to be able to absorb more than one meaning of a word."

His grip tightened on her hand. "Give me an example," he said urgently.

"All right. Yesterday at breakfast we had rolls, and he asked me what they were called. When I told him, he took two of them and went out and gave them to Molly and Bets. 'Here roll,' he said, and Bets said, 'We asked if you could get us a role. In the alien movie. Not this kind of roll,' and threw it at him."

"A regular Shirley Temple. Did you try to explain what a role in a movie was?"

"Yes, I told him there were two words that sounded like roll and that Bets meant an acting job in a movie, but I could tell he didn't understand. He started nodding and smiling the way he always does when I tell him he's got to stop buying things."

"Because there isn't any more room in your apartment," he said, and caught up her hand in both of his. "That's why . . ."

" 'Scuse me," Charmaine said sharply. She had brought Mr. Okeefenokee back. Chris hastily withdrew her hand from Hutchins's.

"You'll never guess who just showed up," Charmaine said. "My old boyfriend. He said he came up to Sony to find me."

"That sounds pretty romantic," Chris said.

"Yeah, I know." She sighed. "I told him I'd go out with him after I get off work, but if he says one word about escrow or closings . . . I gotta go. Thanks, Mr. Fenokee."

Okee had several lipstick prints on the top of his bald head, and his face had smoothed out into that new expression, his mouth straight across, his cheeks bright orange.

"After we see the *sutorippu*," he said, "I would like you to get married."

The waiter appeared suddenly and slammed down three orders of sushi and spaghetti in compartmentalized bento-bako boxes. "Will there be anything else, signor?" he asked Hutchins. "The first show is about to start."

Hutchins didn't answer him. He was still looking worried. Chris wondered if his aspirin was starting to wear off. She hoped not. Between the shuttle-lag and the sake, he would really crash. Okee motioned the waiter over and said something she couldn't hear.

"Please move over next to the gentlemen, signora," the waiter said, and waved her over toward Hutchins, motioning her to turn the chair around so it was facing the wall. She moved the chair so hers and Hutchins's were side by side.

"Chris," Hutchins said, leaning toward her and yawning, "there's something I've got to tell you about this subletting situation. . . ."

There was a sudden blast of music, and the wall in front of Chris rolled up and revealed Omiko and her Orbiting Colonies. Chris was glad she'd moved her chair. She would have fallen over into the orchestra pit. Mr. Okeefenokee was watching the activities on stage, which involved clear plastic stars and tassels, with the broad smile and wobbling nod that usually meant that he was going to buy something.

"If he buys Omiko and her orbiting colonies I'm evicting him," she shouted at Hutchins over the deafening music. He didn't answer. A heavy weight came down on her shoulder. He's probably smiling and nodding at those LaGrangian points, too, and doesn't even realize he's got his hand on my shoulder, she thought. "What about the subletting situation?" she said suspiciously, and turned to glare at him.

He was sound asleep, his mouth a little open and his face looking somehow more tired in sleep. "Well," Chris thought, feeling oddly pleased.

The music ground up to a finale, and Omiko put enough spin on her colonies to induce full gravity. Hutchins began to snore. "My wife does that," Mr. Okeefenokee said, watching the stage, and let out a wail like an air-raid siren.

Hutchins slept all the way home on the bullet. Chris spent the trip explaining to Mr. Okeefenokee why he couldn't buy anything else. He smiled and nodded, trying to juggle the two dozen bento-bako boxes and Fan Tan

Fannie's fan against the uneven motion of the bullet. Chris held the box containing the porcelain sake cups.

"There just isn't any more room in my apartment," Chris said. "Tomorrow I'm going to see my fiancé and ask him if he can store some of the things in his apartment, but . . ."

"Tomorrow you and Hutchins get married. Have closing. Honeymoon." He pronounced honeymoon "hahnahmoon."

"People who get married don't really have closings. They have weddings. And they don't just get married. They have to be in love, they have to know each other."

"No?" Okee said.

"No. I mean, they have to be friends, to talk to each other."

"You and Hutchins talk. You are friends."

Chris glanced at Hutchins, who had his arm slung through one of the hanging straps to keep himself more or less upright, wishing he would wake up and explain things to Mr. Okeefenokee. "You can't just be friends. You have to spend time alone together so you can talk without other people listening, and so you can . . ."

"Neck," Hutchins said, yawning. He eased his arm out of the strap.

"Neck?" Okee said, with the smile starting again that meant he didn't understand. He put his hand on his neck.

"Mr. Hutchins means kissing," Chris said, glaring at Hutchins. He was looking at Okee, though, with that thoughtful expression on his face again. "This is our stop."

It was raining when they came out of the station. People were asleep on the sidewalks, huddled under umbrellas and makeshift tents. There were half a dozen asleep under the overhang of Chris's building. Inside, Mr. Nagisha lay curled up by the front door with his arm around his lap terminal and disk files.

"Shh," she said, and tiptoed to the stairs.

Hutchins tiptoed after her, stopping to take off his shoes. Mr. Okeefenokee followed, juggling his bento-bako boxes. Fan Tan Fannie's fan dragged across Mr. Nagisha's nose. He sneezed but didn't wake up.

Chris started up the stairs. The old man was stretched out like a corpse on the third step up, his hands crossed on his breast and the baseball cap over his face. His running shoes were on the step above him, and his feet in their pink socks stuck through the banisters.

There were at least five extra people sleeping on the landing, each clutching an overnight lease contract. Mr. Nagisha must be making a killing. Molly and Bets's mothers were asleep sitting up against the banister, still holding an open copy of *Variety* between them.

Molly was asleep against the door of Chris's apartment, wrapped in a sleeping bag with blue kittens on it. Chris couldn't get the door open without cracking Molly on the head. Hutchins took hold of a corner of the sleeping bag and pulled her out of the way, yawning. "Here's Dorothy, but where's Lillian?" he said, and yawned again.

"Shh," Chris said, and unlocked the door.

Hutchins and Mr. Okeefenokee both seemed to snap awake at the whirr of her key being read. Okee hoisted up his dragging fan and managed to make it through the door before she did, and Hutchins straightened to his full height and cleared his throat. Chris looked at him warily and opened the door to her room.

The blankets she had left stacked on the end of the couch were draped unevenly over it, the tail of one of the quilts trailing on the floor. In the middle of them, sound asleep, lay Bets, her golden curls spread out endearingly against the pillow and her thumb in her mouth. She was hugging a teddy bear and a frayed pink blanket. Chris glanced at Hutchins, wondering if this was what all the throat-clearing had been about, but he was bending over Bets, shaking his head. "I was wrong about the kid's acting ability. She's doing an amazing imitation of an innocent child asleep."

"Bets," Chris said sternly. "Wake up. What are you doing in here?"

Bets sighed, a sweet, babyish sigh, and turned over.

"I know you're awake, Bets," Chris said. She knelt down and snatched the teddy bear away from her. "Tell me what you're doing in here, or I'll call your agent and tell him both your front teeth fell out."

"You better not," Bets said. She sat up, her cheeks pink and her eyes bright with sleep. "You better give me back my teddy bear."

Chris stuck the teddy bear behind her back. "Not until you tell me what you're doing in here."

"The door was open and I came in here just for a minute and your bed looked so soft I guess I just fell asleep." She shrugged daintily.

"She ate my porridge all up, too," Hutchins said. "Where's your phone, Chris?"

Bets stood up in the middle of the couch. Her pink nightgown had a ruffle around the bottom that almost covered her bare toes. "My mother says we're first on the list and you can't just sublet your room to some boyfriend of yours. She says . . ."

"I did not sublet my room to anybody. Mr. Okeefenokee sublet his room to Mr. Hutchins."

"Oh, yeah?" Bets said. "Then what's that doing in here?" She pointed up at the ceiling.

"What is that?" Chris said, looking up at the hammocklike arrangement of straps and white padding hanging from the ceiling. There was an aluminum ladder hooked onto the wall above the couch.

"It's an astronaut's sleep restraint," Hutchins said. "Okee bought it at the NASA Surplus Store. It was used on the space station, but don't worry. It's been reinforced for seventy percent gravity. It won't fall down."

"It won't fall down because you're taking it down. I

agreed to let you stay in Mr. Okeefenokee's room, not in here."

"I know, but Okee has trouble understanding more than one meaning of a word. That's what I was trying to tell you at Luigi's. You told him there wasn't any more room in your apartment, so he thinks 'room' means 'available storage space.' " He pointed at the ceiling. "He apparently decided this space was available."

Chris didn't wait for him to finish. She marched down the hall and pounded on the door of Mr. Okeefenokee's room. "Mr. Okeefenokee!" she shouted. "I have to talk to you."

"Shh," Hutchins said. "You'll wake up that DeMille crowd scene outside."

"I don't care if I wake the orbiting dead. You're not sleeping in my room."

"You'd better give me back my teddy bear," Bets said.

Okee pushed open his shoji screen an inch and a half and peeked out.

"Mr. Okeefenokee, there's been a misunderstanding. Mr. Hutchins can't sleep in my room. I said you could sublet *your* room." She could see the smile coming.

"Remember 'role'?" Hutchins said. "Remember 'cups'? Remember 'neck'? I spent fifteen minutes trying to explain the difference to him this afternoon."

"And then you suggested that we go out for dinner so we wouldn't get back here until it was too late for me to do anything about it," she said furiously. "You probably timed it so it was raining, too."

"Look, I'm too tired to argue with you, and in about five minutes I'm going to be too lagged to even make it up that ladder and into bed. So if we could please talk about it in the morning . . ."

"There's nothing to talk about. I'm calling Stewart."

"What for? He told you to do whatever Okee wants. Okee wants me to stay."

"Stewart was not talking about a man sleeping in my room."

"I'm not sleeping in your room. I'm sleeping in Okee's room, which happens to be above your room." He shuffled off down the hall. "I'm going to bed. G'night." Bets padded barefoot after him. They disappeared into the living room.

Chris punched in Stewart's number and let it ring. After the first ring, she hit the time key on the screen. It flashed twenty-three o'clock. Stewart's mother went to bed at twenty-one-thirty. Chris hit the hang-up button.

Okee was still peeking at her through the tiny space in the sliding door. "All right," she said, "he can stay tonight, but tomorrow . . ."

"Tomorrow you and Hutchins get married," he said, and slid the screen shut with a bang.

Hutchins was already in the sleep restraint, one arm dangling limply over the side. Bets and Molly were in Molly's sleeping bag, which they had dragged over next to the couch. Their eyes were squeezed shut and their hands were tucked up under their cheeks.

"I said Mr. Hutchins could stay," Chris said. "I didn't say anything about you two. Out."

Molly sat up and rubbed her eyes with her chubby little fists. "We have to thtay to thyaperone you," she said, "tho people won't think you're a thlut."

Chris was suddenly too tired to argue with them. It's the sake, she thought irrationally. He tried to get me drunk so I'd let him stay. He had the whole thing planned.

She undressed in the bathroom and put on her nightshift, even though there wasn't enough room in there to raise her arms over her head. Molly and Bets had kicked their covers off. She put Bets's pink blanket over them, turned off the lights, and got into bed.

She could hear Hutchins breathing above her in the darkness, a heavy, even breathing that meant he was already asleep. Poor guy, she thought in spite of herself.

When she had emigrated to Sony, she'd barely made it through customs and into the Hilton before collapsing. There was no way she could have made it through a dinner and a *sutorippu*. Half a *sutorippu*, she thought, feeling pleased all over again at the way he'd fallen asleep during Omiko's act.

Bets turned over and murmured something that sounded like "I'm going to be a star!" A sound like the shuttle taking off roared from Mr. Okeefenokee's room. It went on for a full minute, subsided, and then started up again.

"What in the hell's that?" Hutchins said. She could hear the sleep restraint creak as if he had sat up.

"It's Mr. Okeefenokee," Chris whispered.

"What's he doing?"

"Snoring, I think. He does it every night."

"You're kidding," he said, and she could hear his head flop back against the pillow. "No wonder you wanted to get rid of him."

"I didn't want to get rid of him. I like him. It's just that it's such a little apartment, and he keeps bringing things home with him, like the piano, and I'm running out of room for . . . where's the piano? It wasn't in the hall."

"I helped him shove it into his room this afternoon," Hutchins said. "It sounds like he's got a spaceship in there, too. You don't suppose he bought one at NASA Surplus when I wasn't looking?"

"He might have," Chris said ruefully. "I didn't see him buy the bento-bako boxes tonight. Or Fan Tan Fannie's fan."

They both listened to the whooshing roar for a while.

"How long does this go on?" Hutchins said finally, in between takeoffs.

"Sometimes he stops," Chris said, thinking how she would have felt if she'd had to put up with this and shuttle-lag, too.

"And sometimes he doesn't. But either way you have

to put up with it because your prospective buyer told you to let him do anything he wants. Has he ever heard him snore?"

Chris didn't answer. She was thinking that the next time Stewart tried to put her on hold she should play a tape of Okeefenokee's snoring.

"I'll bet he has," Hutchins said, answering his own question, "and that's why he pushed him off on you. Why is he staying here anyway? How come he isn't with the rest of the Eahrohhs or keeping your boyfriend and his mother awake tonight?"

"He had to have a place with high ceilings," she said, and hoped he wouldn't ask how high Stewart's mother's ceilings were. "He has vertical claustrophobia."

"Which explains why Okee couldn't stand to ride the bullet tonight or sit in Luigi's. Did your prospective buyer tell you that? Face it, he found out about the snoring."

"How'th a perthon thuppothed to get any thleep around here?" Molly shouted in Chris's ear.

Chris snapped on the light. "You're the one who wanted to sleep in here," she said. Molly was standing over her, clutching her rag doll and Bets's blanket. Bets was rolling up the sleeping bag. "You're doing thith on purpothe to get rid of uth," Molly said darkly, and stomped out in her footed pajamas after Bets.

"She wants to be alone with him so they can—*you know*!" Bets said loudly, and slammed the door. Chris turned out the light.

"It's an ill wind . . . ," Hutchins said. "I wonder why Okee needs high ceilings. Or if that's what he really needs."

"What do you mean?" Chris said.

"Remember the incident of the rolls? Maybe he needed sealings, S-E-A-L-I-N-G-S, whatever they are. The Japanese word for 'ceiling' is *tenjo*, but *tenjo* also means palace. Maybe he really asked for a palace. Have you been in his room since he moved in?"

"No. He comes out when he wants to talk to me, and when he leaves, he locks the door. The first day when we went shopping in the ginza, I was going to go in and help him put things away, but . . ."

"He wouldn't let you. I know. I offered to go get my bicycle and leave it outside. I wonder what he's doing in there besides making lift-off noises," he said thoughtfully. "Do you have a key to his room?"

"No. I gave him mine. And besides . . ."

"I know, your prospective buyer told you to let him do anything he wants to." He was speaking into a sudden silence from the other room. He stopped talking. "You don't suppose we woke him up, do you?" he whispered. The whisper made him seem somehow closer.

Chris didn't answer. There was another long minute of silence, and another sound started up, high-pitched and rising.

"What's that?" Hutchins said.

"It's what he did at Luigi's. When the stripper came on."

"No more *sutorippu* for him. And no more sake."

The sound rose to the same keening note it had in the nightclub and then dropped and rose again. Whether it was because of the high ceilings, though, or because there was a wall between them, it didn't sound like an air-raid siren this time. It sounded like an impossibly high trumpet, sweet and somehow sad.

"I think Omiko and her Orbiting Colonies reminded him of his wife," Chris said.

"Ummm," Hutchins said sleepily. "I missed her. That was when I was sleeping on you."

"I know," Chris said.

"Hutchins?" she said the next time Okee's solo faded, and was answered by a faint snore that was nothing like Mr. Okeefenokee's. "Good night," she said, feeling pleased all over again.

• • •

"I don't believe you," Chris heard Bets say from the hall. "Why would he do that?"

"You don't have to believe me," Hutchins said. He was in the hall, too. That meant he had climbed down the ladder past her and it hadn't even woken her up. She wondered what time it was. "All I said is that if I were Spielberg, I wouldn't want two million little girls following me around, begging me for a part in my movie. I'd come up to Sony in disguise so I could get close to the aliens and decide which little girl I wanted in the movie. Sort of a close encounter of the Hollywood kind."

Chris got up and pulled on a robe.

"He could be anybody," Hutchins went on, and Chris wondered what he was talking about. "Me or Okee or one of Mr. Nagisha's cousins, but whoever he is, he could be watching you right now. He could be giving you a screen test this very minute."

"Mr. Nagithya'th couthinth aren't watching uth. They got thrown out," Molly said.

Chris came into the hall. Hutchins was standing against the wall where the piano had been, holding two towels and two shower bottles. Molly and Bets were sitting on the floor in fuzzy robes and bunny slippers looking at a movie magazine. A young man with blond hair whom Chris had never seen before came out of the bathroom, trailing his shower bottle hose, and grinned at Chris as he went out the door.

"Who was that?" Chris said.

"Charmaine's old boyfriend. The lawyer. He moved in this morning," Hutchins said.

"Mr. Okeefenokee didn't sublet another half of my apartment, did he?"

"No, he's living on the landing. But, listen, speaking of moving in, I want you to know I really appreciate your letting me stay here last night. I was so lagged, I'd probably be dead this morning if you hadn't. And I wanted to tell you why I . . ."

"Mr. Nagisha's cousins got evicted," Bets said, studying a picture in the movie magazine. "We told Mr. Nagisha they were cooking on the stairs in violation of their lease."

"You girls won't even be extras at this rate," Hutchins said.

"I don't believe you," Molly said. "Thpielberg wouldn't dreth up like an alien."

"I didn't say he'd dress up like an alien. Maybe he's dressed up like Charmaine. And if he is, I'll bet he doesn't appreciate being called a thlut."

"I thtill don't believe you," Molly said. "You're jutht doing thith tho we'll act nither."

"Fine. Don't believe me. It's your funeral."

"But Mr. Nagisha's cousins weren't supposed to use the bathroom till after nine," Chris said. "What time is it?"

"Nine-thirty," Hutchins said. He handed her a towel and a shower bottle. "What time's this lunch with your prospective buyer?"

"I'm meeting Stewart at thirteen-thirty," Chris said stiffly. "Nine-thirty! Then what are you doing in line? You were supposed to be"—she squinted at the schedule on the wall—"seven forty-five."

"I traded places with Charmaine. She had a date with her old boyfriend, remember?"

"We mithed our turn, too," Molly said. "And it'th all your fault. If you hadn't kept uth awake with all that thnoring and talking . . ."

"Speaking of thnoring," Hutchins said. "Okee said to give this to you." He handed her a flat metal disk on a short chain. "You wear it around your neck." He opened the odd-looking clasp and moved around behind her. Chris caught a glimpse of metal under his shirt collar.

"When did he buy this?"

"This morning. He got up early and went out to get rolls and coffee for breakfast."

"He went out by himself? What else did he buy? A set of encyclopedias?"

Hutchins fastened the chain. The disk came right to the hollow between her collar bones and seemed almost to stick there. Chris tried to pull it out to see what was on the back, but the chain was too short. "What is this thing?" she said.

"There's an earplug thingee that goes with it," he said, and dropped it into the palm of her outstretched hand.

"My mother says we should have stuck cotton in our ears and stayed right where we were last night," Bets said. "She says possession is nine tenths of the law."

"Did you put her up to this?" Chris said to Hutchins.

"Not me. It's not a bad argument, though. Go ahead. Put it on."

Chris looked warily at the smaller round disk and put it in her ear. "Mr. Okeefenokee didn't go out again, did he?"

(No,) Hutchins said. His lips didn't move. (He's in the bathroom. And after breakfast . . . Oh, that reminds me.) He dug his hand in his pocket and came up with a handful of crumpled yen. (I had to get money out of your purse to give Okee for the rolls and coffee. This is your change.) He handed it to her.

Chris looked at the little girls, but they had their heads together over the movie magazine again.

(After breakfast he's going back to bed,) Hutchins said, still without opening his mouth. (He says our talking kept him awake last night.)

She jammed the yen in her pocket, still watching his mouth and wondering if the thing around her neck was some sort of ventriloquist's device. "What is this thing?"

(Okee called it something that sounded like "the Everglades,") Hutchins said. (It picks up subvocalizations and amplifies them so any other person similarly equipped can hear them. Go ahead, say something. Under your breath. Your lips don't have to move. In fact, all I do is think the words.)

(He said our talking kept him awake?) Chris said cautiously under her breath, her hand on the disk.

(Yep. He said tonight we were supposed to use these, which means he wants me to stay here tonight. And besides, if I spend the whole day moving out, I can't keep an eye on Okee. He'll probably end up buying a steam calliope.)

(You've done a great job of watching him so far,) she thought. (When did he buy these subvocalizers?)

"I don't know," he said thoughtfully, and she could tell by the way the little girls looked up from their movie magazine that he had spoken aloud. It hadn't sounded markedly different from when he used the subvocalizer, only a little farther away.

Molly and Bets were watching Hutchins suspiciously. "Well, I don't know either," Chris said, as if they had been carrying on a rational conversation, "but I'd say his time in the bathroom is definitely up." She tapped on the bathroom door. "Mr. Okeefenokee, your time is up."

He opened the bathroom door and came out, his wispy hair wet and practically invisible. His body looked even lumpier than usual under his Japanese yukata.

Hutchins ducked in. "You could have traded platheth with uth," Molly shouted after him. "We have a holo-interview thith afternoon."

"You are wearing your thuwevrherrnghladdis," Mr. Okeefenokee said, nodding and smiling. It did sound like "the Everglades."

"Yes, thank you. It's lovely." She put her hand up to the disk.

"Have you and Hutchins talked alone?"

"Yes." She looked at Molly and Bets, but they were immersed in their movie magazine again.

Bets was pointing at a picture. "It does look a little

bit like him," she whispered to Molly. "See how lumpy he is."

"But what about his batheball cap? Thpielberg alwayth wearth a batheball cap."

"Good," Mr. Okeefenokee said. His mouth straightened out and his cheeks turned bright orange. "Now you can get married. Have closing. Hahnahmoon."

Both girls looked up. "No! I mean, talking alone isn't enough." She wished Okee were wearing one of the subvocalizers so they could discuss this privately, but he didn't seem to be.

(People have to know each other a long time before they get married,) she thought at Okee, but he only smiled at her.

"People have to know each other a long time before they get married," she said aloud. "They have to . . ." She hesitated, trying to think of a word that he might understand.

"Thyeeth talking about theckth," Molly said wisely. "And if you athk me, they've already . . ."

"Nobody asked you," Chris said. "Why don't you two go find somebody else you can get evicted?" She shoved them out the door.

"Theckth?" Mr. Okeefenokee said.

Chris tried to think what she could tell him. She couldn't just say people had to love each other. "Love" was far too nebulous a term, and he'd already heard Charmaine say she loved Sony and her job and the fans painted on her ath. "Last night you were thinking about your wife, weren't you?" she said, watching for any sign of understanding. To her surprise, he stopped nodding. "And it made you sad?"

"Yes," he said solemnly. "Sad."

"And you wished you could talk to her and see her and be close to her." She put her arms out and brought them back again toward her and hugged herself. "Close."

"Closing," he said.

"Not, not closing. Close."

"Hahnahmoon?"

"No," she said. "See, when two people love each other, they want to be as near each other as they can, and they . . ."

"Wife," he said, "sad," and screwed his face up.

"Oh, Mr. Okeefenokee, I'm sorry. I didn't mean to upset you," she said, but she was too late. He let out a wail like a fire engine.

"What did you do to him?" Hutchins said, coming out of the bathroom.

"He misses his wife," Chris said.

"She probably told him about sex," Bets said. She and Molly came back in.

"What did thyee do to you?" Molly said, patting Okee awkwardly on the back.

"You can have our turn in the bathroom if you want," Bets said, her forefinger stuck in one of her dimples. "We don't really need a shower." She held out her shower bottle to him.

Okee stopped wailing and looked at the little girls, an expression on his face that Chris had never seen before. She had no idea how to interpret it, but at least he had stopped keening.

"Here. You can have my rubber duckie. Hith name ith Tham," Molly said with a sickeningly sweet smile.

Okee continued to look at them for a long moment and then took the yellow duck and the shower bottle and went back into the bathroom.

(How did you do that?) Chris said wonderingly.

(I told them that if I were Spielberg, I'd disguise myself as an alien and do secret screen tests.) It was disconcerting to be watching him grin while he was talking to her. (I thought it might improve their general deportment.)

Chris looked at Molly and Bets, who were whispering about something, curls and hairbows bobbing. "Okay, but we'll have to hurry," Bets said, and they ran out of the hall and down the steps. "He'll be out of the bathroom in a few minutes."

"You don't suppose they'll try to kidnap him and hold him for ransom?" Chris said.

"I hope not," Hutchins said. (What we talked about last night . . . have you noticed Okee having trouble understanding any other words?) He had gone back to using the subvocalizer even though there was nobody else left in the hall.

(He can't seem to tell the difference between closing and close,) she thought (and he has trouble pronouncing some words, like "honeymoon." He still thinks we're getting married, but that's Charmaine's fault. With all her real-estate talk, I think he's gotten the idea marriage is something you can go out and buy.) She tried to think. (He doesn't understand when I tell him he should stop buying things.)

(Has he ever talked to you about the space program thing the Eahrohhs are supposed to be negotiating?)

(No. Stewart said the Japanese linguists had figured out that there was a small core group of officials and a couple of translators and that everybody else was a passenger. Stewart said Okee's one of the passengers. *Noru hito.*)

(*Noru hito*, huh? Did you know that some Japanese words have as many as ten different meanings? *Noru hito* also means . . .)

There was a racket on the steps, and Molly and Bets burst in wearing leotards covered with red, white, and blue sequins, and sequined military hats. Bets was carrying a Sony chip recorder. "Ith he out of the bathroom yet?" Molly said breathlessly.

"No," Hutchins said.

"Good," Molly said. "We'll have time to practith." She adjusted the chin strap on her hat. Bets stuck a music program into the Sony recorder and pushed down the *play* key. They both positioned themselves in front of the bathroom door, clanking as they walked.

"Those are tap shoes," Chris said.

"I know," Hutchins said. "Baby June and Gypsy strike again."

"Ready and . . . ," Bets said. "Hop, shuffle, step. Hop, shuffle, step."

She was late to lunch. Okee had refused to come out of the bathroom until Molly and Bets stopped tap-dancing, and then they demanded their turn in the bathroom. While they were in there, they used the curling iron and blew a fuse. It was almost noon before Chris could have her shower.

By the time she was dressed, Hutchins and Okee had both disappeared. She went out into the hall. Charmaine's lawyer had set up an ancient Apple and two disk drives on a chair. He had the case off the Apple and was digging around inside and swearing to himself. The old man with the baseball cap was playing solitaire on the top three steps. Molly and Bets were on the landing in pink tutus and ballet slippers, hanging on to the railing as if it were a barre and practicing the ballet positions. The chip recorder was blaring, "The Dance of the Sugarplum Fairy."

"Do you know where Mr. Okeefenokee is?" Chris shouted, and then realized it was a stupid question. If they knew, they would be subjecting him to the Sugarplum Fairy.

"Don't interrupt uth," Molly said. "We're trying to practith."

"He's in with Mr. Nagisha," Charmaine said. She was sitting on the second step from the bottom, watching Mr. Nagisha's TV and painting fans on her fingernails. She was dressed in a red strapless dress and spike-heeled shoes. "He asked him to explain leases, but I think he's really hiding from the cast of *Swan Lake*."

"Is Hutchins in there with him?" Chris said, coming down the stairs toward her.

"No. About half an hour ago he said he had something he had to do and left."

Chris looked at her watch. "Oh, dear, I'm supposed to meet Stewart for lunch, and I don't dare leave Mr. Okeefenokee alone."

"I'll keep an eye on him," Charmaine said, blowing on her fingernails. "I don't have anything better to do."

"I thought you had a date."

" 'Had' is right," she said, jabbing the fingernail-polish stylus in the direction of the landing. "He didn't come up here to find me. He came up because he figured with all this overcrowding there'd be lots of real-estate contracts to draw up. And marriage contracts. Only he can't seem to tell the difference." She jammed the cap on the stylus. "He wanted to know if I'd be interested in a lease option. That's where you get to move in before you close the deal. *If* there's a closing. Go on. Don't be late for your lunch."

"All right," Chris said, wondering what had made Hutchins run off like that. "Let Mr. Okeefenokee do anything he wants, but whatever you do, don't let him go shopping."

The bullet was jammed with people carrying flight bags and looking exhausted. Getting off at the ginza, she almost lost her shoe again. This time, since Hutchins wasn't there, she curled her toes and jammed them against the end of the shoe, and it stayed on, but just barely, and she got such a cramp in her foot that she could hardly walk.

The ginza was jammed with bicycles and people carrying huge, bulky suitcases who had a tendency to stop suddenly in the middle of the footwalk to stare at the city far above. It took nearly fifteen minutes to get the half block from the bullet to the Garden of Meditation.

Stewart was standing outside, tapping his foot and

looking at his watch. "Where have you been?" he said. "I've been waiting half an hour."

"I couldn't get into my bathroom," she said. "Molly and Bets . . ."

"Those two cunning moppets I saw on the phone yesterday?" Stewart said, taking her arm and steering her into the restaurant's anteroom. "I don't think I've ever seen two such adorable little girls."

"They're circus midgets," Chris said, but Stewart didn't hear her.

He was waving wildly at a waitress. "For heavens' sake, take your shoes off, so if they do have a table we can sit right down. I don't have much time. If you'd been on time we could have gotten right in, but now we'll probably have to wait." He pulled his shoes off and started through the crowd to find the waitress.

Chris took her shoes off and gave them to the pretty Japanese attendant. She flexed her cramping toes. I should get tap shoes with straps, like those "two charming moppets," she thought.

(Lose your shoe in the bullet again?) Hutchins said at her ear, and she whirled around, but there was no one behind her but the attendant and a wizened old woman who couldn't seem to find her shoes.

"No," Chris said. The attendant was looking at her oddly, which meant she had spoken aloud again. She clamped her mouth shut and said silently, (Where are you?)

(At Luigi's. Sorry to run off this morning, but Charmaine told me about a job waiting tables, and I thought I'd better check it out. I can't keep taking breakfast money out of your purse forever. Is Okee with you?)

(No, I got Charmaine to watch him, but you're not going to be staying long enough to worry about breakfast. I'm going to have Stewart find you and Mr. Okeefenokee another apartment this afternoon and . . .)

Stewart came back, elbowing his way past the wrinkled crone, who was still rummaging through the shoes. "They gave our table to somebody else fifteen minutes ago," he said accusingly, "and they won't have anything else for an hour and a half. We'll have to eat at the sushi counter." He led her through the crowd to the wooden counter and scanned it for seats. "Have you ever seen such a mob?"

"Yes," Chris said. "In line for my bathroom. Stewart, since I talked to you yesterday, Mr. Okeefenokee . . ."

"There aren't two seats together," he said, pointing at the only empty stools, which were separated by an exhausted-looking man with a camera and a shuttle bag, "which is what happens when you aren't on time for your reservations." He motioned her toward one of the stools, sat down on the other, and handed her a menu. A waitress appeared immediately. Stewart snatched the menu out of Chris's hands. "I'll have the jiffy lunch. What is it?"

"Eel. It comes with fries."

"I'll have that, and she'll have the sushi salad."

"I want you to come home with me this afternoon," Chris said across the exhausted-looking man, who had propped his arms on the sushi counter. "You've got to talk to Mr. Okeefenokee. Yesterday he—"

"Okeefenokee?" Stewart said, with the same horrified look he'd had on the phone the day before. "I have asked you repeatedly to learn the correct pronunciation of his name. You obviously don't realize how delicate our relationship with the Eahrohhs is right now or you wouldn't . . ."

"I'm sorry, Stewart, but Mr. Ohghhi . . ." She automatically opened her hand to look at what wasn't written there anymore.

(Ohghhifoehnnahigrheeh,) Hutchins said.

"Ohghhifoehnnahigrheeh," Chris said. "Yesterday he brought home—"

(How delicate is the relationship with the Eahrohhs right now?) Hutchins said.

"Well?" Stewart said. "Don't just stop in the middle of a sentence like that. What did he bring home?"

(Ask him,) Hutchins said insistently. (Ask him what he means by a delicate relationship.)

(How do you know what's he's saying?) Chris said. (I thought these subvocalizers only picked up what the person said under his breath.)

(It does. You're subvocalizing what Stewart's saying. Okee says that happens when the person's upset.)

(I am not upset,) Chris thought. (And would you please stop eavesdropping on this conversation?)

(No. Ask him how the negotiations are going. This is important, Chris. Please.)

"I took the time for this lunch because you told me you had to talk to me," Stewart said, "and now all you do is sit there staring into space."

"I'm sorry, Stewart," Chris said.

(Please,) Hutchins said.

"How are the negotiations going, Stewart?" she said. The exhausted-looking man was lying in his sushi.

"We've had a breakdown in communications. Nothing for you to worry about, though. In fact, it may work to your benefit. The Japanese have decided that because the negotiations are taking longer than we expected, they'll match the compensation NASA's been paying. Which is only fair since this mess is their fault. If they'd allowed NASA to build the size shuttle base they wanted, this overcrowding problem would never have happened."

(What kind of breakdown in communications?) Hutchins said.

"What kind of breakdown in communications?" Chris said.

"It seems the Eahrohhsian the Japanese team thought was their headman isn't in charge, after all, or he used to be and isn't anymore or something. Their concept of roles is apparently different from ours."

"Yes," Chris said, thinking of Molly asking Mr. Okeefenokee to get her a role in Spielberg's movie.

"This mix-up could jeopardize the whole space program, and the American linguistics team is furious. They want to transfer the Eahrohhsians down to Houston immediately, where they can use translation computers to . . ."

(Immediately?) Hutchins said, but Chris had already said it out loud.

"If they can get the Japanese to agree to it. I think they will as soon as they've had time to save face. Two or three more days at the most, and Ohghhifoehnnahigrheeh will be out of your life forever."

And so will Hutchins, Chris thought.

The waitress came back with Stewart's eel and a check, which she stuck under the fingers of the sleeping man. "We're out of sushi salad," the waitress said. "We got tacos and Hungarian goulash. Do you want one of them?"

"Two or three more days, and you'll have your apartment back and we can think seriously about going condo. But in the meantime, you've got to make sure you don't do anything to upset Ohghhifoehnnahigrheeh. The smallest thing, and our chances of negotiating a space program could blow up in our faces."

(Let him do anything he wants,) Hutchins said. (I don't care what it is. Rape and pillage. Anything.)

"Oh, shut up!" Chris said.

"Look, don't take it out on me," the waitress said. "It's not my fault we're out of the sushi salad." She flounced off.

"I realize having to share your apartment with an alien has been a strain," Stewart said stiffly, "but you didn't have to yell at the waitress."

"I didn't," she said, thinking furiously at Hutchins (This is all your fault. Go away and don't say one more word to me.)

"Who were you yelling at, then?" Stewart said. "Me?"

"No," Chris said, "Mr. Ohghhifoehnn . . ." She stopped and waited, listening. Hutchins didn't say anything. Good, she thought, I'm glad he's gone. The waitress reappeared and lifted the sleeping man's head up so she could take the sushi board out from under him. She pointedly did not look at Chris. "Yesterday the alien brought home . . ."

"Can I have the check, please?" Stewart said. "And wrap this up so I can take it with me." He slapped down a credit card and slid off the stool. Three people dived for it. "I've got to be back at the office by fourteen-thirty."

Chris struggled through the crowd after him. By the time she made it to the anteroom, he had found his shoes in the jumble by the door and was pulling them on. "Let him bring home anything he wants," he said, bending down to tie his shoelaces. "And whatever he wants to do, let him do it. I don't care what it is. It's only for a couple of days."

Chris waited for Hutchins to say, even rape and pillage? but he didn't. He'd gone away, and in a couple of days he really would have gone away because Mr. Okeefenokee would have been transferred down to Houston, and he wouldn't be able to use the excuse anymore that Mr. Okeefenokee wanted him to stay, and she'd never see him again.

"Now," Stewart said, straightening up. "What was it you wanted to talk to me about?"

Chris looked around the suddenly quiet anteroom. There was no one in it except the attendant, who was patiently lining up pairs of shoes by the door. The old woman who'd been in there before must have found her shoes.

"Well?" Stewart said.

"I wanted to talk to you about all the things Mr. Ohghhi . . . the alien's been buying, but yesterday after I talked to you, I had a long talk with him, and he promised not to buy anything else. That's what I wanted to tell you."

He looked worried. "Are you sure you should have done that? You don't want to do anything that might . . ."

"Upset negotiations?" Chris said. The waitress brought Stewart his credit card and a cardboard container with a metal handle. Two teenaged girls wearing "Close Encounters of the Fourth Kind" T-shirts came in and began looking for their shoes. "I'm sure I did the right thing. Don't worry. It won't upset your negotiations. I'll go along with anything he wants."

"Good," he said, putting his credit card away. "Oh, and listen, when this is all over, I want you to come over and look at the apartment next to Mother's. With the compensation we could buy it and sublet yours."

He and the teenaged girls left together, and Chris started looking for her shoes. They weren't there. "Very busy. Much shoes," the attendant said in a passable imitation of the way Mr. Okeefenokee used to talk. "Not steal. Wrong take."

Chris thought of Hutchins diving bravely into the bullet to rescue her shoe. You could get my shoes back for me, she thought at him. Where are you?"

There wasn't any answer. "Wrong take. You mine," the attendant said, and removed her getas, which were no more than a size four.

"Not fit. Wear size eight," Chris said in a passable imitation of the way she had talked to Mr. Okeefenokee before she met Hutchins, and wished again that he were here.

The attendant finally found her a pair of disposable tabis. The thick, toed socks were better than nothing, she thought, and smiled and thanked the attendant, but before she had gone twenty steps, she had come to the conclusion that they weren't. She stepped up in a doorway and tried to massage her crushed instep. It was only half a block to the bullet platform, but she would never make it. And even if she did, she'd be crippled for life by the crowd on the bullet.

She leaned out as far as she could from the doorway and peered down the crowded ginza, trying to spot a shoe vendor. There was everything else: a man selling mylar balloons with a picture of the Eahrohhs' ship on them, a Sony outlet selling chip recorders, a flower vendor with a backpack full of cherry blossoms shouting, "*Hana*! Cheap!"

Mr. Okeefenokee would love it here, she thought, and remembering that she had told Charmaine she'd be back by sixteen o'clock gave her the courage to step back down onto the footwalk, where the balloon man stepped squarely on her foot.

She retreated back up into the doorway to peer the other way. I wonder how far Mitsukoshi's Department Store is, she wondered. They'd have shoes.

(It's ten blocks,) Hutchins said in her ear. (We'll have to take the bullet.)

She knew he was miles away and using the subvocalizer again, but the feeling that he was right behind her was irresistible. She turned around. He was standing there, holding a pair of red spike heels by the straps. "You're lucky Charmaine wears a size eight," he said, and handed them to her. "I know these aren't great, but they're not size fours either. And when we get back to Mitsukoshi's, Okee says he'll buy you a new pair."

"Mitsukoshi's?" she said, balancing herself against the doorway to take the tabis off. "You left Okee alone at Mitsukoshi's?"

"I had to come get you. Your exact words, as I recall, were, 'Where the hell is Hutchins? I don't have any shoes.' Do you realize you subvocalize when you're upset?"

"Yes," she said ruefully, and wondered what else he'd heard her think. She stepped into the shoes, which were at least six inches high, and bent down to velcro the red straps.

"Don't worry about Okee," Hutchins said. "He's not alone. I left him with Charmaine. At the makeup counter. She was trying out blusher colors on the top of his head."

"What were you doing at Mitsukoshi's? I thought you had a job interview."

"I did," he said, and helped her out of the doorway. She stepped warily onto the footwalk. It seemed a long way down. "I went in at noon, and Luigi was pretty busy, so he told me to come back this afternoon. You didn't subvocalize what Stewart said when you told him he had to find Okee and me an apartment, which means you're not upset, which must mean he said he would. Which means—"

"I'm starving to death," Chris said. "I didn't get any lunch."

Hutchins bought her a tempura dog on a stick, and she focused her attention on eating it and keeping her balance for the half block to the bullet platform.

"Is Stewart coming over this afternoon to move Okee and me to another apartment or to throw me out?" Hutchins said after they had pushed their way through to the edge of the platform.

"Here comes the bullet," Chris said, looking at her feet so the spindly heels wouldn't catch in the narrow space between the platform and the magnetic rail. The bullet slid to a stop, and the people behind pushed forward. Chris stumbled and looked down at her feet.

"Come on!" Hutchins yelled, and yanked her up onto the bullet by both arms as the doors closed. They slid shut with a whoosh, and she found herself pinned between a lady with a shopping bag and Hutchins. He was still gripping her arms.

"You didn't answer my question," he said. "What did Stewart say?"

"Why do you have to ask?" she said, still looking at her feet. "You listened in on the whole conversation."

"Not that part," he said. "Charmaine asked what I thought of this makeup she was trying on, and the next thing I knew you were hollering for your shoes." He let go of her and put his arms around her.

"Hey," the woman with the shopping bag said, "quit shoving." She hoisted her shopping bag up into her arms, a movement that had the effect of squashing Chris and Hutchins closer together.

"Look," Hutchins said, "I should have told you this morning and now it's probably too late, but it's important that Okee and I stay where we are. I'm not talking about the hammock. I tried to get one of Mr. Nagisha's overnight leases, but he's booked up through next week, so I asked Charmaine if I could bunk on one of her steps. She said she's got a friend moving in with her, but I'll see if her lawyer friend will let me sleep on the landing. The important thing is that Okee stay in his room and do whatever it is he's planning on doing. When did Stewart say he was moving Okee out?"

"He didn't," she said.

"Good," he said, sounding relieved. "Maybe he won't have found anything by tonight and—"

"I didn't tell Stewart."

"What?"

She looked up. Charmaine's shoes put her on a level with him, and when she looked up, it was straight into his eyes. "I didn't tell him Okee sublet the apartment to you."

"Why not?"

"The negotiations are at a very delicate stage," she said, trying not to look at him. She didn't dare duck her head, because they were so close that his lips might brush her forehead, and if she turned her head, he would be whispering in her ear, just as he had been with the subvocalizer. "It's only for a couple of days and . . ."

And I was afraid I'd never see you again, she

thought, and then tried to stifle the thought so Hutchins wouldn't hear her. She would have taken the subvocalizer off if she could, but her arms were pinned against his chest, and she was afraid to move them for fear it would bring her closer to him. "Why is it so important that you and Mr. Okeefenokee stay?" she said.

He was looking at her with that thoughtful expression he had had the night before. She could hear his heart beating in her pinioned arms. "Because he asked for a room with high ceilings. Do you know what else the word for 'high' means in Japanese? It means losing your temper, howling, roaring, growing older, and excelling. Take your pick. I don't know what he wants with that room, and neither does that team of Japanese linguists, but it has something to do with the negotiations that are so delicate right now, and with the space program they're negotiating for. If it's a space program. The word for 'space' also means harmony, leisure, room, or eye. The Eahrohhs could be offering us a new kind of glasses or some time off or a way to beat the house on Vegas Two." He stopped and looked across at her. "Chris . . . ," he said.

He's going to hear what I'm thinking, she thought, and took a frightened step back.

"Quit shoving," the lady with the shopping bag said.

"You heard her," Hutchins said, grinning. He pulled her back against him. "Quit shoving."

"I'm letting you stay," she said, keeping her head averted, "but it's only because of Mr. Okeefenokee. You said you'd asked Charmaine if you could bunk with her. I think maybe that would be a good idea."

(I don't want to sleep with Charmaine,) Hutchins said in her ear. (I want to sleep with you.)

She was so surprised she lifted her head, but he wasn't looking at her. He was watching the station markers through the bullet doors.

Did you know you subvocalize when you're upset? she thought, feeling oddly pleased.

"What?" Hutchins said.

"Get out of the way," the lady with the shopping bag said. "This is my stop."

"I said, this is the stop for Mitsukoshi's," Chris said.

Charmaine was still at the makeup counter. "What do you think of this?" she said, holding up a bright-pink lipstick. "It's called Passion Pink. I'm working up a new single called 'Cherry Blossom Time.' "

"Where's Mr. Okeefenokee?" Chris said.

"Up in Furniture," she said, trying out the pink lipstick on a space above the bodice of her strapless dress. "He said he wanted to buy a bed."

"I'd better go get him," Hutchins said.

"I'll come with you," Chris said.

"Can I have my shoes back first?" Charmaine said. She reached into a shopping bag and pulled out a box. "Mr. Fenokee bought you a new pair."

"I'll catch up with you," Chris said, and leaned against the makeup counter to take off the red heels. "Thanks for loaning them to me," she said, handing them back to Charmaine by the straps.

"I didn't have any choice in the matter," she said, pushing out her chest and looking at it in the mirror. "Hutchins practically knocked me over getting them off. I thought you said you didn't like him."

"I didn't," Chris said. "I mean, I don't. I mean, I'm engaged to Stewart and . . ." She hastily opened the shoe box. "Oh, good," she said brightly. "They're flats. I don't know how you wear such high heels."

"I was trying on green eye makeup, you know, for my fans, and I asked Hutchins what he thought of Jade Royal." She pulled the bodice of her dress down farther and drew a wide line of rose-colored lipstick on the exposed area. "And he said it was fine, but I could tell he wasn't really listening because he had this kind of faraway look on his face, and I mean, gee, most guys want to help me put the makeup on, and then all of a sudden he says, 'What size shoes do you wear? Give me your shoes. Chris needs them,' and takes off."

She pulled the bodice down still farther and tried a bright-coral lipstick. Chris wondered how far down the greens had gotten. "And I turned to Mr. Fenokee and said, 'How does he know Chris needs my shoes?' and you know what he said?"

Chris ducked her head so Charmaine couldn't see her face and put on her new shoes. "Maybe I'd better go see where Mr. Okeefenokee is," she said. "He's probably buying a dining-room set."

"He said you and Hutchins are getting married today and asked me what kinds of things people needed for a honeymoon," Charmaine said. "Only he pronounced it 'hahnahmoon.' "

"What did you tell him?"

"Gee, you know, just the basics. Champagne and a black lace nightie and a bed. And diamonds. I figured diamonds are a girl's best friend."

"A bed?" Chris said. "Oh, no, I told him there wasn't any space in my apartment. I've got to go stop him."

She left as abruptly as Hutchins apparently had and took the escalator up to Furniture. Halfway up, she met Hutchins and Mr. Okeefenokee on their way down. "Did he buy anything?" she shouted after them.

(No,) Hutchins said in her ear. (I caught him just in time. He was looking at a washer and dryer. Meet us at the foot of the escalator.)

Chris ran the rest of the way up to Furniture, wondering if she should check with the clerk to see whether Mr. Okeefenokee had bought a bed that Hutchins didn't know about.

(I'm going to have you take Okee home, if that's all right,) Hutchins said, sounding as if he were on the step above her. (I'm already late to my interview. It's already sixteen o'clock. Why don't you and Okee just stay here and shop and then meet me at Luigi's for dinner? That way you won't have to go home.)

(I don't think that's a good idea,) Chris said. (Mr. Okeefenokee could buy the whole store by suppertime.)

There wasn't any answer, and when Chris arrived at the bottom of the escalator, Hutchins was already gone. Mr. Okeefenokee was at the lingerie counter being handed a large white box. He stuffed it in a bulging shopping bag.

Chris took him back over to the makeup counter. "I'm taking Mr. Okeefenokee home before he buys anything else," Chris told Charmaine. "He has no business being in a place like this."

"Gee, I know," Charmaine said, wiping lipstick off her bosom. "I told Hutchins you'd said he wasn't supposed to go shopping, but he said you wouldn't care if he bought a few souvenirs."

"He said what?" Chris said.

"I need twenty of the Prom Night Pink and fifteen of the Tokyo Rose," Charmaine said to the salesgirl. "Gee, you wouldn't believe how much makeup a person goes through. We ran into him up on the axis this morning, and—"

"What were you doing up on the axis?"

"Mr. Fenokee wanted to go see some of the other arrows guys, I guess he was homesick or something, and you said to let him do anything he wanted as long as it wasn't shopping, and so I took him up there and we ran into Hutchins."

"What was *he* doing on the axis?"

"I don't know. He was coming out of the NASA building. So anyway he suggested we all go shopping and . . ."

"When was this?"

"Gee, I don't know. Around twelve." She turned back to the salesgirl. "I hope this pink is right. You know how lipstick always looks a different color when you try it on your hand than on your lips? Well, I have the same problem with my fans."

"Charmaine," Chris said carefully, "do you happen to know of any job openings at Luigi's?"

"Gee, no. That old guy who lives on the stairs asked me that this morning, and I had to tell him Luigi isn't even taking applications, he's had so many people come in."

"Can you bring Okee home?" Chris said rapidly. "I've got to . . ." She couldn't even think of what excuse to give her. "I have to go," she repeated lamely. I have to follow Hutchins and see why he's been lying to me, she thought, and was infinitely glad Charmaine wasn't wearing a subvocalizer.

"Sure," Charmaine said, and asked to see the eyeliners.

Chris had no idea where Hutchins was going except that it wasn't Luigi's and that he would probably have to take the bullet to get there. If he had to wait for the bullet, she might have a chance of catching up with him and following him. She took off her subvocalizer and put her hand up to her ear, trying to hear any stray thought he might have about where he was going.

Maybe she should use the subvocalizer and just ask him, she thought. She could make up some excuse about needing to go with him to Luigi's. And he would make up an excuse about why she couldn't, the way he had made up the interview with Luigi. Anyway, it was too risky. She might pause, the way she had with Charmaine, unable to think of an excuse, and the truth would come tumbling out because she was upset. She might say, "I need to go with you because that's not where you're going and what were you doing up at the axis this morning and why did you lie to me?" She stuck the subvocalizer in her pocket.

He was still on the bullet platform, though just barely. He was getting on the bullet, and she saw with a sinking feeling that it wasn't the one for Shitamachi. She got on at the farthest door down from him, glad she was wearing flats. She huddled down behind a young woman with a headdress like the one Charmaine wore and watched him through the red-and-black-lacquered chopsticks until he got off.

He looked worried and almost as tired as he had the night before, and she would have felt sorry for him all over again, but his shirt collar was open, and she could see that he wasn't wearing his subvocalizer either.

The young woman got off when he did, and Chris followed her onto the platform and then ducked behind a pillar. She didn't need to see him to know where he was going. This was her stop. Maybe he's still shuttle-lagged, she thought, and he didn't get enough sleep last night with Okee snoring and Molly and Bets and everything, and he's come home to take a nap. But if that was true, why had he taken his subvocalizer off? And why had he lied about the job interview?

She gave him a ten-minute head start and then followed him into her apartment building. She opened the door quietly, afraid that Molly and Bets might have waylaid him with the Sugarplum Fairy, but he was nowhere to be seen, and the little girls were sitting halfway up the stairs talking to a redheaded man with a chip recorder.

They had changed out of their tutus and into navy-sailor dresses and white patent-leather shoes. "I've been in show biz since I was two," Bets was saying in her clear childish voice. "I'm four and a half now."

The old man in the baseball cap had fallen asleep playing solitaire. The cards were still on the step above him, and the young woman with the chopsticks in her hair was leaning over, picking them up. When she leaned over, she looked a lot like Charmaine.

"Hi," she said. She put the cards in a neat stack and laid them next to the old man. "I'm Omiko. I just moved in with Charmaine, and I was wondering if I could use your bathroom."

Chris glanced warily up at the door. "We blew a fuse," she said. "Mr. Hutchins is fixing it, but it'll probably be an hour. Why don't you ask Mr. Nagisha if you can use his bathroom?"

"Would you pleathe be quiet!" Molly said from the landing. "We're being interviewed."

Chris went on up the stairs past Molly and Bets. "I danthed in the road thyow of *Annie Two*," Molly said to the redheaded man and then dropped to a stage whisper as Chris went past. "That'th her!"

"The woman who rents the apartment?" he said.

"Yes," Bets said, and whispered something Chris couldn't hear.

In the hall Charmaine's lawyer was standing by his printer, watching it chug out copies of something. "Tell Okee I'll have these ready for him by tonight."

"All right," Chris said, not really listening to him. She inserted her key in the door, thinking, please let him be taking a nap. But he wasn't in the hammock or the hall, and the door to the bathroom was open. So was the door to Mr. Okeefenokee's room. A key was still in the lock. She pulled it out, put it in her pocket, and went in.

Mr. Okeefenokee had bought a bed. Though he must not have bought it today, Chris thought, because there wouldn't have been time to deliver it, let alone get it in here and pile all those things on it.

The bento-bako boxes were stacked on the foot of the bed next to a tangle of paper umbrellas and a set of encyclopedias. The rest of the bed was piled to the ceiling with boxes that appeared to be microwave ovens.

She came around the end of the bed into a narrow aisle formed by stacks of boxes that went clear to the ceiling. One of the boxes read, "One gross dental floss." Hutchins's bicycle was propped against the boxes. Next to it was a baby buggy with a Christmas tree in it. She couldn't see the piano anywhere, but there were four accordions sitting in the middle of the aisle.

Against the back wall was a trampoline propped on its side with six pairs of roller skates and a wind sock hanging from it. Hutchins was kneeling in front of the trampoline, digging in a box full of Styrofoam packing. He lifted out a lava lamp and looked at it.

"How did you get in here?" Chris said.

He laid the lava lamp back in the box and stood up. "Okee gave me his key," he said. "I thought you were going shopping."

"I thought you had a job interview at Luigi's," Chris said steadily.

"I did, but I called Luigi and told him I'd be a little late. Okee wanted me to check on whether he'd bought a Japanese-English dictionary or not. He couldn't remember. It's no wonder with all the junk he's got in here. At least we know what he wanted the high ceilings for. You don't see a dictionary anywhere, do you?"

"There aren't any job openings at Luigi's," Chris said. "Charmaine told me he's not even taking applications." He stopped pretending to look for the dictionary. "She also told me she saw you on the axis this morning."

"Chris," he said.

She backed away from him into the Christmas tree. The balls rattled. "You're a spy, aren't you?"

He looked genuinely astonished. "A spy? Of course I'm not a spy."

"Then what are you doing in here? And why did you lie to me about the job interview?"

"All right," he said. "I didn't have a job interview. I went up to NASA to get my subvocalizer checked. I wanted to know what made it tick."

"Because you're a spy," Chris said, still backing. "I'm calling Stewart."

"No!" he said, and then in a calmer and even more unsettling tone, "No. You aren't calling anybody. As soon as NASA works out a deal with the Japanese, they're taking Okee down to Houston. I've got maybe two days to figure out what he means by 'space program' before the NASA people start demanding that he deliver a space program he doesn't know anything about. I don't have time to mess with your idiot fiancé."

"He's not an idiot," Chris said, feeling behind her back for something she could hit him with. Her hand closed on a golf club.

"Oh, isn't he? He's engaged to you, for God's sake, and he doesn't even exercise his option. He puts you on hold and goes off and leaves you barefoot in the ginza and lets strange men sleep in your room. If I were engaged to you, I'd . . . I'm not a spy. I'm a linguist."

Chris's grip tightened on the golf club. "I don't believe you," she said. "Stewart said the American linguistics team was at NASA, talking to the Eahrohhs' leaders."

"Okee's the leader."

She let go of the golf club, and the whole bag of clubs went over and spilled out. "But Stewart said he was just a passenger."

"The Eahrohhs told the Japanese linguistics team that Okee was *noru hito*. That means passenger. It also means proclaiming one. That means he's the one who's supposed to deliver the space program, only I don't think he's got one. Do you remember what you said to Okee when I moved in? You said, 'There isn't any space.' "

"Oh, no," Chris said. "And he only understands one meaning of a word."

"The first one he hears. But those idiots over at NASA think that if an alien who has known our language less than two weeks says space program, he has to mean astronauts, rockets, and zero-gravity bathrooms. It never even crosses their minds that 'space' also means a vacuum, that 'program' also means a series of musical numbers. Okee could be giving us radio, for God's sake."

"What are you going to do?"

"I'm going to do what I've been doing for the last two days—try to figure out what the hell he means by 'space program.' He can't pronounce 'honeymoon' right. What if he can't pronounce 'space program' either? What if he's offering us a spice program and NASA's going to find itself with eighty tons of cinnamon? What if it's a spaze program, whatever the hell that is? Or a space pogrom? We've got to find out before he goes down to Houston. That's why I was in here. I thought maybe he was keeping some machine in here or secret plans or something, but all he's got is a swing set and a gross of Girl Scout flashlights. I don't know. Maybe he's a smuggler."

"What about the subvocalizers?" Chris said. "You said you tried to find out what made them work."

"Nothing," Hutchins said. He pulled his out of his pocket and looked at it. "It's two pieces of metal with five millimeters of air between them, not even vacuum, just air." He put the subvocalizer back on. "All they could tell me over at NASA was that it does what it's supposed to."

"It does what it's supposed to," Chris said. She thought about him taking it off so he could come over here without being followed, about talking to her at lunch with it. "Your giving me the subvocalizer, that was all a setup, wasn't it, so you could make sure I didn't tell Stewart about you?"

"I couldn't risk your moving me out. I needed to be where I could talk to Okee."

"Did you really come up on the shuttle yesterday, or was that part of the act, too?"

"It wasn't an act. I was supposed to come up with the rest of the team, but I'd heard how much trouble the Japanese team was having communicating with the Eahrohhs. I figured it was because everybody was trying so hard to get the names pronounced right and learn the language that it made the Eahrohhs nervous. So I thought if I could come up here incognito—"

"Like Spielberg," Chris said bitterly.

" 'Scuse me," Charmaine's cheery voice floated up from downstairs.

"They're home!" Hutchins said. "We can't let him find us in here!" He dashed back into the aisle of boxes. Chris scrambled to pick up the bento-bako boxes and stack them on the bed again. Hutchins jammed the golf clubs back into the bag and came to help her.

"I gotta be at work at nineteen o'clock, Mr. Fenokee," Charmaine said, sounding so close she could have been using a subvocalizer. "We better get all this stuff put away."

Chris and Hutchins dived out the door and slid the shojii screen shut. "Where's the key?" he said.

Chris pulled it out of her pocket and fumbled to lock the door. The lock seemed to take forever to read the key. She pulled it out.

"Can you get the door, please, Molly?" Charmaine said, there was a long pause, and the door of the apartment slid open. Chris put her hands behind her back.

" 'Scuse me," Charmaine said. She was carrying an unsteady stack of boxes and a shopping bag. Hutchins took half of the boxes for her. "Gee, thanks. Would you believe that rotten kid wouldn't even open the door for me? She said after tonight she was going to be a star and wouldn't have to do anything anybody told her." She bent over in her red strapless dress to put the rest of the boxes down.

"Where's Mr. Okeefenokee?" Chris said.

"He stopped to talk to my ex-boyfriend," she said. "Look, I gotta be at work in half an hour, and I don't even have my cherry blossoms on yet, so could you guys help put this stuff away?"

"Sure," Hutchins said. Charmaine grabbed a small sack out of the shopping bag and disappeared into the bathroom.

"Chris," Hutchins said. Chris pretended not to hear

him. She put the key in her pocket and started for her room.

"Did you take our chip recorder?" Bets said indignantly from the door. She was wearing an aproned blue dress. Her yellow curls peeked out from under a turned-up Dutch cap. "It had 'Tiptoe Through the Tulips' on it." She stamped her wooden shoe. "You better give it back."

"I don't have it," Chris said, and amazingly, Bets turned around and stomped out. Chris heard her say loudly, "She says she doesn't have it, but I'll bet she took it. She's always doing mean things like that to us."

"Chris, listen," Hutchins said, putting out his hand to keep her from passing. "I should have told you the truth to begin with."

"Yes," she said. "You should have."

"The first thing I heard you say to Stewart was that you didn't have any room for the piano." He looked thoughtfully at Mr. Okeefenokee's door. "I didn't see the piano in there, did you?"

"No," Chris said. "So you figured if I didn't have room for a piano, I certainly wouldn't have room for you, and you were going to have to romance the landlady into giving you a place to sleep. So you fell asleep on my shoulder and brought me Charmaine's shoes and fed me a tempura dog."

"Now you and Hutchins get married," Mr. Okeefenokee said, carrying two shopping bags full of boxes and Mitsukoshi sacks. His wispy orange-pink hair was flying out in all directions. "Go on hahnahmoon."

"Mr. Okeefenokee, I thought I explained . . . ," Chris said.

"We're thyure you took it," Molly said, with her hands on the hips of her Dutch dress. "If you don't give it back, we're going to tell our interviewer all the thingth you did."

"Fine. Mr. Okeefenokee," she said again, but he had already disappeared through his door.

"I hope we didn't miss any bento-bako boxes," Hutchins whispered to her. The door slid open and Mr. Okeefenokee emerged, picked up the packages Charmaine had left on the floor, and disappeared into the room again.

"You'll be thorry you were mean to uth." Molly slid the apartment door shut with a crash, and Chris and Hutchins were abruptly alone.

"Thanks for not spilling the beans to Okee," Hutchins said.

"What would you have done if I'd tried? Bought me another tempura dog? Fallen asleep on my shoulder again? You're no better than Charmaine's prospective buyer, you know that? Talk about your real-estate deals."

"What do you think of my cherry blossoms?" Charmaine said, emerging from the bathroom with the red dress over her arm. "Do you think that pink's too dark?" She peered over her shoulder. "It always looks different on your—"

"It looks fine," Chris said.

"Omiko said to tell you guys to come to the show tonight, and she'll see that Mr. Fenokee catches her orbiting colonies' tassels," she said, and clattered out. Chris watched her red high heels.

(Chris, listen, I wasn't romancing you for a place to sleep,) Hutchins said in her ear. (I was—)

She turned around furiously, yanked the receiver off her ear, and handed it to him. "It doesn't matter," she said, fishing her subvocalizer out of her pocket and putting it in his outstretched hand. "You can stay. I won't tell Mr. Okeefenokee who you are. Just leave me alone." She pulled the door of her apartment open. "I'll go ask Charmaine if I can bunk with her tonight."

"You don't have to do that," Hutchins said, looking down at the subvocalizer in his hand. "I'll sleep in the bathroom," but she went on out anyway, slamming shut the sliding door with almost as much force as Molly.

Charmaine had already left. She tried to catch her, brushing past Molly and Bets, who stopped in the middle of singing "Tiptoe Through the Tulips" to glare at her from the landing, and practically stepping on the old man in the baseball cap, who was, amazingly, sleeping through it, but by the time she got to the door, Charmaine had already disappeared into the crowd.

She came back up the stairs. Molly and Bets stopped for her again, folding their arms and tapping their wooden shoes impatiently, and then started up again as soon as she was off the landing, singing their own accompaniment in piping, slightly flat voices. Hutchins was at the end of the hall, talking earnestly to Charmaine's lawyer and frowning.

Chris slid her door open. "Why did you refuse to sublet your apartment to Molly and Bets?" the redheaded man said. He stuck a chip-cam in her face. She tried to brush past him. "So you admit you refused to share your apartment with two innocent tykes and then blatantly rented half of it to—"

She got the door shut with some difficulty since his foot was wedged in it, went in the living room and shut and locked that door, too, and then leaned against it, feeling as tired as if she had just come up on the shuttle.

Chris spent the evening huddled on the couch under a blanket.

"I brought you some supper," Hutchins called through the door about nineteen o'clock. "No tempura dogs. I'll leave it outside the door."

Chris opened the door. "I've changed my mind," she said, not looking at him. "I'm sleeping in here. You can sleep with Charmaine," and then was afraid he would say, "I don't want to sleep with Charmaine. I want to sleep with you," but he only said, "I'll sleep in the hall," and handed her a pastrami sandwich and a packet of milk.

He knocked again at twenty-thirty and called out, "Molly and Bets's interview is on. Mr. Nagisha's got his TV set up on the landing. The little girls told me to tell you because, and I quote, 'Thith ith what thyee getth for thtealing our recorder.' I thought maybe you might want to come see what revenge they've cooked up."

"No, thank you."

"Okay," he said, and knocked again immediately.

"Go away," Chris said.

"You and Hutchins get married tonight," Mr. Okeefenokee said. "I must talk to you about closing."

She opened the door. Mr. Okeefenokee came in, wearing his solemn expression. "Why are you not wearing your thuwevrherrnghladdis?"

Chris put her hand up to her throat. "It hurt to wear it," she said. "Charmaine said to ask you if you'd like to go see the show at Luigi's tonight."

"I cannot go. You and Hutchins get married tonight."

"We can't get married, Mr. Okeefenokee," Chris said. "I'm engaged to Stewart, and even if I weren't, Hutchins doesn't want to marry me. He just wanted a place to stay."

"You like my wife," he said, continuing to look at her solemnly, the lines above his nose deepening.

"I thought Omiko reminded you of your wife."

"Omiko sake cups like wife," he said, reverting to pidgin. His cheek knobs were bright orange. "But you like her most."

"You miss your wife, don't you?" Chris said, and then remembered that he wouldn't understand that meaning of "miss." "It makes you sad that she is far away."

"Far away," he said, nodding and smiling vigorously.

"Far away," she said, walking to the end of the hall.

"Far away." She came back and stood in front of him. "Close."

"Closing," he said, and his face smoothed out into his expression of understanding. "Hahnahmoon. I bought bed. Put on subvocalizer. You and Hutchins get married after interview." He went bustling out, his wispy hair trailing behind him, like sunset clouds.

"I don't think so," Chris thought sadly, sliding the door shut. I'm engaged to Stewart and Hutchins just wanted a place to stay. Mr. Okeefenokee hadn't understood her when she'd said that. "I bought bed," he'd said, and he hadn't understood "close" either. Or "far away."

She had a sudden terrible vision of Stewart trying to explain what a space program was. "Space program," she could hear him saying, "go far way," and Mr. Okeefenokee would nod and smile vigorously.

I'd better tell Hutchins about "far away," she thought. She went out in the hall to look for him. He wasn't on the stairs, but everybody else was, including Mr. Nagisha's evicted cousins. They were watching Molly and Bets's holographic images in front of the TV. Molly and Bets, still in costume, were dancing alongside their three-dimensional images, and both Mollys were bawling "Tiptoe Through the Tulipth."

Chris went back inside and went to bed, locking her apartment door but leaving the door of her room slightly open so she could hear Hutchins when he came back. If he comes back, she thought sadly. After a while she heard someone come in, and got up, but it was only Mr. Okeefenokee. He disappeared into his room and began to snore almost before he had the shoji screen shut.

"Chris, wake up," Hutchins said in her ear, and at first she thought he was using the subvocalizer.

"I took it off," she said sleepily, and opened her eyes. He was squatting beside the couch, his hand on her shoulder. He had on jeans and no shirt. "What time is it?" she said, reaching for the light. "And what are you doing in here?"

"Twenty-one o'clock," he whispered. "Don't turn on the light. You'll wake Butch and Sundance." He pointed at the floor, where Molly and Bets were curled up in the pink blanket. "Where's the key to Okee's room? I can't get him to open the door."

"How did *they* get in here?" she said, rummaging through her clothes at the end of the couch.

"I don't know. Probably Molly had another key."

She found the key and handed it to him. "*Another* key?"

"This is Molly's key, too. I threatened to tell her red-headed interviewer that she was really eleven if she didn't give it to me." He stepped over Molly and Bets.

Chris hunted for her robe for nearly a full minute before she realized she was hearing the sound of Mr. Okeefenokee's snoring. "He's asleep," she said, but Hutchins was already out in the hall. She went after him. "He's asleep."

"Remember how he said we woke him up with our talking? Well, I've been shouting through the door at him for the last fifteen minutes. I've done everything short of kicking in his shoji screen." He fitted the key in the door and waited for it to be read. "Something's wrong." He slid the screen open. "Okee? Are you in here?"

The snoring continued. Chris followed him inside and slid the door shut behind her. Hutchins was staring at the bed. Mr. Okeefenokee had cleared off the bento-bako boxes and the microwave ovens and made up the bed with red-and-green-patterned sheets. There was a stack of boxes on the foot of the bed with a piece of paper and a deck of playing cards on top of it. Molly's chip recorder was lying on the pillow.

"Charmaine must have picked out the sheets," Chris said. "There are fans on them."

Hutchins picked up the recorder and hit a button. The snoring stopped. "He's gone," Hutchins said.

"Gone where? And how did he get out? I thought you were sleeping in the hall."

"I didn't come in until after he was asleep." He stopped and corrected himself. "Until I thought he was asleep. I was down in Mr. Nagisha's apartment trying to get Charmaine's boyfriend to tell me what Okee'd been talking to him about, while Okee and everybody else were watching Sacco and Vanzetti tiptoe through the tulips on TV. Charmaine's lawyer kept pleading client confidentiality until the interview was over, and when I came back up here, I could hear Okee snoring." He tapped the recorder on his hand. "He must have hidden in the hall till I came in and then sneaked out."

Chris picked up the piece of paper and looked at it. "Why would he do that?"

"Because he'd found out I'd been lying to him. We probably missed one of the bento-bako boxes or Molly and Bets told him I'd been in here or something. Damn it, coming up here incognito was a truly inspired idea! If I knew where Spielberg was, I'd tell him to come out of hiding before he hurts somebody! Okee's probably halfway back to Eahrohhsani by now!"

"He didn't go home," Chris said. She handed him the list. "He's probably down at Luigi's trying to catch one of Omiko's tassels." She pointed to the middle of the paper. "This is number three: 'Time alone. Talk.' "

He read the list aloud. " 'Be friends, talk, time alone, neck, bed, close, honeymoon.' What is this?"

"It's his list. 'You and Hutchins get married.' I told him people have to have a chance to be alone to talk before they got married." She picked up the deck of cards and looked at it.

"And I said, 'Neck.' "

"Which is number four." There weren't any black cards in the deck. She fanned them out to look at them.

There weren't any hearts either. "You notice those aren't checked off yet. He's trying to give us some time alone."

Hutchins reached for one of the boxes. He took the lid off and held up a black lace nightgown. "It looks like he thought of everything."

"Yeah," she said, spreading out the cards so he could see them. "Charmaine told him diamonds are a girl's best friend."

"So he got you diamonds," he said. He tossed the list on the bed. "God only knows what he thinks a closing is. Or a hahnahmoon."

"Or a space program. We'd better go look for him. Maybe if I asked him about his space program, he'd explain it to me."

"In a minute," he said. He put the nightgown back in the box. "Okee wanted us to talk alone. Your prospective buyer said to do anything Okee wanted."

She was suddenly very aware of her skimpy nightshift and Hutchins's bare chest. "You leave Stewart out of this."

"I'd be glad to. The hell with what Stewart says. The hell with what Okee wants. I want to talk to you alone."

Chris backed away from him, knocking over the bento-bako boxes again. "I don't want to talk to you," she said unsteadily.

"Fine. Don't say anything. I'll do the talking. I didn't 'romance' you, as you call it, because I needed a place to stay. And I didn't pretend to be shuttle-lagged. I was shuttle-lagged, damn it, and all I could think of was keeping close to Okee." He came around the bed, ignoring the scattered bento-bako boxes. "It took about one good look at you to make me realize I should tell you the truth, but every time I tried, we were interrupted by some damned vaudeville act."

Chris kept backing down the narrow aisle between boxes, which was even narrower now that the microwaves were stacked on one side. "And that's why you kept interrupting my lunch with Stewart?" she said, and crashed into the Christmas tree. Two ornaments hit the floor and bounced. "Because you were trying to tell the truth?"

"I was trying to keep you from marrying somebody who only wants your apartment," he shouted. "He doesn't care about you! He pawns some alien off on you without even knowing if he's friendly. What if it is a space pogrom and Okee'd decided to start with you? What if he'd decided to take you home to Eahrohhsani or marry you off to someone else?"

"He did," Chris said.

"And Stewart doesn't know about it, right? No, of course not. Because he's too busy telling you to do whatever Okee wants. So, fine, let's get married!"

There was nowhere left to back. Another ornament hit the floor and rolled, and tinsel shimmered onto Chris's hair and shoulders. "Married?" she said.

"Sure. Why not?" he shouted. "Okee's got everything we need right here: champagne, diamonds, Stewart's permission." He waved his arm at the room. "I'll bet if we dug through this mess, Okee's even got a justice of the peace in here someplace."

Hutchins was very close, and since they were both barefoot, he loomed over her. "I thought you didn't want to get married," Chris said unsteadily.

He looked at her for a long, silent minute. Then he reached forward and plucked a piece of tinsel out of her hair. "I changed my mind," he said.

The shoji screen slid open. "I know they're in here," Molly said. "I heard them thyouting."

"Ohghhifoehnnahigrheeh!" Stewart called. "Chris! Where are you?" He appeared at the end of the hall. "Where's Mr. Ohghhifoehnnahigrheeh?" he said hurriedly, giving Hutchins and Chris the barest of glances. "We need him up at NASA immediately."

"He's not here, Stewart," Chris said.

"Obviouthly," Molly said, her arms folded across her chest.

"Well, where is he, Chris?" Stewart said impatiently.

"I don't know," Chris said, shaking tinsel out of her hair.

"What do you mean, you don't know? This is an emergency. The linguistics team just discovered that Ohghhifoehnnahigrhee's the leader of the Eahrohhs. If they find out up at NASA that he's missing—"

"He's not missing," Hutchins said, stepping forward. "Pete Hutchins, Navy Intelligence Linguistics Unit."

"This is just a little misunderstanding," Stewart said, looking daggers at Chris. "My fiancée doesn't really mean he's missing."

"I know," Hutchins said. "I've had Okee under observation for the last two days."

"That'th not all he'th had under obthervation," Molly said, looking at Chris's bare feet.

"Right now he's at Luigi's Tempura Pizzeria watching the *sutorippu*," Hutchins went on imperturbably. Stewart took out a pad and pencil and began scribbling. "It's down in Shitamachi. On Osaka Street."

"Osaka Street," Stewart said. "I'll call NASA and have him picked up immediately." He started out to the hall.

"Picked up?" Chris said, following him.

"He'th not really there at all," Molly said. "They jutht want you to leave tho they can have theckth."

"Theckth?" Stewart said.

"Too much noise," Mr. Okeefenokee said. He appeared at the end of the aisle, his orange-pink hair mashed down on one side as if he'd been lying on it. "Can't sleep."

"Mr. Okeefenokee, what are you doing here?" Chris said.

"Thee?" Molly said. "I told you he wathn't at Luigi'th."

Mr. Okeefenokee bent over and picked up one of the ornaments and hung it back on the tree. "Too much noise. Fighting. Sleep in back." He gestured in the direction of the back wall, where the trampoline and the roller skates were.

Chris said, "But what about the recorder you—"

"Left a message on saying you were going to Luigi's?" Hutchins interrupted smoothly. "Did you leave it because you didn't want to be disturbed?"

"Message," Mr. Okeefenokee said, smiling and nodding.

"You need to accompany me up to NASA immediately," Stewart said. "You are needed for the negotiations on the space program."

"Space program," he said, his head bobbing even more vigorously. "Closing."

"Hutchins, you'd better come with us to help translate," Stewart said. "I'll call NASA and let them know we're on our way." He went out into the hall to the phone.

Molly picked up the cards on the bed and looked at them. "Doeth that old man know you thtole hith cardth?" she asked Okee. Mr. Okeefenokee beamed at her.

Hutchins pulled Chris back into the aisle. "Where's your subvocalizer?" he said softly.

"I gave it to you. Don't you have it?"

"I gave it to Okee. I asked him to try to talk you into wearing it again."

Chris frowned. "He asked me why I wasn't wearing it and told me to put it on, but he didn't give it back to me."

"Great," Hutchins said. "Now he doesn't understand the word 'give' either, so how can he give us a space program?" He gripped her arms. "Look, I can't let Okee go up to NASA by himself. I've got to go with him."

"I know," Chris said.

"If you had your subvocalizer, you could listen in on what's happening, but . . . I'll call you as soon as I can, okay?" He looked at her. "Maybe it's just as well you don't have it on. I might subvocalize what I'm thinking."

"I knew you thtole my recorder," Molly said. She brandished it at Chris. "Wait till I tell Bets about thith." She stomped out.

"What did you say to upset that poor, dear child?" Stewart said. "I got through to NASA. I told them we were on our way. Perhaps you should get dressed, Mr. Hutchins."

"Yeah," Hutchins said. He went out into the hall. Mr. Okeefenokee followed him.

"I think I should go with you, Stewart," Chris said. "Mr. Okeefenokee doesn't understand English very well, and I couldn't . . ."

"I hardly think you'd have anything to contribute to the space-program negotiations when you haven't even bothered to learn to pronounce his name correctly," Stewart said.

"How do you know it's a space program?"

"What?"

"I said, how do you know *Mr. Okeefenokee*," she said, saying his name with emphasis, "is talking about the same kind of space program you are? What if he's talking about something else?"

"Don't be ridiculous," he said, walking around the bed to look at the microwave boxes. "What else could he possible be talking about?"

A spice program, Chris thought. A space pogrom. Radio. "Aren't you going to ask me what I was doing here in my nightgown with Pete Hutchins?"

Stewart bent over to look to the accordions. "What's all this stuff doing in here?"

"You told me to do whatever Mr. Okeefenokee wanted. He wanted to buy things."

"I meant anything within reason," he said, picking

up one of the bento-bako boxes. "How in heaven's name did he expect to get all this home with him?"

"How *did* he expect to get all this home?" Hutchins said, frowning. He had put on his shirt and a tweed jacket.

"It wath right there!" Molly said, pointing at the bed. "In plain thight."

"She stole it just like she stole our curling iron," Bets said. "That's what I told the interviewer." She struck a pose. "I said, 'She steals things and she won't let us use her phone or her bathroom and . . .' "

"Out," Chris said. She took hold of the pink ribbons on Bets's nightgown and used them to propel her out the door.

"You're just trying to get rid of us so you can be alone with Hutchins, but we fixed you! We—" Chris slid the door shut.

"What was all that about?" Stewart said. "You didn't actually steal that darling tot's recorder, did you?"

"Molly's practicing her lines for a screen test," Hutchins said. "A remake of *The Bad Seed*. Okee, are you ready to go up to NASA?" Okee nodded and smiled. Hutchins herded him downstairs.

"I really think I should go with you, Stewart," Chris said.

He started down the stairs. "It's not necessary," he said, stepping over the old man, who was laying out a hand of solitaire. "You stay here and help the kiddies rehearse for their screen test. Besides, you're not even dressed," he said, and then turned and looked back up at her in surprise.

"Call me," Chris said, and looked over his head at Hutchins standing by the door. "Please."

"I doubt if we'll be able to," Stewart said crisply from the foot of the stairs. "I should imagine we'll be in negotiations all night."

They went out. Chris hesitated a moment and then

started to run back up the stairs to get dressed so she could go with them.

"Wait," Mr. Nagisha said from the door of his apartment. "I have something to give you." She came back down the stairs, stepping carefully over the laid-out cards, and he handed her a folded paper.

"What is it?" Chris said.

"An eviction notice. You are in violation of your lease."

"I am not," she said, unfolding the paper. "How am I in violation?"

"Subletting without landlord's permission to a person not a relative and withholding of rent."

"What? You mean Mr. Okeefenokee? I didn't sublet my apartment to him. NASA requisitioned it, and Stewart paid you. I saw him. Nobody withheld any rent, and if you're talking about Mr. Hutchins, Mr. Okeefenokee was the one who asked him to stay with him. If you think he should be paying rent, too, you'll have to talk to NASA."

"I have evidence. You must be out by seven o'clock tomorrow morning. I have rented your apartment to other tenants."

"What kind of evidence?"

He flourished a chip at her, and for a minute Chris thought it was the missing recording of "Tiptoe Through the Tulips," but Mr. Nagisha walked past the old man, stepping squarely on the cards, and up to the landing, where he stuck the chip into the TV.

The title, "Orphans of the Stairs" appeared in front of the screen followed by a shot of the apartment building. A voice-over, which sounded suspiciously like the red-headed interviewer, said, "Inside this building is one of the apartments NASA has requisitioned so the aliens will have a place to live. But what about all those people on Sony who *don't* have a place to live? Today I met two of them." The interviewer appeared on the landing with

Molly and Bets in their navy-sailor dresses. They curtsied as he introduced them, all their dimples showing.

Mr. Nagisha fast-forwarded and then stopped. The interviewer said, "Let's see these budding performers in action," and Molly and Bets clomped out in their wooden shoes. Mr. Nagisha fast-forwarded it before they could get started on "Tiptoe Through the Tulips." He stopped it.

"Spielberg, are you out there?" the interview said. "All these two talented tots ask is a chance to break into show biz."

He hit the fast-forward button, and when he stopped the chip again, Molly was saying, "Thyee and the alien have thith whole apartment, but thyee won't let uth use the bathroom or the phone or anything, even if we're eckthpecting an important call from our agent."

"And then last night she kicked us out of her room," Bets said, stepping neatly in front of Molly. "We just wanted to sleep on the floor." She began a pretty pout and then seemed to realize that if she stopped talking, Molly would jump in, and added hastily, "I think she wanted us out of there so she could be alone with him."

"Who?" the interviewer said, his ears perking up. "The alien?"

"Of courth not," Molly said, putting her arm up so it was in front of Bets's face. "Mr. Negeethya doethn't know it, but thyee rented her apartment to thith other guy."

"His name's Hutchins," Bets said, wrestling Molly's arm down to where she could see over it. "We saw him give her the rent. It was a whole bunch of yen. She's not supposed to rent to anybody without telling Mr. Nagisha."

"He wasn't paying me rent," Chris said. "He took some money out of my purse to pay for breakfast. He was giving me my change."

The scene in front of the TV cut suddenly to Chris trying to shut the door on the interviewer's foot. "The occupant of the apartment, Ms. Christine Arthur, was unavailable for comment," the interviewer said.

"I did not rent my room to Mr. Hutchins," Chris said. "Mr. Okeefenokee asked him to stay. He doesn't understand English very well, and he thought 'room' meant any available space and . . ."

"Evidence," Mr. Nagisha said.

"Look, I'm sure we can clear this whole thing up if you'll just let me call Stewart."

The interviewer said, peering over Molly's and Bets's simpering faces, "When this reporter checked with NASA, they had no record of having requisitioned Ms. Arthur's apartment, which raises further questions about the alleged alien and Ms. Arthur's refusal to sublet to . . ." Mr. Nagisha popped the chip out of the TV and stepped over the old man in the baseball cap. "Seven o'clock," he said, and went into his apartment and shut the door.

"Molly and Bets are mad at me because they think I stole their chip recorder," Chris shouted at the door. "They told me they'd get even."

The door stayed shut. The old man in the baseball cap looked up blankly and then went back to laying out his cards. He'll never get anywhere without the diamonds, Chris thought irrelevantly, and tore back upstairs, clutching the eviction notice, and tried to call Stewart.

The blond woman who was always laying papers on Stewart's desk for him to sign told her that he couldn't come to the phone. "Have him call me as soon as you can," Chris told her. "This is an emergency!"

She got dressed and tried again. This time the call wouldn't go through. She stared at the screen for a while and then grabbed the eviction notice and her purse and ran downstairs. At the bottom of the steps she collided with Charmaine's lawyer. He was swinging a tassel idly in one hand and whistling.

"Hey!" he said. "Where do you think you're going?"

"Mr. Nagisha's having me evicted because of Hutchins. I've got to go find him."

"And leave your apartment? If you leave, you're liable to find your furniture out on the stairs when you get back." He looked at the eviction notice. "You go back upstairs and sit tight. I'll go try to talk Mr. Nagisha out of this. If it doesn't work, I'll go find Hutchins for you. Go on. Mr. Nagisha's probably already changing the locks."

Chris tore back upstairs, hopelessly scattering the old man's cards. "I'm sorry," she said breathlessly. "You wouldn't have won anyway. Your diamonds are in Mr. Okeefenokee's room."

The locks hadn't been changed, but the door was standing open. Molly and Bets were in the living room, arranging their dolls on the couch.

"I get the bedroom," Molly said. "You can thleep in the hammock."

"*I* get the bedroom," Bets said.

"Out," Chris said. Both of the little girls turned to look at her in surprise.

"Didn't Mr. Nagisha talk to you?" Bets said. "This isn't your apartment anymore. It's ours."

"Either you get out or I'm knocking those pearly little front teeth of yours down your throats, and then we'll see how many parts you get."

"You wouldn't dare," Bets said, but she grabbed one of her dolls by the arm and clutched two others to her stomach. Molly scooped up the rest of them, and they trooped out. "We're moving in at theven o'clock and you'd better be out of here by then," Molly said.

Chris locked the door and shoved a chair against it. She tried Stewart again, and then the operator, but she still couldn't get through. Charmaine's lawyer came up to tell her he hadn't gotten anywhere with Mr. Nagisha. He didn't sound particularly worried, but he said he was going up to NASA to look for Hutchins and Okee. "You don't have to barricade yourself in," he said, pointing at the chair. "Just don't leave. And keep trying to get in touch with Hutchins from this end."

"I will," she promised, trying to think where Mr. Okeefenokee might have put her subvocalizer. As soon as Charmaine's lawyer was gone, she went into Mr. Okeefenokee's room to look for it. She looked through the bento-bako boxes and under the bed and in the baby buggy, and then started in on the endless stacks of boxes. I wonder how he planned on getting all this home, she thought, sticking her hand inside the roller skates.

The phone rang. It was Hutchins. "I've only got a minute," he said rapidly. "Have you found the subvocalizer yet? Okee doesn't have it. They did a metals search on him when we came in. I asked him where he put it, and he said, and I quote, 'You put on. Closing. Hahnahmoon.' Do you realize what that means? There isn't any space program. He hasn't understood a word we've been saying."

"Pete, you've got to come back right away," she said to the suddenly blank screen. "I'm being evicted." She prodded the *reinstate* button until an operator came on-screen. "I was just cut off," she said, and gave her Stewart's number. This time the phone rang. And went on ringing. Chris let it ring twenty-eight times and then went back into the bedroom and sat down on the bed.

She picked up the list Mr. Okeefenokee had written. He had checked off "time alone" and "closing" and crossed off "neck." The only thing left on the list was "hahnahmoon," which he had spelled the way he pronounced it.

"Honeymoon," Chris said out loud. "I wonder what he thinks that means." She picked up the old man's diamonds and took them out to him, but he was asleep again, stretched out across the stairs, his baseball cap in his hands. Chris sat down on the step above him and shuffled the diamonds into his deck. The phone rang.

It was Stewart. "I'm being evicted," Chris said before they could be cut off.

"Evicted?" he said, looking horrified. "What did you do?"

"I didn't do anything. Mr. Nagisha claims I withheld rent from him."

"That's ridiculous," Stewart said. "I paid him myself when Ohghhifoehnnahigrheeh moved in."

"He's not talking about Mr. Okeefenokee. He's talking about Hutchins. You've got to tell him to come back here so he can explain to Mr. Nagisha that he wasn't paying me rent, he was just giving me back my change from breakfast."

"Breakfast?" Stewart said. "How long has Hutchins been over there?"

"Two days. He's got to come explain that Mr. Okeefenokee was the one who asked him to stay. And you've got to bring over the requisition forms that show my apartment was requisitioned by NASA."

"I'll be right over," he said hurriedly.

"Bring Hutchins with you. And Mr. Okeefenokee."

"I can't do that," he said.

"I know they're in negotiations, but they've got to talk to Mr. Nagisha. What if I have Mr. Nagisha come up here and they can talk to him on the phone?"

"That won't work either."

"Why not?"

"They're on their way down to Houston. They left on the shuttle half an hour ago."

" 'Scuse me," Charmaine said, and came into the living room, wearing her pink smock and carrying the red paper umbrella Mr. Okeefenokee had given her. She switched on the light. "I didn't knock 'cause I thought you might be asleep. Did you know Molly's got a key to your apartment?"

Chris nodded numbly. "Hutchins is gone."

"Yeah, I know," she said. She sat down on the couch beside Chris. "How long have you been sitting here in the dark?"

"I don't know. What time is it?"

"Three o'clock."

"They're probably in Houston by now. I hope Hutchins didn't get shuttle lag."

"You look pretty lagged yourself. Why don't you try to get some sleep?"

"I can't. I'm being evicted."

"Yeah, I know that, too. My lawyer stopped by Luigi's to tell me what had happened. The way I figure it, your prospective buyer figured he better get rid of Hutchins before he made you a better offer." She put her arm around Chris. "Don't worry about your apartment. My lawyer say's he's got a plan to fight the eviction. He wouldn't tell me what it was, but he said not to worry, he wouldn't let those brats get your apartment, and I believe him. He knows practically everything there is to know when it comes to real-estate deals."

There was a knock on the door. Charmaine went to answer it and came back in with her lawyer and Stewart.

"Well, you've gotten yourself in a nice mess, Chris," Stewart said. "Mr. Nagisha showed us the chip. How could you jeopardize your apartment by letting some stranger move in?"

"You told me to do whatever Mr. Okeefenokee wanted. He wanted Hutchins to move in. Did you show him the NASA requisition form?"

"There isn't one," Charmaine's lawyer said, looking happier than Stewart. "And we don't have a prayer of taking this to court when he's got two cute kids to testify for him. I guess we'll have to go with my plan after all."

"What do you mean there isn't one?" Chris said.

"I was afraid there'd be a great deal of red tape," Stewart said, "getting you cleared and so on . . ."

"NASA requisitioned dozens of people's apartments.

None of them had any trouble getting cleared. You told NASA he was staying with you, didn't you? So you'd get the compensation?"

"It doesn't really matter which apartment was requisitioned, since we're getting married."

"It matters to me," Chris said. "I'm being evicted."

"No, you're not," Charmaine's lawyer said cheerfully. "We've come up with a plan. All you have to do is marry Hutchins. Then he doesn't have to pay rent because he's a relative."

"I can't," Chris said. "He's in Houston."

"He doesn't have to be here," Stewart said. "We can do a beam-up call, take the vows over the phone, transmit the papers and have them signed on both ends. I've cleared it with NASA."

"I don't understand," Chris said bewilderedly. "How will getting married now help? We weren't married when he stayed here."

"Sony law allows occupancy before closing," Charmaine's lawyer said, looking positively jovial. "What do you say?"

"It's the only way we can save your apartment," Stewart said. "You're not really getting married. There's an automatic buyer-backout clause if the deal isn't closed in twenty-four hours, which of course it won't be. You'll have your apartment back, and with the requisition money I get from NASA we'll be able to buy that apartment next door to Mother's and turn this into a rental."

"What if Mr. Nagisha finds out and tries to stop it?"

"He won't," Charmaine's lawyer said. "Omiko sent him down to Luigi's for the *sutorippu*, and I paid Molly and Bets off."

"I want to talk to Hutchins."

"You can talk to him during the wedding," Stewart said, looking relieved. "I'll call NASA."

"Omiko's out getting a Shinto priest," Charmaine's lawyer beamed. "I'll go get the marriage contracts drawn up. We'll have you married in nothing flat." They both hurried out.

"Gee, this is so exciting," Charmaine said. "I've got a veil from the wedding number you can borrow. I'd loan you the wedding dress to go with it, only it's not a dress exactly."

Charmaine's lawyer came back in with the marriage contracts and one of Mr. Nagisha's evicted cousins. "He's a notary," her lawyer said, and Mr. Nagisha's cousin pulled a seal out of his pocket.

"It'll serve him right," he said. "All we were doing was stir-frying a little blowfish."

"You can sign these now, and then we'll transmit them over the phone. It's a simple death-do-you-part deed, no lease option, no appraisal. Just a minute. I've got to get another witness."

He came back in with the old man in the baseball cap. Chris signed the copies and then watched carefully as the old man countersigned them, but his signature was completely illegible. Charmaine finished witnessing the contracts and scurried out to get the veil.

Omiko came in with the Shinto priest. Molly and Bets were right behind her, wearing frilly lavender dresses and large lavender bows in their hair. Molly was carrying a basket of cherry-blossom petals.

"We're going to be in your wedding," Bets said. "Molly's the flower girl, and I get to be your maid of honor."

"Isn't that sweet?" Stewart said, patting Molly on the head. Chris saw with satisfaction that he was mashing her lavender hair bows. "Someday we'll have two sweet little girls just like these two."

"Over my dead body," Chris said.

"Here's your bouquet," Charmaine said. She had changed back into her strapless red dress. She shoved a bouquet of white silk flowers and ribbons into Chris's hands. "It's really a pastie," she said, putting the veil on

Chris's head, "so I stuck it on one of Mr. Okeefenokee's flashlights."

"The call's coming through," Charmaine's lawyer said from the hall.

"I want to talk to Hutchins first," Chris said.

"I really don't see why that's necessary," Stewart said. "He's already agreed to marry you."

"I'm not going through with this unless I have a chance to talk to him."

"It's almost four o'clock. We've got to do this in the next half hour."

"Fine," Chris said, taking off her veil. "Tell Molly and Bets they can have the apartment. I'll move in with Charmaine and Omiko."

"And lose the apartment!" Stewart said, looking aghast. "I mean, go ahead and talk to him if you have to, but make it quick. If we don't finish this up within the next fifteen minutes, we'll have to wait for satellite relay."

Charmaine's lawyer said, "It'll be a minute or so," and went into the living room and shut the door. Chris locked it and then went over to the screen. It brightened and Hutchins's image appeared in front of the screen. He was wearing the clothes he'd left the apartment in, and he looked tired and drawn.

"Are you all right?" Chris said.

"Yeah," he said, frowning. "They started interrogating Okee as soon as we got here, but they're not getting anywhere. He's clammed up completely." He rubbed his hand across his forehead tiredly.

"You don't have to do this, you know," Chris said. "Marry me, I mean. It's nothing but a real-estate deal."

"It'll make Stewart happy."

"Yeah," Chris said ruefully. "And Mr. Okeefenokee. He kept saying we were going to get married tonight, and here we are."

"Yeah," Hutchins said thoughtfully. "How come they

were able to put this wedding together so fast? I thought Sony marriage contracts were really complicated."

"I don't know. Charmaine's lawyer was the one who came up with the idea."

"Charmaine's lawyer, huh? Maybe Okee's smarter than we thought."

"We really can't wait any longer," Stewart said, opening the door. "We've got to start the ceremony."

He came over to the screen and pressed the *transmit* button. Hutchins's image disappeared, and Charmaine's lawyer held each page of the contract up to the screen by the corners for a full thirty seconds. Stewart pushed another button, and a flat-screen image of Hutchins appeared. He and two men in uniform signed and then held up the copies of the pages the same way.

"Gee, this is so exciting," Charmaine said. She put the veil over Chris's head again and then dashed into the bathroom to get a box of Kleenex, which she passed out to Omiko, the old man in the baseball cap, and Mr. Nagisha's cousin.

"I heard she had to get married," Bets said to the old man in a stage whisper.

Molly said, "Would you pleathe get out of the way?" and began throwing cherry-blossom petals on everyone.

Charmaine's lawyer said, "Okay," and Hutchins's holographic image appeared in front of the screen. He was still holding the copies of the contract.

"Join hands," the Shinto priest said. Hutchins transferred the contracts to his left hand and held out his right. Chris put her hand carefully where the image of his hand was. He closed his hand around her fingers but she couldn't feel anything.

The priest made a speech in Japanese and then said, "Christine Arthur, do you understand the terms of the contract?"

"I do," Chris said.

"Peter Hutchins, do you-under—"

"I do," he said.

"This contract has been duly signed and witnessed. I declare it legally binding."

"Good," Hutchins said. "Now do I get to kiss the bride?" He bent over her.

Stewart hit the *hang-up* button, and Hutchins's image disappeared. "Good. I'm glad that's over," he said happily. He turned to Charmaine's lawyer. "Now we can take these down to Mr. Nagisha."

"In a minute," the lawyer said. He turned to Charmaine. "I'll be back in a few minutes, and then I want to talk to you." She followed him and Stewart out onto the landing.

Chris was still watching the screen. "Ahem," the old man in the baseball cap said, and Chris turned around, but he was talking to Bets. "I've been watching you for several days. I'm directing a new movie and I'd like to cast you in it."

"You don't want her," Molly said. "Thyee dyeth her hair."

"I do not," Bets said, putting a defensive hand up to her curls. "My blond hair is natural, which is more than I can say for your lisp."

"My lisp is not phony!" Molly shouted, and grabbed a handful of yellow curls.

"I want both of you," he said, separating them. "You're perfect for the parts. I've got the contracts in my office downtown."

"I want my name first on the credits," Bets said.

"I want star billing above the title," Molly said.

He herded them out. They nearly collided with Charmaine.

" 'Scuse me," Charmaine said. "What was that all about?"

"That was Spielberg," Chris said. "He just offered Molly and Bets the lead in his new movie."

"Who? The old guy on the stairs? You're kidding.

You'd think he'd know better after living here a whole week." She looked at Chris. "Are you all right?"

"No," Chris said.

"I've got an idea. Why don't we all go down to Luigi's for the early show? Kind of a wedding breakfast."

"Chris has got to stay here until the buyer-beware clause expires," Stewart said.

"What do you think she's gonna do?" Charmaine said. "Jump off Sony and parachute down to earth?"

"Chris has come dangerously close to losing her apartment once today. I don't want anything to interfere with that annulment clause. The safest thing is for her to spend the next twenty-four hours in her apartment."

"Okay, we'll bring the wedding breakfast here. I'll call Luigi and have him deliver some teriyaki ham and eggs and have Omiko bring the girls over and . . ."

"Can I speak to you?" Charmaine's lawyer said, taking hold of her hand and practically yanking her out of the living room.

"I'm not going to let you jeopardize your apartment a second time," Stewart said. He went over to the couch. "I think the best thing for us to do is get married immediately. I've asked the lawyer to draw up the marriage contracts. Where did this Hutchins sleep? In Ohghhifoehnnahigrheeh's room?"

"No," Chris said. "He slept in here. Mr. Okeefenokee didn't understand the concept of 'room.' He thought it meant any space that happened to be available. Hutchins slept up there."

Stewart looked up at the sleep restraint. "In that? Where did you sleep?"

"On the couch."

"I can't believe you let him sleep up there with you not five feet away from him."

"Neither can I," Chris said. She got her nightshift and robe from the end of the couch. "You can sleep in Mr. Okeefenokee's room."

"No!" Charmaine said from the doorway. Her lawyer was with her. They were holding hands. "I mean, 'scuse me, but gee, Mr. Okeefenokee bought all that stuff for you, and it's a shame to let it go to waste."

"What stuff?" Stewart said.

"If you want to be able to testify that Chris didn't leave her apartment for the whole twenty-four hours," Charmaine's lawyer said, "you should be the one to sleep out here. Chris can sleep in the bedroom. That way she can't leave without your knowing it."

"I thought you said this plan was foolproof," Stewart said anxiously.

"It is," Charmaine's lawyer said, grinning.

"Good night," Chris said, and went into Mr. Okeefenokee's room, still carrying the bridal bouquet, and shut the door.

Charmaine immediately slid the shoji screen open a few inches. " 'Scuse me," she said. "Can I come in? I got something to show you." She sidled through the door, shut it behind her, and flashed her hand at Chris. "It's a diamond. We're engaged."

Chris laid the bouquet on the nightstand and started moving boxes off the bed. "I thought you said you weren't going to marry him because he thought marriage was a real-estate deal."

"That was before—" She stopped. "Well, I mean, I think it was pretty romantic the way he got you and Hutchins together."

"We're not exactly together," she said. "Hutchins is in Houston and I'm locked in my room."

"Yeah, but Mr. Fenokee's going to . . ." She stopped again.

Chris looked up.

"Mr. Fenokee's going to what?"

Charmaine fiddled with her ring. "Well, gee, I mean, he's got that space program, right? Maybe he can talk the

NASA people into sending Hutchins back up here. Or maybe you could go down there."

"I don't think so," Chris said sadly. "Stewart'll see to that. Anyway, Sony's got a thirty-day travel-permission law, and the marriage expires in"—she looked at her watch—"about twenty-three hours."

"Gee, that's right. I better go. I promised Omiko I'd be there for the wedding number. Gee, I almost forgot my pastie." She picked it up, untaped it from its makeshift handle, and laid the flashlight back on the nightstand. She pointed at the boxes on the bed. "Why don't you wear that black lace nightie instead of that shift thing?" She flounced out. Chris shut the door and locked it.

She put on her nightshift and her robe and moved the stack of boxes off the bed. "I've just had a great idea, Chris," Stewart called through the door. "I was lying there looking at the hammock, and it suddenly occurred to me that Ohghhifoehnnahigrheeh was right. That is available space. Since we're going to rent this place anyway, we won't need those high ceilings. We can turn this into two apartments. I'm going to go downstairs right now and talk to Mr. Nagisha about it."

She could hear him slide the door to the apartment shut, lock it, and start down the stairs. I hope he trips over the old man in the baseball cap and falls the whole flight, she thought, and then remembered that the old man had gone off with Molly and Bets.

She turned off the light and got into bed. There was something hard under her pillow. It's probably one of Omiko's tassels, she thought, and turned the light back on. It was her subvocalizer.

"Oh," she said, and held it to her heart.

"Mr. Nagisha thinks it's a great idea," Stewart said through the door. "He's going to do it to all the apartments in the building. Good night, darling."

She sat up against the headboard, put the subvocalizer on, and fastened the receiver in her ear. It probably doesn't work except at short distances, she thought. She turned off the light.

It was completely dark in the room. There was a narrow line of light under the shoji screen, but it only seemed to intensify the darkness.

(Pete,) she whispered without making any noise. (Are you there?)

(I'm here,) he said, so close he could have been sitting beside her. (Where are you?)

(In Mr. Okeefenokee's room. My subvocalizer was under his pillow.)

(Where's Stewart?)

(In the living room on the couch. He wants to make sure I don't do anything to jeopardize the annulment clause.)

(Is everything okay?) Hutchins said. (You're not going to be evicted?)

(No.)

(Well, that's good. At least you don't have to sleep out on the stairs with Leopold and Loeb.)

(Molly and Bets aren't here. They got a part in Spielberg's movie.)

He didn't answer for a while. (There isn't any justice, is there?) he said finally.

(No.) Chris said. (I wish you were here.)

(So do I. Chris, look, they've got us locked up tight here until the negotiations are over. I tried to talk Okee into telling NASA I had to come back up to Sony to get the space program, but he said, "No. Be alone on hahnahmoon." Well, we're sure as hell alone.)

(Is he still refusing to talk?)

(No, he's been talking a blue streak ever since we got on the shuttle. And I have a sinking feeling I know why the Eahrohhs came. I don't think it was to negotiate a space program or anything else. I think they just like space travel. Okee had that lump of a nose of his pressed to the port the whole way down, and he told the NASA linguistics team the exciting story of our takeoff and landing twice. He also regaled them with a description of how Omiko orbits her colonies and danced "Tiptoe Through the Tulips" for them. Spielberg blew his big chance. Okee's a lot better than Molly and Bets. He told the linguistics team about you, too. He said you reminded him of his wife.)

(I know,) she said, and wished she had a Kleenex.

(He said I reminded him of himself. No, what he actually said was that I was like him. He then said the reason he'd wanted us to get married was because he knew we liked each other, which shoots our "one word, one meaning" theory all to hell.)

(But if that's true, maybe he understands the word "space," too, and there really is a space program.)

(Maybe.) There was silence for a minute. (He told the linguistics team he'd have a demonstration of the space program for them in twenty-four hours. They asked him what he needed for this demonstration, and he said a room with high ceilings. So they stuck us in an old shuttle hangar with a guard and a couple of army cots, and he went right to sleep on one of the cots.)

She could hear something besides what he was saying, a low whooshing noise that rose to a dull roar and then subsided. (I can hear Mr. Okeefenokee snoring,) she said, and wiped her eyes on the hem of the sheet.

(Chris, listen, if there isn't a space program, Okee's not going to be the only one who's in trouble. I didn't exactly have official clearance to go undercover, and they're going to want somebody they can blame this on. I don't know when I'll be able to get back up there to get you.)

(I know,) she said, sniffling. Charmaine had left her box of Kleenex on the nightstand. She reached for the flashlight. Her hand groped in emptiness where the nightstand was supposed to be. "Hutchins!" she said out loud. "The nightstand's missing." She squinted into the darkness. She could faintly make out the walls of her room. "Mr. Okeefenokee's boxes are gone, too."

(No, they're not,) Hutchins said, and she could hear the rumble of Okee's snoring under his words. (They're here. Did the nightstand have a box of Kleenex on it?)

"Are you all right, darling?" Stewart said through the door. "I heard you call out."

"I'm fine," Chris said. "I was dreaming. Good night."

"Why don't you come out and sleep on the—" Stewart said. His words cut off so abruptly she was afraid he had opened the door, but when she turned her head in that direction, she couldn't see any light, not even the line of light that had been under her door.

(Are you still there, Chris?) Hutchins said.

(Yes,) she said, careful not to speak out loud since Stewart might be trying to unlock the door. I hope Molly took all her keys with her, she thought, and wondered if she should get out of bed and go wedge a chair against the door or something, but she was afraid she wouldn't be able to find her way back to the bed. If the bed was still there. (Pete, what's going on?)

(I don't know,) he said. (This shuttle hangar is now full of Okee's stuff. The microwaves, the trampoline, even the Christmas tree in the baby buggy.)

Chris squinted into the darkness, waiting for her eyes to adjust, but after a long minute she still couldn't see anything.

(He didn't understand when you tried to tell him there wasn't any space in your apartment,) he said slowly (and he didn't understand the words "far away" and "close." And how come? Not because he couldn't understand the words, but because the concept didn't make any sense. Chris, I think he's got a space program, after all.)

It was suddenly not as black in the room. She looked anxiously toward the shoji screen, afraid that Stewart had gotten it open, but the light wasn't coming from that direction. It seemed to be coming from the back wall where the trampoline had been, only she couldn't make out the wall.

(It's not the kind of space program NASA thought they were getting, but so what? I think they'll be happy with this,) he said, sounding excited. (I couldn't figure out how he was going to get all this stuff home in that little ship of theirs, and the answer is, he wasn't. He was going to send it Federal Express. I'll bet he already took the piano home, and that's why we couldn't find it.)

The line of light was under the side walls where the stacks of boxes had been. They were much farther away than they should have been.

(Pete!) Chris said, getting onto her knees on the bed as if she were on a life raft.

(If Okee can send souvenirs home to Eahrohhsani, we've got interstellar trade. Not to mention what this means to Sony. So what if we can only transport freight?)

Now a thin line of pinkish-orange light was under the wall where the shoji screen should be. It wasn't there. (Pete,) she said (I don't think it's limited to transporting freight.)

(I wonder what the high ceilings have to do with this. We can build space colonies on earth and then put them in orbit with—)

His voice cut off. (Just a minute,) Hutchins said after a pause. (The lights went out. I can't see.)

(There's a flashlight on the nightstand,) Chris said.

(I can't find the nightstand. It was right here.) His voice sounded suddenly different, farther away, and she couldn't hear Mr. Okeefenokee's snoring under it. (Chris, I think it's disappeared. It's black as pitch in here. Is the nightstand there?)

(I don't know. Just a minute.) She got up on her knees, waved her hand over where the nightstand was supposed to be, and cracked her knuckles against the corner of it.

"Ouch," she said, nursing her hand. (Yes, it's back.)

"Damn!" Hutchins said. "No, it's not. It's here. I just ran into it."

"But . . . ," Chris said, and then stopped and peered into the darkness. She crawled to the foot of the bed so that the orange-pink light was behind the nightstand and she could make out shapes. "Pete," she said, "take off your subvocalizer." She unfastened the receiver from her ear and closed her hand over it.

"In a minute," he said. "Okee had a box of flashlights right next to the Christmas tree." His voice sounded suddenly softer, as if he had turned away.

She unclasped the subvocalizer with her free hand and took it off. "Take off your subvocalizer and say something." She put it under her pillow and leaned across the bed, feeling carefully for the nightstand.

"Now I can't find the damned boxes," he said. "Damn it, I hit my toe again."

Chris turned on the flashlight. Hutchins had on jeans and no shirt, and he was standing beside the bed, holding his bare foot in one hand. "How did you get here?" he said blankly.

"That's what I should be asking you. This is my room." She shone the flashlight around at the walls. The line of pinkish-orange light was getting wider, as if a curtain were slowly going up. "Sort of." She smiled at him. "Stewart wanted me to stay in my room, but I don't think this is what he had in mind."

Hutchins put his foot down and looked blankly behind him at the wall. "Where's Okee?"

"I don't know. I have a feeling he could be just about anywhere he wants. But I would imagine he's in the shuttle hangar with all his boxes and the Christmas tree and the trampoline. And half of NASA when they realize we're gone. You don't suppose they'll think he disintegrated us or something?"

He limped over to the bed and sat down beside her.

"He said he'd have a space program for them in twenty-four hours. They won't string him up before then, and I have a feeling that at the end of twenty-four hours we'll be able to tell them where we've been ourselves."

"Which is where?" she said.

He looked around at the walls. The band of light was nearly a foot wide now. It looked more pink than orange. Chris switched off the flashlight and put it on the nightstand.

"Damned if I know," he said. "That old faker! He understood every word we said. He knew exactly what kind of space program NASA wanted. And all that stuff about honeymoons and closings and not understanding what kind of roll Bets wanted. 'Time alone. Talk, Neck.' I could just . . . ," he said, smashing his fist against his open hand. He stopped and looked at Chris. "I could kiss him on the top of his lipstick-smeared head," he said. "I thought I was never going to see you again. I figured by the time I made it back up to Sony, you'd have married your prospective buyer."

"I couldn't marry Stewart," Chris said, taking hold of his hand. "I'm already married."

" 'Put on subvocalizer. You and Hutchins get married. Hahnahmoon.' " Hutchins said, shaking his head. "I'll bet he set up this whole thing with Charmaine's lawyer, the marriage, the honeymoon, everything."

He stood up and went over to the wall where the shoji screen had been. When he put out his hand to touch it, the band seemed to spread suddenly in all directions, suffusing the room in pink light.

"The honeymoon!" Chris said, getting up on her knees. "I think I know where we are. And you're wrong. He doesn't understand *every* word we say."

"What do you mean?" he said.

"I'll bet you anything those trees are cherry trees, and that we're on a *hana* moon." A forest of blossoming trees stretched around them in all directions. She could almost smell the cherry blossoms. "It's beautiful here," she said.

"It is," he said, but he wasn't looking at the trees. "And I have the feeling nobody's going to come in to evict us or use the bathroom or do a tap-dance routine." He walked over to the bed. "Spielberg didn't really give Molly and Bets a part in his movie, did he?"

Chris sat back on her heels. "You were right about Spielberg coming up to Sony incognito. You know the old man who lives above Charmaine?"

He pulled her up onto her knees. "In the baseball cap and sneakers? He's not Spielberg," he said. "He's just some chip-cam director who thinks he can bring back slasher movies. He wanted to hire Okee to star in a low-budget remake of *Alien*. When I told him I didn't think Okee was available, he asked me if I thought people would believe in a pair of four-year-olds who were vicious murderers." He put his arms around her. "I said I hoped it was one of those movies where the murderers get what they deserve in the end. I like movies like that, where everybody gets what they deserve."

"So do I," Chris said. Hutchins was even closer than he had been on the bullet. Chris could definitely smell the cherry blossoms. "What's going to happen to Molly and Bets?"

"I don't know," he said, and leaned down to kiss her. "The old guy got this spooky smile on his face and mumbled something about tap shoes."

I DON'T HAVE A LOT OF PATIENCE WITH SHAKESPEARE *conspiracy theories. They all, with the exception of the Bacon theory, seem to be based on an inability to accept the obvious: that Shakespeare was Shakespeare. (The Bacon theory seems to be based on a decoder ring.) They've concluded Shakespeare was the Earl of Oxford or Queen Elizabeth or a committee (A committee!? Who are they trying to kid?) because he* couldn't *have been an Ordinary Person.*

Well, of course he wasn't an Ordinary Person. He was Shakespeare. But that doesn't mean he couldn't have come from Ordinary Circumstances. Say, a log cabin in Illinois. Or a small town in upstate England.

The theories about Anne Hathaway are even worse. Out of a handful of facts—she was six years older, she couldn't read, she was pregnant when they got married—the theorists concoct an aged, ignorant peasant, deservedly abandoned by Queen Elizabeth or the committee or whoever it was.

Honestly. Illiterate doesn't mean stupid, and where do they think Shakespeare got all those wonderful, witty, intelligent women for his plays—Beatrice and Rosalind and Cordelia and Kate—if not from his wife and daughters?

If I *were concocting a Shakespeare conspiracy theory, it would have to take Anne into account. And it wouldn't have any codes or committees. It would have all the things Shakespeare liked so well: secrets and murder and romance. And mistaken identities.*

WINTER'S TALE

"Is the will here?" he said. "I need . . ."

"Thou hast no need of wills," I said, putting my hand upon his poor hot brow. "You have but a fever, husband. You should not have stayed so late last eve with Master Drayton."

"A fever?" he said. "Aye, it must be so. It was raining when I rode home, and now my head is like to split in twain."

"I have sent to John for medicine. It will be here soon."

"John?" he said, alarmed, half rising in the bed. "I had forgot Old John. I must needs bequeath the old man something. When he came to London—"

"I spoke of John Hall, thy son-in-law," I said. "He will bring you somewhat for thy fever."

"I must leave Old John something in my will, that he'll keep silence."

"Old John will not betray you," I said. He hath been silent, lo, these twelve winters, buried in Trinity Church, no danger to anyone. "Hush, thee, and rest awhile."

"I would leave him something of gaud and glitter.

The gilt-and-silver bowl I sent thee from London. Do you remember it?"

"Yea, I remember it," I said.

The bowl had come at midday as I was making the second-best bed. I had already made the best bed for the guests, if any came with him, airing the hangings and putting on a new featherbed, and was going into my room to see to the second-best bed when my daughter Judith called up the stairs that a rider had come. I thought that it was he and left the bed unturned and forgot. Ere I remembered it, it was late afternoon, all the preparations made and we in our new clothes.

"I should have stuffed a new featherbed," I said, laying the coverlid upon the press. "This one is flattened out and full of dust."

"You will spoil your new gown, Mother," Judith said, standing well away. "What matters if the bed be turned? He'll notice not the beds, so glad he'll be to see his family."

"Will he be glad?" Susanna said. "He waited long enough for this homecoming, if it be that. What does he want, I wonder." She took the sheets and folded them. Elizabeth climbed onto the bed to fetch a pillow and brought it me, though it was twice her size.

"To see his daughters, perhaps, or his granddaughter, and make his peace with all of us," Judith said. She took the pillow from Elizabeth gingerly and brushed her skirts when she had laid it down. "It will be dark soon."

" 'Tis light enough for us to make a bed," I said, reaching my hands to lift it up. "Come, help me turn the featherbed, daughters." Susanna took one side, Judith the other, all unwillingly.

"I'll turn it," Elizabeth said, squeezing herself next the wall at the foot, all eagerness to help and like to have her little fingers crushed.

"Wilt thou go out and see if they are coming, granddaughter?" I said. Elizabeth clambered over the bed, kirtle and long hair flying.

"Put on thy cloak, Bess," Susanna cried after her.

"Aye, Mother."

"This room was ever dark," Judith said. "I know not why you took it for your own, Mother. The window is high and small, and the narrow door shuts out the light. Father may be ill pleased at such a narrow bed."

It were well if he were, I thought. It were well if he found it dark and cramped and would sleep elsewhere. "Now," I said, and we three heaved the featherbed up and over the foot of the bedstead. Dust and feathers flew about, filling the room.

"Oh, look at my doublet," Judith said, brushing at the ruffles on her bosom. "Now we shall have to sweep again. Can you not get the serving boy to do this?"

"He is laying the fires," I said, pulling at the underside.

"Well, the cook then."

"She is cooking. Come, one more turn and we'll be done with it."

"Dost thou hear something?" she said, shaking out her skirts. She went out. "Have they come, Bess?" she called.

I waited, listening for the sound of horses' hooves, but I heard naught.

Susanna stood still at the side of the bed, holding the linen sheet. "What think thee of this visitation, Mother? Thou hast said naught of it since word arrived of his coming."

What could I answer her? That I feared this day as I had feared no other? The day the message had come, I'd taken it from Susanna's hand and tried to draw its meaning out, though she had read it out already and I had never learnt to read. "To my wife," it had read. "I will arrive in Stratford on the twelfth day of December." I had kept the message by me from that day to this, trying to see the meaning of it, but I could not cipher its meaning. To my wife, I will arrive in Stratford on the twelfth day of December. To my wife.

"I have had much to do," I said. I gave the featherbed a mighty pull and brought it flat across the bed. "New rushes to be laid within the hall, the baking to be done, the beds to make."

"He came not to his parents' funeral, nor Hamnet's, nor to my wedding. Why comes he now?"

I smoothed the featherbed, pressing the corners so that they lay neat and smooth.

"If the house be too full of guests, you can come to us at the croft, Mother," Susanna said. She folded out the sheet and held it to me. "Or if he . . . you ever have a home with us."

" 'Twas but a passing townsman," Judith said, coming back into the room. "Think you he will bring friends with him from London?"

"His message said he would arrive today," Susanna said, and bellied out the sheet, sweet with lavender, over the bed. "Naught else. Nor who should accompany him or why he comes or whether he will stay."

"Come, he will stay," Judith said, coming to fold the sheet against the side. "I hope his friends are young and handsome."

There was a creak upon the stairs. We stopped, stooped over the bed.

"Bess?" Susanna inquired.

"Nay, my little grandniece stands outside all uncovered," Joan said, and came, creaking, into the room. She wore a yellow ruff so high it seem'd to throttle her. It was the ruff that creak'd, or mayhap her leather farthingale. "I told her she will catch the sweating fever. I bade her put her on a heavier cloak, but she heeded me not."

"Hath it begun to snow, sister-in-law?" I said.

"Nay, but it looks to ere long." She sat upon the bed. "Are you not dressed, and my brother nearly here?" She spread her overskirts on either side that we might see her satin petticoat. "You look a common country wife."

"I am a common country wife," I said. "Good sister, we must make the bed."

She stood up, the ruff creaking as if it were a signboard on a tavern. "A cold welcome for your husband," she said, "the beds unmade, the children unattended, and you in rough, low broadcloth." She sat down on the coverlid on the press. "A winter's welcome."

I stuffed the pillows into their cases with something force. "Where is your husband, madam?" I said, and putting the pillows to the bed, boxed them a blow or two to make them plump.

"Home with the ague," she said, turning to look at Susanna, her ruff making a fearsome sound. "And where is yours?"

"Attending to a patient in Shottery," Susanna said, still sweetly. "He will be here anon."

"Why wear you that unbecoming blue, Susanna?" Joan said. "And Judith, your collar is so small it scarcely shows."

"At least 'tis silent," Judith said.

"He will not know you, Judith, so sharp-tongued have you become. You were a sweet babe when he left. He'll know not you either, Good Sister Anne, so pale and old you look. He'll not look so, I wot. But then, he's not as old as you."

"No, nor so busy," I said. I took the quilt from off the bed-rail and laid it on the bed.

"I remember me when he was gone to London, Anne. You said you would not e'er see him again. What say you now?"

"He is not here, and dusk is fast upon us," Susanna said. "I say he will not come."

"I wonder what my brother will think of the impertinent daughters he hath raised," Joan said.

"He raised us not," Susanna said hotly, and on the

same breath Judith cried out, "At least we do not trick ourselves out like—"

"Let us not quarrel," I said, putting myself between them and their aunt. "We all are tired and vexed with worry that it is so late. Good Sister Joan, I had forgot to tell you. A gift hath come from him this very day. A gilt-and-silver bowl. 'Tis on the table in the hall."

"Gilt?" Joan said.

"Aye, and silver. A broad bowl for the punch. I will with thee to see it."

"Let us go down, then," she said, rising from the chest with a great sound, like a gallows in a wind. I picked the coverlid up.

"They've come!" Elizabeth shouted. She burst into the room, the hood of her cloak flung back from her hair and her cheeks as red as apples. "Four of them! On horses!"

Joan pressed her hands to her bosom momently, then adjusted her ruff. "What does he look like, Bess?" she asked the little girl. "Doth he be very changed?"

Elizabeth gave her an impatient glance. "I never saw him ere this. I know not even which one he is."

"Four of them?" Judith said. "Be the others young?"

"I told thee," Elizabeth said, stamping her little foot. "I know not which is which." She tugged at her mother's sleeve. "Come!"

Susanna plucked a feather from my cap. "Mother . . . ?" she said.

I stood, the coverlid still held against me like a shield. "The bed's not yet made," I said.

"Marry, I'll not leave my brother ungreeted," Joan said. She gathered her skirts. "I'll go down alone."

"No!" I said. I lay the coverlid over the end of the bedstead. "We must all go together," I seized Elizabeth's hand and let her run me down the stairs ahead of them, that Joan might not reach the door before me.

• • •

"Now I remember me," he said. "I left the bowl to Judith. What was bequeath'd to Joan?"

"Thy clothes," I said smilingly. "You said 'twould keep her silent as she walked."

"Ay, she is possessed of strange and several noises of roaring, shrieking, howling, jingling chains. . . ." He took my hand. His own was dry and rough as his night smock, and hot as fire. "Silent. She must keep silent. I should have left her something more."

"The will bequeaths her twenty pounds a year and the house on Henley Street. You have no need of purchasing her silence. She knows naught."

"Aye, but what if she, seeing my cold corpse, should on a sudden realize?"

"What talk is this of corpses?" I said, pulling my hand vexatiously away. I pulled the sheet to cover him. "You had too merry a meeting with thy friends, and now a little fever. You'll soon be well again."

"I was sick when I came," he said. "How long ago it seems. Three years. I was sick, but you made me well again. I am so cold. Is't winter?"

I wished for John to come. " 'Tis April. It is the fever makes thee cold."

" 'Twas winter when I came, do you remember? A cold day."

"Aye, a cold day."

He had sat still on his horse. The others had dismounted, the oldest and broadest of them doubled, his hands to his knees, as though to catch his breath, the younger ones rubbing their hands against the cold. A white dog ran about their legs, foolishly barking. The young men had sharp beards and sharper faces, though their clothes bespoke them gentlemen. The one who was the master of the dog, if he could be called so, had on a collar twice wider than Joan's, the other a brown cap with russet feathers stolen from a barnyard cock.

"I should not have plucked the feather from your cap, Mother," Susanna whispered. "It is the fashion."

"Oh, look," Joan said, squeezing through the door. "He hath not changed a bit!"

"Which one is my grandfather?" Elizabeth said, her little hand clasped to mine.

They turned to look at us, the feathered one with a face canny as a fox's, the collared one with a gawking gaze. The bent man stood with a groan that made the dog run at him. His doublet was quilted and puffed as to make him look twice as broad as his own girth. "Come, come, Will," he said, turning to look at him still on his horse, "we've come to the wrong house. These ladies are too young and fair to be thy family."

Joan laughed, a screeching sound like the cackle of a hen.

"Is he the one on the horse?" Elizabeth said, squeezing my numbed hand and jumping up and down.

"You did not tell me that he was so well-favored, Mother," Judith said in my ear.

He handed down a metal chest behind him. The round man gave it to the feathered one and put a hand up to help him dismount. He came down off the horse oddly, grasping the quilted shoulder with one hand, the horse's neck with the other, and heaving himself over and down on his left leg. He stepped forward, stiff-gaited, watching us.

"See how he limps!" Joan cried.

I could not feel the wind, e'en though it bellied his short cloak and Elizabeth's hair. "Which one is my grandfather?" she said, fairly dancing in her impatience.

I would have made her answer, but I could not speak nor move. I only stood, quiet as a statue, and looked at him. He looked older even than I, the hair half-gone on the crown of his head. I had not thought him to look so old. His face was seamed with lines that gave it a sadness of demeanor, as if he had endured many November's blasts. A winter's face, sad and tired but not unkind, and that I had not thought it to be either.

The round-bellied gentleman turned to us and smiled. "Come, ladies, well met," he said with a merry, booming voice that conquered the wind. "I was long upon the road from London and thought not to find such fair ladies at the end of it. My name is Michael Drayton. And these two gentlemen are Gadshill"—he pointed at the one with the ruff, then at the fox—"and Bardolph. Two actors they, and I a poet and lover of fair ladies." His voice and manner were merry, but he looked troubledly from Joan to me and back again. "Come, tell me your names and which of you his wife and which his daughters, that I speak not amiss."

"Come, Mother, speak and bid them welcome," Judith whispered, and nudged at my elbow, but still I could not speak nor move nor breathe.

He moved not either, though Master Drayton looked at him. I could not read his face. Was he dismayed, or vexed, or only weary?

"If you'll not greet him, I shall," Joan whispered, bending her head to me with a snapping sound. She stretched her arms toward them. "Welcome—"

I stepped down off the porch. "Husband, I bid thee welcome," I said, and kissed him on his lined cheek. "I could not speak at first, my husband, so struck was I to see thee after such an absence." I took his arm and turned to Master Drayton. "I bid thee welcome, too, and thee, and thee," I said, nodding to the young men. The ruffed one wore now a silly grin, though the one with the feathers looked foxy still. " 'Tis a poor country welcome we have to give, but we've warm fires and hot supper and soft beds."

"Aye, and pretty maids," Drayton said. He took my hand and kissed it in the French fashion. "I think that I will stay the winter long."

I smiled at him. "Come then, we'll out of the cold," I said.

"How looks he, Mother?" Susanna whispered to me as I passed. "Find you him very changed?"

"Aye, very changed," I said.

"I have bequeathed naught to Drayton," he said. "I should have done."

"There is no need," I said, laying a cool cloth on his brow. "He is thy friend."

"I would have left him some token of my friendship. And thee some token of my love. You know why I could not bequeath the property to you." He took hold of my hand with his own burning one. "If it were found out after my death, I would not have men say I bought your silence."

"I have my widow's portion, and Susanna and John will care for me," I said, loosing his hand to dip the cloth in the bowl again and wring it. "She is a good daughter."

"Aye, a good daughter, though she loved me not at first. Nor did thee."

"That is not true," I said.

"Come, Mistress Anne, when did you love me?" he said. I laid the cloth across his brow. He closed his eyes and sighed, and seemed to sleep.

"The very instant that I saw you," I said.

We made a slow progress into the house, he leaning on me as we stepp'd over the threshold and into the hall. "My leg grows stiff when I have ridden awhile," he said. "I need but to stand by the fire a little."

Joan crowded close behind, her farthingale filling the door so that the others could not follow till she was through. Master Drayton followed upon her skirts, telling Judith and Susanna in a loud and merry voice of what had passed upon the road from London. "As we came across the bridge, four rogues in buckram thrust at me."

Drayton gestured bravely. Elizabeth stared at him, her eyes round.

The young men, Fox and Frill, entered the hall, bearing bags and the metal chest. They stopped inside the door to hear the tale that Drayton told. Frill dropped his sacks with a thump upon the floor. The Fox set the casket beside it.

"These four began to give me ground, but I followed me close."

"Husband," I said under cover of his windy voice, "thou must needs compliment thy sister Joan Hart on her new ruff. She is most proud of it." He gazed at me, and still I could not decipher his look. "Thy daughters, too, have new finery for this occasion. Susanna hath a blue—"

"Surely a man knows his own daughters," Joan said ere I could finish speaking, "though he hath not had a chance to greet them. Thy wife would keep thee all to herself."

"Good Sister Joan," he said. He bowed to her. "I would have greeted thee outside, but I knew thee not."

Joan said. "Thou did'st not know me?" Her voice was sharp, and I looked anxiously at her, but could see naught in her face but peevishness. The Fox turned to look, too.

"I knew you not for that you seem'd so young."

"Liar," the Fox said, turning back round to Drayton. "Those four were not knaves at all, but beggars. They asked for alms."

"Ah, but it makes a good tale," Drayton said.

"I knew you not. The years have been far kinder to you than to me, Sister," he said.

" 'Tis not true," Joan said, tossing her head. Her ruff groaned. "You look the same as on that day you left for London. Thy wife said on that day she'd not see her husband again. What say you now, Anne?" She smiled with spite at me.

"Thy gown is a most rare fashion, Sister," he said.

"Is't?" she said, spreading her skirts with her hands. "I thought it meet to dress in the fashion for your homecoming, brother." She gazed at my plain gown. "Though thy wife did not. Girls!" she called in a shrill voice that overmastered Drayton's. "Come meet thy father."

I had not had the opportunity to speak and say, "Susanna's gown hath a blue stomacher." They came forward, Bess holding to Judith's hand, and I saw with dismay that Judith's frontlet skirt was blue also.

"Husband," I said, but he had stepped forward already, limping a little. Joan folded her hands across her doublet, waiting to see what he would say.

Judith stepped forward, holding Elizabeth's hand. "I am thy daughter Judith, and this Susanna's little daughter Bess."

"And this must be Susanna," he said. She nodded sharply. He stooped to take Bess's hand. "Is thy true name Elizabeth?"

Bess looked up him. "Who are you?"

"Thy grandsire," Judith said, laughing. "Did you not know it yet?"

"She could not know her grandfather," Susanna said. "She was not born and I a child her age when you left us. Why have you come after all these years away, Father?"

"Susanna!" Joan said.

"I knew not how you looked, if you were fair," he answered quietly, "if you were well and happy. I came to see if there was aught that I could do for you."

"There's somewhat you can do for me, Will," Drayton said, clapping a hand to his shoulder. "Give me a cup of sack, man. I am half-froze and weary and was set upon by thieves. And hungry, too."

"I'll fetch it," Judith said, smiling at the Frill. " 'Tis in the kitchen, already warmed and mixed with sugar."

"I'll help thee," the Frill said.

The Fox said, "Madam, where shall I put these bags and boxes?"

"In the bedchambers," I said. "Husband, where would you have your chest?"

"Leave it," he said. "I'll bear it there myself."

Judith brought in the sack in a ewer with a cloth round it and poured it, steaming, into the bowl.

"I smell sweet savors," Drayton said, holding his cup out to her. "What's in it?"

"Cinnamon," Judith said, smiling the while at the Frill. "And sugar. And divers spices. Father, wilt thou drink a cup?"

He smiled sweetly at her. "I would put this in a safe place first." He raised the chest and turned to me. "Good wife, where would you have me sleep?"

"What's in the chest?" Elizabeth said.

"Infinite riches," Drayton said, and drained his cup.

I led the way up the stairs to my bedchamber, he following behind, dragging his leg a little under the weight of the chest.

"Where would you have me put it, Wife?" he asked when we came into the room. "In the corner?" He set the chest down and leant against the wall, his hand upon his leg. "I am too old for such burdens."

I stood against the door. He stood and looked at me, the lines in his unfamiliar face cut deep and sad.

"Where is my husband?" I said.

"Where is the will?" he said.

I had thought he slept and had stepped quietly to the door to see if John were come. "You must stop this talk of wills and assay to sleep," I said, folding the sheets under the featherbed that he might not cast them off. The featherbed made a rustling sound.

He started up, then lay back down again. "I thought I had heard Joan."

"Fear not," I said. "She'll not come. She is in mourning."

He looked as though he knew not what I spoke of. I said, "Her husband died these ten days since."

"Of the ague? Or overmuch noise?" he said, and smiled at me, and then his face grew sad, the lines deep-carved upon it. "She knew me not."

"Nay, and 'twere well she did not."

"Aye, well," he said. "When they first came to me, I thought not it would succeed. A one would say, I know him by his voice, or by his wit, or by his gait. But none said it. All believed, till at last so did I, and came to think I had a wife and daughters."

"And so thou hast," I said.

"Where is my husband?" I had asked, and he had not answered me at first, but let out his breath sighingly, as if he were relieved.

"I knew not that I had a wife and children till his father came to London to tell me that the boy had died," he said.

"What have you done with my husband?"

He sat down heavily upon the bed. "I cannot long stand on my bad leg," he said. "I killed him."

"When?"

"Near twenty years ago."

These twenty years since, he had lain in his grave. "How came you to kill him? Was it in a fight?"

"Nay, madam." He rubbed his leg. "He was murdered."

He answered me as plainly as I asked, more plainly, for my voice was so light and airy, I thought not it would carry the width of the room.

"How came he to be murdered?" I said.

"He had the misfortune to somewhat resemble me in countenance," he said.

I sat down on the coverlid-drap'd press. Dead. I had never thought him dead.

"I fell into some trouble with the queen," he said at

last. "I had . . . done her a service now and then. It made me overbold. Thinking myself safe from the fire, I spoke in jest of things that had got other men burnt, and was arrested. I fled to friends, asking their help to transport me to France. They told me to lie secretly in London at a certain house until they had arranged passage for me, but when they came, they said that it was all accomplished. The man was dead, and I was free to take his name for mine own."

His hand clutched the bedpost. "They had killed your husband, madam, at a little inn in Deptford and said I was the murdered man, not he. They testified that I had fought them over the reckoning of the bill, and they, in self-defense, had stabbed me. They told me this with pride, as of a job well-done."

He stood, clasping the bedpost as it were a walking stick. "The queen's anger would have passed. The murder never. Your husband has had his revenge on me, madam. He took my life as sure as I took his."

I heard a sound from out the room. I waited, listening. I went, treading softly, into the gallery, but there was no one on the stairs, only the sound of laughter from below, and Drayton's voice. I came back in the room.

"How came my husband to that inn?" I asked.

"They lured him thence with promise of a part to play. He being an actor, they had seen him on the stage and marked his likeness to me. They passed a whole day with him ere they killed him, drawing him out with wine and questions, what were his habits, who his friends, that I might better play the masquerade. He did not tell them that he had a wife and children." He paced the narrow space between the bed and my skirts, and turned and paced again. "They even coaxed him to sign his name to a paper that I might copy it."

"And your deception succeeded?"

"Yes. The lodgings where I had stayed that fortnight since were his. I had already fool'd the owner of the house and all the neighbors without intention." There was another gust of laughter from below.

"What happened to your friends?"

"My friends," he said bitterly. "They were acquitted. Walsingham found me not overgrateful for his help and Poley's and has not seen me since. Skeres is in prison. Of Frizer, I know not. I heard that he was dead, but one cannot believe all that one hears."

"And none knew you?"

"No." He sat him down again. "I have been he this twenty years, and been not found out. Until now." He smiled a little. "What would you have me do, madam, now you have caught me out? Leave you in peace as I found you? I could away tomorrow, called to London, and not return. Or publicly confess my crime. What would you? I will do what you command."

"What's all this?" Drayton's voice bellowed from the stairs. "How now? The coverlet already off the bed? The host and his wife off to slumber so soon?" He lumbered into the room. "The dinner's not yet served, though you two feast your eyes upon each other." He laughed, and his very stomach shook with it, but when he turned his eyes to me, there was no laughter in them. "Good madam, I know we have dallied long upon the road, but tell me not 'tis time for bed so soon, supper missed, and all the trenchers cleared away. Tell me not that, or you shall break my heart."

He had stood up when Drayton came in, taking the weight of his body on his bad leg as if it were some lesson in pain, but he looked not at Drayton.

"For God's sake, come, man!" Drayton said, plucking at his arm. "I grow thinner by the minute!"

"Master Drayton, you are a most importunate guest," he said, looking at me.

"Whatever it is you speak of, sure it bears waiting till after supper."

"Yes," I said, "it hath already waited a long time."

. . .

"I am so cold," he said. I knelt beside the chest and took a quilt from out it. He raised himself to watch me. "What keep you in that chest now?"

I lay the quilt over him. "Sheets and pillowcoats and candles."

" 'Tis better so," he said. "Hast thou burned them all?"

"Aye, husband."

"I copied out his name so oft it was almost my own, but they are in my hand. If any come for them, you must say you burned them with the bedding when I died."

"I hear a sound upon the stairs," I said. I hastened to the door. "I am glad you've come, son-in-law," I said softly. "His fever is worse."

John set a lidded cup upon the press and put his hand upon my husband's brow. "Thou hast a fever."

"I feel no fever," he said. He spoke through chattering teeth. "I am as two people lying side by side in the bed, both like to freeze. A little sack would warm me."

"I have somewhat for you better than sack." He slid his hand behind my husband's head to raise him to sitting. I put the pillows behind. "Drink you this."

"What is it?"

"A decoction of herbs. Flavored with cloves and syrup of violets. Come, father-in-law," John said kindly. " 'Twill help your fever."

He drank a swallow. "Vile potion!" he said. "Why did you not pour it in my ear and be done with it?" His hands shivered so that the liquid splashed onto the bedclothes, but he drank it down and gave the cup to John.

"Would you lie down again, husband?" I said, my hand to the pillows.

"Nay, leave them," he said. " 'Tis easier to breathe."

"Is there naught else I can do to help him?" I said, drawing John aside.

"See he hath warm coverings and clean bedding."

" 'Tis freshly changed, and the featherbed on the bed new. I made it with my own hands."

"The second-best bed," my husband said, and turned, and slept.

We went downstairs, Drayton between us like a father who has caught his children kissing in a corner, prattling of beds and supper so that we could not speak. "Come, man," Drayton said, "you've not had any sack from your own bowl."

The board was already laid. Judith was spreading the cloth, Joan bringing in the salts, little Elizabeth laying the spoons. Joan said, "You once again would steal my brother from me, Anne. You never were so affectionate in the old days."

I know not what I answered her, nor what I did, whether I served the fowl first or the sugar-meats, nor what I ate. All I could think of was that my husband was dead. I had not guessed that, through all the years when no word came and Old John cursed me for a shrew that had driven him away. I had not guessed it e'en when Old John nailed the coat of arms above the door of our new house.

I had thought mayhap my husband had suffered us to be stolen by a thief, as a careless man will let his pocket be picked, or that he'd lost us gaming, staking us all as he had staked my mother's plate, and the winner would come to claim us, house and all. But he had not. He had been murdered and laid in someone else's grave.

He sat at the head of the table, Drayton beside him. Drayton would not allow Elizabeth to be sent from table after she said her grace, but bade her sit on his broad knee. He talked and talked, following one story with another.

Joan sulked and preened by turns. Judith sat between Fox and Frill, feeding first one, then the other, her smiles and glances. "Remember you your father?" the Fox asked. "Had he a limp then?"

She answered him, all innocence, the way her father must have answered his assassins. He would have seen only what his desire showed him, 'twas ever his failing. And his father's, who could not see a stranger's face, so blinded was he by the colors of his coat of arms. His sister's failing, too, who could not e'en see over a starch'd ruff. All blind, and he the worst. He would not even have seen the knife blade coming.

When the meal was already done and the dishes carried away, Susanna's husband John came in, covered with snow, and was sat, and dishes warmed, and questions asked. "This is my grandsire," Elizabeth said.

"Well met, at last," John said, but I saw, watching from the kitchen, that he frowned. "I have been overlong at the birth of a cobbler's son, and overlong coming home."

Drayton called for a toast to the new babe, and then another. "We must toast Elizabeth's birth, for we were not present at her christening," he said. "Ah, and gave her not a christening gift." He bade Elizabeth look in his ear.

She stood on tiptoe, her eyes round. "There's naught in there but dirt," she said.

Drayton laughed merrily. "Thou hast not looked well," he said, and pulled a satin ribbon from out his ear.

" 'Tis a trick," Elizabeth said solemnly, "is it not, grandsire?"

"Aye, a trick," he said. She climbed into his lap.

"He is not as I remembered him," Susanna said, watching him tie the ribbon in Bess's hair.

"Thou wert but four years old and Judith a babe when he left. Dost thou remember him?" I said.

"Only a little. I feared he would be like Aunt Joan, dressed in the fashion, playing the part of master of the house though he did not merit it."

"It is his house," I said, and thought of the name on

the deed, the name that they had cajoled my husband into signing that he might copy it. "And all in it purchased with his money."

"Marry, it is his house, though he never saw it till now," she said. "I feared he would claim the house for his own, and us with it."

He fastened the ribbon clumsily, tying it round a lock of Bess's hair. "But he plays not that part," I said.

"No. Knowest thou what he said to me, Mother, when I brought him his sack? He said, 'Thy father was a fool to ever leave thee.' "

John Hall came and stood beside us, watching the tying of the ribbon. "Look how her ribbon comes loose," Susanna said. "I'll go and tie it."

She went to Bess and would have tied the ribbon, but she tossed her head naughtily.

"My grandsire will do't," she said, and backed against his knees.

"My hands are too clumsy for this business, daughter," he said. The lines had softened already in his face. He looked to her, and she, leaning o'er him, told him to loop the ribbon so and then to pull it through. Judith came and stood beside, smiling and advising.

"Notice you aught amiss about your husband?" John said.

"Amiss?" I said. I could not catch my breath. I had forgot that he had been to Cambridge, and to London, a learned man.

"I fear that he is ill," John said.

Bess ran to us. "Father!" she cried. "Look you at my new ribbon," and ran back again. "Grandsire, is't not pretty?" She fairly leapt into his arms and kissed him on the cheek.

"Sweet Bess, 'twas not my gift, but Drayton's."

"But you tied it."

"Is he very ill?" I said.

John looked kindly at me. "This country air will

make him well again, and your kind ministrations. Shall we into the hall?"

"Nay," I said. "I must go up to make the bed."

I went out through the kitchen. The Fox and Frill stood by the stairs, whispering together. "You are mad," the Frill said. "Look how his family greets him, his daughters gathering round him. It was an idle rumor, and no more."

I hid inside the kitchen door that I might hear their conversation.

"His daughters were but babes when they last saw him," the Fox said.

"The sister says he has changed not at all."

"The sister is a fool. His wife greeted him not so eagerly. Saw you how she stood as a statue when first we came? 'Tis she should be the subject of our watch."

I came into the hall. They bowed to me. The Fox would have spoken, but Drayton came and said, "Good mistress, I had missed you in the hall."

"I'll follow you in a little. I would make up the second-best bed."

"No, I'll accompany thee," he said. "And you two see to the horses. They've not been fed."

The Fox and Frill put on their cloaks and went out into the snow. Drayton climbed the stairs after me, puffing and talking the while. I went into my room and lit the candles.

He looked about him. "A great reckoning in a little room," he said in a gentler voice than before. "I advised against his coming. I said it was not safe while any still lived who knew him, but he would see the daughters. Does the sister know?"

"Nay," I said. I laid the coverlid upon the bed and looked to put it so that it hung straight. I set the bolsters at the head of the bed. "Who is he?"

He sat upon the press, his hands on his stout knees.

"There was a time I could have answered you," he said. "I knew him long ago."

"Before the murder?"

"Before the murders."

"They killed others?" I said. "Besides my husband?"

"Only one other," he said. His voice downstairs had been loud and bold, an actor's voice, but now it was so low I could scarce hear him, as though he spoke to himself. "You asked me who he is. I know not, though he was but a young man when first I knew him, a roguish young man, full of ambition and touched by genius, but reckless, overproud, taking thought only for himself." He stopped and sat, rubbing his hands along his thighs. "Walsingham's henchmen killed more men than they knew that wicked day at Deptford. I saw him on the street afterwards and knew him not, he was so changed. I would show you something," he said, and raised himself awkwardly. He went to the chest in the corner, opened it, and proferred me the papers that lay therein. "Read them," he said.

I gave them back to him. "I cannot read."

"Then all is lost," he said. "I thought to bargain with you for his life with these his plays."

"To buy me."

"I think you cannot be bought, but, aye, I would buy you any way I could to keep him safe. He hath been ill these two winters past. He has need of your refuge. The London air is bad for him, and there are rumors, from whence I know not."

"The young men you brought here have heard them."

"Aye, and wait their chance. I know that naught can replace your husband."

"No," I said, thinking of how he had stolen my honor and my mother's plate and run away to London.

"You cannot bring your husband back from the dead, if you tell all the world. You will but cause another murder. I'll not say one man's life is worth more than another's." He brandished the papers. "No, by God, I will say it! Your husband could not have written words like these. This man is worth a hundred men, and I'll not see him hanged."

He lay the papers back into the chest and closed the lid. "Let us go back to London, and keep silence."

Elizabeth ran into the room. "Come, granddame, come. We are to have a play."

"A play?" Drayton said. He lifted Elizabeth up into his arms. "Madam, he has no life save what you grant him," he said, and carried her down the stairs.

"The decoction will make him sleep," John Hall said.

He slept already, his face less lined in rest. "And quench the fever?"

He shook his head. "I know not if it will. I fear it is his heart that brings it on."

He put the cup into the pouch he carried. "I give you this," he said. He proffered me a sheaf of papers, closely writ.

"What is't?"

"My journal. Thy husband's illness is there, my treatments of it, and all my thoughts. I'd have thee burn it."

"Why?"

"We have been friends these three years. We'd drink a cup of ale, and sit, and talk. One day he chanced to speak of a play he'd writ, a sad play of a man who'd bartered his soul to the devil. He spoke of it as if he had forgot that I was with him: how it was writ and when, where acted. He marked not that I looked at him with wonder, and after a little, we went on to other things."

He closed the pouch. "The play he spoke of was Kit Marlowe's, who was killed in a brawl at Deptford these long years since." He took the papers back from me and thrust them in the candle's flame.

"Hast thou told Susanna?"

"I would not twice deprive her of a father." The pages flamed. He thrust them in the grate and watched them burn.

"His worry is all Susanna's inheritance," I said, "and Judith's. He bade me burn his plays."

"And Marlowe's?" he said, dividing the charring pages with his foot that they might the better burn. "Hast thou done it?"

A little piece of blackened paper flew up, the writing all burnt away. "Yes," I said.

"Judith said we are to have a play," Elizabeth said as we descended the stairs. She freed herself from Drayton's arms and ran into the hall.

"Judith?" I said, and looked to where she stood. The Fox was at her side, his feathered cap wet with snow. He leaned against the wall, seeming not even to listen. The Frill squatted by the hearth, stretching his hands to the fire.

"Oh, grandsire, prithee do!" Elizabeth said, half climbing into his lap. "I never saw a play."

"Yes, brother, a play," Joan said.

Drayton stepped between them. "We are too few for a company, Mistress Bess," he said, pulling at Elizabeth's ribbon to make her laugh, "and the hour too late."

"Only a little one, grandsire?" she begged.

"It is too late," he said, looking at me. "But you shall have your play."

The Fox stepped forward, too quick, taking the Frill by the sleeve and pulling him to his feet. "What shall we, Master Will?" he said, smiling with his sharp teeth. "A play within a play?"

"Aye," Drayton said loudly. "Let us do Bottom's troupe at Pyramus and Thisbe."

The Fox smiled wider. "Or the mousetrap?" All of them looked at him, Judith smiling, the Fox waiting to snap, Master Drayton with a face taken suddenly sober.

But he looked not at them, nor at Bess, who had climbed into his lap. He looked at me.

"A sad tale's best for winter," he said. He turned to the Frill. "Do ye the letter scene from *Measure*. Begin ye, 'Let this Barnardine.' "

The Frill struck a pose, his hand raised in the air as if to strike. " 'Let this Barnardine be this morning executed and his head borne to Angelo,' " he said in a loud voice.

He stopped, his finger pointing toward the Fox, who did not answer.

Drayton said, " 'Tis an old play. They know it not. Come, let's have Bottom. I'll act the ass."

"If they know not the play, then I'll explain it," the Fox said. "The play is called *Measure for Measure*. It is the story of a young man who is in difficulty with the law and would be hanged, but another is killed in his place." He pointed at the Frill. "Play out the play."

" 'Let this Barnardine be this morning executed and his head borne to Angelo.' " the Frill said.

The Fox looked at Drayton. " 'Angelo hath seen them both, and will discover the favor.' "

The Frill smiled, and it was a smile less slack-jawed and more cruel than I had seen, a wolfen smile. " 'Oh, Death's a great disguiser,' " he said.

"An end to this!" I said.

Both of them looked at me, Fox and Frill, disturbed from their prey.

"The child is half-asleep," I said.

"I am not!" Bess said, rubbing at her eyes, which made the party laugh.

I stood her down from off his lap. "Thou mayest have plays tomorrow, and tomorrow, and the next day. Thy grandfather is home to stay."

Susanna hurried forward. "Good night, Father. I am well content that you are home." She fastened Bess's cloak about her neck.

"Will you a play for me tomorrow, grandsire?" Bess said.

He stroked her hair. "Aye, tomorrow."

Bess flung her arms about his neck. "Good night, grandsire."

John Hall picked up the child in his arms. She lay her head upon his shoulder. "I will take the actors with us," John said softly to me. "I trust them not in the house with Judith."

He turned to the Fox and Frill and said in a loud voice, "Gentlemen, you're to bed with us tonight. Will you come now? Aunt Joan, we will walk you home."

"Nay," Joan said haughtily, stretching her neck to look more proud. Her ruff moaned and creaked. "I would stay awhile, and them with me."

John opened the door, and they went out into the snow, Elizabeth already asleep.

"Marry, now they are gone, we'll have our play, brother."

"Nay," I said, kneeling to put my hands in his. "I am a wife long parted from her husband. I would to bed with him ere sunrise."

"You loved not your husband so well in the old days," Joan said, her hands upon her hips. "Brother, you will not let her rule you?"

"I shall do whatever she wills."

"I know a scene will do us perfectly," Drayton said. He spread his arms. " 'Our revels now are ended.' " He donned his wide cloak. "Come, Mistress Joan, I will accompany thee to thy home and these two to Hall's croft and thence to a tavern for a drop or two of sack ere I return."

Judith walked with them to the far end of the hall and opened the door. I knelt still with his hands in mine. "Why did you this?" he asked. "Hath Drayton purchased you with pity?"

"Nay," I said softly. "You cannot leave. Your daughters would be sad to have you go, and you have promised Elizabeth a play. You asked if there was aught that you could do for them. Be thou their father."

"I will and you will answer me one question. Tell me when you discovered me."

"I knew you ere you came."

His hands clasped mine.

"When Hamnet died, and Old John went to London to tell my husband," I said, "he came home with a coat of arms he said his son had got for him, but I believed him not. His son, my husband, would ne'er have raised his hand to help his father or to give his daughters a house to dwell in. I knew it was not he who did us such kindness, but another."

"All these long years I thought that none knew me, that all believed me dead. And so it was as I were dead, and buried in Deptford, and he the one who lived. But you knew me."

"Yes."

"And hated me not, though I had killed your husband."

"I knew not he was dead. I thought he'd lost us dicing, or sold us to a kinder master."

"Sold?" he said. "What manner of man would sell such treasure?"

" 'The iron tongue of midnight hath told twelve. Good night, good rest!' " Drayton called from the door. " 'Sweet suitors, to bed.' "

I rose from where I knelt, holding still to his hands. "Come, husband," I said. "The bed at last is made, in time for bed."

"The bed," he said, so weak I scarce could hear him.

"What is't, husband?"

"I have left you a remembrance in the will." He smiled at me. "I will not tell you of it now. 'Twill please thee to hear it when the will is read."

He had forgot that I sat by him when he made his will.

"John's foul decoction hath made me better," he said. "I am as one again, not split in two."

I laid my hand upon his brow. It was more hot than ever. I went to fetch another quilt from out the chest.

"Nay, come and sit with me and hold my hands," he said. "I have paid the sexton a French crown to write a curse upon my grave, that none will dig me up and say, 'That is not he.' "

"Prithee, speak not of dying," I said.

"I wrote not mine own will, but signed it only. They had him write out his name ere they killed him, that I might copy it."

"I know, husband. Soft, do not fret thyself with—"

"It matters not whose name is on the plays, so that my daughters' inheritance is safe. Hast thou burnst them all?"

"Yes," I said, but I have not. I have sewn them in the new featherbed. I will ensure it is not burnt with the bedding when he dies, and so will keep them safe, save the house itself burns down. I will do naught to endanger their inheritance nor the love they bear their father, but in after years the papers can be found and his true name set on them. The clew lies in the will.

"Wife, come sit by me and hold my hands," he says, though I hold them already. "I have left thee something in the will, a token of that night when first I came. I have bequeathed to thee the second-best bed."

Jack

The night Jack joined our post, Vi was late. So was the Luftwaffe. The sirens still hadn't gone by eight o'clock.

"Perhaps our Violet's tired of the RAF and begun on the aircraft spotters," Morris said, "and they're so taken by her charms, they've forgotten to wind the sirens."

"You'd best watch out, then," Swales said, taking off his tin warden's hat. He'd just come back from patrol. We made room for him at the linoleum-covered table, moving our teacups and the litter of gas masks and pocket torches. Twickenham shuffled his papers into one pile next to his typewriter and went on typing.

Swales sat down and poured himself a cup of tea. "She'll set her cap for the ARP next," he said, reaching for the milk. Morris pushed it toward him. "And none of us will be safe." He grinned at me. "Especially the young ones, Jack."

"I'm safe," I said. "I'm being called up soon. Twickenham's the one who should be worrying."

Twickenham looked up from his typing at the sound of his name. "Worrying about what?" he asked, his hands poised over the keyboard.

ON SEPTEMBER 7, 1940, HITLER'S AIR FORCE BEGAN *systematically bombing London, aiming first for the docks and the oil-storage tanks, and then for the fires. The bombers came over nearly every night for the next four months, dropping high explosive bombs and incendiaries on St. Paul's and Westminster Abbey and Buckingham Palace and killing thirty thousand Londoners.*

The raids were supposed to destroy and demoralize London into surrendering, but it didn't work. Londoners dug in (literally) for their finest hour, and the king and queen had their picture taken, smiling, in the wreckage at Buckingham Palace. The motto of the day, chalked on walls and stuck up in blown-out windows, was "London Can Take It."

The image everyone has of Londoners in the Blitz is of pluck and grim determination as they put out incendiaries and slept in tube stations and rescued children out of the rubble. And it was true for some of them.

But not all. Some of them were continually terrified by the raids, and some of them sank into depression and despair. Most of them were worn down by the rationing and the lack of sleep and the endless, whining sirens and hated every minute of it.

And some of them loved it. For some of them, it was the opportunity of a lifetime.

A FEW YEARS AGO, *I* MOVED BACK HERE TO THE *town where I had gone to college. The campus hadn't changed at all. Well, actually, it had. The college had moved bag and baggage to a new campus half a mile away, and all the buildings on the old campus had been put to new, humiliating uses. But it looked the same—the library (now the administration building) and the student union (now the campus parking authority) and the flagstone walks.*

And the kids. Almost the first thing I saw was a girl leaping out of a car and running across the grass to embrace two other girls, all of them screaming happily. It could have been Tannis and Linda and me, all of us just back from summer vacation with so much to say, we all had to talk at the same time. We hadn't seen each other all summer; we hadn't (in spite of our fervent promises in May) written or called or even thought of each other all summer. But now here we were all back, hugging and shrieking and talking a mile a minute, as if we had never been apart.

Moving back was like that. I hadn't thought of the flagstone walks, of the library, of Phil and Matsu and Pam, in years. Some of them I didn't even know I remembered. But now here I was back, and here they all were, the memories I thought I'd forgotten. Rhonie and Sharon and Chuck, and my own young careless self, who had let them all go.

Chance

On Wednesday Elizabeth's next-door neighbor came over. It was raining hard, but she had run across the yard without a raincoat or an umbrella, her hands jammed in her cardigan sweater pockets.

"Hi," she said breathlessly. "I live next door to you, and I just thought I'd pop in and say hi and see if you were getting settled in." She reached in one of the sweater pockets and pulled out a folded piece of paper. "I wrote down the name of our trash pickup. Your husband asked about it the other day."

She handed it to her. "Thank you," Elizabeth said. The young woman reminded her of Tib. Her hair was short and blond and brushed back in wings. Tib had worn hers like that when they were freshmen.

"Isn't this weather awful?" the young woman said. "It usually doesn't rain like this in the fall."

It had rained all fall when Elizabeth was a freshman. "Where's your raincoat?" Tib had asked her when she unpacked her clothes and hung them up in the dorm room.

Tib was little and pretty, the kind of girl who probably had dozens of dates, the kind of girl who brought all the right clothes to college. Elizabeth hadn't known what kind of clothes to bring. The brochure the college had sent the freshmen had said to bring sweaters and skirts for class, a suit for rush, a formal. It hadn't said anything about a raincoat.

"Do I need one?" Elizabeth had said.

"Well, it's raining right now if that's any indication," Tib had said.

"I thought it was starting to let up," the neighbor said, "but it's not. And it's so cold."

She shivered. Elizabeth saw that her cardigan was damp.

"I can turn the heat up," Elizabeth said.

"No, I can't stay. I know you're trying to get unpacked. I'm sorry you had to move in in all this rain. We usually have beautiful weather here in the fall." She smiled at Elizabeth. "Why am I telling you that? Your husband told me you went to school here. At the university."

"It wasn't a university back then. It was a state college."

"Oh, right. Has the campus changed a lot?"

Elizabeth went over and looked at the thermostat. It showed the temperature as sixty-eight, but it felt colder. She turned it up to seventy-five. "No," she said. "It's just the same."

"Listen, I can't stay," the young woman said. "And you've probably got a million things to do. I just came over to say hello and see if you'd like to come over tonight. I'm having a Tupperware party."

A Tupperware party, Elizabeth thought sadly. No wonder she reminds me of Tib.

"You don't have to come. And if you come you don't have to buy anything. It's not going to be a big party. Just a few friends of mine. I think it would be a good way for you to meet some of the neighbors. I'm really only having the party because I have this friend who's trying to get started selling Tupperware and . . ." She stopped and looked anxiously at Elizabeth, holding her arms against her chest for warmth.

"I used to have a friend who sold Tupperware," Elizabeth said.

"Oh, then you probably have tons of it."

The furnace came on with a deafening whoosh. "No," Elizabeth said. "I don't have any."

"Please come," the young woman had continued to say even on the front porch. "Not to buy anything. Just to meet everybody."

The rain was coming down hard again. She ran back across the lawn to her house, her arms wrapped tightly around her and her head down.

Elizabeth went back in the house and called Paul at his office.

"Is this really important, Elizabeth?" he said. "I'm supposed to meet with Dr. Brubaker in Admissions for lunch at noon, and I have a ton of paperwork."

"The girl next door invited me to a Tupperware party," Elizabeth said. "I didn't want to say yes if you had anything planned for tonight."

"A Tupperware party?!" he said. "I can't believe you called me about something like that. You know how busy I am. Did you put your application in at Carter?"

"I'm going over there right now," she said. "I was going to go this morning, but the . . ."

"Dr. Brubaker's here," he said, and hung up the phone.

Elizabeth stood by the phone a minute, thinking about Tib, and then put on her raincoat and walked over to the old campus.

"It's exactly the same as it was when we were freshmen," Tib had said when Elizabeth told her about Paul's new job. "I was up there last summer to get some transcripts, and I couldn't believe it. It was raining, and I swear the sidewalks were covered with exactly the same worms as they always were. Do you remember that yellow slicker you bought when you were a freshman?"

Tib had called Elizabeth from Denver when they came out to look for a house. "I read in the alumni news that Paul was the new assistant dean," she said as if nothing had ever happened. "The article didn't say anything about you, but I thought I'd call on the off-chance that you two were still married. I'm not." Tib had insisted on taking her to lunch in Larimer Square. She had let her hair grow out, and she was too thin. She ordered a peach daiquiri and told Elizabeth all about her divorce. "I found out Jim was screwing some little slut at the office," she had said, twirling the sprig of mint that had come with her drink, "and I couldn't take it. He couldn't see what I was upset about. 'So I fooled around, so what?' he told me. 'Everybody does it. When are you going to grow up?' I never should have married the creep, but you don't know you're ruining your life when you do it, do you?"

"No," Elizabeth said.

"I mean, look at you and Paul," she said. She talked faster than Elizabeth remembered, and when she called the waiter over to order another daiquiri, her voice shook a little. "Now that's a marriage I wouldn't have taken bets on, and you've been married, what? Fifteen years?"

"Seventeen," Elizabeth said.

"You know, I always thought you'd patch things up with Tupper," she said. "I wonder whatever became of him." The waiter brought the daiquiri and took the empty one away. She took the mint sprig out and laid it carefully on the tablecloth.

"Whatever became of Elizabeth and Tib, for that matter," she said.

The campus wasn't really just the same. They had added a wing onto Frasier and cut down most of the elms. It wasn't even really the campus anymore. The real campus was west and north of here, where there had been room for the new concrete classroom buildings and high-rise dorms. The music department was still in Frasier, and the PE department used the old gym in Gunter for women's sports, but most of the old classroom buildings and the small dorms at the south end of the campus were offices now. The library was now the administration building and Kepner belonged to the campus housing authority, but in the rain the campus looked the same.

The leaves were starting to fall, and the main walk was wet and covered with worms. Elizabeth picked her way among them, watching her feet and trying not to step on them. When she was a freshman, she had refused to walk on the sidewalks at all. She had ruined two pairs of flats that fall by cutting through the grass to get to her classes.

"You're a nut, you know that?" Tib had shouted, sprinting to catch up to her. "There are worms in the grass, too."

"I know, but I can't see them."

When there was no grass, she had insisted on walking in the middle of the street. That was how they had met Tupper. He almost ran them down with his bike.

It had been a Friday night. Elizabeth remembered that, because Tib was in her ROTC Angel Flight uniform, and after Tupper had swerved wildly to miss them, sending up great sprays of water and knocking his bike over, the first thing he said was, "Cripes! She's a cop!"

They had helped him pick up the plastic bags strewn all over the street. "What are these?" Tib had said, stooping because she couldn't bend over in her straight blue skirt and high heels.

"Tupperware," he said. "The latest thing. You girls wouldn't need a lettuce crisper, would you? They're great for keeping worms in."

Carter Hall looked just the same from the outside, ugly beige stone and glass brick. It had been the student union, but now it housed Financial Aid and Personnel. Inside it had been completely remodeled. Elizabeth couldn't even tell where the cafeteria had been.

"You can fill it out here if you want," the girl who gave her the application said, and gave her a pen. Elizabeth hung her coat over the back of a chair and sat down at a desk by a window. It felt chilly, though the window was steamy.

They had all gone to the student union for pizza. Elizabeth had hung her yellow slicker over the back of the booth. Tupper had pretended to wring out his jean jacket and draped it over the radiator. The window by the booth was so steamed up, they couldn't see out. Tib had written "I hate rain" on the window with her finger, and Tupper had told them how he was putting himself through college selling Tupperware.

"They're great for keeping cookies in," he said, hauling up a big pink box he called a cereal keeper. He put a piece of pizza inside and showed them how to put the lid on and burp it. "There. It'll keep for weeks. Years. Come on. You need one. I'll bet your mothers send you cookies all the time."

He was a junior. He was tall and skinny, and when he put his damp jean jacket back on, the sleeves were too short, and his wrists stuck out. He had sat next to Tib on one side of the booth and Elizabeth had sat on the other. He had talked to Tib most of the evening, and when he was paying the check, he had bent toward Tib and whispered something to her. Elizabeth was sure he was asking her out on a date, but on the way home Tib had said, "You know what he wanted, don't you? Your telephone number."

Elizabeth stood up and put her coat back on. She gave the girl in the sweater and skirt back her pen. "I think I'll fill this out at home and bring it back."

"Sure," the girl said.

When Elizabeth went back outside, the rain had stopped. The trees were still dripping, big drops that splattered onto the wet walk. She walked up the wide center walk toward her old dorm, looking at her feet so she wouldn't step on any worms. The dorm had been converted into the university's infirmary. She stopped and stood a minute under the center window, looking up at the room that had been hers and Tib's.

Tupper had stood under the window and thrown pebbles up at it. Tib had opened the window and yelled, "You'd better stop throwing rocks, you . . ." Something hit her in the chest. "Oh, hi, Tupper," she said, and picked it up off the floor and handed it to Elizabeth. "It's for you," she said. It wasn't a pebble. It was a pink plastic gadget, one of the favors he passed out at his Tupperware parties.

"What's this supposed to be?" Elizabeth had said, leaning out of the window and waving it at him. It was raining. Tupper had the collar of his jean jacket turned up and he looked cold. The sidewalk around him was covered with pink plastic favors.

"A present," he said. "It's an egg separator."

"I don't have any eggs."

"Wear it around your neck then. We'll be officially scrambled."

"Or separated."

He grabbed at his chest with his free hand. "Never!" he said. "Want to come out in the worms with me? I've got some deliveries to make." He held up a clutch of plastic bags full of bowls and cereal keepers.

"I'll be right down," she had said, but she had stopped and found a ribbon to string the egg separator on before she went downstairs.

Elizabeth looked down at the sidewalk, but there were no plastic favors on the wet cement. There was a big puddle out by the curb, and a worm lay at the edge of it. It moved a little as she watched, in that horrid boneless way that she had always hated, and then lay still.

A girl brushed past her, walking fast. She stepped in

the puddle, and Elizabeth took a half step back to avoid being splashed. The water in the puddle rippled and moved out in a wave. The worm went over the edge of the sidewalk and into the gutter.

Elizabeth looked up. The girl was already halfway down the center walk, late for class or angry or both. She was wearing an Angel Flight uniform and high heels, and her short blond hair was brushed back in wings along the sides of her garrison cap.

Elizabeth stepped off the curb into the street. The gutter was clogged with dead leaves and full of water. The worm lay at the bottom. She sat down on her heels, holding the application form in her right hand. The worm would drown, wouldn't it? That was what Tupper had told her. The reason they came out on the sidewalks when it rained was that their tunnels filled up with water, and they would drown if they didn't.

She stood up and looked down the central walk again, but the girl was gone, and there was nobody else on the campus. She stooped again and transferred the application to her other hand, and then reached in the icy water, and scooped up the worm in her cupped hand, thinking that as long as it didn't move she would be able to stand it, but as soon as her fingers touched the soft pink flesh, she dropped it and clenched her fist.

"I can't," Elizabeth said, rubbing her wet hand along the side of her raincoat, as if she could wipe off the memory of the worm's touch.

She took the application in both hands and dipped it into the water like a scoop. The paper went a little limp in the water, but she pushed it into the dirty, wet leaves and scooped the worm up and put it back on the sidewalk. It didn't move.

"And thank God they do come out on the sidewalks!" Tupper had said, walking her home in the middle of the street from his Tupperware deliveries. "You think they're disgusting lying there! What if they didn't come out on the sidewalks? What if they all stayed in their holes and drowned? Have you ever had to do mouth-to-mouth resuscitation on a worm?"

Elizabeth straightened up. The job application was wet and dirty. There was a brown smear where the worm had lain, and a dirty line across the top. She should throw it away and go back to Carter to get another one. She unfolded it and carefully separated the wet pages so they wouldn't stick together as they dried.

"I had first aid last semester, and we had to do mouth-to-mouth resuscitation in there," Tupper had said, standing in the middle of the street in front of her dorm. "What a great class! I sold twenty-two square rounds for snake-bite kits. Do you know how to do mouth-to-mouth resuscitation?"

"No."

"It's easy," Tupper had said, and put his hand on the back of her neck under her hair and kissed her, in the middle of the street in the rain.

The worm still hadn't moved. Elizabeth stood and watched it a little longer, feeling cold, and then went out in the middle of the street and walked home.

Paul didn't come home until after seven. Elizabeth had kept a casserole warm in the oven.

"I ate," he said. "I thought you'd be at your Tupperware party."

"I don't want to go," she said, reaching into the hot oven to get the casserole out. It was the first time she had felt warm all day.

"Brubaker's wife is going. I told him you'd be there, too. I want you to get to know her. Brubaker's got a lot of influence around here about who gets tenure."

She put the casserole on top of the stove and then stood there with the oven door half-open. "I went over to apply for a job today," she said, "and I saw this worm. It had fallen in the gutter and it was drowning and I picked it up and put it back on the sidewalk."

"And did you apply for the job or do you think you can make any money picking up worms?"

She had turned up the furnace when she got home and put the application on the vent, but it had wrinkled as it dried, and there was a big smear down the middle where the worm had lain. "No," she said. "I was going to, but when I was over on the campus, there was this worm lying on the sidewalk. A girl walked by and stepped in a puddle, and that was all it took. The worm was right on the edge, and when she stepped in the puddle, it made a kind of wave that pushed it over the edge. She didn't even know she'd done it."

"Is there a point to this story, or have you decided to stand here and talk until you've completely ruined my chance at tenure?" He shut off the oven and went into the living room. She followed him.

"All it took was somebody walking past and stepping in a puddle, and the worm's whole life was changed. Do you think things happen like that? That one little action can change your whole life forever?"

"What I think," he said, "is that you didn't want to move here in the first place, and so you are determined to sabotage my chances. You know what this move is costing us, but you won't go apply for a job. You know how important my getting tenure is, but you won't do anything to help. You won't even go to a goddamn Tupperware party!" He turned the thermostat down. "It's like an oven in here. You've got the heat turned up to seventy-five. What's the matter with you?"

"I was cold," Elizabeth said.

She was late to the Tupperware party. They were in the middle of a game where they told their name and something they liked that began with the same letter.

"My name's Sandy," an overweight woman in brown

polyester pants and a rust print blouse was saying, "and I like sundaes." She pointed at Elizabeth's neighbor. "And you're Meg, and you like marshmallows, and you're Janice," she said, glaring at a woman in a pink suit with her hair teased and sprayed the way girls had worn it when Elizabeth was in college. "You're Janice and you like Jesus," she said, and moved rapidly on to the next person. "And you're Barbara and you like bananas."

She went all the way around the circle until she came to Elizabeth. She looked puzzled for a moment, and then said. "And you're Elizabeth, and you went to college here, didn't you?"

"Yes," she said.

"That doesn't begin with an *E*," the woman in the center said. Everyone laughed. "I'm Terry, and I like Tupperware," she said, and there was more laughter. "You got here late. Stand up and tell us your name and something you like."

"I'm Elizabeth," she said, still trying to place the woman in the brown slacks. Sandy. "And I like . . ." She couldn't think of anything with an *E*.

"Eggs," Sandy whispered loudly.

"And I like eggs," Elizabeth said, and sat back down.

"Great," Terry said. "Everybody else got a favor, so you get one, too." She handed Elizabeth a pink plastic egg separator.

"Somebody gave me one of those," she said.

"No problem," Terry said. She held out a shallow plastic box full of plastic toothbrush holders and grapefruit slicers. "You can put it back and take something else if you've already got one."

"No. I'll keep this." She knew she should say something good-natured and funny, in the spirit of things, but all she could think of was what she had said to Tupper when he gave it to her. "I'll treasure this always," she had told him. A month later she had thrown it away.

"I'll treasure it always," Elizabeth said, and everyone laughed.

They played another game, unscrambling words like "autumn" and "schooldays" and "leaf," and then Terry passed out order forms and pencils and showed them Tupperware.

It was cold in the house, even though Elizabeth's neighbor had a fire going in the fireplace, and after she had filled out her order form, Elizabeth went over and sat in front of the fire, looking at the plastic egg separator.

The woman in the brown pants came over, holding a coffee cup and a brownie on a napkin. "Hi, I'm Sandy Konkel. You don't remember me, do you?" she said. "I was an Alpha Phi. I pledged the year after you did."

Elizabeth looked earnestly at her, trying to remember her. She did not look like she had ever been an Alpha Phi. Her mustard-colored hair looked as if she had cut it herself. "I'm sorry, I . . . ," Elizabeth said.

"That's okay," Sandy said. She sat down next to her. "I've changed a lot. I used to be skinny before I went to all these Tupperware parties and ate brownies. And I used to be a lot blonder. Well, actually, I never was any blonder, but I looked blonder, if you know what I mean. You look just the same. You were Elizabeth Wilson, right?"

Elizabeth nodded.

"I'm not really a whiz at remembering names," she said cheerfully, "but they stuck me with being alum rep this year. Could I come over tomorrow and get some info from you on what you're doing, who you're married to? Is your husband an alum, too?"

"No," Elizabeth said. She stretched her hands out over the fire, trying to warm them. "Do they still have Angel Flight at the college?"

"At the university, you mean," Sandy said, grinning. "It used to be a college. Gee, I don't know. They dropped the whole ROTC thing back in sixty-eight. I don't know if they ever reinstated it. I can find out. Were you in Angel Flight?"

"No," Elizabeth said.

"You know, now that I think about it, I don't think they did. They always had that big fall dance, and I don't remember them having it since. . . . What was it called, the Autumn Something?"

"The Harvest Ball," Elizabeth said.

Thursday morning Elizabeth walked back over to the campus to get another job application. Paul had been late going to work. "Did you talk to Brubaker's wife?" he had said on his way out the door. Elizabeth had forgotten all about Mrs. Brubaker. She wondered which one she had been, Barbara who liked bananas or Meg who liked marshmallows.

"Yes," she said. "I told her how much you liked the university."

"Good. There's a faculty concert tomorrow night. Brubaker asked if we were going. I invited them over for coffee afterwards. Did you turn the heat up again?" he said. He looked at the thermostat and turned it down to sixty. "You had it turned up to eighty. I can hardly wait to see what our first gas bill is. The last thing I need is a two-hundred-dollar gas bill, Elizabeth. Do you realize what this move is costing us?"

"Yes," Elizabeth said. "I do."

She had turned the thermostat back up as soon as he left, but it didn't seem to do any good. She put on a sweater and her raincoat and walked over to the campus.

The rain had stopped sometime during the night, but the central walk was still wet. At the far end, a girl in a yellow slicker stepped up on the curb. She took a few steps on the sidewalk, her head bent, as if she were looking at something on the ground, and then cut across the wet grass toward Gunter.

• • •

Elizabeth went into Carter Hall. The girl who had helped her the day before was leaning over the counter, taking notes from a textbook. She was wearing a pleated skirt and sweater like Elizabeth had worn in college.

"The styles we wore have all come back," Tib had said when they had lunch together. "Those matching sweater-and-skirt sets and those horrible flats that we never could keep on our feet. And penny loafers." She was on her third peach daiquiri and her voice had gotten calmer with each one, so that she almost sounded like her old self. "And cocktail dresses! Do you remember that rust formal you had, with the scoop neck and the long skirt with the raised design? I always loved that dress. Do you remember that time you loaned it to me for the Angel Flight dance?"

"Yes," Elizabeth said, and picked up the bill.

Tib tried to stir her peach daiquiri with its mint sprig, but it slipped out of her fingers and sank to the bottom of the glass. "He really only took me to be nice."

"I know," Elizabeth had said. "Now how much do I owe? Six-fifty for the crepes and two for the wine cooler. Do they add on the tip here?"

"I need another job application," Elizabeth said to the girl.

"Sure thing." When the girl walked over to the files to get it, Elizabeth could see that she was wearing flat-heeled shoes like she had worn in college. Elizabeth thanked her and put the application in her purse.

She walked up past her dorm. The worm was still lying there. The sidewalk around it was almost dry, and the worm was a darker red than it should have been. "I should have put it in the grass," she said out loud. She knew it was dead, but she picked it up and put it in the grass anyway, so no one would step on it. It was cold to the touch.

Sandy Konkel came over in the afternoon wearing a gray polyester pantsuit. She had a wet high-school letter jacket over her head. "John loaned me his jacket," she said. "I wasn't going to wear a coat this morning, but John told me I was going to get drenched. Which I was."

"You might want to put it on," Elizabeth said. "I'm sorry it's so cold in here. I think there's something wrong with the furnace."

"I'm fine," Sandy said. "You know, I wrote that article on your husband being the new assistant dean, and I asked him about you, but he didn't say anything about your having gone to college here."

She had a thick notebook with her. She opened it at tabbed sections. "We might as well get this alum stuff out of the way first, and then we can talk. This alum-rep job is a real pain, but I must admit I get kind of a kick out of finding out what happened to everybody. Let's see," she said, thumbing through the sections. "Found, lost, hopelessly lost, deceased. I think you're one of the hopelessly lost. Right? Okay." She dug a pencil out of her purse. "You were Elizabeth Wilson."

"Yes," Elizabeth said. "I was." She had taken off her light sweater and put on a heavy wool one when she got home, but she was still cold. She rubbed her hands along her upper arms. "Would you like some coffee?"

"Sure," she said. She followed Elizabeth to the kitchen and asked her questions about Paul and his job and whether they had any children while Elizabeth made coffee and put out the cream and sugar and a plate of the cookies she had baked for after the concert.

"I'll read you some names off the hopelessly lost list, and if you know what happened to them, just stop me. Carolyn Waugh, Pam Callison, Linda Bohlender." She was several names past Cheryl Tibner before Elizabeth realized that was Tib.

"I saw Tib in Denver this summer," she said. "Her married name's Scates, but she's getting a divorce, and I don't know if she's going to go back to her maiden name or not."

"What's she doing?" Sandy said.

She's drinking too much, Elizabeth thought, and she let her hair grow out, and she's too thin. "She's working for a stockbroker," she said, and went to get the address Tib had given her. Sandy wrote it down and then flipped to the tabbed section marked "Found" and entered the name and address again.

"Would you like some more coffee, Mrs. Konkel?" Elizabeth said.

"You still don't remember me, do you?" Sandy said. She stood up and took off her jacket. She was wearing a short-sleeved gray knit shell underneath it. "I was Karen Zamora's roommate. Sondra Dickeson?"

Sondra Dickeson. She had had pale-blond hair that she wore in a pageboy, and a winter-white cashmere sweater and a matching white skirt with a kick pleat. She had worn it with black heels and a string of real pearls.

Sandy laughed. "You should see the expression on your face. You remember me now, don't you?"

"I'm sorry. I just didn't . . . I should have . . ."

"Listen, it's okay," she said. She took a sip of coffee. "At least you didn't say, 'How could you let yourself go like that?' like Janice Brubaker did." She bit into a cookie. "Well, aren't you going to ask me whatever became of Sondra Dickeson? It's a great story."

"What happened to her?" Elizabeth said. She felt suddenly colder. She poured herself another cup of coffee and sat back down, wrapping her hands around the cup for warmth.

Sandy finished the cookie and took another one. "Well, if you remember, I was kind of a snot in those days. I was going to this Sigma Chi dinner dance with Chuck Pagano. Do you remember him? Well, anyway, we were going to this dance clear out in the country somewhere, and he stopped the car and got all clutchy-grabby, and I got mad because he was messing up my hair and my makeup so I got out of the car. And he drove off. So there

I was, standing in the middle of nowhere in a formal and high heels. I hadn't even grabbed my purse or anything, and it's getting dark, and Sondra Dickeson is such a snot that it never even occurs to her to walk back to town or try to find a phone or something. No, she just stands there like an idiot in her brocade formal and her orchid corsage and her dyed satin pumps and thinks, 'He can't do this to me. Who does he think he is?' "

She was talking about herself as if she had been another person, which Elizabeth supposed she had been, an ice-blond with a pageboy and a formal like the one Elizabeth had loaned Tib for the Harvest Ball, a rust satin bodice and a bell skirt out of sculptured rust brocade. After the dance Elizabeth had given it to the Salvation Army.

"Did Chuck come back?" she said.

"Yes," Sandy said, frowning, and then grinned. "But not soon enough. Anyway, it's almost dark and along comes this truck with no lights on, and this guy leans out and says, 'Hiya, gorgeous Wanta ride?' " She smiled at her coffee cup as if she could still hear him saying it. "He was awful. His hair was down to his ears and his fingernails were black. He wiped his hand on his shirt and helped me up into the truck. He practically pulled my arm out of its socket, and then he said, 'I thought there for a minute I was going to have to go around behind and shove. You know, you're lucky I came along. I'm not usually out after dark on account of my lights being out, but I had a flat tire.' "

She's happy, Elizabeth thought, putting her hand over the top of her cup to try to warm herself with the steam.

"And he took me home and I thanked him and the next week he showed up at the Phi house and asked me out for a date, and I was so surprised that I went, and I married him, and we have four kids."

The furnace kicked on, and Elizabeth could feel the air coming out of the vent under the table, but it felt cold. "You went out with him?" she said.

"Hard to believe, isn't it? I mean, at that age all you can think about is your precious self. You're so worried about getting laughed at or getting hurt, you can't even see anybody else. When my sorority sister told me he was downstairs, all I could think of was how he must look, his hair all slicked back with water and cleaning those black fingernails with a penknife, and what everybody would say. I almost told her to tell him I wasn't there."

"What if you had done that?"

"I guess I'd still be Sondra Dickeson, the snot, a fate worse than death."

"A fate worse than death," Elizabeth said, almost to herself, but Sandy didn't hear her. She was plunging along, telling the story that she got to tell everytime somebody new moved to town, and no wonder she liked being alum rep.

"My sorority sister said, 'He's really got intestinal fortitude coming here like this, thinking you'd go out with him,' and I thought about him, sitting down there being laughed at, being hurt, and I told my roommate to go to hell and went downstairs and that was that." She looked at the kitchen clock. "Good lord, is it that late? I'm going to have to go pick up the kids pretty soon." She ran her finger down the hopelessly lost list. "How about Dallas Tindall, May Matsumoto, Ralph DeArvill?"

"No," Elizabeth said. "Is Tupper Hofwalt on that list?"

"Hofwalt." She flipped several pages over. "Was Tupper his real name?"

"No. Phillip. But everybody called him Tupper because he sold Tupperware."

She looked up. "I remember him. He had a Tupperware party in our dorm when I was a freshman." She flipped back to the Found section and started paging through it.

He had talked Elizabeth and Tib into having a Tupperware party in the dorm. "As co-hostesses you'll be eligible to earn points toward a popcorn popper," he had said. "You don't have to do anything except come up with some refreshments, and your mothers are always sending you cookies, right? And I'll owe you guys a favor."

They had had the party in the dorm lounge. Tupper pinned the names of famous people on their backs, and they had to figure out who they were by asking questions about themselves.

Elizabeth was Twiggy. "Am I a girl?" she asked Tib.

"Yes."

"Am I pretty?"

"Yes," Tupper had said before Tib could answer.

After she guessed it, she went over and stooped down next to the coffee table where Tupper was setting up his display of plastic bowls. "Do you really think Twiggy's pretty?" she asked.

"Who said anything about Twiggy?" he said. "Listen, I wanted to tell you . . ."

"Am I alive?" Sharon Oberhausen demanded.

"I don't know," Elizabeth said. "Turn around so I can see who you are."

The sign on her back said Mick Jagger.

"It's hard to tell," Tupper said.

Tib was King Kong. It had taken her forever to figure it out. "Am I tall?" she asked.

"Compared to what?" Elizabeth had said.

She stuck her hands on her hips. "I don't know. The Empire State Building."

"Yes," Tupper said.

He had had a hard time getting them to stop talking so he could show them his butter keeper and cake taker and popsicle makers. While they were filling out their order forms, Sharon Oberhausen said to Tib, "Do you have a date yet for the Harvest Ball?"

"Yes," Tib said.

"I wish I did," Sharon said. She leaned across Tib.

"Elizabeth, do you realize everybody in ROTC has to have a date or they put you on weekend duty? Who are you going with, Tib?"

"Listen, you guys," Tib said, "the more you buy, the better our chances at that popcorn popper, which we are willing to share."

They had bought a cake and chocolate-chip ice cream. Elizabeth cut the cake in the dorm's tiny kitchen while Tib dished it up.

"You didn't tell me you had a date to the Harvest Ball," Elizabeth said. "Who is it? That guy in your ed-psych class?"

"No." She dug into the ice cream with a plastic spoon.

"Who?"

Tupper came into the kitchen with a catalog. "You're only twenty points away from a popcorn popper," he said. "You know what you girls need?" He folded back a page and pointed to a white plastic box. "An ice-cream keeper. Holds a half gallon of ice cream, and when you want some, all you do is slide this tab out"—he pointed to a flat rectangle of plastic—"and cut off a slice. No more digging around in it and getting your hands all messy."

Tib licked ice cream off her knuckles. "That's the best part."

"Get out of here, Tupper," Elizabeth said. "Tib's trying to tell me who's taking her to the Harvest Ball."

Tupper closed the catalog. "I am."

"Oh," Elizabeth said. Sharon stuck her head around the corner. "Tupper, when do we have to pay for this stuff?" she said. "And when do we get something to eat?"

Tupper said, "You pay before you eat," and went back out to the lounge.

Elizabeth drew the plastic knife across the top of the cake, making perfectly straight lines in the frosting. When she had the cake divided into squares, she cut the corner piece and put it on the paper plate next to the melting ice cream. "Do you have anything to wear?" she said. "You can borrow my rust formal."

Sandy was looking at her, the thick notebook opened almost to the last page. "How well did you know Tupper?" she said.

Elizabeth's coffee was ice cold, but she put her hand over it, as if to try to catch the steam. "Not very well. He used to date Tib."

"He's on my deceased list, Elizabeth. He killed himself five years ago."

Paul didn't get home till after ten. Elizabeth was sitting on the couch wrapped in a blanket.

He went straight to the thermostat and turned it down. "How high do you have this thing turned up?" He squinted at it. "Eighty-five. Well, at least I don't have to worry about you freezing to death. Have you been sitting there like that all day?"

"The worm died," she said. "I didn't save it after all. I should have put it over on the grass."

"Ron Brubaker says there's an opening for a secretary in the dean's office. I told him you'd put in an application. You have, haven't you?"

"Yes," Elizabeth said. After Sandy left, she had taken the application out of her purse and sat down at the kitchen table to fill it out. She had had it nearly filled out before she realized it was a retirement fund withholding form.

"Sandy Konkel was here today," she said. "She met her husband on a dirt road. They were both there by chance. By chance. It wasn't even his route. Like the worm. Tib just walked by, she didn't even know she did it, but the worm was too near the edge, and it went over into the water and drowned." She started to cry. The tears felt cold running down her cheeks. "It drowned."

"What did you and Sandy Konkel do? Get out the cooking sherry and reminisce about old times?"

"Yes," she said. "Old times."

In the morning Elizabeth took back the retirement fund withholding form. It had rained off and on all night, and it had turned colder. There were patches of ice on the central walk.

"I had it almost all filled out before I realized what it was," she told the girl. A boy in a button-down shirt and khaki pants had been leaning on the counter when Elizabeth came in. The girl was turned away from the counter, filing papers.

"I don't know what you're so mad about," the boy had said, and then stopped and looked at Elizabeth. "You've got a customer," he said, and stepped away from the counter.

"All these dumb forms look alike," the girl said, handing the application to Elizabeth. She picked up a stack of books. "I've got a class. Did you need anything else?"

Elizabeth shook her head and stepped back so the boy could finish talking to her, but the girl didn't even look at him. She shoved the books into a backpack, slung it over her shoulder, and went out the door.

"Hey, wait a minute," the boy said, and started after her. By the time Elizabeth got outside, they were halfway up the walk. Elizabeth heard the boy say, "So I took her out once or twice. Is that a crime?"

The girl jerked the backpack out of his grip and started off down the walk toward Elizabeth's old dorm. In front of the dorm a girl in a yellow slicker was talking to another girl with short upswept blond hair. The girl in the slicker turned suddenly and started down the walk.

A boy went past Elizabeth on a bike, hitting her elbow and knocking the application out of her hand. She grabbed for it and got it before it landed on the walk.

"Sorry," he said without glancing back. He was wearing a jean jacket. Its sleeves were too short, and his bony wrists stuck out. He was steering the bike with one hand and holding a big plastic sack full of pink and green bowls in the other. That was what he had hit her with.

"Tupper," she said, and started to run after him.

She was down on the ice before she even knew she was going to fall, her hands splayed out against the sidewalk and one foot twisted under her. "Are you all right, ma'am?" the boy in the button-down shirt said. He knelt down in front of her so she couldn't see up the walk.

Tupper would call me "ma'am," too, she thought. He wouldn't even recognize me.

"You shouldn't try to run on this sidewalk. It's slicker than shit."

"I thought I saw somebody I knew."

He turned, balancing himself on the flat of one hand, and looked down the long walk. There was nobody there now. "What did they look like? Maybe I can still catch them."

"No," Elizabeth said. "He's long gone."

The girl came over. "Should I go call 911 or something?" she said.

"I don't know," he said to her, and then turned back to Elizabeth. "Can you stand up?" he said, and put his hand under her arm to help her. She tried to bring her foot out from its twisted position, but it wouldn't come. He tried again, from behind, both hands under her arms and hoisting her up, then holding her there by brute force till he could come around to her bad side. She leaned shamelessly against him, shivering.

"If you can get my books and this lady's purse, I think I can get her up to the infirmary," he said. "Do you think you can walk that far?"

"Yes," Elizabeth said, and put her arm around his neck. The girl picked up Elizabeth's purse and her job fund application.

"I used to go to school here. The central walk was heated back then." She couldn't put any weight on her foot at all. "Everything looks the same. Even the college kids. The girls wear skirts and sweaters just like we wore and those little flat shoes that never will stay on your feet, and the boys wear button-down shirts and jean jackets, and they look just like the boys I knew when I went here to school, and it isn't fair. I keep thinking I see people I used to know."

"I'll bet," the boy said politely. He shifted his weight, hefting her up so her arm was more firmly on his shoulder.

"I could maybe go get a wheelchair. I bet they'd loan me one," the girl said, sounding concerned.

"You know it can't be them, but it looks just like them, only you'll never see them again, never. You'll never even know what happened to them." She had thought she was getting hysterical, but instead her voice was getting softer and softer until her words seemed to fade away to nothing. She wondered if she had even said them aloud.

The boy got her up the stairs and into the infirmary.

"You shouldn't let them get away," she said.

"No," the boy said, and eased her onto the couch. "I guess you shouldn't."

"She slipped on the ice on the central walk," the girl told the receptionist. "I think maybe her ankle's broken. She's in a lot of pain." She came over to Elizabeth.

"I can stay with her," the boy said. "I know you've got a class."

She looked at her watch. "Yeah. Ed-psych. Are you sure you'll be all right?" she said to Elizabeth.

"I'm fine. Thank you for all your help, both of you."

"Do you have a way to get home?" the boy said.

"I'll call my husband to come and get me. There's really no reason for either of you to stay. I'm fine. Really."

"Okay," the boy said. He stood up. "Come on," he said to the girl. "I'll walk you to class and explain to old

Harrigan that you were being an angel of mercy." He took the girl's arm, and she smiled up at him.

They left, and the receptionist brought Elizabeth a clipboard with some forms on it. "They were having a fight," Elizabeth said.

"Well, I'd say whatever it was about, it's over now."

"Yes," Elizabeth said. Because of me. Because I fell down on the ice.

"I used to live in this dorm," Elizabeth said. "This was the lounge."

"Oh," the receptionist said. "I bet it's changed a lot since then."

"No," Elizabeth said. "It's just the same."

Where the reception desk was, there had been a table with a phone on it where they had checked in and out of the dorm, and along the far wall the couch that she and Tib had sat on at the Tupperware party. Tupper had been sitting on it in his tuxedo when she came down to go to the library.

The receptionist was looking at her. "I bet it hurts," she said.

"Yes," Elizabeth said.

She had planned to be at the library when Tupper came, but he was half an hour early. He stood up when he saw her on the stairs and said, "I tried to call you this afternoon. I wondered if you wanted to go study at the library tomorrow." He had brought Tib a corsage in a white box. He came over and stood at the foot of the stairs, holding the box in both hands.

"I'm studying at the library tonight," Elizabeth said, and walked down the stairs past him, afraid he would put his hand out to stop her, but they were full of the corsage box. "I don't think Tib's ready yet."

"I know. I came early because I wanted to talk to you."

"You'd better call her so she'll know you're here," she said, and walked out the door. She hadn't even checked out, which could have gotten her in trouble with the dorm mother. She found out later that Tib had done it for her.

The receptionist stood up. "I'm going to see if Dr. Larenson can't see you right now," she said. "You are obviously in a lot of pain."

Her ankle was sprained. The doctor wrapped it in an Ace bandage. Halfway through, the phone rang, and he left her sitting on the examining table with her foot propped up while he took the call.

The day after the dance Tupper had called her. "Tell him I'm not here," Elizabeth had told Tib.

"You tell him," Tib had said, and stuck the phone at her, and she had taken the receiver and said, "I don't want to talk to you, but Tib's here. I'm sure she does," and handed the phone back to Tib and walked out of the room. She was halfway across campus before Tib caught up with her.

It had turned colder in the night, and there was a sharp wind that blew the dead leaves across the grass. Tib had brought Elizabeth her coat.

"Thank you," Elizabeth said, and put it on.

"At least you're not totally stupid," Tib said. "Almost, though."

Elizabeth jammed her hands deep in the pockets. "What did Tupper have to say? Did he ask you out again? To one of his Tupperware parties?"

"He didn't ask me out. I asked him to the Harvest Ball because I needed a date. They put you on weekend duty if you didn't have a date, so I asked him. And then after I did it, I was afraid you wouldn't understand."

"Understand what?" Elizabeth said. "You can date whoever you want."

"I don't want to date Tupper, and you know it. If you don't stop acting this way, I'm going to get another roommate."

And she had said, without any idea how important

little things like that could be, how hanging up a phone or having a flat tire or saying something could splash out in all directions and sweep you over the edge, she had said, "Maybe you'd better do just that."

They had lived in silence for two weeks. Sharon Oberhausen's roommate didn't come back after Thanksgiving, and Tib moved in with her until the end of the quarter. Then Elizabeth pledged Alpha Phi and moved into the sorority house.

The doctor came back and finished wrapping her ankle. "Do you have a ride home? I'm going to give you a pair of crutches. I don't want you walking on this any more than absolutely necessary."

"No, I'll call my husband." The doctor helped her off the table and onto the crutches. He walked back out to the waiting room and punched buttons on the phone so she could make an outside call.

She dialed her own number and told the ringing to come pick her up. "He'll be over in a minute," she told the receptionist. "I'll wait outside for him."

The receptionist helped her through the door and down the steps. She went back inside, and Elizabeth went out and stood on the curb, looking up at the middle window.

After Tupper took Tib to the Angel Flight dance, he had come and thrown things at her window. She would see them in the mornings when she went to class, plastic jar openers and grapefruit slicers and kitchen scrubber holders, scattered on the lawn and the sidewalk. She had never opened the window, and after a while he had stopped coming.

Elizabeth looked down at the grass. At first she couldn't find the worm. She parted the grass with the tip of her crutch, standing on her good foot. It was there, where she had put it, shrivelled now and darker red, almost black. It was covered with ice crystals.

Elizabeth looked in the front window at the receptionist. When she got up to go file Elizabeth's chart, Elizabeth crossed the street and walked home.

The walk home had made Elizabeth's ankle swell so badly, she could hardly move by the time Paul came home.

"What's the matter with you?" he said angrily. "Why didn't you call me?" He looked at his watch. "Now it's too late to call Brubaker. He and his wife were going to dinner. I suppose you don't feel like going to the concert."

"No," Elizabeth said. "I'll go."

He turned down the thermostat without looking at it. "What in the hell were you doing anyway?"

"I thought I saw a boy I used to know. I was trying to catch up to him."

"A boy you used to know?" Paul said disbelievingly. "In college? What's he doing here? Still waiting to graduate?"

"I don't know," Elizabeth said. She wondered if Sandy ever saw herself on the campus, dressed in the winter-white sweater and pearls, standing in front of her sorority house talking to Chuck Pagano. She's not there, Elizabeth thought. Sandy had not said, "Tell him I'm not here." She had not said, "Maybe you'd better just do that," and because of that and a flat tire, Sondra Dickeson isn't trapped on the campus, waiting to be rescued. Like they are.

"You don't even realize what this little move of yours has cost, do you?" Paul said. "Brubaker told me this afternoon he'd gotten you the job in the dean's office."

He took off the Ace bandage and looked at her ankle. She had gotten the bandage wet walking home. He went to look for another one. He came back carrying the wrinkled job application. "I found this in the bureau drawer. You told me you turned your application in."

"It fell in the gutter," she said.

"Why didn't you throw it away?"

"I thought it might be important," she said, and hobbled over on her crutches and took it away from him.

They were late to the concert because of her ankle, so they didn't get to sit with the Brubakers, but afterward they came over. Dr. Brubaker introduced his wife.

"I'm so sorry about this," Janice Brubaker said. "Ron's been telling them for years they should get that central walk fixed. It used to be heated." She was the woman Sandy had pointed at at the Tupperware party and said was Janice who loved Jesus. She was wearing a dark-red suit and had her hair teased into a bouffant, the way girls had worn their hair when Elizabeth was in college. "It was so nice of you to ask us over, but of course now with your ankle we understand."

"No," Elizabeth said. "We want you to come. I'm doing great, really. It's just a little sprain."

The Brubakers had to go to talk to someone backstage. Paul told the Brubakers how to get to their house and took Elizabeth outside. Because they were late, there hadn't been anyplace to park. Paul had had to park up by the infirmary. Elizabeth said she thought she could walk as far as the car, but it took them fifteen minutes to make it three fourths of the way up the walk.

"This is ridiculous," Paul said angrily, and strode off up the walk to get the car.

She hobbled slowly on up to the end of the walk and sat down on one of the cement benches that had been vents for the heating system. Elizabeth had worn a wool dress and her warmest coat, but she was still cold. She laid her crutches against the bench and looked across at her old dorm.

Someone was standing in front of the dorm, looking up at the middle window. He looked cold. He had his hands jammed in his jean-jacket pockets, and after a few minutes he pulled something out of one of the pockets and threw it at the window.

It's no good, Elizabeth thought, she won't come.

He had made one last attempt to talk to her. It was spring quarter. It had been raining again. The walk was covered with worms. Tib was wearing her Angel Flight uniform, and she looked cold.

Tib had stopped Elizabeth after she came out of the dorm and said, "I saw Tupper the other day. He asked about you, and I told him you were living in the Alpha Phi house."

"Oh," Elizabeth had said, and tried to walk past her, but Tib had kept her there, talking as if nothing had happened, as if they were still roommates. "I'm dating this guy in ROTC. Jim Scates. He's gorgeous!" she had said, as if they were still friends.

"I'm going to be late for class," she said. Tib glanced nervously down the walk, and Elizabeth looked, too, and saw Tupper bearing down on them on his bike. "Thanks a lot," she said angrily.

"He just wants to talk to you."

"About what? How he's taking you to the Alpha Sig dinner dance?" she had said, and turned and walked back into the dorm before he could catch up to her. He had called her on the dorm phone for nearly half an hour, but she hadn't answered, and after a while he had given up.

But he hadn't given up. He was still there, under her windows, throwing grapefruit slicers and egg separators at her, and she still, after all these years, wouldn't come to the window. He would stand there forever, and she would never, never come.

She stood up. The rubber tip of one of her crutches skidded on the ice under the bench, and she almost fell. She steadied herself against the hard cement bench.

Paul honked and pulled over beside the curb, his turn lights flashing. He got out of the car. "The Brubakers are already going to be there, for God's sake," he said. He took the crutches away from her and hurried her to the car, his hand jammed under her armpit. When they pulled away, the boy was still there, looking up at the window, waiting.

The Brubakers were there, waiting in the driveway. Paul left her in the car while he unlocked the door. Dr. Brubaker opened the car door for her and tried to help her with her crutches. Janice kept saying, "Oh, really, we would have understood." They both stood back, looking helpless, while Elizabeth hobbled into the house.

Janice offered to make the coffee, and Elizabeth let her, sitting at the kitchen table, her coat still on. Paul had set out the cups and saucers and the plate of cookies before they left.

"You were at the Tupperware party, weren't you?" Janice said, opening the cupboards to look for the coffee filters. "I never really got a chance to meet you. I saw Sandy Konkel had her hooks in you."

"At the party you said you like Jesus," Elizabeth said. "Are you a Christian?"

Janice had been peeling off a paper filter. She stopped and looked hard at Elizabeth. "Yes," she said. "I am. You know, Sandy Konkel told me a Tupperware party was no place for religion, and I told her that any place was the place for a Christian witness. And I was right, because that witness spoke to you, didn't it, Elizabeth?"

"What if you did something, a long time ago, and you found out it had ruined everything?"

"'For behold your sin will find you out,' " Janice said, holding the coffeepot under the faucet.

"I'm not talking about sin," Elizabeth said. "I'm talking about little things that you wouldn't think would matter so much, like stepping in a puddle or having a fight with somebody. What if you drove off and left somebody standing in the road because you were mad, and it changed their whole life, it made them into a different person? Or what if you turned and walked away from somebody because your feelings were hurt or you wouldn't open your window, and because of that one little thing their whole lives were changed and now she drinks too much, and he killed himself, and you didn't even know you did it."

Janice had opened her purse and started to get out a Bible. She stopped with the Bible only half out of the purse and stared at Elizabeth. "You made somebody kill himself?"

"No," Elizabeth said. "I didn't make him kill himself and I didn't make her get a divorce, but if I hadn't turned and walked away from them that day, everything would have been different."

"Divorce?" Janice said.

"Sandy was right. When you're young all you think about is yourself. All I could think about was how much prettier she was and how she was the kind of girl who had dozens of dates, and when he asked her out, I thought that he'd liked her all along, and I was so hurt. I threw away the egg separator, I was so hurt, and that's why I wouldn't talk to him that day, but I didn't know it was so important! I didn't know there was a puddle there and it was going to sweep me over into the gutter."

Janice laid the Bible on the table. "I don't know what you've done, Elizabeth, but whatever it is, Our Lord can forgive you. I want to read you something." She opened the Bible at a cross-shaped bookmark. "'For God so loved the world that He gave his only begotten Son that whosoever believeth in Him should not perish, but have everlasting life.' Jesus, God's own son, died on a cross and rose again so we could be forgiven for our sins."

"What if he didn't?" Elizabeth said impatiently. "What if he just lay there in the tomb getting colder and colder, until ice crystals formed on him and he never knew if he'd saved them or not?"

"Is the coffee ready yet?" Paul said, coming into the kitchen with Dr. Brubaker. "Or did you womenfolk get to talking and forget all about it?"

"What if they were waiting here for Jesus to save them, they'd been waiting for him all those years and he didn't know it? He'd have to try to save them, wouldn't he? He couldn't just leave them there, standing in the cold looking up at her window? And maybe he couldn't. Maybe they'd get a divorce or kill themselves anyway." Her teeth had started to chatter. "Even if he did save them, he wouldn't be able to save himself. Because it was too late. He was already dead."

Paul moved around the table to her. Janice was paging through the Bible, looking frantically for the right scripture. Paul took hold of Elizabeth's arm, but she shook it off impatiently. "In Matthew we see that he was raised from the dead and is alive today. Right now," Janice said, sounding frightened. "And no matter what sin you have in your heart, he will forgive you if you accept him as your personal Savior."

Elizabeth brought her fist down hard on the table so that the plate of cookies shook. "I'm not talking about sin. I'm talking about opening a window. She stepped in the puddle and the worm went over the edge and drowned. I shouldn't have left it on the sidewalk." She hit the table with her fist again. Dr. Brubaker picked up the stack of coffee cups and put them on the counter, as if he were afraid she might start throwing them at the wall. "I should have put it in the grass."

Paul left for work without even having breakfast. Elizabeth's ankle had swollen up so badly she could hardly get her slippers on, but she got up and made the coffee. The filters were still lying on the counter where Janice Brubaker had left them.

"Weren't you satisfied that you'd ruined your chances for a job, you had to ruin mine, too?"

"I'm sorry about last night," she said. "I'm going to fill out my job application today and take it over to the campus. When my ankle heals . . ."

"It's supposed to warm up today," Paul said. "I turned the furnace off."

After he was gone, she filled out the application. She tried to erase the dark smear that the worm had left, but it wouldn't come out, and there was one question that she couldn't read. Her fingers were stiff with cold, and she had to stop and blow on them several times but she filled in as many questions as she could and folded it up and took it over to the campus.

The girl in the yellow slicker was standing at the end of the walk, talking to a girl in an Angel Flight uniform. She hobbled toward them with her head down, trying to hurry, listening for the sound of Tupper's bike.

"He asked about you," Tib said, and Elizabeth looked up.

She didn't look at all the way Elizabeth remembered her. She was a little overweight and not very pretty, the kind of girl who wouldn't have been able to get a date for the dance. Her short hair made her round face look even plumper. She looked hopeful and a little worried.

Don't worry, Elizabeth thought. I'm here. She didn't look at herself. She concentrated on getting up even with them at the right time.

"I told him you were living in the Alpha Phi house," Tib said.

"Oh," she heard her own voice, and under it the hum of a bicycle.

"I'm dating this guy in ROTC. He's absolutely gorgeous!"

There was a pause, and then Elizabeth's voice said, "Thanks a lot," and Elizabeth pushed the rubber end of her crutch against a patch of ice and went down.

For a minute she couldn't see anything for the pain. "I've broken it," she thought, and clenched her fists to keep from screaming.

"Are you all right?" Tib said, kneeling in front of her so she couldn't see anything. No, not you! Not you! For a minute she was afraid that it hadn't worked, that the girl had turned and walked away. But after all, this was not a stranger but only herself, who was too kind to let a worm drown. She had only gone around to Elizabeth's other side, where she couldn't see her. "Did she break it?" she said. "Should I go call an ambulance or something?"

No. "No," Elizabeth said. "I'm fine. If you could just help me up."

The girl who had been Elizabeth Wilson put her books down on the cement bench and came and knelt down by Elizabeth. "I hope we don't collapse in a heap," she said, and smiled at Elizabeth. She was a pretty girl. I didn't know that either, Elizabeth thought, even when Tupper told me. She took hold of Elizabeth's arm and Tib took hold of the other.

"Tripping innocent passersby again, I see. How many times have I told you not to do that?" And here, finally, was Tupper. He had laid his bike flat in the grass and put his bag of Tupperware beside it.

Tib and the girl that had been herself let go and stepped back and he knelt beside her. "They're not bad girls, really. They just like to play practical jokes. But banana peels is going too far, girls," he said, so close she could feel his warm breath on her cheek. She turned to look at him, suddenly afraid that he would be different, too, but it was only Tupper, who she had loved all these years. He put his arm around her. "Now just put your arm around my neck, sweetheart. That's right. Elizabeth, come over here and atone for your sins by helping this pretty lady up."

She had already picked her books up and was holding them against her chest, looking angry and eager to get away. She looked at Tib, but Tib was picking up the crutches, stooping down in her high heels because she couldn't bend over in her Angel Flight skirt.

She put her books down again and came around to Elizabeth's other side to take hold of her arm, and Elizabeth grabbed for her hand instead and held it tightly so she couldn't get away. "I took her to the dance because she helped with the Tupperware party. I told her I owed her a favor," he said, and Elizabeth turned and looked at him.

He was not looking at her really. He was looking past her at the other Elizabeth, who would not answer the phone, who would not come to the window, but he seemed to be looking at her, and on his young remembered face there was a look of such naked, vulnerable love that it was like a blow.

"I told you so," Tib said. She laid the crutches against the bench.

"I'm sure this lady doesn't want to hear this," Elizabeth said.

"I was going to tell you at the party, but that idiot Sharon Oberhausen . . ."

Tib brought over the crutches. "After I asked him, I thought, 'What if she thinks I'm trying to steal her boyfriend?' and I got so worried I was afraid to tell you. I really only asked him to get out of weekend duty. I mean, I don't like him or anything."

Tupper grinned at Elizabeth. "I try to pay my debts, and this is the thanks I get. You wouldn't get mad at me if I took your roommate to a dance, would you?"

"I might," Elizabeth said. It was cold sitting on the cement. She was starting to shiver. "But I'd forgive you."

"You see that?" he said.

"I see," Elizabeth said disgustedly, but she was smiling at him now. "Don't you think we'd better get this innocent passerby up off the sidewalk before she freezes to death?"

"Upsy-daisy, sweetheart," Tupper said, and in one easy motion she was up and sitting on the stone bench.

"Thank you," she said. Her teeth were chattering with the cold.

Tupper knelt in front of her and examined her ankle.

"It looks pretty swollen," he said. "Do you want us to call somebody?"

"No, my husband will be along any minute. I'll just sit here till he comes."

Tib fished Elizabeth's application out of the puddle. "I'm afraid it's ruined," she said.

"It doesn't matter."

Tupper picked up his bag of bowls. "Say," he said, "you wouldn't be interested in having a Tupperware party? As hostess, you could earn valuable points toward . . ."

"Tupper!" Tib said.

"Will you leave this poor lady alone?" Elizabeth said.

He held up the sack. "Only if you'll go with me to deliver my lettuce crispers to the Sigma Chi house."

"I'll go," Tib said. "There's this darling Sigma Chi I've been wanting to meet."

"And I'll go," Elizabeth said, putting her arm around Tib. "I don't trust the kind of boyfriend you find on your own. Jim Scates is a real creep. Didn't Sharon tell you what he did to Marilyn Reed?"

Tupper handed Elizabeth the sack of bowls while he stood his bike up. Elizabeth handed them to Tib.

"Are you sure you're all right?" Tupper said. "It's cold out here. You could wait for your husband in the student union."

She wished she could put her hand on his cheek just once. "I'll be fine," she said.

The three of them went down the walk toward Frasier, Tupper pushing the bike. When they got even with Carter Hall, they cut across the grass toward Frasier. She watched them until she couldn't see them anymore, and then sat there a while longer on the cold bench. She had hoped that something might happen, some sign that she had rescued them, but nothing happened. Her ankle didn't hurt anymore. It had stopped the minute Tupper touched it.

She continued to sit there. It seemed to her to be getting colder, though she had stopped shivering, and after a while she got up and walked home, leaving the crutches where they were.

It was cold in the house. Elizabeth turned the thermostat up and sat down at the kitchen table, still in her coat, waiting for the heat to come on. When it didn't, she remembered that Paul had turned the furnace off, and she went and got a blanket and wrapped up in it on the couch. Her ankle did not hurt at all, though it felt cold. When the phone rang, she could hardly move it. It took her several rings to make it to the phone.

"I thought you weren't going to answer," Paul said. "I made an appointment with a Dr. Jamieson for you this afternoon at three. He's a psychiatrist."

"Paul," she said. She was so cold it was hard to talk. "I'm sorry."

"It's a little late for that, isn't it?" he said. "I told Dr. Brubaker you were on muscle relaxants for your ankle. I don't know whether he bought it or not." He hung up.

"Too late," Elizabeth said. She hung up the phone. The back of her hand was covered with ice crystals. "Paul," she tried to say, but her lips were stiff with cold, and no sound came out.

THESE ARE THE BEST AND WORST OF TIMES FOR WRIT*ing comedy. On the one hand, there's plenty of material out there. If you don't believe me, tune in Oprah-Sally-Phil-Geraldo for a few days. (Last week they had strippers who'd been separated at birth, Elvis's diet specialist, and women whose husbands don't listen to them.) On the other hand, nobody has a sense of humor.*

You're not supposed to laugh at global warming or low self-esteem or cholesterol. This is the age of political correctness, a movement devoted to the stamping out of "inappropriate laughter," and the battle cry of every anti-(choose one: smoking, animal research, logging, abortion, Columbus) activist seems to be, "That's not *funny. These are serious issues."*

Of course, seriousness and self-importance are what comedy is all about—tragedy, too. Does the word "hubris" ring a bell?—and I feel it's my bounden duty to laugh at them. Besides, it's fun sitting up here on the fence taking potshots at Newspeak and predators and faculty teas. As Jane Austen (a regular Annie Oakley when it comes to fancy shooting) says, "For what do we live, but to make sport of our neighbors, and laugh at them in our turn?"

And it's either that, or cry. Or scream.

In the Late Cretaceous

"It was in the late Cretaceous that predators reached their full flowering," Dr. Othniel said. "Of course, carnivorous dinosaurs were present from the Middle Triassic on, but it was in the Late Cretaceous, with the arrival of the albertosaurus, the velociraptor, the deinonychus, and of course, the tyrannosaurus rex, that the predatory dinosaur reached its full strength, speed, and sophistication."

Dr. Othniel wrote "LATE CRETACEOUS—PREDATORS" on the board. He suffered from arthritis and a tendency to stoop, and the combination made him write only on the lower third of the chalkboard. He wrote "ALBERTOSAURUS, COELOPHYSIS, VELOCIRAPTOR, DEINONYCHUS, TYRANNOSAURUS REX," in a column under "LATE CRETACEOUS—PREDATORS," which put "TYRANNOSAURUS REX" just above the chalk tray.

"Of all these," Dr. Othniel said, "tyrannosaurus rex is the most famous, and deservedly so."

Dr. Othniel's students wrote in their notebooks "#1 LC. predator TRX" or "No predators in the Late Cretaceous" or "I have a new roommate. Her name is Traci.

Signed, Deanna." One of them composed a lengthy letter protesting the unfairness of his parking tickets.

"This flowering of the predators was partly due to the unprecedented abundance of prey. Herbivores such as the triceratops, the chasmosaurus, and the duck-billed hadrosaur roamed the continents in enormous herds."

He had to move an eraser so he could write "PREY—HADROSAURS" under "TYRANNOSAURUS REX." His students wrote "Pray—duck-billed platypus," and "My new roommate Traci has an absolutely *wow* boyfriend named Todd," and "If you think I'm going to pay this ticket, you're crazy!"

"The hadrosaurs were easy prey. They had no horns or bony frills like the triceratops," he said. "They did, however, have large bony crests, which may have been used to trumpet warnings to each other or to hear or smell the presence of predators." He squeezed "HOLLOW BONY CREST" in under "HADROSAURS" and raised his head, as if he had heard something.

One of his sophomores, who was writing "I don't even have a car," glanced toward the door, but there wasn't anyone there.

Dr. Othniel straightened, vertebra by vertebra, until the top of his bald head was nearly even with the top of the blackboard. He lifted his chin, as if he were sniffing the air, and then bent over again, frowning. "Warnings, however, were not enough against the fifty-foot-tall tyrannosaurus rex, with his five-foot-long jaws and seven-inch-long teeth," he said. He wrote "JAWS—5 FT., TEETH—7 IN." down among the erasers.

His students wrote "The Parking Authority is run by a bunch of Nazis," and "Deanna + Todd," and "TRX had five feet."

After her Advanced Antecedents class, Dr. Sarah Wright collected her mail and took it to her office. There was a manila envelope from the State Department of Education, a letter from the Campus Parking Authority marked "Third Notice: Pay Your Outstanding Tickets Immediately," and a formal-looking square envelope from the dean's office, none of which she wanted to open.

She had no outstanding parking tickets, the legislature was going to cut state funding of universities by another eighteen percent, and the letter from the dean was probably notifying her that the entire amount was going to come out of Paleontology's hide.

There was also a stapled brochure from a flight school she had written to during spring break after she had graded 143 papers, none of which had gotten off the ground. The brochure had an eagle, some clouds, and the header "Do you ever just want to get away from it all?"

She pried the staple free and opened it. "Do you ever get, like, fed up with your job and want to blow it off?" it read. "Do you ever feel like you just want to bag everything and do something really neat instead?"

It went on in this vein, which reminded her of her students' papers, for several illustrated paragraphs before it got down to hard facts, which were that the Lindbergh Flight Academy charged three thousand dollars for their course, "including private, commercial, instrument, CFI, CFII, written tests, and flight tests. Lodging extra. Not responsible for injuries, fatalities, or other accidents."

She wondered if the "other accidents" covered budget cuts from the legislature.

Her TA, Chuck, came in, eating a Twinkie and waving a formal-looking square envelope. "Did you get one of these?" he asked.

"Yes," Sarah said, picking up hers. "I was just going to open it. What is it, an invitation to a slaughter?"

"No, a reception for some guy. The dean's having it this afternoon. In the Faculty Library."

Sarah looked at the invitation suspiciously. "I thought the dean was at an educational conference."

"She's back."

Sarah tore open the envelope and pulled out the invitation. "The dean cordially invites you to a reception for Dr. Jerry King," she muttered. "Dr. Jerry King?" She opened the manila envelope and scanned through the legislature report, looking for his name. "Who is he, do you know?"

"Nope."

At least he wasn't one of the budget-cut supporters. His name wasn't on the list. "Did the rest of the department get these?"

"I don't know. Othniel got one. I saw it in his box," Chuck said. "I don't think he can reach it. His box is on the top row."

Dr. Robert Walker came in, waving a piece of paper. "Look at this! Another ticket for not having a parking sticker! I have a parking sticker! I have two parking stickers! One on the bumper and one on the windshield. Why can't they see them?"

"Did you get one of these, Robert?" Sarah asked, showing him the invitation. "The dean's having a reception this afternoon. Is it about the funding cuts?"

"I don't know," Robert said. "They're right there in plain sight. I even drew an arrow in Magic Marker to the one on the bumper."

"The legislature's cut our funding again," Sarah said. "I'll bet you anything the dean's going to eliminate a position. She was over here last week looking at our enrollment figures."

"The whole university's enrollment is down," Robert said, going over to the window and looking out. "Nobody can afford to go to college anymore, especially when it costs eighty dollars a semester for a parking sticker. Not that the stickers do any good. You still get parking tickets."

"We've got to fight this," Sarah said. "If she eliminates one of our positions, we'll be the smallest department on campus, and the next thing you know, we'll have been merged with Geology. We've got to organize the department and put up a fight. Do you have any ideas, Robert?"

"You know," Robert said, still looking out the window, "maybe if I posted someone out by my car—"

"Your car?"

"Yeah. I could hire a student to sit on the back bumper, and when the Parking Authority comes by, he could point to the sticker. It would cost a lot, but—Stop that!" he shouted suddenly. He wrenched the window open and leaned out. "You can't give me a parking ticket!" he shouted down at the parking lot. "I have two stickers! What are you, blind?" He pulled his head in and bolted out of the office and down the stairs, yelling, "They just gave me another ticket! Can you believe that?"

"No," Sarah said. She picked up the flight-school brochure and looked longingly at the picture of the eagle.

"Do you think they'll have food?" Chuck said. He was looking at the dean's invitation.

"I hope not," Sarah said.

"Why not?"

"Grazing," she said. "The big predators always attack when the hadrosaurs are grazing."

"If they do have food, what kind do you think they'll have?" Chuck asked wistfully.

"It depends," Sarah said, turning the brochure over. "Tea and cookies, usually."

"Homemade?"

"Not unless there's bad news. Cheese and crackers means somebody's getting the ax. Liver pâté means a budget cut. Of course, if the budget cut's big enough, there won't be any money for refreshments."

On the back of the brochure it said in italics "*Become Upwardly Mobile,*" and underneath, in boldface:

FAA-APPROVED
TUITION WAIVERS AVAILABLE
FREE PARKING

• • •

"There have been radical changes in our knowledge of the dinosaurs over the past few years," Dr. Albertson said, holding the micropaleontology textbook up, "so radical that what came before is obsolete." He opened the book to the front. "Turn to the introduction."

His students opened their books, which had cost $64.95.

"Have you all turned to the introduction?" Dr. Albertson asked, taking hold of the top corner of the first page. "Good. Now tear it out." He ripped out the page. "It's useless, completely archaic."

Actually, although there had been some recent revisions in theories regarding dinosaur behavior and physiology, particularly in the larger predators, there hadn't been any at all at the microscopic level. But Dr. Albertson had seen Robin Williams do this in a movie and been very impressed.

His students, who had been hoping to sell them back to the university bookstore for $32.47, were less so. One of them asked hopefully, "Can't we just promise not to read it?"

"Absolutely not," Dr. Albertson said, yanking out a handful of pages. "Come on. Tear them out."

He threw the pages in a metal wastebasket and held the wastebasket out to a marketing minor who was quietly tucking the torn-out pages into the back of the book with an eye to selling it as a pre-edited version. "That's right, all of them," Dr. Albertson said. "Every outdated, old-fashioned page."

Someone knocked on the door. He handed the wastebasket to the marketing minor and left the slaughter to open it. It was Sarah Wright with a squarish envelope.

"There's a reception for the dean this afternoon," she said. "We need the whole department there."

"Do we have to tear out the title page, too?" a psychology minor asked.

"The legislature's just cut funding another eighteen

percent, and I'm afraid they're going to try to eliminate one of our positions."

"You can count on my support one hundred percent," he said.

"Good," Sarah said, sighing with relief. "As long as we stick together, we've got a chance."

Dr. Albertson shut the door behind her, glancing at his watch. He had planned to stand on his desk before the end of class, but now there wouldn't be time. He had to settle for the inspirational coda.

"Ostracods, diatoms, fusilinids, these are what we stay alive for," he said. "Carpe diem! Seize the day!"

The psych minor raised his hand. "Can I borrow your Scotch tape?" he asked. "I accidentally tore out Chapters One and Two."

There was brie at the reception. And sherry and spinach puffs and a tray of strawberries with cellophane-flagged toothpicks stuck like daggers into them. Sarah took a strawberry and a rapid head count of the department. Everyone else seemed to be there except Robert, who was probably parking his car, and Dr. Othniel.

"Did you make sure Dr. Othniel saw his invitation?" she asked her TA, who was eating strawberries two at a time.

"Yeah," Chuck said with his mouth full. "He's here." He gestured with his plate toward a high-backed wing chair by the fire.

Sarah went over and checked. Dr. Othniel was asleep. She went back over to the table and had another strawberry. She wondered which one was Dr. King. There were only three men she didn't recognize. Two of them were obviously Physics Department—they were making a fusion reactor out of a Styrofoam cup and several of the fancy toothpicks. The third looked likely. He was tall and distinguished and was wearing a tweed jacket with patches on the elbows, but after a few minutes he disappeared into the kitchen and came back with a tray of liver pâté and crackers.

Robert came in, carrying his suit jacket and looking out of breath. "You will *not* believe what happened to me," he said.

"You got a parking ticket," Sarah said. "Were you able to find out anything about this Dr. King?"

"He's an educational consultant," Robert said. "What *is* the point of spending eighty dollars a semester for a parking sticker when there are never any places to park in the permit lots? You know where I had to park? Behind the football stadium! That's five blocks farther away than my house!"

"An educational consultant?" Sarah said. "What's the dean up to?" She stared thoughtfully at her strawberry. "An educational consultant . . ."

"Author of *What's Wrong with Our Entire Educational System*," Dr. Albertson said. He took a plate and put a spinach puff on it. "He's an expert on restructionary implementation."

"What's that?" Chuck said, making a sandwich out of the liver pâté and two bacon balls.

Dr. Albertson looked superior. "Surely they teach you graduate assistants about restructionary implementation," he said, which meant he didn't know either. He took a bite of spinach puff. "You should try these," he said. "I was just talking to the dean. She told me she made them herself."

"We're dead," Sarah said.

"There's Dr. King now," Dr. Albertson said, pointing to a lumbering man wearing a polo shirt and Sansabelt slacks.

The dean went over to greet him, clasping his hands in hers. "Sorry I'm late," he boomed out. "I couldn't find a parking place so I parked out in front."

Dr. Othniel suddenly emerged from the wing chair, looking wildly around. Sarah beckoned to him with her toothpick, and he stooped his way over to them, sat down next to the brie, and went back to sleep.

The dean moved to the center of the room and clapped her hands for attention. Dr. Othniel jerked at the sound. "I don't want to interrupt the fun," the dean said, "And *please*, do go on eating and drinking, but I just wanted you all to meet Dr. Jerry King. Dr. King will be working with the Paleontology Department on something I'm sure you'll all find terribly exciting. Dr. King, would you like to say a few words?"

Dr. King smiled, a large friendly grin that reminded Sarah of the practice jaw in Field Techniques. "We all know the tremendous impactization technology has had on our modern society," he said.

"Impactization?" Chuck said, eating a lemon tart the distinguished-looking gentleman had just brought out from the kitchen. "I thought 'impact' was a verb."

"It is," Sarah said. "And once, back in the Late Cretaceous, it was a noun."

"Shh," Dr. Albertson said, looking disapproving.

"As we move into the twenty-first century, our society is transformizing radically, but is education? No. We are still teaching the same old subjects in the same old ways." He smiled at the dean. "Until today. Today marks the beginning of a wonderful innovationary experiment in education, a whole new instructionary dynamic in teaching paleontology. I'll be thinktanking with you dinosaur guys and gals next week, but until then I want you to think about one word."

"Extinction," Sarah murmured.

"That word is 'relevantness.' Does paleontology have relevantness to our modern society? How can we *make* it have relevantness? Think about it. Relevantness."

There was a spattering of applause from the departments Dr. King would not be thinktanking with. Robert poured a large glass of sherry and drank it down. "It's not fair," he said. "First the Parking Authority and now this."

"Pilots make a lot of money," Sarah said. "And the only word they have to think about is 'crash.' "

Dr. Albertson raised his hand.

"Yes?" the dean asked.

"I just wanted Dr. King to know," he said, "that he can count on my support one hundred percent."

"Are you supposed to eat this white crust thing on the cheese?" Chuck asked.

Dr. King put a memo in the Paleontology Department's boxes the next day. It read "Group ideating session next Mon. Dr. Wright's office. 2 P.M. J. King. P.S. I will be doing observational datatizing this Tues. and Thurs."

"We'll all do some observational datatizing," Sarah said, even more alarmed by Dr. King's preempting her office without asking her than by the brie.

She went to find her TA, who was in her office eating a Snickers. "I want you to go find out about Dr. King's background," she told him.

"Why?"

"Because he used to be a junior-high girl's basketball coach. Maybe we can get some dirt on him and one of his seventh grade forwards."

"How do you know he used to be a junior-high coach?"

"All educational consultants used to be junior-high coaches. Or social-studies teachers." She looked at the memo disgustedly. "What do you suppose observational datatizing consists of?"

Observational datatizing consisted of wandering around the halls of the Earth Sciences building with a clipboard listening to Dr. Albertson.

"Okay, how much you got?" Dr. Albertson was saying to his class. He was wearing a butcher's apron and a paper fast-food hat and was cutting apples into halves, quarters, and thirds with a cleaver, which had nothing to do with depauperate fauna, but which he had seen Edward James Olmos do in *Stand and Deliver*. He had been very impressed.

"Yip, that'll do it," he was saying in an Hispanic accent when Dr. King appeared suddenly at the back of the room with his clipboard.

"But the key question here is *relevantness*," Dr. Albertson said hastily. "How do the depauperate fauna affectate on our lives today?"

His students looked wary. One of them crossed his arms protectively over his textbook as though he thought he was going to be asked to tear out more pages.

"Depauperate fauna have a great deal of relevantness to our modern society," Dr. Albertson said, but Dr. King had wandered back into the hall and into Dr. Othniel's class.

"The usual mode of the tyrannosaurus rex was to approach a herd of hadrosaurs from cover," Dr. Othniel, who did not see Dr. King because he was writing on the board, said. "He would then attack suddenly and retreat." He wrote "1. OBSERVE, 2. ATTACK, 3. RETREAT," in a column on the board, the letters of each getting smaller and squinchier as he approached the chalk tray.

His students wrote "1. Sneak up, 2. Bite ass, 3. Beat it," and "Todd called last night. I told him Traci wasn't there. We talked forever."

Dr. King wrote "RELEVANTNESS?" in large block letters on his clipboard and wandered out again.

"The jaws and teeth of the tyrannosaurus were capable of inflicting a fatal wound with a single bite. It would then follow at a distance, waiting for its victim to bleed to death." Dr. Othniel said.

Robert was late to the meeting on Monday. "You will not believe what happened to me!" he said. "I had to park in the daily permit lot, and while I was getting the permit out of the machine, they gave me a ticket!"

Dr. King, who was sitting at Sarah's desk wearing a pair of gray sweats, a whistle, and a baseball cap with "Dan Quayle Junior High" on it, said, "I know you're all as excited about this educationing experiment we're about to embarkate on as I am."

"More," Dr. Albertson said.

Sarah glared at him. "Will this experiment involve eliminating positions?"

Dr. King smiled at her. His teeth reminded her of some she'd seen at the Denver Museum of Natural History. " 'Positions,' 'classes,' 'departments,' all those terms are irrelevantatious. We need to reassessmentize our entire concept of education, its relevantatiousness to modern society. How many of you are using paradigmic bonding in your classes?"

Dr. Albertson raised his hand.

"Paradigmic bonding, experiential role-playing, modular cognition. I assessmentized some of your classes last week. I saw no computer-learner linkages, no multimedial instruction, no cognitive tracking. In one class"—Dr. King smiled largely at Dr. Othniel—"I saw a blackboard being used. Methodologies like that are extinct."

"So are dinosaurs," Sarah muttered. "Why don't you say something, Robert?"

"Dr. King," Robert said, "do you plan to extend this reorganization to other departments?"

Good, Sarah thought, send him over to pester English Lit.

"Yes," Dr. King said, beaming. "Paleontology is only an initiatory pretest. Eventually we intend to expand it to encompassate the entire university. Why?"

"There's one department that drastically needs reorganization," Robert said. "I don't know if you're aware of this, but the Parking Authority is completely out of control. The sign distinctly says you're supposed to park your car first and *then* go get the daily permit out of the machine."

• • •

"What did you find out about Dr. King?" Sarah asked Chuck Tuesday morning.

"He didn't coach junior-high girl's basketball," he said, drinking a lime Slurpee. "It was junior-high wrestling."

"Oh," Sarah said. "Then find out where he got his doctorate. Maybe we can get the college to rescind it for using words like 'assessmentize.' "

"I don't think I'd better," Chuck said. "I mean, I've only got one semester till I graduate. And besides," he said, sucking on the Slurpee, "some of his ideas made sense. I mean, a lot of that stuff we learn in class does seem kind of pointless. I mean, what does the Late Cretaceous have to do with us, really? It might be fun to role-play and stuff."

"Fine," Sarah said. "Role-play this. You are a coryhosaurus. You're smart and fast, but not fast enough because a tyrannosaurus rex has just taken a bite out of your flank. What do you do?"

"Gosh, that's a tough one," Chuck said, slurping meditatively. "What would you do?"

"Grow a wishbone."

Tuesday afternoon, as soon as her one o'clock class was over, Sarah went to Robert's office. He wasn't there. She waited outside for half an hour, reading the announcement for a semester at sea, and then went over to the Parking Authority office.

He was standing near the front of a line that wound down the stairs and out the door. It was composed mostly of students, though the person at the head of the line was a frail-looking old man. He was flapping a green slip at the young man behind the counter. The young man had a blond crew cut and looked like an adolescent Himmler.

". . . a heart attack," the old man at the head of the line was saying. Sarah wondered if he had had one when he got his parking ticket or if he intended to have one now.

Sarah tried to get to Robert, but two students were

blocking the door. She recognized one of the freshmen from Dr. Othniel's class. "Oh, Todd," the freshman was saying to a boy in a tank undershirt and jeans, "I knew you'd help me. I tried to get Traci to come with me—I mean, after all, it was her car—but I think she had a date."

"A date?" Todd said.

"Well, I don't know for sure. It's hard to keep track of all her guys. I couldn't do that. I mean"—she lowered her eyes demurely—"if you were *my* boyfriend, I'd never even think about other guys."

"Excuse me," Sarah said, "but I need to talk to Dr. Walker."

Todd stepped to one side, and instead of stepping to the other, the freshman from Dr. Othniel's class squeezed over next to him. Sarah slid past and worked her way up to Robert, ignoring the nasty looks of the other people in line.

"Don't tell me you got a ticket, too," Robert said.

"No," she said. "We have to do something about Dr. King."

"We certainly do," Robert said indignantly.

"Oh, I'm so glad you feel that way. Dr. Othniel's useless. He doesn't even realize what's going on, and Dr. Albertson's giving a lecture on 'The Impactization of Microscopic Fossils on Twentieth-Century Society.' "

"Which is what?"

"I have no idea. When I was in there, he was showing a videotape of *The Land Before Time*."

"I had a coronary thrombosis!" the old man shouted.

"Unauthorized vehicles are not allowed in permit lots," the Hitler Youth said. "However, we have initiated a preliminary study of the incident."

"A preliminary study!" the old man said, clutching his left arm. "The last one you did took five years!"

"We need another meeting with Dr. King," Sarah said. "We need to tell him relevance is not the issue, that paleontology is important in and of itself, and not because brontosaurus earrings are trendy. Surely he'll see reason. We have science and logic on our side."

Robert looked at the old man at the counter.

"What is there to study?" he was saying. "You ticketed the ambulance while the paramedics were giving me CPR!"

"I'm not sure reason will work," Robert said doubtfully.

"Well, then, how about a petition? We've got to do something, or we'll all be showing episodes of *The Flintstones*. He's a dangerous man!"

"He certainly is," Robert said. "Do you know what I just got? A citation for parking in front of the Faculty Library."

"Will you forget about your stupid parking tickets for a minute?" Sarah said. "You won't have any reason to park unless we get rid of King. I know Albertson's students would all sign a petition. Yesterday he made them cut the illustrations out of their textbooks and make a collage."

"The Parking Authority doesn't acknowledge petitions," Robert said. "You heard what Dr. King told the dean at the reception. He said, 'I'm parked right outside.' He left a note on his windshield that said the Paleontology Department had given him permission to park there." He waved the green paper at her. "Do you know where *I* parked? Fifteen blocks away. And I'm the one who gets a citation for improperly authorizing parking permission!"

"Good-bye, Robert," Sarah said.

"Wait a minute! Where are you going? We haven't figured out a plan of action yet."

Sarah worked her way back through the line. The two students were still blocking the door. "I'm sure Traci will understand," the freshman from Dr. Othniel's class was saying, "I mean, it isn't like you two were *serious* or anything."

"Wait a minute!" Robert shouted from his place in line. "What are you going to do?"

"Evolve," Sarah said.

• • •

On Wednesday there was another memo in Paleontology's boxes. It was on green paper, and Robert snatched it up and took off for the Parking Authority office, muttering dark threats. He was already there and standing in line behind a young woman in a wheelchair and two firemen when he finally unfolded it and read it.

"I *know* I was parking in a handicapped spot," the young woman was saying when Robert let out a whoop and ran back to the Earth Sciences building.

Sarah had a one o'clock class, but she wasn't there. Her students, who were spending their time waiting erasing marks in their textbooks so they could resell them at the bookstore, didn't know where she was. Neither did Dr. Albertson, who was making a papier-mâché foraminifer.

Robert went into Dr. Othniel's class. "The prevalence of predators in the Late Cretaceous," Dr. Othniel was saying, "led to severe evolutionary pressures, resulting in aquatic and aeronautical adaptations."

Robert tried to get his attention, but he was writing "BIRDS" in the chalk tray.

He went out in the hall. Sarah's TA was standing outside her office, eating a bag of Doritos.

"Have you seen Dr. Wright?" Robert asked.

"She's gone," Chuck said, munching.

"Gone? You mean, resigned?" he said, horrified. "But she doesn't have to." He waved the green paper at Chuck. "Dr. King's going to do a preliminary study, a—what does he call it?—a preinitiatory survey of prevailing paleontological pedagogy. We won't have to worry about him for another five years at least."

"She saw it," Chuck said, pulling a jar of salsa out of his back pocket. "She said it was too late. She'd already paid her tuition." He unscrewed the lid.

"Her tuition?" Robert said. "What are you talking about? Where did she go?"

"She flew the coop." He dug in the bag and pulled out a chip. He dipped it in the sauce. "Oh, and she left something for you." He handed Robert the jar of salsa and the chips and dug in his other back pocket. He handed Robert the flight brochure and a green plastic square.

"It's her parking sticker," Robert said.

"Yeah," Chuck said. "She said she won't be needing it where she's going."

"That's all? She didn't say anything else?"

"Oh, yeah," he said, dipping a chip into the salsa Robert still held. "She said to watch out for falling rocks."

"The predatory dinosaurs flourished for the entire Late Cretaceous," Dr. Othniel said, "and then, along with their prey, disappeared. Various theories have been advanced for their extinction, none of which has been authoritatively proved."

"I'll bet they couldn't find a parking place," a student who had written one of the letters to the Parking Authority and who had finally given up and traded his Volkswagen in on a skateboard, whispered.

"What?" Dr. Othniel said, looking vaguely around. He turned back to the board. "The diminishing food supply, the rise of mammals, the depradations of smaller predators, all undoubtedly contributed."

He wrote: "1. FOOD SUPPLY
2. MAMMALS
3. COMPETITION," on the bottom one fifth of the board.

His students wrote "I thought it was an asteroid," and "My new roommate Terri is trying to steal Todd away from me! Can you believe that? Signed, Deanna."

"The demise of the dinosaurs—" Dr. Othniel said, and stopped. He straightened slowly, vertebra by vertebra, until he was nearly erect. He lifted his chin, as if he were sniffing the air, and then walked over to the open window, leaned out, and stood there for several minutes, scanning the clear and empty sky.

WHEN YOU TELL PEOPLE YOU WRITE SCIENCE FICtion, *they say, "Oh, spaceships and aliens," and then want to know your qualifications. "How do you think up those strange worlds?" they ask. "I suppose you majored in science."*

It's best to nod, even if you majored in English. You won't get anywhere trying to explain that you subscribe to the Miss Marple theory of literature, which maintains that you don't have to go farther than your front yard to understand the universe. (Even though Jane Austen subscribed to it, too.) And it's no good telling them that your qualifications are that you've seen some strange worlds, all right, and you didn't need a spaceship to get to them. They probably wouldn't understand.

I've sung in church choirs, had Mary Kay facials, put on garage sales. I've been to the mall and the orthodontist and the second-grade Valentine's party. I've even been to Tupperware parties—only slightly stranger than Venusian eyestalk-bonding ceremonies—at which you participate in arcane contests ("How many words can you make out of 'Tupperware'?" "Warp, put, upper, rue . . ." I always win. It's the only thing majoring in English is good for) and eat ritual preparations of Cool Whip and graham-cracker crumbs and purchase plastic boxes that burp.

Science fiction? Piece of cake. ("Pert, rat, paw, tarp, prate, weep, apt, true, wart, Ra . . .")

TIME OUT

"I want you to come with me to the airport, Dr. Lejeune," Dr. Young said. "I've got to pick up Andrew Simons."

It was the first time he'd spoken to Dr. Lejeune since she'd told him his project proposal was idiotic, and during the intervening three weeks she'd thought quite a bit about what she would say to him when he did speak to her, but now he sounded so much like the old sensible, sane Max Young that she picked up her purse and said, "Who's Andrew Simons?"

"He's coming from Tibet," Dr. Young said, leading the way out of the physics building and over to the parking lot. "He's with Duke University. Been studying the cultural aspects of time perception in a lamasery in the Himalayas. He's perfect. I read a monograph of his on déjà vu three months ago and got in touch with Duke." He stopped next to a red Porsche.

"When did you get a Porsche?" Dr. Lejeune said, looking at the license plates. They spelled WITHIT1, which was a bad sign. So was the Porsche. "And why exactly is this Simons person coming here?"

"He's going to work on the time displacement project," Dr. Young said as if it were obvious, and squeezed himself into the Porsche. "Come on. Get in. His plane gets in at four-nineteen."

She attempted to get into the Porsche. She had hoped he'd given up on the time-displacement project. She had attempted to argue him out of it, with the result that he hadn't spoken to her in three weeks, and she had hoped he had come to his senses, but apparently he hadn't.

The project *was* idiotic. He had decided that time was a quantum object like space and leaped from there to the idea that it could be separated into pieces called hodiechrons, shaken up, and moved around. Quantum time travel. Only he was calling it hodiechron displacement and the silly gadget that was supposed to do all this a temporal oscillator instead of a time machine.

She had decided he was having some kind of midlife crisis, and now the Porsche confirmed it. "I am too old for sports cars," she said, slamming the door shut on the tail of her lab coat. "And so are you."

Dr. Young reached across her to the glove compartment and pulled out a tweed cap and a pair of leather driving gloves.

"Simons is extremely enthusiastic about the project. He accepted the job before I even had a chance to fully explain it to him."

Which, considering what the project involves, is probably a good thing, Dr. Lejeune thought, clutching the dashboard as the Porsche shot out of the parking lot, down College Avenue, and onto the highway.

"How old is he?" she shouted over the roar of the wind.

"Forty-two," Dr. Young shouted back.

"Is he married?"

"Of course not. He's been in a lamasery in Tibet for five years."

"No wonder he accepted," Dr. Lejeune said. "I should fix him up with Bev Frantz. She's forty. You know her, she's teaching Intro to Nursing this semester. She'd be perfect for him."

"Absolutely not," Dr. Young shouted. "I will not have you endangering this project." He swooped into the airport parking lot. He took off his cap and gloves, shoved them into the glove compartment, and got out. "Are you aware that matchmaking is a substitute for sex? It's one of the classic symptoms of a midlife crisis."

Which is a clear case of the pot psychoanalyzing the kettle, Dr. Lejeune thought, struggling up out of the car. "What do you call buying a Porsche?" she said, following him into the airport. "How about suddenly abandoning your work on subatomic particles and trying to build a time machine? Wouldn't you call those *classic* symptoms?"

"It's a temporal oscillator, not a time machine," Dr. Young said. He walked through the security gate. It buzzed. The guard motioned him back through and held out a plastic bowl for him to empty his pockets into. "The university has complete faith in the project. Dr. Gillis has promised me full university support. And complete freedom in choosing my staff."

"Obviously," Dr. Lejeune said. "If you're hiring Tibetan lamas."

"Dr. Simons is a research psychologist," he said stiffly, putting his keys in the dish and trying again. This time it buzzed before he was even halfway through. Some of the guards from other security gates came over to watch. "Are you aware that resistance to new ideas is a classic symptom in postmenopausal women?" He took off his belt. "The federal government doesn't share your opinion of my project either. If they did, I'd hardly have gotten my funding, would I?"

"You got your funding?" Dr. Lejeune said, astonished. "The new administration must be as senile as the old one."

He walked through the gate. It buzzed. "It is that

kind of negative attitude that has already put this project a month behind schedule!" he said.

"You're sure it isn't displaced hodiechrons?" she said, and swept through the gate. "It's his neck chains," she told the guard. "He's postmenopausal. Classic symptom."

"Mom, when's supper?" Liz asked, opening the refrigerator. "Lisa and I are going to start filling out college applications tonight."

"As soon as your father gets home," Carolyn said. She squeezed past Liz and got the radishes and a tomato out of the crisper drawer. "He had to stay for gymnastics."

"But, Mom, I have to be at volleyball practice at six," Wendy said.

"I thought the eighth-grade practices were at four," Carolyn said, rummaging through the utensils drawer for a paring knife.

"On Mondays, Tuesdays, and every other Friday," Wendy said. "This is Wednesday, Mom."

The only knife in the entire drawer was a serrated bread knife. Carolyn tried slicing the tomato with it. It wouldn't even cut through the skin.

"How come Dad's having gymnastics practice?" Liz asked. "I thought the season didn't start till next week."

"It doesn't," Carolyn said. "Shut the refrigerator. He's interviewing assistant coaches."

"I have to have new hightops," Wendy said.

"You had new hightops when school started."

"These are for volleyball. Coach Nicotero says we need ones with bank and turn heels and spike insteps."

The phone rang. Liz dived for it. "It's for you," she said disgustedly, and handed Carolyn the phone.

"Hi, this is Sherri at the elementary school," the voice on the phone said. "I tried to catch you when you were doing your volunteer stuff, but you would not believe what our beloved principal Old Paperwork decided his secretary should do now! He's having me call every parent and check to make sure the information is correct. Just in case, he says. Are you aware that you are the 'person to be contacted if parents cannot be reached' on fourteen separate emergency cards?"

"Yes," Carolyn said. "It's because I'm at home during the day. I may well be the last woman in America at home during the day."

"No, Heidi Dreismeier's mother doesn't work either. Anyway, Old Paperwork decided I should call every single 'person to be contacted if parents cannot be reached' just to make sure they really can be contacted and their phones are in working order. The man's a menace."

"Mom, it's *five o'clock*," Wendy said.

"Anyway," Sherri said, "I need to read you the names of all these kids. Heidi Dreismeier, Monica Morales, Ricky Morales—"

"Mom, I'm not going to have time to eat," Wendy said.

"Troy Yoder," Sherri said, "Brendan James. Speaking of which, did you know Brendan's parents are getting a divorce?"

"You're kidding," Carolyn said. "She's PTA vice president."

"Not anymore she's not. You remember that Make Me Marvy guy who was going around doing color consultations? Well, apparently Brendan's mother didn't stop with a few swatches."

"Mother, Coach Nicotero said we're supposed to let our food settle before we practice."

"Look, Sherri, I'm going to have to go," Carolyn said. "Whoever put my name on the emergency card, it's fine."

"Wait, wait, that isn't really what I called about. Do you remember that fat, bald guy from the university who had you take all those tests last March?"

"Dr. Young?"

"Yeah. Well, he's coming back with some kind of research team, and he wants you to work for him. It'd be every day all day for about a month, he said. It pays better than volunteering."

"Oh, gosh, I don't know," Carolyn said, thinking about Wendy's hightops. "Don starts gymnastics practice next week, and the PTA Fair's coming up. Did he say how much he'd pay?"

"Yeah, and he must really want you because he said he'd pay anything you asked. And you wouldn't have to start till October second."

Carolyn tried to lift up the September page of the calendar with the hand that was still holding the bread knife. "That's next Wednesday, right?"

"I have my orthodontist appointment on Wednesday," Wendy said.

"I'll have to see if I can reschedule some stuff. How long will you be at school?"

"Oh, till about midnight if Old Paperwork has his way. After I'm done with the emergency cards, he wants the recess-duty schedule redone alphabetically."

"I'll call you back," Carolyn said, and hung up.

"There's no way that meat loaf is going to be done by six," Wendy said.

Carolyn poked some holes in a hot dog with the end of the bread knife and put it in the microwave. Then she called the orthodontist and changed Wendy's appointment to four-fifteen on Tuesday.

"I have practice at four on Tuesdays," Wendy said. "Coach Nicotero says if we miss even one practice, we can't play."

"What do you have on Thursday?" Carolyn asked the orthodontist's receptionist.

"We have a five forty-five," she said.

"How's five forty-five?" Carolyn asked Wendy.

"Fine," Wendy said.

"Thursday's the College Fair," Liz said. "You promised you'd drive Lisa and me."

"I have a three-thirty on Wednesday," the receptionist said.

"Oh, good. That's after school. I'll take it," Carolyn said.

Before she could get the phone back in its cradle, it rang again.

"Hi, this is Lisa. Can I talk to Liz?"

Carolyn handed the phone to Liz and got Wendy's hot dog out of the microwave. She poured her a glass of milk.

"Coach Nicotero says we're supposed to have something from each of the four food groups. Meat, grains, dairy products—"

"Fruits and vegetables," Carolyn said. She handed Wendy the tomato.

Liz hung up the phone. "I'm eating supper at Lisa's," she said. "Can you drop me off when you take Wendy?" She ran into her room and came out with a stack of college catalogs. "Where did you say you went to college, Mom?"

"NSC," Carolyn said.

"Did you like it?"

I had all the time in the world, Carolyn thought. I didn't have to take anybody anywhere, and I'd never heard of the four basic food groups. My favorite food was a suicide, which my roommate Allison and I made by mixing different flavors of pop together.

"I loved it," Carolyn said.

The phone rang.

"Sorry to call so late, honey," Don said. "We're not even half-done. Don't wait supper for me. You and the girls go ahead and eat."

The plane taxied to a stop, and everyone made a dash for the aisles. Andrew was in the window seat. He pulled his duffel bag out from under the seat in front of him and leaned back against the upright seat back. He shouldn't have had the Scotch on the L.A.-to-Denver leg. He had hoped it might put him to sleep so he wouldn't have to listen to the obviously unhappily married couple in the seats next to him.

Instead it had sent him off into a sentimental reverie of his junior year in college, which was possibly the worst year of his life. He had nearly flunked out of prelaw, he had gotten serious about Stephanie Forrester, and he had been an usher at her wedding. There was no reason to remember that misbegotten year at all, and especially not nostalgically.

"I didn't say I didn't want you to play tennis," the male half of the unhappy couple said. He stood up, opened the overhead compartment, and got down a suitcase and his raincoat. "I just said I thought four lessons a day was a little too much."

"For your information," the woman said, "Carlos thinks I have real potential." She reached in the elasticized seat-back pocket, pulled out a paperback of *Passages*, and jammed it in her purse.

Andrew remembered Dr. Young's project proposal and got it out of his seat pocket. That was the real reason he'd had the Scotch, to try to blot out the memory of Dr. Young's harebrained ideas. Dr. Young's theory was that time existed not as a continuous flow but as a series of discrete quantum objects. They were perceived as a flow because of a "persistence" phenomenon that was learned in childhood. That part of the theory wasn't so bad. Ashtekar's research at Syracuse University had already suggested the quantum nature of time, and the idea of perceptual time blocks of some duration was generally accepted by temporal psychologists. Without it, there couldn't be phenomena like music, which depended on relationships between notes. If time were a continuous flow, music would be perceived as a single note replaced immediately in the consciousness by another instead of as a pattern of interval and duration.

But the concept of time blocks, or hodiechrons, as Dr. Young had christened them, was a perceptual concept, not a physical reality. Not only did Dr. Young think his hodiechrons were real, he also thought they were much longer than any temporal psychologist had suggested—minutes or even hours long instead of the seconds it took to hear a melody. But the truly crazy part of his theory was that these hodiechrons could be moved around like toy blocks, even stacked one on top of the other.

It had nothing to do with cultural aspects of time perception or déjà vu, and if he'd read it all the way through before this, he'd never have accepted Dr. Young's offer, but he hadn't checked Dr. Young out at all. Dr. Young had checked him out—he'd had him take a whole battery of tests before he offered Andrew the job. And Andrew had leaped at it without even reading the proposal. Andrew stood up in a semicrouch and looked ahead at the line of people in the aisle. He willed it to move.

"For your information," the woman said, "Carlos says I have the most beautiful backhand he's ever seen."

"For *your* information," the man said, wrestling with something in the overhead compartment, "Carlos is paid to say things like that to overweight, middle-aged women."

Andrew took his plastic safety-instructions card out of the seat pocket and began reading the emergency-exit diagrams.

"I've been thinking about going on tour," the woman said.

"Now that's what I mean," the man said, pulling down a tennis racket in a zippered lavender cover. "You're getting carried away with this tennis thing!"

"The way you got carried away with those Managua municipal bonds? The way you got carried away with that little blond in securities?" She grabbed the tennis racket out of his hands.

According to the safety card there were emergency slides over both wings. If he could climb back over the seats till he got to row H and then pull down the handle on the emergency door . . .

"I thought we agreed not to talk about Vanessa," the man said.

"I am not talking about Vanessa. I am talking about Heather."

Andrew sat back down in his seat, fastened his seat belt, and pretended to read the proposal until everybody but the flight attendants had gotten off the plane. The proposal didn't make any more sense now than when he had read it in earnest.

He looked longingly at the emergency-slide handle and then stuck the proposal in his duffel bag and walked out through the covered walkway and into the terminal. Dr. Young and a fiftyish woman with disorganized hair were the only people left at the gate. The woman was looking interestedly down the hall.

"Dr. Simons," Dr. Young said, coming forward to shake his hand. "I want you to meet Dr. Lejeune. Dr. Lejeune, Dr. Simons is going to run the psychology end of our little project. Dr. Lejeune?"

Dr. Lejeune came over and shook his hand, still trying to peer down the corridor. "This woman just hit some man over the head with a tennis racket," she said.

"She found out about Heather," Andrew said.

"We're very excited to have you working with us," Dr. Young said. "I'll be working with the oscillator, and Dr. Lejeune will be running the computer interp."

"Since when?" Dr. Lejeune said.

Andrew began looking for emergency exits. There didn't appear to be any.

"Dr. Gillis told me I could choose whatever staff I

needed. I told him I wanted you as my second in command."

Dr. Lejeune was glancing around as if she were looking for a tennis racket to hit Dr. Young over the head with. "Did you also tell him I think your project is completely addlepated?"

I should have had at least two more Scotches, Andrew thought. Or what were those things he had drunk when he ushered at Stephanie Forrester's wedding? Clockstoppers. He should have had a clockstopper.

"Addlepated?" Dr. Young said. "Addlepated! Dr. Simons here doesn't think it's addlepated. He came all the way from Tibet to work on this project. Tell us, Dr. Simons, is 'addlepated' the word that springs to mind about this project?"

The word that sprang to mind was disaster. He should have had a lot of clockstoppers. Ten. Or fifteen.

"No," he said.

"You see?" Dr. Young said triumphantly to Dr. Lejeune. He took Andrew's bag. "We'll go straight back to the lab and I'll show you the oscillator. And then I'll outline my theory in more detail."

His junior year hadn't been half-bad, all things considered, Andrew thought, walking out to the car with them. He had had to usher at Stephanie Forrester's wedding, and when the minister had read that part about, "let him speak now or forever hold his peace," the entire congregation had turned and looked at him, but otherwise it hadn't been half bad.

Dr. Lejeune didn't speak to Dr. Young on the way home from the airport even though he didn't realize until they got to the Porsche that there wasn't room for all three of them and then told her to take Andrew's duffel bag and go find a taxi. Andrew, who was looking either jet-lagged or sorry he had ever left Tibet, insisted on being the one to take the taxi, and Dr. Young spent the trip back to the university telling her how her attitude was undermining the project. She maintained a stony silence.

She maintained it through his announcing that their research was not going to be done at the university but at an elementary school in a town called Henley that was halfway across the state and through his unveiling of the temporal oscillator, even though it was close on that one. It looked like a giant lava lamp.

She talked to Dr. Gillis instead, but she didn't get anywhere. Dr. Gillis refused to take her refusal to work on the project seriously. Worse, he thought shiftable hodiechrons and temporal oscillation were entirely plausible, and when she told him she thought Max was having some kind of midlife crisis, Dr. Gillis stiffened and said, "Dr. Young is three years younger than I am. I would hardly call him middle-aged. Besides, he is far too intelligent and sensible a man to have a midlife crisis."

"That's what I thought," Dr. Lejeune said, "till I saw the Porsche."

She went back to the lab and Andrew Simons, who was staring at the temporal oscillator. He looked terrible. Max hadn't given him a minute's rest since he got there, but she had the feeling it was more than that. He looked unhappy. He needs to get married, she thought. I really should introduce him to Bev Frantz. She's pretty and smart and unmarried. She'd be perfect.

"How can this be a temporal oscillator?" Andrew said. "It looks like a lava lamp."

Dr. Young came in, beaming. "I've just been talking to the school secretary in Henley." The top of his head was bright pink with excitement. "I decided you needed an assistant, Dr. Simons, and they just called to say they'd hired someone. Her name's Carolyn Hendricks. She's perfect. She'll be helping you with the screening and getting coffee and things like that."

"Why does she need to be perfect if all she's doing is

getting the coffee?" Dr. Lejeune almost asked, and then remembered she wasn't speaking to him.

"She's forty years old, married, secretary of the PTA, and has two daughters. Her husband coaches the girls' gymnastics team. The seasons' just started," he added, as if that were perfect, too. "Which reminds me—" he said, and hurried out.

Why is her husband's coaching a bunch of teenaged girls in leotards perfect? she thought. Does he expect her to fly off the uneven bars and into the past?

"Have you ever heard of a drink called a clockstopper?" Andrew asked, still staring at the lava lamp. "I used to drink them in college."

"No," Dr. Lejeune said, frowning at the door Dr. Young had just left by.

"Beer and wine," Andrew said. "That's what they were made out of. The clockstoppers."

"Oh," said Dr. Lejeune, still frowning. "We called them cataclysms."

Carolyn dropped Wendy at the middle school and drove over to the elementary.

"Where am I supposed to go?" she asked Sherri in the office. "The library?"

"No," Sherri said, handing Carolyn a sheaf of papers. "You're downstairs in the music room."

"Where's music?"

"In with the PE classes. They divided the gym in half with masking tape."

"And the music teacher stood for that?"

"She had to. Old Paperwork told her how much money Dr. Young was paying to use the school for this project."

"If he's paying so much, why didn't he let him use the library?"

"I don't know. The music room *is* pretty cramped."

"I know," Carolyn said. "I did hearing tests in there

last year. The room's L-shaped, and the light switch is at the top of this hall part next to the door and about a million miles from the main part of the room. The third-graders were always switching it off on their way to recess and leaving me in the dark, because there aren't any windows. Can't you see if we can be in the library instead?"

"I'll ask Old Paperwork," Sherri said. "I don't know what you're griping about, though. I'd love being stuck in a small space with a gorgeous-looking man like that."

"Dr. *Young*?"

"No. The guy you're working with." She fumbled through the papers on the counter. "Andrew Something." She picked up a pink sheet and looked at it. "Andrew Simons. Speaking of gorgeous looking, how's that adorable husband of yours?"

"Adorable," Carolyn said, smiling. "When I get to see him. Gymnastics is our worst time of the year. And this year's been even worse because of his having to hire a new assistant coach."

"I heard they hired some twenty-year-old who looks like Farrah Fawcett."

"They did," Carolyn said, looking through her collection of forms. "Don was really upset. He spent two whole weeks doing interviews and then the board hires this Linda person, who never even applied."

"I'll bet he's not all that upset," Sherri said. "He gets to work with Farrah Fawcett, you get to work with this absolute hunk of a psychologist—why don't I ever get to work with anybody gorgeous?" Sherri asked. "Do you know what happened to me when I had the Make Me Marvy guy at my house? He wrapped a dish towel around my head, held up a few swatches, and told me I look sallow in pink. It isn't fair. The married women are grabbing all the eligible bachelors. Like Shannon Williams's mother."

"Shannon Williams's mother?" Carolyn said, looking

up from her papers. "I thought it was Brendan's mother who ran off with the colors guy."

"It was. Shannon's mother is messing around with some guy she works with at the bank. It seems they had to spend all this time in the vault together, and the next thing you know . . . Speaking of which, how much time will Don have to spend with this Linda person?"

"I think I'd better get down to the music room before the bell rings," Carolyn said. "Is this Dr. Simons down there?"

"I don't know. He's been in and out all morning, carrying stuff. I'll check with Old Paperwork about the library. And in the meantime, you watch out for this Andrew Simons guy. That music room is even smaller than the vault." She held the pink paper up to her neck. "Do you really think pink makes me look sallow?"

"Yes," Carolyn said.

Andrew hooked the temporal oscillator up to the response monitors and plugged the whole thing into the only outlet he could find in the music room. The lights stayed on.

Good, he thought, and started hooking up the rest of the response wires, which were supposed to register reactions in the students they tested.

According to Dr. Young they would be screening to find children who saw time as blocks rather than a continuous flow. These children would have longer hodiechrons since, according to Dr. Young, their hodiechrons got progressively shorter as they learned to perceive time as a flow.

After Andrew had found these children, they would be hooked up to the temporal oscillator and worked into an excited emotional state and they would begin switching their hodiechrons around. Dr. Young claimed he had been able to make it happen on a subatomic level.

"Maximum agitation," Dr. Young had said. "Simple

bombardment won't do it. The key is maximum agitation."

"But even if it does happen at the microcosmic level, what makes you think you can make it happen in macro?" Dr. Lejeune had asked, the first thing she'd said to Dr. Young in a week and a half.

"It already happens," Dr. Young had said. "You've both experienced it. The sensation of déjà vu. The now is displaced for a millisecond by a hodiechron from the past, and you have the sensation of having seen or heard something before. It usually occurs when you're in an excited emotional state. Déjà vu is temporal displacement, and what we're going to do in this project is to produce it in longer hodiechrons so the displacement lasts a second, a minute, as long as several hours."

Andrew didn't believe a word of it. He had told Dr. Lejeune so while they packed the equipment for the trip to the elementary school in Henley.

"I don't believe it either," she'd said.

"Then why are you staying?"

She'd shrugged. "Somebody needs to be around to save him from himself, or at least to pick up the pieces when his precious oscillator doesn't work. But that's no reason for you to stay. So why are you?"

I don't know, he'd thought. Why did I agree to usher at Stephanie Forrester's wedding? "Maybe I'm having a midlife crisis," he said.

"Along with everybody else around here," Dr. Lejeune had said, and then looked thoughtful. "You're forty-two, right?" she said. "Hmm. Did you have a girlfriend in Tibet?"

"I was in a lamasery in the Himalayas."

"Hmm," she'd said, and handed him another piece of equipment.

There was too much equipment. He didn't even know what some of it was. There was a medium-size gray box with only an on-off switch on it and two smaller ones without even that, and no jacks to plug any of them into anything else. He wondered if they were something the music teacher had left behind. He set them on the piano along with the photon counter and the spectroscope.

The lights went off. "Hey!" he said. The lights went back on.

"Sorry," a woman's voice said. She came down the ell and into the room. She had short dark hair and was wearing a skirt and blazer. She extended her hand. "I'm Carolyn Hendricks. I couldn't tell if you were here or not, and I didn't want to get locked in. Sherri forgot to give me a key. I called a couple of times, but the room's soundproofed unless you really yell."

He shook her hand. "Which you knew I'd do if you turned off the lights?"

"Yes," she said. "I had to do hearing tests in here last year, and the third graders think it's funny to flip the light switch on their way out to recess." She smiled. "I yelled a lot." She had a nice smile.

"For a minute there I thought maybe I'd blown the lights," he said, indicating the jumble of wires. "Would you believe there's only one outlet in the whole room?"

"Yes," she said. She watched him plug the spectrum analyzer into the power supply. "Maybe it would be a good idea if I brought in a flashlight tomorrow, just in case we blow a fuse."

"Or a miner's lamp," he said, peering at the back of the spectrum analyzer. "It got awfully black in here when you turned off the light."

" 'Black as the pit from pole to pole,' " she said.

He looked up at her.

"I know you," he said.

"Oh?" she said, squinting at him the way people did when they were trying to decide if someone looked familiar or not.

"Were you ever at Duke University?"

"No," she said warily.

"And I don't suppose you've been in Tibet lately."

"No," she said even more warily, and he realized suddenly how that must sound, especially down here in the black hole of Calcutta.

"Sorry," he said. "That wasn't meant to sound like the oldest line in the book. You must remind me of somebody," he said, frowning.

That was a lie. She didn't remind him of anybody. He was positive he'd never seen her before, but for a fraction of a second there, when she said, "Black as the pit from pole to pole," he could have sworn he knew her.

She was still looking wary. He said, "What I need you to do is help me get this equipment arranged so we can actually move in here. If we could move *that*," he pointed to the resonant converter, "over next to the blackboard and then do something with the chairs to get them out of the way—"

"Sure," she said, squeezing between the oscilloscope and the magnetometer to get to him. Together they hefted the resonant converter, carried it over to the blackboard, and set it down. "We can move some of these chairs out of the room if you don't need them," she said. "We can store them in the supply closet."

"Great," he said.

"I'll go get the key from the janitor," she said. She started to pick up one of the chairs and knocked it over instead.

"I—" he said, and clamped it off.

She picked up the chair and looked inquiringly at him.

"Leave a couple for us," he said lamely. "And one for the child we'll be testing. And maybe you'd better leave a couple for Dr. Young and Dr. Lejeune in case they want to observe. Five. Leave five chairs."

"Okay," she said, and went down the hall.

"I know you," he said, looking after her. "I *know you.*"

• • •

Dr. Lejeune spent half the day setting up her computer equipment and the other half looking for Dr. Young.

"Have you been down in that broom closet of a music room?" she asked when he finally came in. "My purse is bigger. I was down there this morning, and there was hardly room for the two of them to even move, let alone try to get kids in there."

"Perfect," Dr. Young said.

"Perfect?" Dr. Lejeune said suspiciously. He had said Carolyn Hendricks was perfect. Come to think of it, he had called Andrew that, too. "He's perfect," he had said. "He's forty-two years old and spent the last five years in a Tibetan lamasery."

"Why is it perfect?" Dr. Lejeune said.

"Your computer setup," Dr. Young said. "I knew the kindergarten was the perfect place for you to work."

"Well, the music room isn't."

"No, I know," he said, shaking his bald head sadly. "I tried to get the library, but Mr. Paprocki said they needed it for Fire Prevention Week. Maybe after that's over, we can move them," he said, and left before she could ask him anything else.

She went up to the office. "Is Mr. Paprocki in?" she asked Sherri, who was folding a stack of orange papers in half one at a time.

"He's out on the playground. Brendan James got into a fight. It's his third fight today. His mother ran off with the Make Me Marvy man."

Dr. Lejeune took one of the folded sheets and unfolded it. It said, "ATTN PARENTS: IT'S CHICKEN-POX TIME!" Dr. Lejeune folded it back up. "Make Me Marvy?" she said.

"Yeah, you know, he tells you what colors you can wear by examining your skin tones. And then he runs off with you, at least if you're Brendan James's mother. All he did to me was tell me to wear fuchsia."

Dr. Lejeune took part of the stack of orange sheets and started folding them.

"Actually, I wasn't all that surprised it happened. There was this article in *Woman's Day* about the Donkey Doldrums. You know, that point in a marriage where you feel like all you are is a pack animal, and just the week before she'd been in to bring Brendan his lunch that he forgot, and she told me the only time her husband noticed her anymore was when he needed her to find his keys. It still makes me mad, though. I mean, the Make Me Marvy man was just about the only single guy in town."

"Is Mr. Paprocki married?" Dr. Lejeune asked, folding.

"Old Paperwork?" Sherri asked, surprised. She folded the last sheet in her pile and got a stamp and stamp pad out of the desk drawer. "Married? Are you kidding? He never looks up from his triplicate forms long enough to see you're a woman, let alone marry you!" She pounded the stamp into the stamp pad two or three times and banged it onto the folded sheet. It was a smiley face. She whacked the next sheet. "What about Dr. Simons? I suppose he's too good-looking not to be married."

"No," Dr. Lejeune said, thinking of something else. "He spent the last five years in a lamasery in Tibet."

"You're kidding!" Sherri said. "That's perfect!"

Dr. Lejeune narrowed her eyes. "Why do you say that?"

"Well, because he's probably desperate. Five years and no sex would make me desperate," she said, stamping. "What am I talking about? Five years and no sex *have* made desperate. But I'll bet the first woman who comes along can have him for the taking."

"I'll try to catch Mr. Paprocki later," Dr. Lejeune said, handing the stack of folded sheets to Sherri. "Just tell him I want to talk to him about the music room."

"What about it?"

"It's too small. They've got all that equipment in

there, and they can hardly move. I was just wondering if there was some other room they could use."

"Carolyn Hendricks asked about that this morning, and I asked Old—Mr. Paprocki about. He said he knew it was too small and he'd offered Dr. Young the library instead, but Dr. Young had insisted on the music room. He said it was perfect for what he was going to do."

While Carolyn was waiting for Wendy at the orthodontist, she unstapled the orange flyer Sherri had handed her on her way out and read it.

"ATTN PARENTS: IT'S CHICKEN-POX TIME!" it said in all caps. There were subheadings: Be Aware, Be Prepared, and Be Informed, each with a cute picture of a bee next to it. "Be Aware. Sixteen cases have been reported in the state since school started, two in Henley, though so far we have had no cases in the schools."

The Be Prepared section listed the symptoms of the disease, and the Be Informed section talked about the incubation period, which was from thirteen to seventeen days, and concluded, "Chicken pox is most contagious the day before any symptoms appear and during the first few days of breaking out."

Great, Carolyn thought. Neither Liz nor Wendy had had the chicken pox even though they'd both been exposed when they were little.

After Wendy was done, Carolyn ran to the cleaners and the bank and went to the grocery store.

"Don't forget we're out of pop," Wendy said. "And Coach Nicotero said we were supposed to have—"

"The four basic food groups," Carolyn said. "Are you aware that pop is not a basic food group?"

"Are we going to the mall to get my hightops after this?" Wendy asked. "My shoelaces came untied during practice today and I called a time out and Sarah Perkins said there weren't any time outs in volleyball and I said there were time outs in every game. So are we?"

"Are we what?" Carolyn said, staring at the two-liter bottles of pop. When she was in college, pop had come in reasonable-sized bottles. They had bought one bottle each of Coke and orange and lemon-lime for their suicides, and what else? Root beer? Cream soda?

"Getting my hightops. At the mall."

Carolyn looked at her watch. "It's a quarter to five already, and Dad said he'd be home early tonight. We'll have to do it tonight after supper."

"Mother," Wendy said, somehow managing to get several extra syllables in "mother," "it's Wednesday. I have practice at six."

Carolyn bought two-liter bottles of cola, orange, cream soda, root beer, and lemon-lime and some new batteries for the flashlight and raced Wendy out to the mall to get her hightops. They didn't get home till five-thirty.

"I'm eating supper over at Lisa's," Liz said. "We're going to do our applications on her computer."

"I have to be at practice at six," Wendy said, lacing up her hightops.

Carolyn made Wendy a peanut-butter sandwich and began unpacking the groceries. "Did your father call, Liz?"

"No. Sherri did, though. She wants you to call her at school. What kind of microcomputers did your college have?"

"None." Carolyn took out the bottles of pop and set them on the counter. "There weren't any microcomputers in those days."

"You're kidding! What did you have, then?"

"It's twenty to six," Wendy said, munching on her sandwich.

Carolyn handed Wendy an apple and called Sherri.

"I talked to Monica and Ricky Morales's mother after school, and she says she's not surprised Brendan James's mother ran off with that Make Me Marvy man. She read this article in *Cosmopolitan* on the seven warning signs of Over-Forty-Frenzy, and she had them all. She was forty-three, her husband was never home, her kids were right at two of the most demanding ages—"

"What? Thirteen and seventeen?" Carolyn asked.

"No. Two and five. The article said she was easy prey for the first man who said two nice words to her."

"Mom, it's a quarter to six," Wendy said.

"I know the feeling," Carolyn said.

"And I know you," Sherri said. "You'd never run off with anybody. You're crazy about Don, and your girls are two of the nicest girls I know."

"Mom," Wendy said, pointing at the kitchen clock.

"I'm in kind of a hurry," Carolyn said. "Can I call you back?"

"You don't have to do that. I just wanted to warn you that Heidi Dreismeier's mother called. She heard you were doing tests and wanted to know how Heidi should study for them. I told her not to worry, but you know how she is. She'll probably call you next. I'll talk to you tomorrow," she said, and hung up.

Carolyn pulled her coat on and fished her car keys out of her purse. The phone rang. She handed Liz the keys and picked up the receiver.

"Hi, sweetheart," Don said. "How was your first day of work?"

"Fine," she said, waving good-bye to the girls. "We moved equipment all day. And chairs. I'm still not sure what this project is all about. There's one machine that looks like a giant lava lamp. And the guy I work with—" She stopped.

"The guy you work with what?"

"Nothing. Did you know Brendan James's mother ran off with the Make Me Marvy man? And there have been two cases of chicken pox in Henley."

"Great," Don said. "The girls will probably both get it. You've had it, haven't you?"

"What? Chicken pox?" Carolyn said. "Of course

I—" She stopped. "I don't remember." She frowned. "I must have. I had to have had it as a kid: I mean, all those times the girls were exposed when they were little, I was exposed, too, and I never got it, but . . . isn't that funny? I don't remember whether I've had it or not."

"It'll come to you if you don't think about it," Don said. "You're probably just tired."

"I am," she said. "Wendy had her orthodontist appointment and then dragged me all over the mall looking for volleyball shoes, and then Sherri called and Wendy had to go to practice."

"*And* you moved equipment all day. No wonder you're exhausted. Linda says she doesn't know how you do it all, taking care of the kids and all and now this job. She said she wondered if you had any time left over for being a wife."

"And what did you tell her?"

"I said you were a terrific wife and I—" Don said something to somebody else and then came back on the line. "Sorry. Linda just came in. She went out to get us some sandwiches. That's what I called about. I thought I was going to make it home early, but Linda is feeling real insecure about the meet tomorrow. She wanted to go over the floor ex routines again. But, listen, sweetheart, I can tell the girls to come in before school tomorrow."

"No, that's okay," Carolyn said. "I'm just being tired and cranky." She had a sudden thought. "I'll make myself a suicide," she said.

"A what?" Don said.

"A suicide," she said. "We used to drink them in college when we'd had a bad day."

She told Don good-bye, hung up, and opened all the bottles of pop.

We used to drink them in college, she thought, pouring some Coke into the glass. She added some orange and a little root beer. My roommate Allison and I used to sit on the floor and drink them and talk about what we were going to do with our lives. I do not remember our ever discussing driving people to the orthodontist or volleyball practice or the mall. She added a dollop of grape, filled the glass up with lemon lime, and stirred it with the knife she had used for peanut butter.

I don't' remember us ever discussing being married to a coach with a snotty assistant.

She took the suicide into the living room, sat down on the floor, and took a sip. It didn't taste anything like the suicides she and Allison had made, probably because Allison was the one who always made them. That one fall quarter when Allison was in Europe, she had had to experiment for days before she got the recipe right. That had been a bad fall quarter. It had snowed all the time, and she had sat by the window and drunk suicides and thought about falling in love, and being pursued by handsome men, and sex.

Which reminded her. She set the suicide on the coffee table and went and got the flashlight and put the batteries in.

Andrew got to school early, hoping he'd have a few minutes to try to figure out why he kept thinking he knew Carolyn Hendricks, but she was already there.

"I brought the flashlight," she said. "Where shall we put it so we both know where it is in case of emergency?"

"How about the top of the piano?" he said.

She set it on end between two gray boxes that didn't plug into anything. She didn't look familiar today, which Andrew was grateful for. It was bad enough working on a nutty project without behaving like a nut yourself.

"We're just going to do some screening today," he said. "The Idelman-Ponoffo Short-Term Memory Inventory. It consists of reading strings of numbers, letters, and words and having the child repeat them back to you, forward, backward, from the middle—"

"I know," Carolyn said. "Dr. Young gave it to me when he tested me last year."

"Oh," Andrew said. He had had the idea Dr. Young didn't know her, that she had been picked at random by the elementary school. "Good. You'll be asking the questions, and I'll be monitoring their responses. They'll be hooked up to an EKG and autonomic response sensors, and I'll be videotaping the testing."

"Don't you think all this equipment is liable to scare five-year-olds?"

"That's what you're here for. They know you already, and you'll be the one interacting with them. Don't start the test immediately. Talk to them awhile, and then we'll hook them up as unobtrusively as possible and start the test."

She went and got the first kindergartner and brought him in. "This is Matt Rothaus," she said.

"Wow, neat!" Matt said, racing over to look at the temporal oscillator. "*Star Trek: The Next Generation*!"

Carolyn laughed. She leaned forward. "Do you like *Star Trek*?"

I know you, Andrew thought. I've never seen you before, but I've heard you laugh and lean forward just like that.

"What did you do in Show and Tell today?" Carolyn was asking Matt.

"Heidi threw up," Matt said. "It was gross to the max."

At lunch Dr. Lejeune set her tray down next to Sherri's. "How's Heidi?" she asked. "It isn't the chicken pox, is it?"

"No. Nervous stomach. Her mother—"

"Don't tell me. She ran off with the man who installed their cable TV."

"You're kidding!" Sherri said. "Where did you hear that?"

"I was kidding. What about her mother?"

"Oh, she just lessons Heidi to death. Ballet, tap, swimming, tae kwon do. The poor kid probably wishes her mother would run off with somebody and leave her alone." She sighed. "I wish somebody would run off with me."

"What about Mr. Paprocki?" Dr. Lejeune said.

"Old Paperwork? Are you kidding? He's never even looked at me." She took a bite of macaroni, hamburger, and tomato sauce. "I think my timing must be off or something. I always meet guys after they're already married or engaged. Would you believe I was out with strep throat when Dr. Young did all that testing last March or I could have been the one down there in that cozy little music room with Dr. Simons?"

"All what testing?" Dr. Lejeune said.

"The testing he did to find somebody to work with Dr. Simons," Sherri said, eating her peach slices. "He did all kinds of interviews and stuff and then gave the finalists all these psychological tests. If I'd known how gorgeous Dr. Simons was, I'd have taken a few tests myself, but I thought whoever Dr. Young picked was going to work with *him*!"

Dr. Young had gone up to Fermilab in February and been gone two months. She had assumed—correction, he had let her assume—he was working with the cyclotron that whole time, trying to get his subatomic hodiechrons to switch phases. "The school wouldn't have copies of those tests, would it?"

"Are you kidding? Old Paperwork makes me make copies of *everything*." She stacked her silverware and milk carton on top of her plate. "My timing's always been off. In college I kept meeting guys who'd just been drafted." She stood up and pushed her chair in. "It'd be great if this time-machine thing of Dr. Young's worked, wouldn't it? You'd be able to go back and get the timing right for once."

"Yes," Dr. Lejeune said. "It would."

• • •

Wendy called after school and told Carolyn they had an out-of-town volleyball game and could Carolyn bring her money for McDonald's and some Gatorade to drink on the bus. "Coach Nicotero says we have to have lots of electrolytes." She and Andrew weren't done testing Heidi Dreismeier, but he told her to go on and he'd finish the last few questions.

Carolyn ran by the grocery store and bought the Gatorade and a two-liter bottle of black-cherry pop, which she'd decided was the secret ingredient in the suicides. She took Wendy the Gatorade and the money and picked up Liz at the high school.

"Can you drop me over at Lisa's?" Liz sad. "Harvard sent her a recruitment video. I don't know, though. How important do you think coed dorms are?"

"I don't know," Carolyn said, stopping in front of Lisa's. "We didn't have them."

"You're kidding. How did you meet guys?" She gathered up her books and got out of the car. "Oh, I almost forgot. I saw Dad. He said to tell you he and Linda had to go out to the mall to look at warm-ups. He said not to wait supper."

Carolyn went home and made herself a suicide, adding a very small amount of black cherry to try it out. Not only did we not have coed dorms, she thought, we weren't even allowed to have boys in the dorm. The dorm mother ran a bed check at midnight, and you could be expelled for sneaking a boy into your room, but I still managed somehow to meet boys, Liz. They sat next to me in class, and they danced with me at mixers, and they called me on the phone.

The phone rang. "Thanks a lot for running out on me," Andrew said.

"What happened?" Carolyn asked. "Did Heidi throw up?"

"Worse. Her mother came in. It took me an hour and fifteen minutes to convince her Heidi doesn't need hodiechronicity lessons."

"Sherri says she read this article about Housewife Hysteria, and that's what she thinks Heidi's mother has," Carolyn said. She took a sip of the suicide. Black cherry was not the secret ingredient. "She can't find a socially acceptable outlet for her frustrations and longings."

"So she makes poor Heidi take belly-dancing. She spent forty-five minutes telling me about their Suzuki lessons. I felt like I was caught in some horrible time dilation. It serves me right for going into this business."

"How did you get into this business anyway?" Carolyn said, opening the refrigerator and peering inside to see if there were any other flavors of pop she could try.

"You mean why did I decide to study time? Well, I . . ." There was a long pause and then he said in an odd voice, "Isn't that funny? I don't remember."

"You mean you just sort of gradually got into it?" There was a jar of maraschino cherries in the refrigerator door with one cherry left in it. She ate the cherry and poured the juice into the suicide. "You just drifted into it?"

"Temporal psychology isn't something you just drift into," he said. "This is ridiculous. I can't for the life of me remember."

"Maybe you still haven't gotten used to the altitude or something," Carolyn said, trying out the suicide. Maraschino-cherry juice wasn't the secret ingredient either. "And you're probably under a lot of stress with the project and all. People forget things when they're under stress."

"You forget phone numbers and where you put your keys. You don't forget why you picked your chosen vocation."

"I can't remember whether I had the chicken pox," Carolyn said. "I even called my mother. She said I didn't have it when I was little, but she thought I'd had it when I was in college, and when she said that, it sounded right, but I can't for the life of me remember. It's like there's a big hole where the—"

"Nebraska State College," Andrew said.

"What?" Carolyn said.

"Your college. You went to Nebraska State College. That's where I know you from."

"You're kidding. You went to NSC, too?"

"No, Stanford, but—" He stopped. "You didn't ever go to California when you were in college, did you? For spring break or something?"

"No," Carolyn said. "Did you ever come to Nebraska?"

"No, and you still think I'm trying the old 'Don't I know you from somewhere?' routine, don't you?"

"No," Carolyn said. "I think you probably had a girlfriend in college that I remind you of."

"Not a chance. Stephanie Forrester was blond and malicious."

She certainly was, Carolyn thought. Making him usher at her wedding.

"Brown and gold," he said suddenly.

"What?"

"Your school colors. Brown and gold."

She looked at the suicide and then poured it down the sink. Her school colors were brown and gold, and Andrew had never said a word about Stephanie Forrester until this minute, but she knew all about it, how the head usher was in love with her, too, how they'd gone out drinking clockstoppers and—

"I've got to go fix supper before my husband gets home," she said, and hung up the phone.

Dr. Lejeune had hoped Sherri would look for the tests right away, but when she went into the office after school, Sherri said. "Oh, I forgot all about that. Old Paperwork suddenly decided he wanted me to take an inventory of the supply closet, *including* counting the individual sheets of construction paper."

"How old is Mr. Paprocki?" Dr. Lejeune asked.

"Six, seven," Sherri said, counting green. "Forty-three."

"Forty-three," Dr. Lejeune said thoughtfully, watching Sherri count. "Are you aware that obsessive attention to detail is a classic symptom of sexual repression?"

"Nineteen—you're kidding," Sherri said. She looked at the half-counted stack. "Where was I?"

"Nineteen," Dr. Lejeune said. "Are you sure he's never noticed you?"

"I'm sure. I've been wearing fuchsia for a week." She finished the stack and tamped it down and along the side to straighten the sheets back into line. "I'll try to look for those tests as soon as I finish this inventory."

Dr. Lejeune went down to the music room to see what she could find out from Carolyn, but she wasn't there and neither was Andrew. They had probably gotten lost in all the equipment, Dr. Lejeune thought, looking at the metal boxes stacked next to the piano and lined up under the blackboard. She wondered what he needed the photon counter for. And the spectrum analyzer. She didn't even know what some of this stuff was. She picked up a gray metal box that wasn't plugged into anything. There were no dials or markings on it except an on-off switch. Whatever it was, it was turned on.

The lights went off. "Hey!" Dr. Lejeune shouted. She took a step in the direction of the door. She crashed into the wastebasket. "Hey!" she said again.

"Sorry," Dr. Young said, and the light came on. He came down the narrow ell and into the main part of the room, looking oddly guilty, as if she had just caught him at something. "I didn't know anybody was in here, and I saw the light on. It's a waste of electricity to leave a light on in an empty room and—" He stopped. "What are you doing?"

"Nothing," Dr. Lejeune said, surprised.

He was looking at the box she was still holding. She set it down on the piano. "I was looking for Dr. Simons."

"What for?" he said suspiciously. "You weren't going to try to fix him up with Bev Frantz, were you?"

"I wanted to ask him what he thought of the children he'd tested so far," Dr. Lejeune said stiffly. "The computer isn't showing even a glimmer of a hodiechron, long or short. You should check before you turn out the light. It got black as a coal mine in here."

Dr. Young looked guilty all over again, and he still couldn't take his eyes off the box on the piano.

"I've got to go finish running the extrapolations," Dr. Lejeune said, and went back up to the office.

Sherri was counting yellow construction paper. Dr. Lejeune asked if she could use the phone in Mr. Paprocki's office to call the university. "Forty-two, forty-three," Sherri said. "Sure. You have to fill out these." She handed Dr. Lejeune a sheaf of forms an inch thick.

"I'll call collect," Dr. Lejeune said. She went into the office, shut the door, and called the physics department. "I need to talk to somebody who worked on the temporal oscillator with Dr. Young," she told the graduate assistant who answered the phone. "I want to know exactly what it does."

"The main unit?"

"I suppose so," Dr. Lejeune said. She hadn't been aware the thing had more than one part.

"It has two functions. It produces the agitational stimuli, and it stores the temporal energy collected by the portable transmitter-receivers."

"Agitational stimuli?"

"Yes. A combination of subsonic emissions and subliminal messages that produce an excited emotional state in the experimental subjects."

Yes, and I'll bet I know what those subliminal messages are saying, Dr. Lejeune thought.

"I don't suppose this 'main unit' looks like a lava lamp, does it?"

"A lava lamp? Why on earth would a temporal oscillator look like a lava lamp?"

"Good question," Dr. Lejeune said. "Tell me about these portable transmitter-receivers."

It took two more days to finish kindergarten. Brendan James was the last one on the list. "Maybe we should just skip him," Carolyn said. "He's under a lot of stress."

"I'm not sure we have enough time left today anyway," Andrew said. It was nearly two-thirty. He could tell because the third grade was rattling past on their way out to recess. "Let's put it off till tomorrow, and I'll ask—"

The lights went out.

"Just a minute," Andrew said. "I'll get the flashlight. You can't see a thing in here."

That was an understatement. It was as black as pitch, as black as a mine shaft in there. It was so black, it seemed to destroy his sense of direction as well. He took a step toward the piano and cracked his knee against the desk. Wrong way. He turned around and started in the opposite direction, his hands out in front of him.

"I'll try to find the light switch," Carolyn said, and there was a loud metallic crash.

"Stay right where you are," Andrew said. His hands hit the keyboard in a clatter of notes. "I'm almost there." He grabbed for the piano top and got hold of one of the square metal boxes and then the other. The flashlight wasn't there. He patted his hands over the surface of the piano. "Did you move the flashlight?" he asked.

"No," she said. "Did you?"

"No," he said, turning in the direction her voice was coming from. He crashed into the wastebasket. "I can't see a thing," he said. "It's black as the pit from pole to pole in here. Where are you?"

She didn't answer for a moment, but he didn't need her to tell him. He suddenly knew exactly where she was. He couldn't see a thing; there was not enough light for his eyes even to make an attempt at adjusting, but he knew exactly where she was.

"I'm by the blackboard, I think," she said. She wasn't. She was between the photon counter and the oscilloscope, and all he had to do was reach out his arm and pull her toward him. Her face was already turned up toward his in the pitch darkness. All he had to do was say her name.

And then what? Make her be the next piece of gossip for Sherri to spread? Well, you know what happened to Wendy and Liz's mother, don't you? She ran off with the hodiechronicity man.

"The blackboard's over here," he said, putting his hand on her shoulder and turning her gently toward it. He patted the surface with his free hand, completely sure now of where everything was. He could have walked straight down the narrow tunnel to the light switch and never have made a misstep. "You have a better idea than I do where the light switch is," he said, letting go of her shoulder. "Just keep your hand on the chalk tray, and when you get to the end of it, feel along the wall."

"It's against the rules," she said. "The music teacher doesn't let the kids run their hands against the wall like this."

There was nothing in her voice to indicate she had any idea of how close they'd come to disaster, and probably she didn't. She was happily married to the gymnastics coach. She had a teenaged daughter who was getting ready for college and one who was out for volleyball. She probably hadn't even noticed that they couldn't move in here without touching each other.

"I'm sure the music teacher will make an exception this time," he said. "This is an emergency."

He could tell she had stopped, her hand already on the switch. "I know."

She turned on the light. "I guess I'd better go talk to the third-grade teacher," she said, and opened the door.

"I guess you'd better," he said.

After school Dr. Lejeune went up to the office to ask Mr. Paprocki if she could use his phone to place a long-distance call to Fermilab.

"I can't believe it," Sherri said. "The last single man in the state and he quits."

"Who quit?" Dr. Lejeune said. "Dr. Simons?"

"Yes. He came up about two-thirty and said he was leaving, to tell Dr. Young he was going back to Tibet."

"Is that all he said? Did he leave a note?"

"No," Sherri said. "It's not fair. I went out and bought a whole new fuchsia wardrobe."

Dr. Lejeune went and found Dr. Young. He was in the third grade passing out lollipops. "Andrew's quit," she said.

"I know," he said. He handed her a lollipop.

"He says he's going to Tibet," she said. "Aren't you going to try and stop him?"

"Stop him?" he said. "Why would I do that? If he's unhappy, he's not much use to the project, is he? Besides"—he unwrapped a lollipop—"you can run a video camera, can't you?"

"You sent all the way to Tibet for him. You said he was perfect."

"I know," he said, looking speculatively at the lollipop. "Well, we all make mistakes."

"I should have introduced him to Bev Frantz while I had the chance," Dr. Lejeune said under her breath.

"What?" Dr. Young said.

"I said, what about the project?"

"The project," Dr. Young said, sticking a lollipop in his mouth, "is proceeding right on schedule."

"I've got bad news," Sherri said when Carolyn got to school in the morning.

"Don't tell me," Carolyn said, looking at the testing schedule. "Pam Lopez's mother ran off with the Lutheran minister."

Sherri didn't rise to the bait. "Dr. Simons left," she said.

"Oh," Carolyn said, moving Brendan James's name to the end of first grade. "Where did he go?"

"Tibet."

Good, Carolyn thought. Maybe now you'll stop acting like a college girl. You are not nineteen and living in the dorm. You are forty-one years old. You are married and have two children, and it is just as well he is in Tibet instead of down there in that music room, where you can't even move without brushing against him. "Is Dr. Young going to continue the project?" she said.

"Yes."

Brendan James's mother was married and had two children, Carolyn thought, and what on earth is the matter with you? Brendan James's mother is a complete flake and always has been, and you love your husband, you love Liz and Wendy, and just because they are a little preoccupied with gymnastics and volleyball and college right now is no reason to act like a college girl with a crush. "I wonder who they're going to have replace him? Dr. Young?"

"I don't know. Honestly, you don't seem very upset that he left," Sherri said. "Well, maybe you don't care that the last single man around just departed for another continent, but I do."

Another continent, Carolyn thought. The university wasn't far enough. Even Duke University wasn't far enough. He had to go all the way to Tibet to get away from me.

"There's always Mr. Paprocki," Carolyn said, and went down to the music room.

"Dr. Simons was called away suddenly," Dr. Young told her. He was showing Dr. Lejeune how to use the video camera. "Some kind of emergency," he said.

Some kind of emergency. "This is an emergency," Andrew had said, and he hadn't known the half of it. She had known exactly where he was, standing there in the pitch darkness. She hadn't been able to see her own hand in front of her face, she hadn't been able to find the spectrum analyzer even when she crashed into it, but she had known exactly where he was. All she would have had to do was put her hand on the back of his neck and pull him down to her.

"Sorry to interrupt," Sherri said, holding out a note to Carolyn. "I've got bad news. The senior high just called. Liz has the chicken pox."

Andrew took the Greyhound bus back to the university. Someone had left a *McCall's* on the seat beside him. The cover had a picture of Elizabeth Taylor and the headline, "Are You Ready for an Affair? Our Test Can Help You Tell."

He took the test, answering the questions the way he thought Carolyn would. He remembered her saying her husband was a coach, so he answered yes to "I am lonely a lot of the time." He also answered yes to the question that said, "I sometimes fantasize about someone I know," even though he was sure that was wishful thinking.

Under the test it said, "Give yourself one point for every yes. 0-5: You're not ready. 6-10: Getting there. 11-15: Ready or not, here it comes. 16 and up: DANGER!"

Carolyn got a four.

He stared out the window a while and then took the

test himself, rewording the questions so they would apply to him. To eliminate sexual bias, he answered no to every other PMS question and no to the one that said, "I find myself thinking a lot about an old flame." Stephanie Forrester was not who he thought about while he was staring out the window, and he didn't see how Carolyn Hendricks could qualify as an old flame when all he had ever done was know where she was in the dark.

He scored a twenty-two. He went back and marked all the PMS questions no. He still got a seventeen.

Dr. Young didn't seem any more upset about losing Carolyn than he had about losing Andrew. In fact, as he recited number strings to Troy Yoder, he looked positively cheerful. As soon as he was finished, Dr. Lejeune offered to get the next first grader and went up to the office. "Have you found those tests yet?" she asked Sherri.

"No," Sherri said disgustedly. "I am knee-deep in chicken pox, and *he* decides the milk money accounts should be double entry. The second I get a chance, I promise I'll look for them."

"It's okay," Dr. Lejeune said.

"If you're in a hurry, you might ask Heidi Dreismeier's mother," Sherri said. "She probably sneaked copies of the tests home to try on Heidi."

"Heidi Dreismeier's mother?" Dr. Lejeune asked. "How many people exactly did Dr. Young test?"

"Well, he started out by screening the staff and volunteers and all the homeroom mothers, but that was just an interview kind of thing. Then he narrowed it down to five or so and gave them the whole battery."

"Who were those five?"

"Well, Carolyn Hendricks, of course, and Heidi's mother, and Francine Williams . . ."

"Shannon's mother?" Dr. Lejeune asked.

"Yes, and who else?" She thought a minute. "Oh. Brendan James's mother. It's a good thing she didn't come in first, isn't it? And Maribeth Greenberg. She taught fourth grade here last year."

"How old was she?" Dr. Lejeune asked.

"Forty," Sherri said promptly. "We had a birthday party for her right before she quit."

"She didn't happen to run off with anybody, did she?"

"Maribeth?" Sherri said. "Are you kidding? She left to become a nun."

Liz didn't look too bad when Carolyn picked her up at the high school, but by the next morning she was covered. "What am I going to do?" she wailed. "My senior picture appointment is next week."

"I'll call and change it," Carolyn said, but the phone rang before she could find the number.

"More bad news," Sherri said.

"Wendy?" Carolyn said, thinking, please let them get it at the same time.

"No. Monica and Ricky Morales. I can't get in touch with their mother. She's in real estate. And your name was on the emergency card."

"I'll be right there," Carolyn said. She checked on Liz, who was sleeping on the living-room couch, and drove to the elementary. On the way over she stopped at the grocery store and stocked up on 7-Up, Popsicles, and calamine lotion. She also bought some Dr. Pepper, which she had decided was the missing ingredient in Allison's suicides.

When she got to school, Monica and Ricky were sitting in the office looking flushed and bright-eyed. "We've had five cases since this morning," Sherri told her. "Five cases! And Heidi Dreismeier threw up, but I think it's just her nervous stomach." She helped Monica into her jacket. "I'll keep trying their mother. The office said she was showing apartments to some bachelor."

Carolyn took Monica and Ricky out to the car. Ricky

promptly lay down on the backseat and wouldn't budge. Carolyn had to put the groceries in the trunk so Monica could sit up front beside her. She fastened Monica into the seat belt and started the car.

"Wait, wait!" Sherri yelled, pounding on the window on Monica's side. Carolyn leaned across and opened the window. "You've got another one," she said breathlessly. "It wasn't nervous stomach. Heidi's chest is covered with them. Oh, and I forgot to tell you. Don called. He tried to get you at home. He's going to be late. Two of his girls have got it, and he and Linda have to work up a beam routine with one of the freshmen."

Carolyn shut off the car. "Why do I have to take Heidi?" she said. "Her mother doesn't work."

"She's at a three-day seminar on Spending More Time with Your Child."

Andrew went straight to Dr. Gillis's office as soon as he got back to the university to tell him he'd resigned. "Yes, yes, Max called and told me all about it," Dr. Gillis said. "It's too bad, but if they need you in Tibet, well, then, I guess our project will just have to wait. Now what can we do to expedite your getting back to Tibet?" He called Duke University and the U.S. envoy to China, made arrangements for Bev Frantz to give him a cholera booster, and found a place he could stay on campus until he left.

That last was a bad idea. The dorm room reminded him of the one he had had his junior year at Stanford when he had been in love with Stephanie Forrester. He should have met Carolyn Hendricks his junior year instead of Stephanie. She wouldn't have been Carolyn Hendricks then. She wouldn't have been married and had two kids, and he could have fallen in love with her instead of the kind of girl who would ask her old boyfriends to usher at her wedding. The head usher had been an old boyfriend, too. He had told Andrew that, after a half-dozen clockstoppers or so, and they had both decided they needed a few more. He didn't know how many, but it must have been enough, because the next morning he hadn't been able to remember a thing, and he was completely over Stephanie.

A sure-fire cure. It was too bad liquor wasn't allowed in dorms.

Dr. Young refused to give up on the project, even though by the end of the first week there was almost no one left to test. "We'll work with the data we've got until the epidemic's over," he said, not at all upset. "How long does it take to get over the chicken pox?"

"Two weeks," Dr. Lejeune said, "but Sherri says these outbreaks usually last at least a month. Why don't we go back to the university until it's over? We could leave the equipment here."

"Absolutely not!" Dr. Young thundered. "It is that kind of attitude that has undermined this project from the start!" He stomped off, presumably to go to work with the data they had.

We don't have any data, Dr. Lejeune thought, going up to the office, and my attitude is not what's undermining this project. She wondered why he was so upset. Andrew's leaving hadn't upset him, Carolyn's leaving hadn't upset him, not even the chicken pox had upset him. But the suggestion of leaving here had turned the top of his bald head bright pink.

Sherri was dabbing calamine lotion on a fourth-grader. "I finally found the tests," she said. She handed them to Dr. Lejeune. "Sorry it took so long, but I had six kids go home this morning, three of them to Carolyn Hendricks's house."

Dr. Lejeune looked at the tests. The one on the top was the Idelman-Ponoffo that they'd been giving the kids, and under it were an assortment of psychological tests.

"And as if that isn't bad enough, Old Paperwork decides he wants me to alphabetize the field-trip release slips."

The last test was something called the Rick. Dr. Lejeune didn't recognize it. She asked Sherri if she could use Mr. Paprocki's office and place a call to the psych department at the university.

"It tests logical thinking, responsibility, and devotion to duty," the graduate assistant said.

"How about fidelity?" Dr. Lejeune asked.

"Oh, yes. In fact, Dr. Young over in the physics department just used it in a project of his. He wanted to test the likelihood of affairs among forty-year-olds."

"Say someone scored a six hundred ninety-two on the Rick, what would their chances of having an extramarital affair be?"

"Six hundred ninety-two?" the graduate assistant said. "Nonexistent. Seven hundred's a perfect score."

Perfect, Dr. Lejeune thought. "You wouldn't happen to have Dr. Andrew Simons's score on file, would you?"

"I know Dr. Young did a Rick on him, but I'm not sure where it—"

"Never mind," Dr. Lejeune said. "I already know what he got."

Carolyn checked Wendy's stomach every morning for two weeks, but she didn't show any signs of getting the chicken pox, even though at one point Carolyn had five patients on Wendy's bed, her and Don's bed, and the family-room couch. "I can't get sick," Wendy told her, yanking her T-shirt down after Carolyn had checked her stomach. "We've got a game this afternoon. I have to start. Sarah Perkins got sick yesterday. Coach Nicotero had to call a time out and everything."

That's what I need, Carolyn thought, driving her to practice. A time out. Only there aren't any in this game.

"I've narrowed it down to Vassar, Carleton, and Tufts," Liz said when Carolyn got back. She was lying on the couch dabbing calamine lotion on her legs and reading college catalogs. "How important do you think VCRs in the dorms are, Mom?"

The phone rang. "I am *so* sorry to do this to you," Sherri said, "but I didn't know what else to do. It's Shannon Williams. I called her mother at the bank. Do you think I should have done that?"

"Was she there?"

"I don't know," Sherri said, lowering her voice. "*He* answered the phone and he said she wasn't there, but he sounded really angry and I think she was. So can you come pick her up?"

"I'll be right there," Carolyn said.

She settled Erin in Wendy's bed with her popsicle and some of Wendy's comics. "I've got to go get Shannon Williams," she told Liz, who had given up on the catalog and was watching *All My Children.*

"Is her mother in real estate, too?"

"No," Carolyn said. Her mother is in deep trouble if her husband finds out. And how did that happen? I know how it happened, Carolyn thought. She knew exactly where he was, and she wasn't thinking about her husband or her kids because right then they didn't exist. Talk about time displacement. It was as if that moment, as she stood there in the dark, knowing all she had to do was put her hand on the back of his neck and pull him down to her, was out of time altogether.

Only it wasn't. Shannon Williams's mother was just kidding herself that it was. It would be wonderful if people could step out of time as Dr. Young seemed to think they could, go back to when they were in college and unencumbered with families and responsibilities, but they couldn't. And standing there in the dark, Shannon's mother should have been thinking about how much this was going to hurt her husband. She should have been thinking about who was going to take Shannon to volleyball practice and the orthodontist after the divorce was final.

The phone rang. It was Don. "How are things going?" he asked.

"Great," she said. "Erin Peterson is on the couch, I am on my way to pick up Shannon Williams, we are all out of Popsicles *and* calamine lotion, and you have just called to tell me you're going to be late again."

"Yeah," he said. "I'm sorry to do this to you when you've got all those kids to take care of, but somebody erased all the floor ex music, and we've got a big invitational tomorrow. Luckily, Linda's got a dual tape deck at her apartment, so we're going over there. I'll get home as soon as I can. And listen, you take it easy. You sound terrible."

"Thank you," Carolyn said coldly. She opened the refrigerator. They were all out of pop, too.

"That's what I mean. You're so edgy. Linda thinks you're doing way too much with all these poxy kids. She says a woman your age has to be careful not to overdo."

"Or my arthritis might kick up again?" she said. She hung up, called the bank, and asked for the head loan officer.

"You tell Shannon Williams's mother that I don't care if she's there or not, but she has a sick child and she'd better come pick her up," she said, and hung up.

The phone rang. "I have bad news," Sherri said.

"I don't care who it is," Carolyn said. "Their mother has got to come and get them."

"It's Wendy," Sherri said.

By the end of three weeks, a few scabby children had started to trickle back, but Dr. Young showed no interest in screening them.

"If we're not going to use the music room, why don't we at least move some of that equipment out so the music teacher can get back in?" Dr. Lejeune suggested.

"You are not moving anything anywhere," Dr. Young shouted, his bald head turning fuchsia. "It is that kind of attitude—"

"I know, I know," Dr. Lejeune said, but she went down to the music room anyway. She could at least shift things around so the music teacher could get to the piano.

She dismantled the video camera and stuck it in the music cupboard. At the back between two xylophones was a flashlight. That would come in handy if the lights went out, Dr. Lejeune thought. She put it in her pocket and sidled over to the piano to get the temporal oscillator. The gray box that didn't plug into anything was still on top of the piano, but the two smaller flat ones weren't.

She went upstairs to the office and called Carolyn. "Did Dr. Young send anything home with you?" she asked.

"The interview transcripts," Carolyn said, sounding exhausted. "He thought I might have time to go over them, but I've got a whole bunch of—"

"There wouldn't be a flat gray box in with them, would there?" Dr. Lejeune interrupted.

"I don't think so. Just a minute," Carolyn said. She was gone a long time. "Yeah, it's here. I don't know how it got in with the transcripts. Do you want me to bring it back to school?"

"No," Dr. Lejeune said. "We can get it when we pick up the transcripts. Don't worry about it."

"Is the other one missing, too? There were two of them on top of the piano."

"No, it's not missing," Dr. Lejeune said. "I know right where it is."

Even with Dr. Gillis helping, it took three weeks to arrange everything, and then Andrew had trouble getting a flight to L.A. The one he finally got on was jammed. He was sandwiched in between a sleeping man and a little girl. When the flight attendant came around with the drinks cart, he ordered a clockstopper.

"I'm sorry, sir," she said. "I don't know that drink. How is it made?"

"I wanta Coke," the little girl said.

"Just give me a beer and a wine and I'll mix it myself," he said.

"I'm sorry, sir. I can only sell you one drink at a time."

"Fine," he said, pointing at the sleeping man in the window seat. "Give him a beer and me a wine, and I'll pay for both of them."

The flight attendant slapped a napkin down on his tray and followed it with a vile-looking pinkish-brown drink in a squat plastic glass. It was not anywhere near the amount to do anything but taste the way it looked. He drank it anyway.

The little girl picked her glass up with both hands and then tried to maneuver the straw into her mouth by moving the glass around and grabbing for it with her teeth. "I'm going to see my mom," she said between grabs. "She lives in Santa Monica. My dad lives in Philadelphia. They're getting a divorce."

"Oh?" Andrew said. He twisted around in his seat and tried to catch the attendant's eye, but the cart was already fifteen rows back.

"My mom went to California to find herself," the little girl said. She put down her glass and began blowing bubbles into it with the straw. "She lives with this guy named Carlos. He plays tennis."

The drinks cart disappeared into the recesses of the plane.

"My dad has a new girlfriend named Heather."

A different flight attendant came up with headphones. "Would you like to see the movie? It's Nostalgia Month."

"What's the movie?" the little girl said, bending her straw in half trying to drink upside down.

"An Affair to Remember."

Andrew bought a headset. He put it on, turned the volume all the way down, and closed his eyes.

"My psychiatrist says the divorce has had a traumatic effect on me," the little girl said, holding her straw above her head and catching the drips with her tongue. "He says I feel abandoned and neglected."

Andrew took off the headphones and put them on the little girl. He put his seat back, snatched the blanket away from the sleeping man, and stared out the window of the plane. It looked like it was snowing.

Dr. Lejeune waited till nearly all the teachers had left the building and then went down to the music room and got the gray box with the on-off switch. She took it upstairs to the office and asked Sherri where Mr. Paprocki was.

"He's got late bus duty," Sherri said. "One of the second-grade teachers went home with the chicken pox at noon."

"Oh," Dr. Lejeune said. "Did he tell you about the music room?"

Sherri shook her head. She looked a little haggard, and she wasn't wearing fuchsia, but that wouldn't matter.

"He wants you to file all the sheet music according to key signature," she said.

As soon as Sherri started downstairs, Dr. Lejeune walked out to the playground. She met Mr. Paprocki coming in. "Sherri sent me to get you. She's in the music room. I'm afraid she's coming down with the chicken pox."

Mr. Paprocki took off at a dead run. Dr. Lejeune followed, still carrying the gray box, and as soon as he was all the way in the music room, she turned off the light.

"Hey!" Sherri and Mr. Paprocki said.

Dr. Lejeune locked the door and went up to the kindergarten. "I want to know what's going on," she said.

Dr. Young was sitting at the computer. "Going on?" he said, turning around. "What do you mean?" He saw the gray box. The top of his bald head went pale. "What are you doing with that?"

"I'm turning the temporal oscillator off in about ten seconds if you don't tell me what's going on," she said, holding her hand over the switch. "This *is* the temporal oscillator, isn't it? Along with the portable transmitter-receivers you sent home with Carolyn—where's Andrew Simons's? In his luggage?"

"Yes," Dr. Young said. "Don't—what do you want to know?"

"I want to know what your project really is, and don't tell me you're testing kindergartners' hodiechrons, because I know that's just a blind," she said. "What are you really doing? You hired a housewife whose husband is never home and a psychologist who hasn't had sex in five years, and you stuck them down in a tiny room where they couldn't move without touching each other, and then you turned off the lights and started subsonically whispering in their ears." She moved her hand closer to the switch. "You obviously wanted them to have an affair, and what I want to know is why."

"I didn't want them to have an affair," he said.

"I don't believe you," she said, taking hold of the switch.

"It's true! All right, all right, I'll tell you everything! Just take your hand away from the switch."

Dr. Lejeune did. Dr. Young sank down on one of the tiny kindergarten chairs. "I needed to have maximum agitation, but subsonics and subliminals aren't enough to produce an excited emotional state, so I had to have subjects who were already under stress. People going through midlife crises experience a lot of stress. They worry about growing old, they think about death, they long for the past. Most of them find some outlet for that longing—"

"Like running off with the Make Me Marvy man," Dr. Lejeune said.

"Or finding God," Dr. Young said, "or becoming obsessive about their children or their work."

"But people who score a six-ninety on the Rick don't have any outlets."

"Right. So their hodiechrons would be in a maximum state of agitation."

"And if they weren't, you'd see to it that they were," Dr. Lejeune said grimly. "What did you do besides the subsonics? Hire Sherri to talk about Shannon Williams's mother's boyfriend at the bank? Release some chicken pox virus into the air?"

"I had nothing to do with Sherri or the chicken pox," he said stiffly. "I was simply trying to maximize their agitation so their hodiechrons would be destabilized. Hodiechrons can't be switched when they're stable."

"What about Carolyn and Andrew?"

"They're simply supplying temporal energy, which is then stored in the oscillator. The actual time-displacement experiments will be carried out on laboratory rats."

"Oh. They're simply supplying temporal energy. And what about what's going to happen to them afterwards?"

"Nothing's going to happen to them afterwards," Dr. Young said, looking as if he were getting ready to lunge for the storage unit. "The temporal oscillator has no effect on them whatsoever."

"No effect on them? What about all those feelings you've churned up? What are they supposed to do with those?"

"They'll get over them as soon as they're removed from contact with the temporal oscillator. Their agitation level will gradually drop back to normal, and they'll forget about it. I don't know what you're so worried about. They can't have an affair with Andrew on the way to Tibet, and I plan to send Linda back to central casting as soon as—"

"You hired Linda!" Dr. Lejeune said, her hand trembling on the switch.

"I had to. Carolyn scored a six-ninety on the Rick. Nobody else got above a five hundred. But she was too happily married."

"And you wanted maximum agitation, so you had to ruin her marriage."

"Oh, I don't think so," Dr. Young said, walking carefully towards her. "Her husband scored a four-eighty, and Linda was under strict orders—"

"You wanted maximum agitation," Dr. Lejeune said, so angry she could hardly speak, "so you took probably the only two people left in the world who wouldn't cheat on their spouses and you poked and prodded them and subjected them to subliminals till they were in love and miserable, and you planned to go off and leave them like that, sitting ducks for the next Tibetan bar girl or colors consultant to come along, didn't you? Didn't you?"

Dr. Young took a few more cautious steps forward. "I think you're exaggerating. They scored above six hundred on the Rick. They won't go off with someone else. Andrew will go back to the lamasery and Carolyn will go back to her husband."

"And what about all the resentment and distrust and desire that's been built up in the meantime? What about all that longing for the past?"

"It will be used in my time-displacement experiments," Dr. Young said.

"The hell it will."

Dr. Young grabbed for the temporal oscillator and got it away from her before she could flip the switch. "I couldn't let you turn it off," he said. "There's no telling what the sudden release of all that temporal energy might do."

"It's too late," Dr. Lejeune said. "I already did."

• • •

Linda called just after Don left for the state meet. "I was just wondering if I should bring an overnight bag. The weather report looks like we might have to stay overnight. Is it still chicken-pox city over there?"

"Yes," Carolyn said, "and it's highly contagious, so you'd better not get too close to Don. He's never had the chicken pox, and it would be terrible if you got it with those French-cut leotards and all."

After she hung up, she went in and checked on the patients. Liz was asleep on the couch with a Texas A & M brochure in her hand. Susy Hopkins was in her and Don's bed. Her mother had called to say she had to work the late shift in the pediatrics ward because of all the chicken pox. Wendy still hadn't finished breaking out. She looked flushed.

Carolyn put her hand on Wendy's forehead, expecting it to be warm, but it felt cool. She felt her own forehead. Warm, too warm. I must not have had the chicken pox after all, she thought. But she had. In college. She'd been the only person in her whole dorm to get it, and the doctor hadn't been able to figure out how she'd caught it.

She covered Wendy up. There was an afghan at the foot of the bed. She took it into Liz's room and lay down under it.

She had been in the infirmary ten days, and the doctor had made her make a list of everybody she might have exposed, and she had written Don's name down because he sat next to her in psychology, and that was how they met.

She was shivering badly, hunched under the too-small afghan. Her throat ached. I'm definitely catching chicken pox, she thought. Only I can't be. I had it fall quarter of my sophomore year. The quarter Allison was in Europe. I remember now. She put her hand under her burning cheek and fell asleep.

• • •

The lights went out, and he couldn't see anything. He took a step forward and crashed into something. A wastebasket. He didn't remember there being a wastebasket next to the bar. He tried to set it back up and cracked his knee against something else. A chair. There hadn't been any chairs in the bar either. And no bar stools either. He and Stephanie Forrester's head usher had had to kind of lean on the bar to drink their clockstoppers. He must be back in his dorm room.

"Who's there?" a female voice said. "Is somebody there?"

He was not in his room. He took a step backward and crashed into the wastebasket again.

"I know there's somebody there," the voice said, sounding frightened. He heard a crash, and then she must have opened the curtains or pulled a shade or something, because he could see her in the pale light thrown from a street lamp outside.

She was sitting up on a bed, wrapped in a blanket on top of the covers. There was a book open on the bed beside her. She must have fallen asleep reading. There was a clock on the desk. It said three-thirty. The lamp she'd just tried to turn on was lying on its side on the floor. He moved to pick it up.

"Don't you come near me!" the girl said, scrambling back to the head of the bed, the blanket held up tight against her. "How did you get in here?"

"I don't know," he said. He looked around the room. There was a chain on the door. The window. Maybe he'd come in the window and shut it behind him. It was snowing. Snowflakes drifted past the street lamp outside, and he could see it piled up on the windowsill. "I don't know," he said helplessly.

The girl was looking at the window and the chained door, too. "Are you a friend of Allison's?" she asked.

"No." Stephanie Forrester. He had been ushering at

Stephanie Forrester's wedding and . . . "Are you a friend of Stephanie's?"

"No," she said. "Are you drunk?"

That must be it. He was drunk. It would explain a number of things, such as why he couldn't remember what he was doing in some strange girl's room in the middle of the night. "I'm drunk," he said, suddenly remembering. "I was drinking clockstoppers with Stephanie's head usher. Beer and wine. Together."

"That'll do it," she said, not sounding particularly frightened anymore. She had let the blanket slip a little, and he could see that she was wearing a brown T-shirt that barely covered her hips. Nebraska State College, the yellow letters on the T-shirt said. He tried not to feel worried about that. And the snow.

There was a simple explanation for all this. It had started snowing while he and the head usher were in the bar. It snowed sometimes in California. Her boyfriend from Nebraska had given her the T-shirt.

"Do you have a boyfriend?" he said, and instantly regretted it. She looked wildly around for something to defend herself with. "Your T-shirt," he said hastily. "I figured your boyfriend gave it to you or something since it's not from this school."

"It *is* from this school," she said. "Nebraska State College."

"In Nebraska?" he said. He grabbed for the back of the desk chair and almost tipped it over again.

"Where exactly were you drinking these clockstoppers?" the girl asked.

"California."

Neither of them said anything for a minute. Finally the girl said, "Don't you remember anything about how you got here?"

"Yes," he said. "I was . . . no."

"It'll come to you if you don't think about it," the girl said, and then looked scared. "I feel like I said that before, or somebody said it to me. Only I have this funny feeling it hasn't happened yet."

She leaned forward on her hands and looked hard at him. "I know you," she said. "You're a temporal psychologist."

"I'm an English major," he said. "I was drinking clockstoppers with Stephanie Forrester's head usher, and all of a sudden it got as black as—"

"The pit from pole to pole," the girl said.

He knocked over the chair. "I know you," he said. "You're Carolyn Hendricks."

She shook her head. "I'm Carolyn Rutherford."

"That's your maiden name. Your married name is Hendricks."

"I'm not married," she said, starting to look scared again.

"Not yet you're not. But you will be. You'll have two daughters."

"You're Dr. Andrew Simons," she said suddenly. "You spent the last five years in Tibet studying déjà vu."

"I spent the last five years in high school and going to Stanford. And why would I study déjà vu? I'm an English major."

"*Were* an English major. I think after tonight you'll probably switch your major to psychology." She sat back on her heels. "Hendricks, huh? I think there's a guy named Hendricks in my psych class."

"But you haven't met him yet," he said, no longer bewildered, no longer uneasy. "And I haven't met you yet. But I will. In about twenty years."

"Yes," she said, "and I'll be married and have two daughters, and you'll be in Tibet."

"And there won't be any possible way for us to get together because the timing will be all wrong," he said.

"All things are possible," she said. "It's three-thirty." She smiled a little, leaning toward him on her hands. "They never check the rooms after midnight."

"What about your roommate?" he said, and her sudden look of surprised joy almost staggered him.

"Oh," she said happily, "this is the quarter Allison's in Europe."

"I couldn't find you," Don said. He was standing over her with a mug.

"Susy was in our bed," she said sleepily. "How was the meet?" She sat up and pulled the afghan over her knees.

"We took second." He got down on the bed and handed her the mug. "Jennifer Whipple got sick and couldn't do her bar routine, and Linda quit. How are you doing?"

"Fine," she said, taking a sip. "What is this?"

"A suicide," he said. "I remembered you were crazy about them in college, so I stopped at the 7-Eleven and bought some ginger ale and—"

"Ginger ale!" Carolyn said. "That was what I couldn't remember." She took another sip. "It tastes just like the ones Allison used to make. Oh, and speaking of Allison, I finally remembered when I had the chicken pox. It was the quarter Allison was in Europe. It was the strangest thing. I . . . Linda quit?"

"Halfway through the vaulting. She didn't even come home on the bus with us. I tried to call you."

"To tell me she quit?"she said.

"No. To tell you you'd had the chicken pox. Jennifer got sick, and all of a sudden I remembered you'd had it in college. It beats me how I could have forgotten, since that's how we met. I came to see you in the infirmary."

"I know," Carolyn said. "The doctor made me make a list of who I might have exposed, and I put your name down because you sat next to me in my psych class."

"You looked terrible when I came to see you in the infirmary," he said, grinning at her. "You were all covered with scabs. And sitting there looking at you, I had this funny kind of vision of the two of us married with two kids and both of them with the chicken pox. I don't think Linda understood that part."

"You told Linda?"

"Yeah. She was talking about how touchy you were on the phone. She said nobody could be that crabby unless they were coming down with something, and all of a sudden I remembered how I'd met you, and so I told her."

"No wonder she quit," Carolyn said.

"Yeah, I guess it was probably boring for a kid like her to have to listen to an old geezer like me talking about things that happened a long time ago. The funny thing is, it doesn't feel like a long time ago, though, you know. It feels like it just happened yesterday."

"I know," Carolyn said. "That isn't the only funny thing. I—"

"Listen, honey, I've got to go back to school," Don said. He patted her knee. "I've got to unload the equipment. I just thought I'd better come check on you since you didn't answer the phone."

She draped the afghan over her shoulders and followed him into the living room. "I didn't hear it ring," she said. "And that's not the only funny thing. I—"

"I decided on a college," Liz said. She was sitting up on the couch dabbing calamine lotion on her arms. "NSC."

"NSC?" Carolyn said. "I thought you'd narrowed it down to Vassar, Carleton, and Tufts."

"Well, I had, but I couldn't sleep because I was itching, and I got to thinking about how you and Dad are always saying how great NSC was, so I decided to go there instead."

"It was great," Don said. "That's where I met your mother. She had the chicken pox and—"

"I *know*," Liz said. "You've told that story about a million times."

"The old geezer strikes again," Don said. He kissed

Carolyn. "I'll be back in an hour if I don't suddenly go senile while I'm unloading the bus." He kissed Carolyn again.

"I don't see how having the chicken pox could have been all that romantic," Liz said after he'd left.

"It was," Carolyn said.

Dr. Lejeune went to see Andrew in the university infirmary. "Sherri Paprocki said to say hello," she said. "She wants to know how you managed to get the chicken pox. The incubation period is only two weeks, and you didn't catch it till five weeks after you'd left."

"On the plane to L.A. I sat next to a little girl who must have been contagious," he said. "It's a good thing I decided not to go to Tibet."

"Excuse me," Bev Frantz said. She came in with a thermometer. "I need to take your temp."

"Great," Andrew said. "I was hoping I'd see you agai—"

She stuck the thermometer in his mouth and looked at the box. He smiled up at her. She concentrated fiercely on the LED readout.

He didn't look sick except for the calamine-covered scabs all over his face and arms. In fact, he looked better than Dr. Lejeune had ever seen him look. Happier.

The box beeped. Bev took the sensor out of his mouth and shoved it back in its carrier. She turned to Dr. Lejeune. "Dr. Young's been asking for you."

"You really should go see him," Andrew said. "I think he wants to apologize."

"You're the one he should apologize to," she said, and then looked closely at him. "Or should he? Are you sure you got the chicken pox from that little girl?"

"Max really cares about you, you know," Andrew said. "He told me the reason he started the project in the first place was to impress you."

"Hmm," Dr. Lejeune said. She told Andrew good-bye and went out in the hall.

"I wondered if I could talk to you about Dr. Simons for a minute," Bev said. "I really like him, but when he was in here before for his cholera booster, I got the idea he was in love with somebody else."

"He was," Dr. Lejeune said. "A girl he knew in college. But that was a long time ago. I wouldn't worry about it."

She started out the door and then turned around and went into Max's room. He looked terrible. He had chicken pox on the top of his bald head, and he was wearing a pair of mittens that were taped at the wrist. "Well?" he said. "Has he asked her out yet?"

"Who?" Dr. Lejeune said.

"Andrew. Has he asked Bev out? I told him he'd better latch on to her while he still has the chance. I've been trying to get them together ever since I got in here. It's the least I can do."

"I thought you said matchmaking was a substitute for sex."

"It is," he said. "So was my time machine. I wanted to go back in time and be young again."

"You're not that old. You caught the chicken pox, didn't you?"

"Nothing happened, did you know that? All that energy released at once, and nothing. Carolyn slept through the whole thing." He reached up with his mittened hand to scratch his face and then laid his hand back in his lap. She had never felt so sorry for anyone in her whole life.

"Would you like me to rub on some calamine?" she asked.

"Nothing happened to him either."

"He caught the chicken pox." She opened the bottle of calamine and dabbed some on his cheek. "Did you know when Carolyn had it in college, she was the only person in her dorm to get it? Nobody could figure out where she caught it from. Personally, I think she caught it from that poxy bunch of kids at her house. And now Andrew has the chicken pox, and nobody can figure out where he got it from."

"He said he caught it from a little girl he sat next to on the plane."

"Personally, I think he caught it from Carolyn." She stood up and dabbed calamine on the top of his head.

"You mean—" he said, perking up noticeably.

"Your theory says that an entire hodiechron could be displaced. Including chicken-pox viruses. Suppose Carolyn caught the chicken pox from one of those kids she was taking care of and was contagious but she didn't have any symptoms yet. Suppose she gave the chicken pox to Andrew when they were in college."

"We could call the airlines and find out who the little girl was and if she came down with the chicken pox," he said excitedly. He began trying to get the tape off his wrists with his mittened hands. "We can run the experiment again. Heidi Dreismeier's mother scored a four-ninety, and we can surely find—" He stopped and laid his hands back in his lap. "We can't run the experiment again. You were right. I had no business messing with people's lives."

"Who said anything about messing with people's lives? Why can't we run the experiment on ourselves? I worry about being old, I long for the past, and I'm about as desperate for sex as they come. I'd love to be shut in a cramped little room with you."

Dr. Young took hold of her hands with his mittened ones. "I don't think you're old," he said. He leaned forward to peck her on the cheek.

Bev came in carrying her thermometer. "Oops, sorry," she said. "I'm obviously in the wrong place at the wrong time."

"We may be able to do something about that," Dr. Lejeune said.

"Our Violet setting her cap for you," Swales said. "Girls always go for poets."

"I'm a journalist, not a poet. What about Renfrew?" He nodded his head toward the cots in the other room.

"Renfrew!" Swales boomed, pushing his chair back and starting into the room.

"Shh," I said. "Don't wake him. He hasn't slept all week."

"You're right. It wouldn't be fair in his weakened condition." He sat back down. "And Morris is married. What about your son, Morris? He's a pilot, isn't he? Stationed in London?"

Morris shook his head. "Quincy's up at North Weald."

"Lucky, that," Swales said. "Looks as if that leaves you, Twickenham."

"Sorry," Twickenham said, typing. "She's not my type."

"She's not anyone's type, is she?" Swales said.

"The RAF's," Morris said, and we all fell silent, thinking of Vi and her bewildering popularity with the RAF pilots in and around London. She had pale eyelashes and colorless brown hair she put up in flat little pin curls while she was on duty, which was against regulations, though Mrs. Lucy didn't say anything to her about them. Vi was dumpy and rather stupid, and yet she was out constantly with one pilot after another, going to dances and parties.

"I still say she makes it all up," Swales said. "She buys all those things she says they give her herself, all those oranges and chocolate. She buys them on the black market."

"On a full-time's salary?" I said. We only made two pounds a week, and the things she brought home to the post—sweets and sherry and cigarettes—couldn't be bought on that. Vi shared them round freely, though liquor and cigarettes were against regulations as well. Mrs. Lucy didn't say anything about them, either.

She never reprimanded her wardens about anything, except being malicious about Vi, and we never gossiped in her presence. I wondered where she was. I hadn't seen her since I came in.

"Where's Mrs. Lucy?" I asked. "She's not late as well, is she?"

Morris nodded toward the pantry door. "She's in her office. Olmwood's replacement is here. She's filling him in."

Olmwood had been our best part-time, a huge out-of-work collier who could lift a house beam by himself, which was why Nelson, using his authority as district warden, had had him transferred to his own post.

"I hope the new man's not any good," Swales said. "Or Nelson will steal *him*."

"I saw Olmwood yesterday," Morris said. "He looked like Renfrew, only worse. He told me Nelson keeps them out the whole night patrolling and looking for incendiaries."

There was no point in that. You couldn't see where the incendiaries were falling from the street, and if there was an incident, nobody was anywhere to be found. Mrs. Lucy had assigned patrols at the beginning of the Blitz, but within a week she'd stopped them at midnight so we could get some sleep. Mrs. Lucy said she saw no point in our getting killed when everyone was already in bed anyway.

"Olmwood says Nelson makes them wear their gas masks the entire time they're on duty and holds stirrup-pump drills twice a shift," Morris said.

"Stirrup-pump drills!" Swales exploded. "How difficult does he think it is to learn to use one? Nelson's not getting me on his post, I don't care if Churchill himself signs the transfer papers."

The pantry door opened. Mrs. Lucy poked her head

out. "It's half past eight. The spotter'd better go upstairs even if the sirens haven't gone," she said. "Who's on duty tonight?"

"Vi," I said, "but she hasn't come in yet."

"Oh, dear," she said. "Perhaps someone had better go look for her."

"I'll go," I said, and started pulling on my boots.

"Thank you, Jack," she said. She shut the door.

I stood up and tucked my pocket torch into my belt. I picked up my gas mask and slung it over my arm in case I ran into Nelson. The regulations said they were to be worn while patrolling, but Mrs. Lucy had realized early on that you couldn't see anything with them on. Which is why, I thought, she has the best post in the district, including Admiral Nelson's.

Mrs. Lucy opened the door again and leaned out for a moment. "She usually comes by underground. Sloane Square," she said. "Take care."

"Right," Swales said. "Vi might be lurking outside in the dark, waiting to pounce!" He grabbed Twickenham round the neck and hugged him to his chest.

"I'll be careful," I said, and went up the basement stairs and out onto the street.

I went the way Vi usually came from Sloane Square Station, but there was no one in the blacked-out streets except a girl hurrying to the underground station, carrying a blanket, a pillow, and a dress on a hanger.

I walked the rest of the way to the tube station with her to make sure she found her way, though it wasn't that dark. The nearly full moon was up, and there was a fire still burning down by the docks from the raid of the night before.

"Thanks awfully," the girl said, switching the hanger to her other hand so she could shake hands with me. She was much nicer looking than Vi, with blond, very curly hair. "I work for this old stewpot at John Lewis's, and she won't let me leave even a minute before closing, will she, even if the sirens have gone."

I waited outside the station for a few minutes and then walked up to the Brompton Road, thinking Vi might have come in at South Kensington instead, but I didn't see her, and she still wasn't at the post when I got back.

"We've a new theory for why the sirens haven't gone," Swales said. "We've decided our Vi's set her cap for the Luftwaffe, and they've surrendered."

"Where's Mrs. Lucy?" I asked.

"Still in with the new man," Twickenham said.

"I'd better tell Mrs. Lucy I couldn't find her," I said, and started for the pantry.

Halfway there the door opened, and Mrs. Lucy and the new man came out. He was scarcely a replacement for the burly Olmwood. He was not much older than I was, slightly built, hardly the sort to lift housebeams. His face was thin and rather pale, and I wondered if he was a student.

"This is our new part-time, Mr. Settle," Mrs. Lucy said. She pointed to each of us in turn. "Mr. Morris, Mr. Twickenham, Mr. Swales, Mr. Harker." She smiled at the part-time and then at me. "Mr. Harker's name is Jack, too," she said. "I shall have to work at keeping you straight."

"A pair of jacks," Swales said. "Not a bad hand."

The part-time smiled.

"Cots are in there if you'd like to have a lie-down," Mrs Lucy said, "and if the raids are close, the coal cellar's reinforced. I'm afraid the rest of the basement isn't, but I'm attempting to rectify that." She waved the papers in her hand. "I've applied to the district warden for reinforcing beams. Gas masks are in there," she said, pointing at a wooden chest, "batteries for the torches are in here"—she pulled a drawer open—"and the duty roster's posted on this wall." She pointed at the neat columns. "Patrols here and watches here. As you can see, Miss Westen has the first watch for tonight."

"She's still not here," Twickenham said, not even pausing in his typing.

"I couldn't find her," I said.

"Oh, dear," she said. "I do hope she's all right. Mr. Twickenham, would you mind terribly taking Vi's watch?"

"I'll take it," Jack said. "Where do I go?"

"I'll show him," I said, starting for the stairs.

"No, wait," Mrs. Lucy said. "Mr. Settle, I hate to put you to work before you've even had a chance to become acquainted with everyone, and there really isn't any need to go up till after the sirens have gone. Come and sit down, both of you." She took the flowered cozy off the teapot. "Would you like a cup of tea, Mr. Settle?"

"No, thank you," he said.

She put the cozy back on and smiled at him. "You're from Yorkshire, Mr. Settle," she said as if we were all at a tea party. "Whereabouts?"

"Newcastle," he said politely.

"What brings you to London?" Morris said.

"The war," he said, still politely.

"Wanted to do your bit, eh?"

"Yes."

"That's what my son Quincy said. 'Dad,' he says, 'I want to do my bit for England. I'm going to be a pilot.' Downed twenty-one planes, he has, my Quincy," Morris told Jack, "and been shot down twice himself. Oh, he's had some scrapes, I could tell you, but it's all top secret."

Jack nodded.

There were times I wondered whether Morris, like Violet with her RAF pilots, had invented his son's exploits. Sometimes I even wondered if he had invented the son, though if that were the case, he might surely have made up a better name than Quincy.

" 'Dad,' he says to me out of the blue, 'I've got to do

my bit,' and he shows me his enlistment papers. You could've knocked me over with a feather. Not that he's not patriotic, you understand, but he'd had his little difficulties at school, sowed his wild oats, so to speak, and here he was, saying, 'Dad, I want to do my bit.' "

The sirens went, taking up one after the other. Mrs. Lucy said, "Ah, well, here they are now," as if the last guest had finally arrived at her tea party, and Jack stood up.

"If you'll just show me where the spotter's post is, Mr. Harker," he said.

"Jack," I said. "It's a name that should be easy for you to remember."

I took him upstairs to what had been Mrs. Lucy's cook's garret bedroom—unlike the street, a perfect place to watch for incendiaries. It was on the fourth floor, higher than most of the buildings on the street so one could see anything that fell on the roofs around. One could see the Thames, too, between the chimney pots, and in the other direction the searchlights in Hyde Park.

Mrs. Lucy had set a wing-backed chair by the window, from which the glass had been removed, and the narrow landing at the head of the stairs had been reinforced with heavy oak beams that even Olmwood couldn't have lifted.

"One ducks out here when the bombs get close," I said, shining the torch on the beams. "It'll be a swish and then a sort of rising whine." I led him into the bedroom. "If you see incendiaries, call out and try to mark exactly where they fall on the roofs." I showed him how to use the gunsight mounted on a wooden base that we used for a sextant and handed him the binoculars. "Anything else you need?" I asked.

"No," he said soberly. "Thank you."

I left him and went back downstairs. They were still discussing Violet.

"I'm really becoming worried about her," Mrs. Lucy

said. One of the ack-ack guns started up, and there was the dull crump of bombs far away, and we all stopped to listen.

"ME 109's," Morris said. "They're coming in from the south again."

"I do hope she has the sense to get to a shelter," Mrs. Lucy said, and Vi burst in the door.

"Sorry I'm late," she said, setting a box tied with string on the table next to Twickenham's typewriter. She was out of breath and her face was suffused with color. "I know I'm supposed to be on watch, but Harry took me out to see his plane this afternoon, and I had a horrid time getting back." She heaved herself out of her coat and hung it over the back of Jack's chair. "You'll never believe what he's named it! The *Sweet Violet*!" She untied the string on the box. "We were so late we hadn't time for tea, and he said, 'You take this to your post and have a good tea, and I'll keep the jerries busy till you've finished,' " She reached in the box and lifted out a torte with sugar icing. "He's painted the name on the nose and put little violets in purple all round it," she said, setting it on the table. "One for every jerry he's shot down."

We stared at the cake. Eggs and sugar had been rationed since the beginning of the year, and they'd been in short supply even before that. I hadn't seen a fancy torte like this in over a year.

"It's raspberry filling," she said, slicing through the cake with a knife. "They hadn't any chocolate." She held the knife up, dripping jam. "Now, who wants some, then?"

"I do," I said. I had been hungry since the beginning of the war and ravenous since I'd joined the ARP, especially for sweets, and I had my piece eaten before she'd finished setting slices on Mrs. Lucy's Wedgwood plates and passing them round.

There was still a quarter left. "Who's upstairs taking

my watch?" she said, sucking a bit of raspberry jam off her finger.

"The new part-time," I said. "I'll take it up to him."

She cut a slice and eased it off the knife and onto the plate. "What's he like?" she asked.

"He's from Yorkshire," Twickenham said, looking at Mrs. Lucy. "What did he do up there before the war?"

Mrs. Lucy looked at her cake, as if surprised that it was nearly eaten. "He didn't say," she said.

"I meant, is he handsome?" Vi said, putting a fork on the plate with the slice of cake. "Perhaps I should take it up to him myself."

"He's puny. Pale," Swales said, his mouth full of cake. "Looks as if he's got consumption."

"Nelson won't steal him anytime soon, that's certain," Morris said.

"Oh, well, then," Vi said, and handed the plate to me.

I took it and went upstairs, stopping on the second-floor landing to shift it to my left hand and switch on my pocket torch.

Jack was standing by the window, the binoculars dangling from his neck, looking out past the rooftops toward the river. The moon was up, reflecting whitely off the water like one of the German flares, lighting the bombers' way.

"Anything in our sector yet?" I said.

"No," he said, without turning round. "They're still to the east."

"I've brought you some raspberry cake," I said.

He turned and looked at me.

I held the cake out. "Violet's young man in the RAF sent it."

"No, thank you," he said. "I'm not fond of cake."

I looked at him with the same disbelief I had felt for Violet's name emblazoned on a Spitfire. "There's plenty," I said. "She brought a whole torte."

"I'm not hungry, thanks. You eat it."

"Are you sure? One can't get this sort of thing these days."

"I'm certain," he said, and turned back to the window.

I looked hesitantly at the slice of cake, guilty about my greed but hating to see it go to waste and still hungry. At the least I should stay up and keep him company.

"Violet's the warden whose watch you took, the one who was late," I said. I sat down on the floor, my back to the painted baseboard, and started to eat. "She's full-time. We've got five full-timers. Violet and I and Renfrew—you haven't met him yet, he was asleep. He's had rather a bad time. Can't sleep in the day—and Morris and Twickenham. And then there's Petersby. He's part-time like you."

He didn't turn around while I was talking or say anything, only continued looking out the window. A scattering of flares drifted down, lighting the room.

"They're a nice lot," I said, cutting a bite of cake with my fork. In the odd light from the flares the jam filling looked black. "Swales can be rather a nuisance with his teasing sometimes, and Twickenham will ask you all sorts of questions, but they're good men on an incident."

He turned around. "Questions?"

"For the post newspapers. Notice sheet, really, information on new sorts of bombs, ARP regulations, that sort of thing. All Twickenham's supposed to do is type it and send it round to the other posts, but I think he's always fancied himself an author, and now he's got his chance. He's named the notice sheet *Twickenham's Twitterings*, and he adds all sorts of things—drawings, news, gossip, interviews."

While I had been talking, the drone of engines overhead had been growing steadily louder. It passed, there was a sighing whoosh and then a whistle that turned into a whine.

"Stairs," I said, dropping my plate. I grabbed his arm

and yanked him into the shelter of the landing. We crouched against the blast, my hands over my head, but nothing happened. The whine became a scream and then sounded suddenly farther off. I peeked round the reinforcing beam at the open window. Light flashed and then the crump came, at least three sectors away. "Lees," I said, going over to the window to see if I could tell exactly where it was. "High explosive bomb." Jack focused the binoculars where I was pointing.

I went out to the landing, cupped my hands, and shouted down the stairs, "HE. Lees." The planes were still too close to bother sitting down again. "Twickenham's done interviews with all the wardens," I said, leaning against the wall. "He'll want to know what you did before the war, why you became a warden, that sort of thing. He wrote up a piece on Vi last week."

Jack had lowered the binoculars and was watching where I had pointed. The fires didn't start right away with a high explosive bomb. It took a bit for the ruptured gas mains and scattered coal fires to catch. "What was she before the war?" he asked.

"Vi? A stenographer," I said. "And something of a wallflower, I should think. The war's been rather a blessing for our Vi."

"A blessing," Jack said, looking out at the high explosive in Lees. From where I was sitting, I couldn't see his face except in silhouette, and I couldn't tell whether he disapproved of the word or was merely bemused by it.

"I didn't mean a blessing exactly. One can scarcely call something as dreadful as this a blessing. But the war's given Vi a chance she wouldn't have had otherwise. Morris says without it she'd have died an old maid, and now she's got all sorts of beaux." A flare drifted down, white and then red. "Morris says the war's the best thing that ever happened to her."

"Morris," he said, as if he didn't know which one that was.

"Sandy hair, toothbrush mustache," I said. "His son's a pilot."

"Doing his bit," he said, and I could see his face clearly in the reddish light, but I still couldn't read his expression.

A stick of incendiaries came down over the river, glittering like sparklers, and fires sprang up everywhere.

The next night there was a bad incident off Old Church Street, two HEs. Mrs. Lucy sent Jack and me over to see if we could help. It was completely overcast, which was supposed to stop the Luftwaffe but obviously hadn't, and very dark. By the time we reached the King's Road, I had completely lost my bearings.

I knew the incident had to be close, though, because I could smell it. It wasn't truly a smell; it was a painful sharpness in the nose from the plaster dust and smoke and whatever explosive the Germans put in their bombs. It always made Vi sneeze.

I tried to make out landmarks, but all I could see was the slightly darker outline of a hill on my left. I thought blankly, We must be lost. There aren't any hills in Chelsea, and then realized it must be the incident.

"The first thing we do is find the incident officer," I told Jack. I looked round for the officer's blue light, but I couldn't see it. It must be behind the hill.

I scrabbled up it with Jack behind me, trying not to slip on the uncertain slope. The light was on the far side of another, lower hill, a ghostly bluish blur off to the left. "It's over there," I said. "We must report in. Nelson's likely to be the incident officer, and he's a stickler for procedure."

I started down, skidding on the broken bricks and plaster. "Be careful," I called back to Jack. "There are all sorts of jagged pieces of wood and glass."

"Jack," he said.

I turned around. He had stopped halfway down the

hill and was looking up, as if he had heard something. I glanced up, afraid the bombers were coming back, but couldn't hear anything over the antiaircraft guns. Jack stood motionless, his head down now, looking at the rubble.

"What is it?" I said.

He didn't answer. He snatched his torch out of his pocket and swung it wildly round.

"You can't do that!" I shouted. "There's a blackout on!"

He snapped it off. "Go and find something to dig with," he said, and dropped to his knees. "There's someone alive under here."

He wrenched the bannister free and began stabbing into the rubble with its broken end.

I looked stupidly at him. "How do you know?"

He jabbed viciously at the mess. "Get a pickax. This stuff's hard as rock." He looked up at me impatiently. "Hurry!"

The incident officer was someone I didn't know. I was glad. Nelson would have refused to give me a pickax without the necessary authorization of duties. This officer, who was younger than me and broken out in spots under his powdering of brick dust, didn't have a pickax, but he gave me two shovels without any argument.

The dust and smoke were clearing a bit by the time I started back across the mounds, and a shower of flares drifted down over by the river, lighting everything in a fuzzy, overbright light like headlights in a fog. I could see Jack on his hands and knees halfway down the mound, stabbing with the bannister. He looked like he was murdering someone with a knife, plunging it in again and again.

Another shower of flares came down, much closer. I ducked and hurried across to Jack, offering him one of the shovels.

"That's no good," he said, waving it away.

"What's wrong? Can't you hear the voice anymore?"

He went on jabbing with the bannister. "What?" he said, and looked in the flare's dazzling light like he had no idea what I was talking about.

"The voice you heard," I said. "Has it stopped calling?"

"It's this stuff," he said. "There's no way to get a shovel into it. Did you bring any baskets?"

I hadn't, but farther down the mound I had seen a large tin saucepan. I fetched it for him and began digging. He was right, of course. I got one good shovelful and then struck an end of a floor joist and bent the blade of the shovel. I tried to get it under the joist so I could pry it upward, but it was wedged under a large section of beam farther on. I gave it up, broke off another of the bannisters, and got down beside Jack.

The beam was not the only thing holding the joist down. The rubble looked loose—bricks and chunks of plaster and pieces of wood—but it was as solid as cement. Swales, who showed up out of nowhere when we were three feet down, said, "It's the clay. All London's built on it. Hard as statues." He had brought two buckets with him and the news that Nelson had shown up and had had a fight with the spotty officer over whose incident it was.

" 'It's *my* incident.' Nelson says, and gets out the map to show him how this side of King's Road is in his district," Swales said gleefully, "and the incident officer says, '*Your* incident? Who wants the bloody thing, I say,' he says."

Even with Swales helping, the going was so slow, whoever was under there would probably have suffocated or bled to death before we could get to him. Jack didn't stop at all, even when the bombs were directly overhead. He seemed to know exactly where he was going, though none of us heard anything in those brief intervals of silence, and Jack seemed scarcely to listen.

The bannister he was using broke off in the iron-hard

clay, and he took mine and kept digging. A broken clock came up, and an egg cup. Morris arrived. He had been evacuating people from two streets over where a bomb had buried itself in the middle of the street without exploding. Swales told him the story of Nelson and the spotty young officer and then went off to see what he could find out about the inhabitants of the house.

Jack came up out of the hole. "I need braces," he said. "The sides are collapsing."

I found some unbroken bed slats at the base of the mound. One of the slats was too long for the shaft. Jack sawed it halfway through and then broke it off.

Swales came back. "Nobody in the house," he shouted down the hole. "The colonel and Mrs. Godalming went to Surrey this morning." The all clear sounded, drowning out his words.

"Jack," Jack said from the hole.

"Jack," he said again, more urgently.

I leaned over the tunnel.

"What time is it?" he said.

"About five," I said. "The all clear just went."

"Is it getting light?"

"Not yet," I said. "Have you found anything?"

"Yes," he said. "Give us a hand."

I eased myself into the hole. I could understand his question; it was pitch-dark down here. I switched my torch on. It lit up our faces from beneath like spectres.

"In there," he said, and reached for a bannister just like the one he'd been digging with.

"Is he under a stairway?" I said, and the bannister clutched at his hand.

It only took a minute or two to get him out. Jack pulled on the arm I had mistaken for a bannister, and I scrabbled through the last few inches of plaster and clay to the little cave he was in, formed by an icebox and a door leaning against each other.

"Colonel Godalming?" I said, reaching for him.

He shook off my hand. "Where the bleeding hell have you people been?" he said. "Taking a tea break?"

He was in full evening dress, and his big mustache was covered with plaster dust. "What sort of country is this, leaving a man to dig himself out?" he shouted, brandishing a serving spoon full of plaster in Jack's face. "I could have dug all the way to China in the time it took you blighters to get me out!"

Hands came down into the hole and hoisted him up. "Blasted incompetents!" he yelled. We pushed on the seat of his elegant trousers. "Slackers, the lot of you! Couldn't find the nose in front of your own face!"

Colonel Godalming had in fact left for Surrey the day before but had decided to come back for his hunting rifle, in case of invasion. "Can't rely on the blasted Civil Defence to stop the jerries," he had said as I led him down to the ambulance.

It was starting to get light. The incident was smaller than I'd thought, not much more than two blocks square. What I had taken for a mound to the south was actually a squat office block, and beyond it the row houses hadn't even had their windows blown out.

The ambulance had pulled up as near as possible to the mound. I helped him over to it. "What's your name?" he said, ignoring the doors I'd opened. "I intend to report you to your superiors. And the other one. Practically pulled my arm out of its socket. Where's he got to?"

"He had to go to his day job," I said. As soon as we had Godalming out, Jack had switched on his pocket torch again to glance at his watch and said, "I've got to leave."

I told him I'd check him out with the incident officer and started to help Godalming down the mound. Now I was sorry I hadn't gone with him.

"Day job!" Godalming snorted. "Gone off to take a

nap is more like it. Lazy slacker. Nearly breaks my arm and then goes off and leaves me to die. I'll have his job!"

"Without him we'd never even have found you," I said angrily. "He's the one who heard your cries for help."

"Cries for help!" the colonel said, going red in the face. "Cries for help! Why would I cry out to a lot of damned slackers!"

The ambulance driver got out of the car and came round to see what the delay was.

"Accused me of crying out like a damned coward!" he blustered to her. "I didn't make a sound. Knew it wouldn't do any good. Knew if I didn't dig myself out, I'd be there till Kingdom Come! Nearly had myself out, too, and then he comes along and accuses me of blubbering like a baby! It's monstrous, that's what it is! Monstrous!"

She took hold of his arm.

"What do you think you're doing, young woman? You should be at home instead of out running about in short skirts! It's indecent, that's what it is!"

She shoved him, still protesting, onto a bunk and covered him up with a blanket. I slammed the doors to, watched her off, and then made a circuit of the incident, looking for Swales and Morris. The rising sun appeared between two bands of cloud, reddening the mounds and glinting off a broken mirror.

I couldn't find either of them, so I reported in to Nelson, who was talking angrily on a field telephone and who nodded and waved me off when I tried to tell him about Jack, and then went back to the post.

Swales was already regaling Morris and Vi, who were eating breakfast, with an imitation of Colonel Godalming. Mrs. Lucy was still filling out papers, apparently the same form as when we'd left.

"Huge mustaches," Swales was saying, his hands two feet apart to illustrate their size, "like a walrus's, and tails, if you please. 'Oi siy, this is disgriceful!' " he sputtered, his right eye squinted shut with an imaginary monocle. " 'Wot's the Impire coming to when a man cahn't even be rescued!' " He dropped into his natural voice. "I thought he was going to have our two Jacks court-martialed on the spot." He peered round me. "Where's Settle?"

"He had to go to his day job," I said.

"Just as well," he said, screwing the monocle back in. "The colonel looked like he was coming back with the Royal Lancers." He raised his arm, gripping an imaginary sword. "Charge!"

Vi tittered. Mrs. Lucy looked up and said, "Violet, make Jack some toast. Sit down, Jack. You look done in."

I took my helmet off and started to set it on the table. It was caked with plaster dust, so thick it was impossible to see the red *W* through it. I hung it on my chair and sat down.

Morris shoved a plate of kippers at me. "You never know what they're going to do when you get them out," he said. "Some of them fall all over you, sobbing, and some act like they're doing you a favor. I had one old woman acted all offended, claimed I made an improper advance when I was working her leg free."

Renfrew came in from the other room, wrapped in a blanket. He looked as bad as I thought I must, his face slack and gray with fatigue. "Where was the incident?" he asked anxiously.

"Just off Old Church Street. In Nelson's sector," I added to reassure him.

But he said nervously, "They're coming closer every night. Have you noticed that?"

"No, they aren't," Vi said. "We haven't had anything in our sector all week."

Renfrew ignored her. "First Gloucester Road and then Ixworth Place and now Old Church Street. It's as if they're circling, searching for something."

"London," Mrs. Lucy said briskly. "And if we don't

enforce the blackout, they're likely to find it." She handed Morris a typed list. "Reported infractions from last night. Go round and reprimand them." She put her hand on Renfrew's shoulder. "Why don't you go have a nice lie-down, Mr. Renfrew, while I cook you breakfast?"

"I'm not hungry," he said, but he let her lead him, clutching his blanket, back to the cot.

We watched Mrs. Lucy spread the blanket over him and then lean down and tuck it in around his shoulders, and then Swales said, "You know who this Godalming fellow reminds me of? A lady we rescued over in Gower Street," he said, yawning. "Hauled her out and asked her if her husband was in there with her. 'No,' she says, 'the bleedin' coward's at the front.' "

We all laughed.

"People like this colonel person don't deserve to be rescued," Vi said, spreading oleo on a slice of toast. "You should have left him there awhile and seen how he liked that."

"He was lucky they didn't leave him there altogether," Morris said. "The register had him in Surrey with his wife."

"Lucky he had such a loud voice," Swales said. He twirled the end of an enormous mustache. "Oi siy," he boomed. "Get me out of here im-meejutly, you slackers!"

But he said he didn't call out, I thought, and could hear Jack shouting over the din of the antiaircraft guns, the drone of the planes, "There's someone under here."

Mrs. Lucy came back to the table. "I've applied for reinforcements for the post," she said, standing her papers on end and tamping them into an even stack. "Someone from the Town Hall will be coming to inspect in the next few days." She picked up two bottles of ale and an ashtray and carried them over to the dustbin.

"Applied for reinforcements?" Swales asked. "Why? Afraid Colonel Godalming'll be back with the heavy artillery?"

There was a loud banging on the door.

"Oi siy," Swales said. "Here he is now, and he's brought his hounds."

Mrs. Lucy opened the door. "Worse," Vi whispered, diving for the last bottle of ale. "It's Nelson." She passed the bottle to me under the table, and I passed it to Renfrew, who tucked it under his blanket.

"Mr. Nelson," Mrs. Lucy said as if she were delighted to see him, "do come in. And how are things over your way?"

"We took a beating last night," he said, glaring at us as though we were responsible.

"He's had a complaint from the colonel," Swales whispered to me. "You're done for, mate."

"Oh, I'm so sorry to hear that," Mrs. Lucy said. "Now, how may I help you?"

He pulled a folded paper from the pocket of his uniform and carefully opened it out. "This was forwarded to me from the City Engineer," he said. "All requests for material improvements are to be sent to the district warden, *not* over his head to the Town Hall."

"Oh, I'm so *glad,*" Mrs. Lucy said, leading him into the pantry. "It is such a comfort to deal with someone who knows, rather than a faceless bureaucracy. If I had realized you were the proper person to appeal to, I should have contacted you *immediately.*" She shut the door.

Renfield took the ale bottle out from under his blanket and buried it in the dustbin. Violet began taking out her bobby pins.

"We'll never get our reinforcements now," Swales said. "Not with Adolf von Nelson in charge."

"Shh," Vi said, yanking at her snaillike curls. "You don't want him to hear you."

"Olmwood told me he makes them keep working at an incident, even when the bombs are right overhead. Thinks all the posts should do it."

"Shh!" Vi said.

"He's a bleeding Nazi!" Swales said, but he lowered his voice. "Got two of his wardens killed that way. You better not let him find out you and Jack are good at finding bodies, or you'll be out there dodging shrapnel, too."

Good at finding bodies. I thought of Jack, standing motionless, looking at the rubble and saying, "There's someone alive under here. Hurry."

"That's why Nelson steals from the other posts," Vi said, scooping her bobby pins off the table and into her haversack. "Because he does his own in." She pulled out a comb and began yanking it through her snarled curls.

The pantry door opened and Nelson and Mrs. Lucy came out, Nelson still holding the unfolded paper. She was still wearing her tea-party smile, but it was a bit thin. "I'm sure you can see it's unrealistic to expect nine people to huddle in a coal cellar for hours at a time," she said.

"There are people all over London 'huddling in coal cellars for hours at a time,' as you put it," Nelson said coldly, "who do not wish their Civil Defence funds spent on frivolities."

"I do not consider the safety of my wardens a frivolity," she said, "though it is clear to me that you do, as witnessed by your very poor record."

Nelson stared for a full minute at Mrs. Lucy, trying to think of a retort, and then turned on me. "Your uniform is a disgrace, warden," he said, and stomped out.

Whatever it was Jack had used to find Colonel Godalming, it didn't work on incendiaries. He searched as haphazardly for them as the rest of us, Vi, who had been on spotter duty, shouting directions: "No, farther down Fulham Road. In the grocer's."

She had apparently been daydreaming about her pilots, instead of spotting. The incendiary was not in the grocer's but in the butcher's three doors down, and by the time Jack and I got to it, the meat locker was on fire. It wasn't hard to put out, there were no furniture or curtains to catch, and the cold kept the wooden shelves from catching, but the butcher was extravagantly grateful. He insisted on wrapping up five pounds of lamb chops in white paper and thrusting them into Jack's arms.

"Did you really have to be at your day job so early, or were you only trying to escape the colonel?" I asked Jack on the way back to the post.

"Was he that bad?" he said, handing me the parcel of lamb chops.

"He nearly took my head off when I said you'd heard him shouting. Said he didn't call for help. Said he was digging himself out." The white butcher's paper was so bright, the Luftwaffe would think it was a searchlight. I tucked the parcel inside my overalls so it wouldn't show. "What sort of work is it, your day job?" I asked.

"War work," he said.

"Did they transfer you? Is that why you came to London?"

"No," he said. "I wanted to come." We turned into Mrs. Lucy's street. "Why did you join the ARP?"

"I'm waiting to be called up," I said, "so no one would hire me."

"And you wanted to do your bit."

"Yes," I said, wishing I could see his face.

"What about Mrs. Lucy? Why did she become a warden?"

"Mrs. Lucy?" I said blankly. The question had never even occurred to me. She was the best warden in London. It was her natural calling, and I'd thought of her as always having been one. "I've no idea," I said. "It's her house, she's a widow. Perhaps the Civil Defence commandeered it, and she had to become one. It's the tallest in the street." I tried to remember what Twickenham had written about her in his interview. "Before the war she had something to do with a church."

"A church," he said, and I wished again I could see

his face. I couldn't tell in the dark whether he spoke in contempt or longing.

"She was a deaconess or something," I said. "What sort of war work is it? Munitions?"

"No," he said, and walked on ahead.

Mrs. Lucy met us at the door of the post. I gave her the package of lamb chops, and Jack went upstairs to replace Vi as spotter. Mrs. Lucy cooked the chops up immediately, running upstairs to the kitchen during a lull in the raids for salt and a jar of mint sauce, standing over the gas ring at the end of the table and turning them for what seemed an eternity. They smelled wonderful.

Twickenham passed round newly run-off copies of *Twickenham's Twitterings*. "Something for you to read while you wait for your dinner," he said proudly.

The lead article was about the change in address of Sub-Post D, which had taken a partial hit that broke the water mains.

"Had Nelson refused them reinforcements, too?" Swales asked.

"Listen to this," Petersby said. He read aloud from the news sheet. " 'The crime rate in London has risen twenty-eight percent since the beginning of the blackout.' "

"And no wonder," Vi said, coming down from upstairs. "You can't see your nose in front of your face at night, let alone someone lurking in an alley. I'm always afraid someone's going to jump out at me while I'm on patrol."

"All those houses standing empty, and half of London sleeping in the shelters," Swales said. "It's easy pickings. If I was a bad'un, I'd come straight to London."

"It's disgusting," Morris said indignantly. "The idea of someone taking advantage of there being a war to commit crimes."

"Oh, Mr. Morris, that reminds me. Your son telephoned," Mrs. Lucy said, cutting into a chop to see if it was done. Blood welled up. "He said he'd a surprise for you, and you were to come out to"—she switched the fork to her left hand and rummaged in her overall pocket till she found a slip of paper—"North Weald on Monday, I think. His commanding officer's made the necessary travel arrangements for you. I wrote it all down." She handed it to him and went back to turning the chops.

"A surprise?" Morris said, sounding worried. "He's not in trouble, is he? His commanding officer wants to see me?"

"I don't know. He didn't say what it was about. Only that he wanted you to come."

Vi went over to Mrs. Lucy and peered into the skillet. "I'm glad it was the butcher's and not the grocer's," she said. "Rutabagas wouldn't have cooked up half so nice."

Mrs. Lucy speared a chop, put it on a plate, and handed it to Vi. "Take this up to Jack," she said.

"He doesn't want any," Vi said. She took the plate and sat down at the table.

"Did he say why he didn't?" I asked.

She looked curiously at me. "I suppose he's not hungry," she said. "Or perhaps he doesn't like lamb chops."

"I do hope he's not in any trouble," Morris said, and it took me a minute to realize he was talking about his son. "He's not a bad boy, but he does things without thinking. Youthful high spirits, that's all it is."

"He didn't eat the cake either," I said. "Did he say why he didn't want the lamb chop?"

"If Mr. Settle doesn't want it, then take it to Mr. Renfrew," Mrs. Lucy said sharply. She snatched the plate away from Vi. "And don't let him tell you he's not hungry. He must eat. He's getting very run-down."

Vi sighed and stood up. Mrs. Lucy handed her back the plate, and she went into the other room.

"We all need to eat plenty of good food and get lots of sleep," Mrs. Lucy said reprovingly. "To keep our strength up."

"I've written an article about it in the *Twitterings,*" Twickenham said, beaming. "It's known as 'walking death.' It's brought about by lack of sleep and poor nutrition, with the anxiety of the raids. The walking dead exhibit slowed reaction time and impaired judgment, which result in increased accidents on the job."

"Well, I won't have any walking dead among *my* wardens," Mrs. Lucy said, dishing up the rest of the chops. "As soon as you've had these, I want you all to go to bed."

The chops tasted even better than they had smelled. I ate mine, reading Twickenham's article on the walking dead. It said that loss of appetite was a common reaction to the raids. It also said that lack of sleep could cause compulsive behavior and odd fixations. "The walking dead may become convinced that they are being poisoned or that a friend or relative is a German agent. They may hallucinate, hearing voices, seeing visions, or believing fantastical things."

"He was in trouble at school, before the war, but he's steadied down since he joined up," Morris said. "I wonder what he's done."

At three the next morning a land mine exploded in almost the same spot off Old Church Street as the HEs. Nelson sent Olmwood to ask for help, and Mrs. Lucy ordered Swales, Jack, and me to go with him.

"The mine didn't land more'n two houses away from the first crater," Olmwood said while we were getting on our gear. "The jerries couldn't have come closer if they'd been aiming at it."

"I know what they're aiming at," Renfrew said from the doorway. He looked terrible, pale and drawn as a ghost. "And I know why you've applied for reinforcements for the post. It's me, isn't it? They're after me."

"They're not after any of us," Mrs. Lucy said firmly. "They're two miles up. They're not aiming at anything."

"Why would Hitler want to bomb you more than the rest of us?" Swales said.

"I don't know." He sank down on one of the chairs and put his head in his hands. "I don't *know*. But they're after me. I can feel it."

Mrs. Lucy had sent Swales, Jack, and me to the incident because "you've been there before. You'll know the terrain." But that was a fond hope. Since they explode above ground, land mines do considerably more damage then HEs. There was now a hill where the incident officer's tent had been, and three more beyond it, a mountain range in the middle of London. Swales started up the nearest peak to look for the incident officer's light.

"Jack, over here!" somebody called from the hill behind us, and both of us scrambled up a slope toward the voice.

A group of five men were halfway up the hill looking down into a hole.

"Jack!" the man yelled again. He was wearing a blue foreman's arm band, and he was looking straight past us at someone toiling up the slope with what looked like a stirrup pump. I thought, surely they're not trying to fight a fire down that shaft, and then saw it wasn't a pump. It was, in fact, an automobile jack, and the man with the blue arm band reached between us for it, lowered it down the hole, and scrambled in after it.

The rest of the rescue squad stood looking down into the blackness as if they could actually see something. After a while they began handing empty buckets down into the hole and pulling them out heaped full of broken bricks and pieces of splintered wood. None of them took any notice of us, even when Jack held out his hands to take one of the buckets.

"We're from Chelsea," I shouted to the foreman over the din of the planes and bombs. "What can we do to help?"

They went on bucket-brigading. A china teapot came

up on the top of one load, covered with dust but not even chipped.

I tried again. "Who is it down there?"

"Two of 'em," the man nearest me said. He plucked the teapot off the heap and handed it to the man wearing a balaclava under his helmet. "Man and a woman."

"We're from Chelsea," I shouted over a burst of antiaircraft fire. "What do you want us to do?"

He took the teapot away from the man with the balaclava and handed it to me. "Take this down to the pavement with the other valuables."

It took me a long while to get down the slope, holding the teapot in one hand and the lid on with the other and trying to keep my footing among the broken bricks, and even longer to find any pavement. The land mine had heaved most of it up, and the street with it.

I finally found it, a square of unbroken pavement in front of a blown-out bakery, with the "valuables" neatly lined up against it: a radio, a boot, two serving spoons like the one Colonel Godalming had threatened me with, a lady's beaded evening bag. A rescue worker was standing guard next to them.

"Halt!" he said, stepping in front of them as I came up, holding a pocket torch or a gun. "No one's allowed inside the incident perimeter."

"I'm ARP," I said hastily. "Jack Harker. Chelsea." I held up the teapot. "They sent me down with this."

It was a torch. He flicked it on and off, an eye blink. "Sorry," he said. "We've had a good deal of looting recently." He took the teapot and placed it at the end of the line next to the evening bag. "Caught a man last week going through the pockets of the bodies laid out in the street waiting for the mortuary van. Terrible how some people will take advantage of a thing like this."

I went back up to where the rescue workers were digging. Jack was at the mouth of the shaft, hauling buckets up and handing them back. I got in line behind him.

"Have they found them yet?" I asked him as soon as there was a lull in the bombing.

"Quiet!" a voice shouted from the hole, and the man in the balaclava repeated, "Quiet, everyone! We must have absolute quiet!"

Everyone stopped working and listened. Jack had handed me a bucket full of bricks, and the handle cut into my hands. For a second there was absolute silence, and then the drone of a plane and the distant swish and crump of an HE.

"Don't worry," the voice from the hole shouted, "we're nearly there." The buckets began coming up out of the hole again.

I hadn't heard anything, but apparently down in the shaft they had, a voice or the sound of tapping, and I felt relieved, both that one of them at least was still alive, and that the diggers were on course. I'd been on an incident in October where we'd had to stop halfway down and sink a new shaft because the rubble kept distorting and displacing the sound. Even if the shaft was directly above the victim, it tended to go crooked in working past obstacles, and the only way to keep it straight was with frequent soundings. I thought of Jack digging for Colonel Godalming with the bannister. He hadn't taken any soundings at all. He had seemed to know exactly where he was going.

The men in the shaft called for the jack again, and Jack and I lowered it down to them. As the man below it reached up to take it, Jack stopped. He raised his head, as if he were listening.

"What is it?" I said. I couldn't hear anything but the ack-ack guns in Hyde Park. "Did you hear someone calling?"

"Where's the bloody jack?" the foreman shouted.

"It's too late," Jack said to me. "They're dead."

"Come along, get it down here," the foreman shouted. "We haven't got all day."

He handed the jack down.

"Quiet," the foreman shouted, and above us, like a ghostly echo, we could hear the balaclava call, "Quiet, please, everyone."

A church clock began to chime, and I could hear the balaclava say irritatedly, "We must have absolute quiet."

The clock chimed four and stopped, and there was a skittering sound of dirt falling on metal. Then silence, and a faint sound.

"Quiet!" the foreman called again, and there was another silence, and the sound again. A whimper. Or a moan. "We hear you," he shouted. "Don't be afraid."

"One of them's still alive," I said.

Jack didn't say anything.

"We just *heard* them," I said angrily.

Jack shook his head.

"We'll need lumber for bracing," the man in the balaclava said to Jack, and I expected him to tell him it was no use, but he went off immediately and came back dragging a white-painted bookcase.

It still had three books in it. I helped Jack and the balaclava knock the shelves out of the case and then took the books down to the store of "valuables." The guard was sitting on the pavement going through the beaded evening bag.

"Taking inventory," he said, scrambling up hastily. He jammed a lipstick and a handkerchief into the bag. "So's to make certain nothing gets stolen."

"I've brought you something to read," I said, and laid the books next to the teapot. "*Crime and Punishment.*"

I toiled back up the hill and helped Jack lower the bookshelves down the shaft, and after a few minutes buckets began coming up again. We re-formed our scraggly bucket brigade, the balaclava at the head of it and me and then Jack at its end.

The all clear went. As soon as it wound down, the

foreman took another sounding. This time we didn't hear anything, and when the buckets started again, I handed them to Jack without looking at him.

It began to get light in the east, a slow graying of the hills above us. Two of them, several stories high, stood where the row houses that had escaped the night before had been, and we were still in their shadow, though I could see the shaft now, with the end of one of the white bookshelves sticking up from it like a gravestone.

The buckets began to come more slowly.

"Put out your cigarettes!" the foreman called up, and we all stopped, trying to catch the smell of gas. If they were dead, as Jack had said, it was most likely gas leaking in from the broken mains that had killed them, and not internal injuries. The week before we had brought up a boy and his dog, not a scratch on them. The dog had barked and whimpered almost up to when we found them, and the ambulance driver said she thought they'd only been dead a few minutes.

I couldn't smell any gas, and after a minute the foreman said excited, "I see them!"

The balaclava leaned over the shaft, his hands on his knees. "Are they alive?"

"Yes! Fetch an ambulance!"

The balaclava went leaping down the hill, skidding on broken bricks that skittered down in a minor avalanche.

I knelt over the shaft. "Will they need a stretcher?" I called down.

"No," the foreman said, and I knew by the sound of his voice they were dead.

"Both of them?" I said.

"Yes."

I stood up. "How did you know they were dead?" I said, turning to look at Jack. "How did—"

He wasn't there. I looked down the hill. The balaclava was nearly to the bottom—grabbing at a broken window sash to stop his headlong descent, his wake a smoky cloud of brick dust—but Jack was nowhere to be seen.

It was nearly dawn. I could see the gray hills and at the far end of them the warden and his "valuables." There was another rescue party on the third hill over, still digging. I could see Swales handing down a bucket.

"Give a hand here," the foreman said impatiently, and hoisted the jack up to me. I hauled it over to the side and then came back and helped the foreman out of the shaft. His hands were filthy, covered in reddish-brown mud.

"Was it the gas that killed them?" I asked, even though he was already pulling out a packet of cigarettes.

"No," he said, shaking a cigarette out and taking it between his teeth. He patted the front of his coverall, leaving red stains.

"How long have they been dead?" I asked.

He found his matches, struck one, and lit the cigarette. "Shortly after we last heard them, I should say," he said, and I thought, but they were already dead by then. And Jack knew it. "They've been dead at least two hours."

I looked at my watch. I read a little past six. "But the mine didn't kill them?"

He took the cigarette between his fingers and blew a long puff of smoke. When he put the cigarette back in his mouth, there was a red smear on it. "Loss of blood."

The next night the Luftwaffe was early. I hadn't gotten much sleep after the incident. Morris had fretted about his son the whole day, and Swales had teased Renfrew mercilessly. "Göring's found out about your spying," he said, "and now he's sent his Stukas after you."

I finally went up to the fourth floor and tried to sleep in the spotter's chair, but it was too light. The afternoon was cloudy, and the fires burning in the East End gave the sky a nasty reddish cast.

Someone had left a copy of *Twickenham's Twitterings* on the floor. I read the article on the walking dead again, and then, still unable to sleep, the rest of the news sheet. There was an account of Hitler's invasion of Transylvania, and a recipe for butterless strawberry tart, and the account of the crime rate. "London is currently the perfect place for the criminal element," Nelson was quoted as saying. "We must constantly be on the lookout for wrongdoing."

Below the recipe was a story about a Scottish terrier named Bonny Charlie who had barked and scrabbled wildly at the ruins of a collapsed house till wardens heeded his cries, dug down, and discovered two unharmed children.

I must have fallen asleep reading that, because the next thing I knew Morris was shaking me and telling me the sirens had gone. It was only five o'clock.

At half past we had an HE in our sector. It was just three blocks from the post, and the walls shook, and plaster rained down on Twickenham's typewriter and on Renfrew, lying awake in his cot.

"Frivolities, my foot," Mrs. Lucy muttered as we dived for our tin hats. "We need those reinforcing beams."

The part-times hadn't come on duty yet. Mrs. Lucy left Renfrew to send them on. We knew exactly where the incident was—Morris had been looking in that direction when it went—but we still had difficulty finding it. It was still evening, but by the time we had gone half a block, it was pitch-black.

The first time that had happened, I thought it was some sort of after-blindness from the blast, but it's only the brick and plaster dust from the collapsed buildings. It rises up in a haze that's darker than any blackout curtain, obscuring everything. When Mrs. Lucy set up shop on a stretch of sidewalk and switched on the blue incident light, it glowed spectrally in the man-made fog.

"Only two families still in the street," she said, holding the register up to the light. "The Kirkcuddy family and the Hodgsons."

"Are they an old couple?" Morris asked, appearing suddenly out of the fog.

She peered at the register. "Yes. Pensioners."

"I found them," he said in that flat voice that meant they were dead. "Blast."

"Oh, dear," she said. "The Kirkcuddys are a mother and two children. They've an Anderson shelter." She held the register closer to the blue light. "Everyone else has been using the tube shelter." She unfolded a map and showed us where the Kirckcuddys' backyard had been, but it was no help. We spent the next hour wandering blindly over the mounds, listening for sounds that were impossible to hear over the Luftwaffe's comments and the ack-ack's replies.

Petersby showed up a little past eight and Jack a few minutes later, and Mrs. Lucy set them to wandering in the fog, too.

"Over here," Jack shouted almost immediately, and my heart gave an odd jerk.

"Oh, good, he's heard them," Mrs. Lucy said. "Jack, go and find him."

"Over here," he called again, and I started off in the direction of his voice, almost afraid of what I would find, but I hadn't gone ten steps before I could hear it, too. A baby crying, and a hollow, echoing sound like someone banging a fist against tin.

"Don't stop," Vi shouted. She was kneeling next to Jack in a shallow crater. "Keep making noise. We're coming." She looked up at me. "Tell Mrs. Lucy to ring the rescue squad."

I blundered my way back to Mrs. Lucy through the darkness. She had already rung up the rescue squad. She sent me to Sloane Square to make sure the rest of the inhabitants of the block were safely there.

The dust had lifted a little but not enough for me to see where I was going. I pitched off a curb into the street and tripped over a pile of debris and then a body. When I shone my torch on it, I saw it was the girl I had walked to the shelter two nights before.

She was sitting against the tiled entrance to the station, still holding a dress on a hanger in her limp hand. The old stewpot at John Lewis's never let her off even a minute before closing, and the Luftwaffe had been early. She had been killed by blast, or by flying glass. Her face and neck and hands were covered with tiny cuts, and glass crunched underfoot when I moved her legs together.

I went back to the incident and waited for the mortuary van and went with them to the shelter. It took me three hours to find the families on my list. By the time I got back to the incident, the rescue squad was five feet down.

"They're nearly there," Vi said, dumping a basket on the far side of the crater. "All that's coming up now is dirt and the occasional rosebush."

"Where's Jack?" I said.

"He went for a saw." She took the basket back and handed it to one of the rescue squad, who had to put his cigarette into his mouth to free his hands before he could take it. "There was a board, but they dug past it."

I leaned over the hole. I could hear the sound of banging but not the baby. "Are they still alive?"

She shook her head. "We haven't heard the baby for an hour or so. We keep calling, but there's no answer. We're afraid the banging may be something mechanical."

I wondered if they were dead, and Jack, knowing it, had not gone for a saw at all but off to that day job of his.

Swales came up. "Guess who's in hospital?" he said.

"Who?" Vi said.

"Olmwood. Nelson had his wardens out walking patrols during a raid, and he caught a piece of shrapnel from one of the ack-acks in the leg. Nearly took it off."

The rescue worker with the cigarette handed a heaping basket to Vi. She took it, staggering a little under the weight, and carried it off.

"You'd better not let Nelson see you working like that," Swales called after her, "or he'll have you transferred to his sector. Where's Morris?" he said, and went off, presumably to tell him and whoever else he could find about Olmwood.

Jack came up, carrying the saw.

"They don't need it," the rescue worker said, the cigarette dangling from the side of his mouth. "Mobile's here," he said, and went off for a cup of tea. Jack knelt and handed the saw down the hole.

"Are they still alive?" I asked.

Jack leaned over the hole, his hands clutching the edges. The banging was incredibly loud. It must have been deafening inside the Anderson. Jack stared into the hole as if he heard neither the banging nor any voice.

He stood up, still looking into the hole. "They're farther to the left," he said.

How can they be farther to the left? I thought. We can hear them. They're directly under us. "Are they alive?" I said.

"Yes."

Swales came back. "He's a spy, that's what he is," he said. "Hitler sent him here to kill off our best men one by one. I told you his name was Adolf von Nelson."

The Kirkcuddys were farther to the left. The rescue squad had to widen the tunnel, cut the top of the Anderson open, and pry it back, like opening a can of tomatoes. It took till nine o'clock in the morning, but they were all alive.

Jack left sometime before it got light. I didn't see him

go. Swales was telling me about Olmwood's injury, and when I turned around, Jack was gone.

"Has Jack told you where this job of his is that he has to leave so early for?" I asked Vi when I got back to the post.

She had propped a mirror against one of the gas masks and was putting her hair up in pin curls. "No," she said, dipping a comb in a glass of water and wetting a lock of her hair. "Jack, could you reach me my bobby pins? I've a date this afternoon, and I want to look my best."

I pushed the pins across to her. "What sort of job is it? Did Jack say?"

"No. Some sort of war work, I should think." She wound a lock of hair around her finger. "He's had ten kills. Four Stukas and six 109's."

I sat down next to Twickenham, who was typing up the incident report. "Have you interviewed Jack yet?"

"When would I have had time?" Twickenham asked. "We haven't had a quiet night since he came."

Renfrew shuffled in from the other room. He had a blanket wrapped round him Indian style and a bedspread over his shoulders. He looked terrible, pale and drawn as a ghost.

"Would you like some breakfast?" Vi asked, prying a pin open with her teeth.

He shook his head. "Did Nelson approve the reinforcements?"

"No," Twickenham said in spite of Vi's signaling him not to.

"You must tell Nelson it's an emergency," he said, hugging the blanket to him as if he were cold. "I know why they're after me. It was before the war. When Hitler invaded Czechoslovakia. I wrote a letter to the *Times*."

I was grateful Swales wasn't there. A letter to the *Times*.

"Come, now, why don't you go and lie down for a

bit?" Vi said, securing a curl with a bobby pin as she stood up. "You're tired, that's all, and that's what's getting you so worried. They don't even get the *Times* over there."

She took his arm, and he went docilely with her into the other room. I heard him say, "I called him a lowland bully. In the letter." The person suffering from severe sleep loss may hallucinate, hearing voices, seeing visions, or believing fantastical things.

"Has he mentioned what sort of day job he has?" I asked Twickenham.

"Who?" he asked, still typing.

"Jack."

"No, but whatever it is, let's hope he's as good at it as he is at finding bodies." He stopped and peered at what he'd just typed. "This makes five, doesn't it?"

Vi came back. "And we'd best not let von Nelson find out about it," she said. She sat down and dipped the comb into the glass of water. "He'd take him like he took Olmwood, and we're already shorthanded, with Renfrew the way he is."

Mrs. Lucy came in carrying the incident light, disappeared into the pantry with it, and came out again carrying an application form. "Might I use the typewriter, Mr. Twickenham?" she asked.

He pulled his sheet of paper out of the typewriter and stood up. Mrs. Lucy sat down, rolled in the form, and began typing. "I've decided to apply directly to Civil Defence for reinforcements," she said.

"What sort of day job does Jack have?" I asked her.

"War work," she said. She pulled the application out, turned it over, rolled it back in. "Jack, would you mind taking this over to headquarters?"

"Works days," Vi said, making a pin curl on the back of her head. "Raids every night. When does he sleep?"

"I don't know," I said.

"He'd best be careful," she said. "Or he'll turn into one of the walking dead, like Renfrew."

Mrs. Lucy signed the application form, folded it in half, and gave it to me. I took it to Civil Defence headquarters and spent half a day trying to find the right office to give it to.

"It's not the correct form," the sixth girl said. "She needs to file an A-114, Exterior Improvements."

"It's not exterior," I said. "The post is applying for reinforcing beams for the cellar."

"Reinforcements are classified as exterior improvements," she said. She handed me the form, which looked identical to the one Mrs. Lucy had already filled out, and I left.

On the way out Nelson stopped me. I thought he was going to tell me my uniform was a disgrace again, but instead he pointed to my tin hat and demanded, "Why aren't you wearing a regulation helmet, warden? 'All ARP wardens shall wear a helmet with the letter *W* in red on the front,' " he quoted.

I took my hat off and looked at it. The red *W* had partly chipped away so that it looked like a *V*.

"What post are you?" he barked.

"Forty-eight. Chelsea," I said, and wondered if he expected me to salute.

"Mrs. Lucy is your warden," he said disgustedly, and I expected his next question to be what was I doing at Civil Defence, but instead he said, "I heard about Colonel Godalming. Your post has been having good luck locating casualties these last few raids."

"Yes, sir," was obviously the wrong answer, and "No, sir," would make him suspicious. "We found three people in an Anderson last night," I said. "One of the children had the wits to bang on the roof with a pair of pliers."

"I've heard that the person finding them is a new

man, Settle." He sounded friendly, almost jovial. Like Hitler at Munich.

"Settle?" I said blankly. "Mrs. Lucy was the one who found the Anderson."

Morris's son Quincy's surprise was the Victoria Cross. "A medal," he said over and over. "Who'd have thought it, my Quincy with a medal? Fifteen planes he shot down."

It had been presented at a special ceremony at Quincy's commanding officer's headquarters, and the Duchess of York herself had been there. Morris had pinned the medal on Quincy himself.

"I wore my suit," he told us for the hundredth time. "In case he was in trouble I wanted to make a good impression, and a good thing, too. What would the Duchess of York have thought if I'd gone looking like this?"

He looked pretty bad. We all did. We'd had two breadbaskets of incendiaries, one right after the other, and Vi had been on watch. We had had to save the butcher's again, and a baker's two blocks farther down, and a thirteenth-century crucifix.

"I *told* him it went through the altar roof," Vi had said disgustedly when she and I finally got it out. "Your friend Jack couldn't find an incendiary if it fell on him."

"You told Jack the incendiary came down on the church?" I said, looking up at the carved wooden figure. The bottom of the cross was blackened, and Christ's nailed feet, as if he had been burnt at the stake instead of crucified.

"Yes," she said. "I even told him it was the altar." She looked back up the nave. "And he could have seen it as soon as he came into the church."

"What did he say? That it wasn't there?"

Vi was looking speculatively up at the roof. "It could have been caught in the rafters and come down after. It hardly matters, does it? We put it out. Come on, let's get back to the post," she said, shivering. "I'm freezing."

I was freezing, too. We were both sopping wet. The AFS had stormed up after we had the fire under control and sprayed everything in sight with icy water.

"Pinned it on myself, I did," Morris said. "The Duchess of York kissed him on both cheeks and said he was the pride of England." He had brought a bottle of wine to celebrate the Cross. He got Renfrew up and brought him to the table, draped in his blankets, and ordered Twickenham to put his typewriter away. Petersby brought in extra chairs, and Mrs. Lucy went upstairs to get her crystal.

"Only eight, I'm afraid," she said, coming back with the stemmed goblets in her blackened hands. "The Germans have broken the rest. Who's willing to make do with the tooth glass?"

"I don't care for any, thank you," Jack said. "I don't drink."

"What's that?" Morris said jovially. He had taken off his tin helmet, and below the white line it left, he looked like he was wearing blackface in a music-hall show. "You've got to toast my boy at least. Just imagine. My Quincy with a medal."

Mrs. Lucy rinsed out the porcelain tooth glass and handed it to Vi, who was pouring out the wine. They passed the goblets round. Jack took the tooth glass.

"To my son Quincy, the best pilot in the RAF!" Morris said, raising his goblet.

"May he shoot down the entire Luftwaffe!" Swales shouted. "And put an end to this bloody war!"

"So a man can get a decent night's sleep!" Renfrew said, and everyone laughed.

We drank. Jack raised his glass with the others, but when Vi took the bottle round again, he put his hand over the mouth of it.

"Just think of it," Morris said. "My son Quincy with

a medal. He had his troubles in school, in with a bad lot, problems with the police. I worried about him, I did, wondered what he'd come to, and then this war comes along and here he is a hero."

"To heroes!" Petersby said.

We drank again, and Vi dribbled out the last of the wine into Morris's glass. "That's the lot, I'm afraid." She brightened. "I've a bottle of cherry cordial Charlie gave me."

Mrs. Lucy made a face. "Just a minute," she said, disappeared into the pantry, and came back with two cobwebbed bottles of port, which she poured out generously and a little sloppily.

"The presence of intoxicating beverages on post is strictly forbidden," she said. "A fine of five shillings will be imposed for a first offence, one pound for subsequent offences." She took out a pound note and laid it on the table. "I wonder what Nelson was before the war?"

"A monster," Vi said.

I looked across at Jack. He still had his hand over his glass.

"A headmaster," Swales said. "No, I've got it. An Inland Revenue collector!"

Everyone laughed.

"I was a horrid person before the war," Mrs. Lucy said.

Vi giggled.

"I was a deaconess, one of those dreadful women who arranges the flowers in the sanctuary and gets up jumble sales and bullies the rector. 'The Terror of the Churchwardens,' that's what I used to be. I was determined that they should put the hymnals front side out on the backs of the pews. Morris knows. He sang in the choir."

"It's true," Morris said. "She used to instruct the choir on the proper way to line up."

I tried to imagine her as a stickler, as a petty tyrant like Nelson, and failed.

"Sometimes it takes something dreadful like a war for one to find one's proper job," she said, staring at her glass.

"To the war!" Swales said gaily.

"I'm not sure we should toast something so terrible as that," Twickenham said doubtfully.

"It isn't all that terrible," Vi said. "I mean, without it, we wouldn't all be here together, would we?"

"And you'd never have met all those pilots of yours, would you, Vi?" Swales said.

"There's nothing wrong with making the best of a bad job," Vi said, miffed.

"Some people do more than that," Swales said. "Some people take positive advantage of the war. Like Colonel Godalming. I had a word with one of the AFS volunteers. Seems the colonel didn't come back for his hunting rifle, after all." He leaned forward confidingly. "Seems he was having a bit on with a blond dancer from the Windmill. *Seems* his wife thought he was out shooting grouse in Surrey, and now she's asking all sorts of unpleasant questions."

"He's not the only one taking advantage," Morris said. "That night you got the Kirkcuddys out, Jack, I found an old couple killed by blast. I put them by the road for the mortuary van, and later I saw somebody over there, bending over the bodies, doing something to them. I thought, he must be straightening them out before the rigor sets in, but then it comes to me. He's robbing them. Dead bodies."

"And who's to say they were killed by blast?" Swales said. "Who's to say they weren't murdered? There's lot of bodies, aren't there, and nobody looks close at them. Who's to say they were all killed by the Germans?"

"How did we get onto this?" Petersby said. "We're supposed to be celebrating Quincy Morris's medal, not talking about murderers." He raised his glass. "To Quincy Morris!"

"And the RAF!" Vi said.

"To making the best of a bad job," Mrs. Lucy said.

"Hear, hear," Jack said softly, and raised his glass, but he still didn't drink.

Jack found four people in the next three days. I did not hear any of them until well after we had started digging, and the last one, a fat woman in striped pyjamas and a pink hair net, I never did hear, though she said when we brought her up that she had "called and called between prayers."

Twickenham wrote it all up for the *Twitterings*, tossing out the article on Quincy Morris's medal and typing up a new master's. When Mrs. Lucy borrowed the typewriter to fill out the A-114, she said, "What's this?"

"My lead story," he said. " 'Settle Finds Four in Rubble.' " He handed her the master's.

" 'Jack Settle, the newest addition to Post Forty-eight,' " she read, " 'located four air-raid victims last night. "I wanted to be useful," says the modest Mr. Settle when asked why he came to London from Yorkshire. And he's been useful since his very first night on the job when he—' " She handed it back to him. "Sorry. You can't print that. Nelson's been nosing about, asking questions. He's already taken one of my wardens and nearly gotten him killed. I won't let him have another."

"That's censorship!" Twickenham said, outraged.

"There's a war on," Mrs. Lucy said, "and we're shorthanded. I've relieved Mr. Renfrew of duty. He's going to stay with his sister in Birmingham. And I wouldn't let Nelson have another one of my wardens if we were overstaffed. He's already gotten Olmwood nearly killed."

She handed me the A-114 and asked me to take it to Civil Defence. I did. The girl I had spoken to wasn't there, and the girl who was said, "This is for *interior* improvements. You need to fill out a D-268."

"I did," I said, "and I was told that reinforcements qualified as exterior improvements."

"Only if they're on the outside." She handed me a D-268. "Sorry," she said apologetically. "I'd help you if I could, but my boss is a stickler for the correct forms."

"There's something else you can do for me," I said. "I was supposed to take one of our part-times a message at his day job, but I've lost the address. If you could look it up for me. Jack Settle? If not, I've got to go all the way back to Chelsea to get it."

She looked back over her shoulder and then said, "Wait a mo," and darted down the hall. She came back with a sheet of paper.

"Settle?" she said. "Post Forty-eight, Chelsea?"

"That's the one," I said. "I need his work address."

"He hasn't got one."

He had left the incident while we were still getting the fat woman out. It was starting to get light. We had a rope under her, and a makeshift winch, and he had abruptly handed his end to Swales and said, "I've got to leave for my day job."

"You're certain?" I said.

"I'm certain." She handed me the sheet of paper. It was Jack's approval for employment as a part-time warden, signed by Mrs. Lucy. The spaces for work and home addresses had been left blank. "This is all there was in the file," she said. "No work permit, no identity card, not even a ration card. We keep copies of all that, so he must not have a job."

I took the D-268 back to the post, but Mrs. Lucy wasn't there. "One of Nelson's wardens came round with a new regulation," Twickenham said, running off copies on the duplicating machine. "All wardens will be out on patrol unless on telephone or spotter duty. *All* wardens. She went off to give him what-for," he said, sounding pleased. He was apparently over his anger at her for censoring his story on Jack.

I picked up one of the still-wet copies of the news sheet. The lead story was about Hitler's invasion of Greece. He had put the article about Quincy Morris's medal down in the right-hand corner under a list of "What the War Has Done for Us." Number one was, "It's made us discover capabilities we didn't know we had."

"Mrs. Lucy called him a murderer," Twickenham said.

A murderer.

"What did you want to tell her?" Twickenham said.

That Jack doesn't have a job, I thought. Or a ration card. That he didn't put out the incendiary in the church even though Vi told him it had gone through the altar roof. That he knew the Anderson was farther to the left.

"It's still the wrong form," I said, taking out the D-268.

"That's easily remedied," he said. He rolled the application into the typewriter, typed for a few minutes, handed it back to me.

"Mrs. Lucy has to sign it," I said, and he snatched it back, whipped out a fountain pen, and signed her name.

"What were you before the war?" I asked. "A forger?"

"You'd be surprised." He handed the form back to me. "You look dreadful, Jack. Have you gotten any sleep this last week?"

"When would I have had the chance?"

"Why don't you lie down now while no one's here?" he said, reaching for my arm the way Vi had reached for Renfrew's. "I'll take the form back to Civil Defence for you."

I shook off his arm. "I'm all right."

I walked back to Civil Defence. The girl who had tried to find Jack's file wasn't there, and the first girl was. I was sorry I hadn't brought the A-114 along as well, but she scrutinized the form without comment and stamped the back. "It will take approximately six weeks to process," she said.

"Six weeks!" I said. "Hitler could have invaded the entire Empire by then."

"In that case, you'll very likely have to file a different form."

I didn't go back to the post. Mrs. Lucy would doubtless be back by the time I returned, but what could I say to her? I suspect Jack. Of what? Of not liking lamb chops and cake? Of having to leave early for work? Of rescuing children from the rubble?

He had said he had a job, and the girl couldn't find his work permit, but it took the Civil Defence six weeks to process a request for a few beams. It would probably take them till the end of the war to file the work permits. Or perhaps his had been in the file, and the girl had missed it. Loss of sleep can result in mistakes on the job. And odd fixations.

I walked to Sloane Square Station. There was no sign of where the young woman had been. They had even swept the glass up. Her stewpot of a boss at John Lewis's never let her go till closing time, even if the sirens had gone, even if it was dark. She had had to hurry through the blacked-out streets all alone, carrying her dress for the next day on a hanger, listening to the guns and trying to make out how far off the planes were. If someone had been stalking her, she would never have heard him, never have seen him in the darkness. Whoever found her would think she had been killed by flying glass.

He doesn't eat, I would say to Mrs. Lucy. He didn't put out an incendiary in a church. He always leaves the incidents before dawn, even when we don't have the casualties up. The Luftwaffe is trying to kill me. It was a letter I wrote to the *Times*. The walking dead may hallucinate, hearing voices, seeing visions, or believing fantastical things.

The sirens went. I must have been standing there for hours, staring at the sidewalk. I went back to the post. Mrs. Lucy was there. "You look dreadful, Jack. How long's it been since you've slept?"

"I don't know," I said. "Where's Jack?"

"On watch," Mrs. Lucy said.

"You'd best be careful," Vi said, setting chocolates on a plate. "Or you'll turn into one of the walking dead. Would you like a sweet? Eddie gave them to me."

The telephone pipped. Mrs. Lucy answered it, spoke a minute, hung up. "Slaney needs help on an incident," she said. "They've asked for Jack."

She sent both of us. We found the incident without any trouble. There was no dust cloud, no smell except from a fire burning off to one side. "This didn't just happen," I said. "It's a day old, at least."

I was wrong. It was two days old. The rescue squads had been working straight through, and there were still at least thirty people unaccounted for. Some of the rescue squad were digging halfheartedly halfway up a mound, but most of them were standing about, smoking and looking like they were casualties themselves. Jack went up to where the men were digging, shook his head, and set off across the mound.

"Heard you had a bodysniffer," one of the smokers said to me. "They've got one in Whitechapel, too. Crawls round the incident on his hands and knees, sniffing like a bloodhound. Yours do that?"

"No," I said.

"Over here," Jack said.

"Says he can read their minds, the one in Whitechapel does," he said, putting out his cigarette and taking up a pickax. He clambered up the slope to where Jack was already digging.

It was easy to see because of the fire, and fairly easy

to dig, but halfway down we struck the massive headboard of a bed.

"We'll have to go in from the side," Jack said.

"The hell with that," the man who'd told me about the bodysniffer said. "How do you know somebody's down there? I don't hear anything."

Jack didn't answer him. He moved down the slope and began digging into its side.

"They've been in there two days," the man said. "They're dead and I'm not getting overtime." He flung down the pickax and stalked off to the mobile canteen. Jack didn't even notice he was gone. He handed me baskets, and I emptied them, and occasionally Jack said, "Saw," or "Tin-snips," and I handed them to him. I was off getting the stretcher when he brought her out.

She was perhaps thirteen. She was wearing a white nightgown, or perhaps it only looked white because of the plaster dust. Jack's face was ghastly with it. He had picked her up in his arms, and she had fastened her arms about his neck and buried her face against his shoulder. They were both outlined by the fire.

I brought the stretcher up, and Jack knelt down and tried to lay her on it, but she would not let go of his neck. "It's all right," he said gently. "You're safe now."

He unclasped her hands and folded them on her chest. Her nightgown was streaked with dried blood, but it didn't seem to be hers. I wondered who else had been in there with her. "What's your name?" Jack said.

"Mina," she said. It was no more than a whisper.

"My name's Jack," he said. He nodded at me. "So's his. We're going to carry you down to the ambulance now. Don't be afraid. You're safe now"

The ambulance wasn't there yet. We laid the stretcher on the sidewalk, and I went over to the incident officer to see if it was on its way. Before I could get back, somebody shouted, "Here's another," and I went and helped dig out a hand that the foreman had found, and then the body all the blood had come from. When I looked down the hill, the girl was still lying there on the stretcher, and Jack was bending over it.

I went out to Whitechapel to see the bodysniffer the next day. He wasn't there. "He's a part-time," the post warden told me, clearing off a chair so I could sit down. The post was a mess, dirty clothes and dishes everywhere. An old woman in a print wrapper was frying up kidneys in a skillet. "Works days in munitions out to Dorking," she said.

"How exactly is he able to locate the bodies?" I asked. "I heard—"

"That he reads their minds?" the woman said. She scraped the kidneys onto a plate and handed it to the post warden. "He's heard it, too, more's the pity, and it's gone straight to his head. 'I can feel them under here,' he says to the rescue squads, like he was Houdini or something, and points to where they're supposed to start digging."

"Then how does he find them?"

"Luck," the warden said.

"*I* think he smells 'em," the woman said. "That's why they call 'em bodysniffers."

The warden snorted. "Over the stink the jerries put in the bombs and the gas and all the rest of it?"

"If he were a—" I said, and didn't finish it. "If he had an acute sense of smell, perhaps he could smell the blood."

"You can't even smell the bodies when they've been dead a week," the warden said, his mouth full of kidneys. "He hears them screaming, same as us."

"He's got better hearing than us," the woman said, switching happily to his theory. "Most of us are half-deaf from the guns, and he isn't."

I hadn't been able to hear the fat woman in the pink hair net, although she'd said she had called for help. But Jack, just down from Yorkshire, where they hadn't been deafened by antiaircraft guns for weeks, could. There was nothing sinister about it. Some people had better hearing than others.

"We pulled an army colonel out last week who claimed he didn't cry out," I said.

"He's lying," the warden said, sawing at a kidney. "We had a nanny, two days ago, prim and proper as you please, swore the whole time we was getting her out, words to make a sailor blush, and then claimed she didn't. 'Unclean words have *never* crossed my lips and never will,' she says to me." He brandished his fork at me. "Your colonel cried out, all right. He just won't admit it."

"I didn't make a sound," Colonel Godalming had said, brandishing his serving spoon. "Knew it wouldn't do any good," and perhaps the warden was right, and it was only bluster. But he hadn't wanted his wife to know he was in London, to find out about the dancer at the Windmill. He had had good reason to keep silent, to try to dig himself out.

I went home and rang up a girl I knew in the ambulance service and asked her to find out where they had taken Mina. She rang me back in a few minutes with the answer, and I took the tube over to St. George's Hospital. The others had all cried out, or banged on the roof of the Anderson, except Mina. She had been so frightened when Jack got her out, she couldn't speak above a whisper, but that didn't mean she hadn't cried or whimpered.

"When you were buried last night, did you call for help?" I would ask her, and she would answer me in her mouse voice, "I called and called between prayers. Why?" And I would say, "It's nothing, an odd fixation brought on by lack of sleep. Jack spends his days in Dorking, at a munitions plant, and has exceptionally acute hearing." And there is no more truth to my theory than to Renfrew's belief that the raids were brought on by his letter to the *Times*.

St. George's had an entrance marked "Casualty

Clearing Station." I asked the nursing sister behind the desk if I could see Mina.

"She was brought in last night. The James Street incident."

She looked at a penciled and crossed-over roster. "I don't show an admission by that name."

"I'm certain she was brought here," I said, twisting my head round to read the list. "There isn't another St. George's, is there?"

She shook her head and lifted up the roster to look at a second sheet.

"Here she is," she said, and I had heard the rescue squads use that tone of voice often enough to know what it meant, but that was impossible. She had been under that headboard. The blood on her nightgown hadn't even been hers.

"I'm so sorry," the sister said.

"When did she die?" I said.

"This morning," she said, checking the second list, which was much longer than the first.

"Did anyone else come to see her?"

"I don't know. I've just been on since eleven."

"What did she die of?"

She looked at me as if I were insane.

"What was the listed cause of death?" I said.

She had to find Mina's name on the roster again. "Shock due to loss of blood," she said, and I thanked her and went to find Jack.

He found me. I had gone back to the post and waited till everyone was asleep and Mrs. Lucy had gone upstairs and then sneaked into the pantry to look up Jack's address in Mrs. Lucy's files. It had not been there, as I had known it wouldn't. And if there had been an address, what would it have turned out to be when I went to find it? A gutted house? A mound of rubble?

I had gone to Sloane Square Station, knowing he

wouldn't be there, but having no other place to look. He could have been anywhere. London was full of empty houses, bombed-out cellars, secret places to hide until it got dark. That was why he had come here.

"If I was a bad'un, I'd head straight for London," Swales had said. But the criminal element weren't the only ones who had come, drawn by the blackout and the easy pickings and the bodies. Drawn by the blood.

I stood there until it started to get dark, watching two boys scrabble in the gutter for sweets that had been blown out of a confectioner's front window, and then walked back to a doorway down the street from the post, where I could see the door, and waited. The sirens went. Swales left on patrol. Petersby went in. Morris came out, stopping to peer at the sky as if he were looking for his son Quincy's plane. Mrs. Lucy must not have managed to talk Nelson out of the patrols.

It got dark. The searchlights began to crisscross the sky, catching the silver of the barrage balloons. The planes started coming in from the east, a low hum. Vi hurried in, wearing high heels and carrying a box tied with string. Petersby and Twickenham left on patrol. Vi came out, fastening her helmet strap under her chin and eating something.

"I've been looking for you everywhere," Jack said.

I turned around. He had driven up in a lorry marked ATS. He had left the door open and the motor running. "I've got the beams," he said. "For reinforcing the post. The incident we were on last night, all these beams were lying on top, and I asked the owner of the house if I could buy them from him."

He gestured to the back of the lorry, where jagged ends of wood were sticking out. "Come along, then, we can get them up tonight if we hurry." He started toward the truck. "Where were you? I've looked everywhere for you."

"I went to St. George's Hospital," I said.

He stopped, his hand on the open door of the truck.

"Mina's dead," I said, "but you knew that, didn't you?"

He didn't say anything.

"The nurse said she died of loss of blood," I said. A flare drifted down, lighting his face with a deadly whiteness. "I know what you are."

"If we hurry, we can get the reinforcements up before the raid starts," he said. He started to pull the door to.

I put my hand on it to keep him from closing it. "War work," I said bitterly. "What do you do, make sure you're alone in the tunnel with them or go to see them in hospital afterward?"

He let go of the door.

"Brilliant stroke, volunteering for the ARP," I said. "Nobody's going to suspect the noble air-raid warden, especially when he's so good at locating casualties. And if some of those casualties die later, if somebody's found dead on the street after a raid, well, it's only to be expected. There's a war on."

The drone overhead got suddenly louder, and a whole shower of flares came down. The searchlights wheeled, trying to find the planes. Jack took hold of my arm.

"Get down," he said, and tired to drag me into the doorway.

I shook his arm off. "I'd kill you if I could," I said. "But I can't, can I?" I waved my hand at the sky. "And neither can they. Your sort don't die, do they?"

There was a long swish, and the rising scream. "I *will* kill you, though," I shouted over it. "If you touch Vi or Mrs. Lucy."

"Mrs. Lucy," he said, and I couldn't tell if he said it with astonishment or contempt.

"Or Vi or any of the rest of them. I'll drive a stake through your heart or whatever it takes," I said, and the air fell apart.

There was a long sound like an enormous monster growling. It seemed to go on and on. I tried to put my hands over my ears, but I had to hang on to the road to keep from falling. The roar became a scream, and the sidewalk shook itself sharply, and I fell off.

"Are you all right?" Jack said.

I was sitting next to the lorry, which was on its side. The beams had spilled out the back. "Were we hit?" I said.

"No," he said, but I already knew that, and before he had finished pulling me to my feet, I was running toward the post that we couldn't see for the dust.

Mrs. Lucy had told Nelson having everyone out on patrol would mean no one could be found in an emergency, but that was not true. They were all there within minutes, Swales and Morris and Violet, clattering up in her high heels, and Petersby. They ran up, one after the other, and then stopped and looked stupidly at the space that had been Mrs. Lucy's house, as if they couldn't make out what it was.

"Where's Renfrew?" Jack said.

"In Birmingham," Vi said.

"He wasn't here," I explained. "He's on sick leave." I peered through the smoke and dust, trying to see their faces. "Where's Twickenham?"

"Here," he said.

"Where's Mrs. Lucy?" I said.

"Over here," Jack said, and pointed down into the rubble.

We dug all night. Two different rescue squads came to help. They called down every half hour, but there was no answer. Vi borrowed a light from somewhere, draped a blue head scarf over it, and set up as incident officer. An ambulance came, sat awhile, left to go to another incident, came back. Nelson took over as incident officer, and Vi came back up to help. "Is she alive?" she asked.

"She'd better be," I said, looking at Jack.

It began to mist. The planes came over again, dropping flares and incendiaries, but no one stopped work. Twickenham's typewriter came up in the baskets, and one of Mrs. Lucy's wineglasses.

At around three Morris thought he heard something, and we stopped and called down, but there was no answer. The mist turned into a drizzle. At half past four I shouted to Mrs. Lucy, and she called back, from far underground, "I'm here."

"Are you all right?" I shouted.

"My leg's hurt. I think it's broken," she shouted, her voice calm. "I seem to be under the table."

"Don't worry," I shouted. "We're nearly there."

The drizzle turned the plaster dust into a slippery, disgusting mess. We had to brace the tunnel repeatedly and cover it with a tarpaulin, and then it was too dark to see to dig. Swales lay above us, holding a pocket torch over our heads so we could see. The all clear went.

"Jack!" Mrs. Lucy called up.

"Yes!" I shouted.

"Was that the all clear?"

"Yes," I shouted. "Don't worry. We'll have you out soon now."

"What time is it?"

It was too dark in the tunnel to see my watch. I made a guess. "A little after five.

"Is Jack there?"

"Yes."

"He mustn't stay," she said. "Tell him to go home."

The rain stopped, and it began to get light. Jack glanced vaguely up at the sky.

"Don't even think about it," I said. "You're not going anywhere." We ran into one and then another of the oak beams that had reinforced the landing on the fourth floor and had to saw through them. Swales reported that

Morris had called Nelson "a bloody murderer." Vi brought us paper cups of tea.

We called down to Mrs. Lucy, but there wasn't any answer. "She's probably dozed off," Twickenham said, and the others nodded as if they believed him.

We could smell the gas long before we got to her, but Jack kept on digging, and like the others, I told myself that she was all right, that we would get to her in time.

She was not under the table after all, but under part of the pantry door. We had to call for a jack to get it off her. It took Morris a long time to come back with it, but it didn't matter. She was lying perfectly straight, her arms folded across her chest and her eyes closed as if she were asleep. Her left leg had been taken off at the knee. Jack knelt beside her and cradled her head.

"Keep your hands off her," I said.

I made Swales come down and help get her out. Vi and Twickenham put her on the stretcher. Petersby went for the ambulance. "She was never a horrid person, you know," Morris said. "Never."

It began to rain again, the sky so dark, it was impossible to tell whether the sun had come up yet or not. Swales brought a tarp to cover Mrs. Lucy.

Petersby came back. "The ambulance has gone off again," he said. "I've sent for the mortuary van, but they said they doubt they can be here before half past eight."

I looked at Jack. He was standing over the tarp, his hands slackly at his sides. He looked worse then Renfrew ever had, impossibly tired, his face gray with wet plaster dust. "We'll wait," I said.

"There's no point in all of us standing here in the rain for two hours," Morris said. "I'll wait here with the . . . I'll wait here. Jack"—he turned to him—"go and report to Nelson."

"I'll do it," Vi said. "Jack needs to get to his day job."

"Is she up?" Nelson said. He clambered over the

fourth-floor beams to where we were standing. "Is she dead?" He glared at Morris and then at my hat, and I wondered if he were going to reprimand me for the condition of my uniform.

"Which of you found her?" he demanded.

I looked at Jack. "Settle did," I said. "He's a regular wonder. He's found six this week alone."

Two days after Mrs. Lucy's funeral, a memo came through from Civil Defence transferring Jack to Nelson's post, and I got my official notice to report for duty. I was sent to basic training and then on to Portsmouth. Vi sent me food packets, and Twickenham posted me copies of his *Twitterings*.

The post had relocated across the street from the butcher's in a house belonging to a Miss Arthur, who had subsequently joined the post. "Miss Arthur loves knitting and flower arranging and will make a valuable addition to our brave little band," Twickenham had written. Vi had got engaged to a pilot in the RAF. Hitler had bombed Birmingham. Jack, in Nelson's post now, had saved sixteen people in one week, a record for the ARP.

After two weeks I was shipped to North Africa, out of the reach of the mails. When I finally got Morris's letter, it was three months old. Jack had been killed while rescuing a child at an incident. A delayed-action bomb had fallen nearby, but "that bloody murderer Nelson" had refused to allow the rescue squad to evacuate. The DA had gone off, the tunnel Jack was working in had collapsed, and he'd been killed. They had gotten the child out, though, and she was unhurt except for a few cuts.

But he isn't dead, I thought. It's impossible to kill him. I had tried, but even betraying him to von Nelson hadn't worked, and he was still somewhere in London, hidden by the blackout and the noise of the bombs and the number of dead bodies, and who would notice a few more?

In January I helped take out a tank battalion at Tobruk. I killed nine Germans before I caught a piece of shrapnel. I was shipped to Gibraltar to hospital, where the rest of my mail caught up with me. Vi had gotten married, the raids had let up considerably, Jack had been awarded the George Cross posthumously.

In March I was sent back to hospital in England for surgery. It was near North Weald, where Morris's son Quincy was stationed. He came to see me after the surgery. He looked the very picture of an RAF pilot, firm-jawed, steely-eyed, rakish grin, not at all like a delinquent minor. He was flying nightly bombing missions over Germany, he told me, "giving Hitler a bit of our own back."

"I heard you're to get a medal," he said, looking at the wall above my head as if he expected to see violets painted there, nine of them, one for each kill.

I asked him about his father. He was fine, he told me. He'd been appointed Senior Warden. "I admire you ARP people," he said, "saving lives and all that."

He meant it. He was flying nightly bombing missions over Germany, reducing their cities to rubble, creating incidents for their air-raid wardens to scrabble through looking for dead children. I wondered if they had bodysniffers there, too, and if they were monsters like Jack.

"Dad wrote to me about your friend Jack," Quincy said. "It must have been rough, hearing so far away from home and all."

He looked genuinely sympathetic, and I supposed he was. He had shot down twenty-eight planes and killed who knows how many fat women in hair nets and thirteen-year-old girls, but no one had ever thought to call him a monster. The Duchess of York had called him the pride of England and kissed him on both cheeks.

"I went with Dad to Vi Westen's wedding," he said. "Pretty as a picture she was."

I thought of Vi, with her pin curls and her plain face.

It was as though the war had transformed her into someone completely different, someone pretty and sought after.

"There were strawberries and two kinds of cake," he said. "One of the wardens—Tottenham?—read a poem in honor of the happy couple. Wrote it himself."

It was as if the war had transformed Twickenham as well, and Mrs. Lucy, who had been the terror of the churchwardens. What the War Has Done for Us. But it hadn't transformed them. All that was wanted was for someone to give Vi a bit of attention for all her latent sweetness to blossom. Every girl is pretty when she knows she's sought after.

Twickenham had always longed to be a writer. Nelson had always been a bully and a stickler, and Mrs. Lucy, in spite of what she said, had never been either. "Sometimes it takes something dreadful like a war for one to find one's proper job," she'd said.

Like Quincy, who had been, in spite of what Morris said, a bad boy, headed for a life of petty crime or worse, when the war came along. And suddenly his wildness and daring and "high spirits" were virtues, were just what was needed.

What the War Has Done for Us, Number Two. It has made jobs that didn't exist before. Like RAF pilot. Like post warden. Like bodysniffer.

"Did they find Jack's body?" I asked, though I knew the answer. No, Quincy would say, we couldn't find it, or there was nothing left.

"Didn't Dad tell you?" Quincy said with an anxious look at the transfusion bag hanging above the bed. "They had to dig past him to get to the little girl. It was pretty bad, Dad said. The blast from the DA had driven the leg of a chair straight through his chest."

So I had killed him after all. Nelson and Hitler and I.

"I shouldn't have told you that," Quincy said, watching the blood drip from the bag into my veins as if it were a bad sign. "I know he was a friend of yours. I wouldn't have told you only Dad said to tell you yours was the last name he said before he died. Just before the DA went up. 'Jack,' he said, like he knew what was going to happen, Dad said, and called out your name."

He didn't though, I thought. And "that bloody murderer Nelson" hadn't refused to evacuate him. Jack had just gone on working, oblivious to Nelson and the DA, stabbing at the rubble as though he were trying to murder it, calling out "saw" and "wire cutters" and "braces." Calling out "jack." Oblivious to everything except getting them out before the gas killed them, before they bled to death. Oblivious to everything but his job.

I had been wrong about why he had joined the ARP, about why he had come to London. He must have lived a terrible life up there in Yorkshire, full of darkness and self-hatred and killing. When the war came, when he began reading of people buried in the rubble, of rescue wardens searching blindly for them, it must have seemed a godsend. A blessing.

It wasn't, I think, that he was trying to atone for what he'd done, for what he was. It's impossible, at any rate. I had killed only ten people, counting Jack, and had helped rescue nearly twenty, but it doesn't cancel out. And I don't think that was what he wanted. What he had wanted was to be useful.

"Here's to making the best of a bad job," Mrs. Lucy had said, and that was all any of them had been doing: Swales with his jokes and gossip, and Twickenham, and Jack, and if they found friendship or love or atonement as well, it was no less than they deserved. And it was still a bad job.

"I should be going," Quincy said, looking worriedly at me. "You need your rest, and I need to be getting back to work. The German army's halfway to Cairo, and Yugoslavia's joined the Axis." He looked excited, happy. "You must rest and get well. We need you back in this war."

"I'm glad you came," I said.

"Yes, well, Dad wanted me to tell you that about Jack calling for you." He stood up. "Tough luck, your getting it in the neck like this." He slapped his flight cap against his leg. "I hate this war," he said, but he was lying.

"So do I," I said.

"They'll have you back killing jerries in no time," he said.

"Yes."

He put his cap on at a rakish angle and went off to bomb lecherous retired colonels and children and widows who had not yet managed to get reinforcing beams out of the Hamburg Civil Defence and paint violets on his plane. Doing his bit.

A sister brought in a tray. She had a large red cross sewn to the bib of her apron.

"No, thanks, I'm not hungry," I said.

"You must keep your strength up," she said. She set the tray beside the bed and went out.

"The war's been rather a blessing for our Vi," I had told Jack, and perhaps it was. But not for most people. Not for girls who worked at John Lewis's for old stewpots who never let them leave early even when the sirens had gone. Not for those people who discovered hidden capabilities for insanity or betrayal or bleeding to death. Or murder.

The sirens went. The nurse came in to check my transfusion and take the tray away. I lay there for a long time, watching the blood come down into my arm.

"Jack," I said, and didn't know who I called out to, or if I had made a sound.

I FOUND OUT WHO *MAY ROBSON* WAS THE OTHER *day. She was in an old Frank Capra movie,* Lady for a Day, *and I realized when I saw her as Apple Annie that I'd seen her in dozens of movies. So have you. She was the Queen of Hearts in* Alice in Wonderland *and Katherine Hepburn's scatterbrained aunt in* Bringing up Baby. *You know, the one who kept calling Cary Grant "Mr. Bone." So she definitely was a star and deserves her square at Graumann's Chinese along with Freddie Bartholomew and Trigger.*

I wasn't sure. You never know with Hollywood. She could have been a starlet with a good publicist or somebody's girlfriend or something. And I suppose it's appropriate that in Lady for a Day *she was pretending she was somebody else, because in Hollywood nothing is quite what it appears. The bottle broken over your head is breakaway glass, love is a special effect (though not always, even in Hollywood), voices are dubbed in afterward, and you're only dead until the sequel.*

But what else would you expect from a place where it's possible to store time in round metal tins? It's as if the laws of physics have been suspended in Hollywood. Or other laws altogether are in force.

At the Rialto

Seriousness of mind was a prerequisite for understanding Newtonian physics. I am not convinced it is not a handicap in understanding quantum theory.

—Excerpt from Dr. Gedanken's
keynote address to the
1988 International Congress
of Quantum Physicists Annual
Meeting, Hollywood, California

I got to Hollywood around one-thirty and started trying to check into the Rialto.

"Sorry, we don't have any rooms," the girl behind the desk said. "We're all booked up with some science thing."

"I'm with the science thing," I said. "Dr. Ruth Baringer. I reserved a double."

"There are a bunch of Republicans here, too, and a tour group from Finland. They told me when I started work here that they got all these movie people, but the only one so far was that guy who played the friend of that other guy in that one movie. You're not a movie person, are you?"

"No," I said. "I'm with the science thing. Dr. Ruth Baringer."

"My name's Tiffany," she said. "I'm not actually a hotel clerk at all. I'm just working here to pay for my transcendental posture lessons. I'm really a model/actress."

"I'm a quantum physicist," I said, trying to get things back on track. "The name is Ruth Baringer."

She messed with the computer for a minute. "I don't show a reservation for you."

"Maybe it's in Dr. Mendoza's name. I'm sharing a room with her."

She messed with the computer some more. "I don't show a reservation for her either. Are you sure you don't want the Disneyland Hotel? A lot of people get the two confused."

"I want the Rialto," I said, rummaging through my bag for my notebook. "I have a confirmation number. W-three-seven-four-two-oh."

She typed it in. "Are you Dr. Gedanken?" she asked.

"Excuse me," an elderly man said.

"I'll be right with you," Tiffany told him. "How long do you plan to stay with us, Dr. Gedanken?" she asked me.

"*Excuse* me," the man said, sounding desperate. He had bushy white hair and a dazed expression, as if he had just been through a horrific experience or had been trying to check into the Rialto.

He wasn't wearing any socks. I wondered if *he* was Dr. Gedanken. Dr. Gedanken was the main reason I'd decided to come to the meeting. I had missed his lecture on wave-particle duality last year, but I had read the text of it in the *ICQP Journal*, and it had actually seemed to make sense, which is more than you can say for most of quantum theory. He was giving the keynote address this year, and I was determined to hear it.

It wasn't Dr. Gedanken. "My name is Dr. Whedbee," the elderly man said. "You gave me the wrong room."

"All our rooms are pretty much the same," Tiffany said. "Except for how many beds they have in them and stuff."

"My room has a *person* in it!" he said. "Dr. Sleeth. From the University of Texas at Austin. She was changing her clothes." His hair seemed to get wilder as he spoke. "She thought I was a serial killer."

"And your name is Dr. Whedbee?" Tiffany asked,

fooling with the computer again. "I don't show a reservation for you."

Dr. Whedbee began to cry. Tiffany got out a paper towel, wiped off the counter, and turned back to me. "May I help you?" she said.

Thursday, 7:30–9 P.M. *Opening Ceremonies*. Dr. Halvard Onofrio, University of Maryland at College Park, will speak on the topic, "Doubts Surrounding the Heisenberg Uncertainty Principle." Ballroom.

I finally got my room at five, after Tiffany went off duty. Till then I sat around the lobby with Dr. Whedbee, listening to Abey Fields complain about Hollywood.

"What's wrong with Racine?" he said. "Why do we always have to go to these exotic places, like Hollywood? And St. Louis last year wasn't much better. The Institute Henri Poincaré people kept going off to see the arch and Busch Stadium."

"Speaking of St. Louis," Dr. Takumi said, "have you seen David yet?"

"No," I said.

"Oh, really?" she said. "Last year at the annual meeting you two were practically inseparable. Moonlight riverboat rides and all."

"What's on the programming tonight?" I said to Abey.

"David was just here," Dr. Takumi said. "He said to tell you he was going out to look at the stars in the sidewalk."

"That's exactly what I'm talking about," Abey said. "Riverboat rides and movie stars. What do those things have to do with quantum theory? Racine would have been an appropriate setting for a group of physicists. Not like this . . . this . . . do you realize we're practically across the street from Grauman's Chinese Theatre? And

Hollywood Boulevard's where all those gangs hang out. If they catch you wearing red or blue, they'll—"

He stopped. "Is that Dr. Gedanken?" he asked, staring at the front desk.

I turned and looked. A short roundish man with a mustache was trying to check in. "No," I said. "That's Dr. Onofrio."

"Oh, yes," Abey said, consulting his program book. "He's speaking tonight at the opening ceremonies. On the Heisenberg uncertainty principle. Are you going?"

"I'm not sure," I said, which was supposed to be a joke, but Abey didn't laugh.

"I must meet Dr. Gedanken. He's just gotten funding for a new project."

I wondered what Dr. Gedanken's new project was—I would have loved to work with him.

"I'm hoping he'll come to my workshop on the wonderful world of quantum physics," Abey said, still watching the desk. Amazingly enough, Dr. Onofrio seemed to have gotten a key and was heading for the elevators. "I think his project has something to do with understanding quantum theory."

Well, that let me out. I didn't understand quantum theory at all. I sometimes had a sneaking suspicion nobody else did either, including Abey Fields, and that they just weren't willing to admit it.

I mean, an electron is a particle except it acts like a wave. In fact, a neutron acts like two waves and interferes with itself (or each other), and you can't really measure any of this stuff properly because of the Heisenberg uncertainty principle, and that isn't the worst of it. When you set up a Josephson junction to figure out what rules the electrons obey, they sneak past the barrier to the other side, and they don't seem to care much about the limits of the speed of light either, and Schrödinger's cat is neither alive nor dead till you open the box, and it all makes about as much sense as Tiffany's calling me Dr. Gedanken.

Which reminded me, I had promised to call Darlene and give her our room number. I didn't have a room number, but if I waited much longer, she'd have left. She was flying to Denver to speak at CU and then coming on to Hollywood sometime tomorrow morning. I interrupted Abey in the middle of his telling me how beautiful Cleveland was in the winter and went to call her.

"I don't have a room yet," I said when she answered. "Should I leave a message on your answering machine or do you want to give me your number in Denver?"

"Never mind all that," Darlene said. "Have you seen David yet?"

To illustrate the problems of the concept of wave function, Dr. Schrödinger imagines a cat being put into a box with a piece of uranium, a bottle of poison gas, and a Geiger counter. If a uranium nucleus disintegrates while the cat is in the box, it will release radiation, which will set off the Geiger counter and break the bottle of poison gas. It is impossible in quantum theory to predict whether a uranium nucleus will disintegrate while the cat is in the box, and only possible to calculate uranium's probable half-life; therefore, the cat is neither alive nor dead until we open the box.

From "The Wonderful World of Quantum Physics,"
A seminar presented at the ICQP Annual Meeting
by A. Fields, Ph.D., University of Nebraska at Wahoo

I completely forgot to warn Darlene about Tiffany, the model-slash-actress.

"What do you mean you're trying to avoid David?" she had asked me at least three times. "Why would you do a stupid thing like that?"

Because in St. Louis I ended up on a riverboat in the

moonlight and didn't make it back until the conference was over.

"Because I want to attend the programming," I said the third time around, "Not a wax museum. I am a middle-aged woman."

"And David is a middle-aged man who, I might add, is absolutely charming."

"Charm is for quarks," I said, and hung up, feeling smug until I remembered I hadn't told her about Tiffany. I went back to the front desk, thinking maybe Dr. Onofrio's success signaled a change. Tiffany asked, "May I help you?" and left me standing there.

After a while I gave up and went back to the red-and-gold sofas.

"David was here again," Dr. Takumi said. "He said to tell you he was going to the wax museum."

"There *are* no wax museums in Racine," Abey said.

"What's the programming for tonight?" I said, taking Abey's program away from him.

"There's a mixer at six-thirty and the opening ceremonies in the ballroom and then some seminars." I read the descriptions of the seminars. There was one on the Josephson junction. Electrons were able to somehow tunnel through an insulated barrier even though they didn't have the required energy. Maybe I could somehow get a room without checking in.

"If we were in Racine," Abey said, looking at his watch, "we'd already be checked in and on our way to dinner."

Dr. Onofrio emerged from the elevator, still carrying his bags. He came over and sank down on the sofa next to Abey.

"Did they give you a room with a seminaked woman in it?" Dr. Whedbee asked.

"I don't know," Dr. Onofrio said. "I couldn't find it." He looked sadly at the key. "They gave me twelve eighty-two, but the room numbers go only up to seventy-five."

"I think I'll attend the seminar on chaos," I said.

The most serious difficulty quantum theory faces today is not the inherent limitation of measurement capability or the EPR paradox. It is the lack of a paradigm. Quantum theory has no working model, no metaphor that properly defines it.

Excerpt from Dr. Gedanken's keynote address

I got to my room at six, after a brief skirmish with the bellboy-slash-actor, who couldn't remember where he'd stored my suitcase, and unpacked. My clothes, which had been permanent press all the way from MIT, underwent a complete wave-function collapse the moment I opened my suitcase and came out looking like Schrödinger's almost-dead cat.

By the time I had called housekeeping for an iron, taken a bath, given up on the iron, and steamed a dress in the shower, I had missed the "Mixer with Munchies" and was half an hour late for Dr. Onofrio's opening remarks.

I opened the door to the ballroom as quietly as I could and slid inside. I had hoped they would be late getting started, but a man I didn't recognize was already introducing the speaker. "—and an inspiration to all of us in the field."

I dived for the nearest chair and sat down.

"Hi," David said. "I've been looking all over for you. Where were you?"

"Not at the wax museum," I whispered.

"You should have been," he whispered back. "It was great. They had John Wayne, Elvis, and Tiffany the model-slash-actress with the brain of a pea-slash-amoeba."

"Shh," I said.

"—the person we've all been waiting to hear, Dr. Ringgit Dinari."

"What happened to Dr. Onofrio?" I asked.

"Shhh," David said.

Dr. Dinari looked a lot like Dr. Onofrio. She was short, roundish, and mustached and was wearing a rainbow-striped caftan. "I will be your guide this evening into a strange new world," she said, "a world where all that you thought you knew, all common sense, all accepted wisdom, must be discarded. A world where all the rules have changed and it sometimes seems there are no rules at all."

She sounded just like Dr. Onofrio, too. He had given this same speech two years ago in Cincinnati. I wondered if he had undergone some strange transformation during his search for room 1282 and was now a woman.

"Before I go any further," Dr. Dinari said, "how many of you have already channeled?"

Newtonian physics had as its model the machine. The metaphor of the machine, with its interrelated parts, its gears and wheels, its causes and effects, was what made it possible to think about Newtonian physics.

Excerpt from Dr. Gedanken's keynote address

"You *knew* we were in the wrong place," I hissed at David when we got out to the lobby.

When we stood up to leave, Dr. Dinari had extended her pudgy hand in its rainbow-striped sleeve and called out in a voice a lot like Charlton Heston's, "O Unbelievers! Leave not, for here only is reality!"

"Actually, channeling would explain a lot," David said, grinning.

"If the opening remarks aren't in the ballroom, where are they?"

"Beats me," he said. "Want to go see the Capitol Records building? It's shaped like a stack of records."

"I want to go to the opening remarks."

"The beacon on top blinks out 'Hollywood' in Morse code."

I went over to the front desk.

"Can I help you?" the clerk behind the desk said. "My name is Natalie, and I'm an—"

"Where is the ICQP meeting this evening?" I said.

"They're in the ballroom."

"I'll bet you didn't have any dinner," David said. "I'll buy you an ice-cream cone. There's this great place that has the ice-cream cone Ryan O'Neal bought for Tatum in *Paper Moon*."

"A channeler's in the ballroom," I told Natalie. "I'm looking for the ICQP."

She fiddled with the computer. "I'm sorry. I don't show a reservation for them."

"How about Grauman's Chinese?" David said. "You want reality? You want Charlton Heston? You want to see quantum theory in action?" He grabbed my hands. "Come with me," he said seriously.

In St. Louis I had suffered a wave-function collapse a lot like what had happened to my clothes when I opened the suitcase. I had ended up on a riverboat halfway to New Orleans that time. It happened again, and the next thing I knew, I was walking around the courtyard of Grauman's Chinese, eating an ice-cream cone and trying to fit my feet into Myrna Loy's footprints.

She must have been a midget or had her feet bound as a child. So, apparently, had Debbie Reynolds, Dorothy Lamour, and Wallace Beery. The only footprints I came close to fitting were Donald Duck's.

"I see this as a map of the microcosm," David said, sweeping his hand over the slightly irregular pavement of printed and signed cement squares. "See, there are all these tracks. We know something's been here, and the prints are pretty much the same, only every once in a while you've got this"—he knelt down and pointed at the print of John Wayne's clenched fist—"and over here"—he walked toward the box office and pointed to the print of Betty Grable's leg—"and we can figure out the signatures, but what is this reference to 'Sid' that keeps popping up? And what does this mean?"

He pointed at Red Skelton's square. It said, "Thanks Sid We Dood It."

"You keep thinking you've found a pattern," David said, crossing over to the other side, "but Van Johnson's square is kind of sandwiched in here at an angle between Esther Williams and Cantinflas, and who the hell is May Robson? And why are all these squares over here empty?"

He had managed to maneuver me over behind the display of Academy Award winners. It was an accordionlike wrought-iron screen. I was in the fold between 1944 and 1945.

"And as if that isn't enough, you suddenly realize you're standing in the courtyard. You're not even in the theater."

"And that's what you think is happening in quantum theory?" I said weakly. I was backed up into Bing Crosby, who had won for Best Actor in *Going My Way*. "You think we're not in the theater yet?"

"I think we know as much about quantum theory as we can figure out about May Robson from her footprints," he said, putting his hand up to Ingrid Bergman's cheek (Best Actress, *Gaslight*) and blocking my escape. "I don't think we understand anything *about* quantum theory, not tunneling, not complementarity." He leaned toward me. "Not passion."

The best movie of 1945 was *Lost Weekend*. "Dr. Gedanken understands it," I said, disentangling myself from the Academy Award winners and David. "Did you know he's putting together a new research team for a big project on understanding quantum theory?"

"Yes," David said. "Want to see a movie?"

"There's a seminar on chaos at nine," I said, stepping over the Marx Brothers. "I have to get back."

"If it's chaos you want, you should stay right here," he said, stopping to look at Irene Dunne's handprints. "We could see the movie and then go have dinner. There's this place near Hollywood and Vine that has the mashed potatoes Richard Dreyfuss made into Devil's Tower in *Close Encounters.*"

"I want to meet Dr. Gedanken," I said, making it safely to the sidewalk. I looked back at David. He had gone back to the other side of the courtyard and was looking at Roy Rogers's signature.

"Are you kidding? He doesn't understand it any better than we do."

"Well, at least he's trying."

"So am I. The problem is, how can one neutron interfere with itself, and why are there only two of Trigger's hoofprints here?"

"It's eight fifty-five," I said. "I am going to the chaos seminar."

"If you can find it," he said, getting down on one knee to look at the signature.

"I'll find it," I said grimly. He stood up and grinned at me, his hands in his pockets. "It's a great movie," he said.

It was happening again. I turned and practically ran across the street.

"*Benji IX* is showing," he shouted after me. "He accidentally exchanges bodies with a Siamese cat."

Thursday, 9–10 P.M. "The Science of Chaos." I. Durcheinander, University of Leipzig. A seminar on the structure of chaos. Principles of chaos will be discussed, including the Butterfly Effect, fractals, and insolid billowing. Clara Bow Room.

• • •

I couldn't find the chaos seminar. The Clara Bow Room, where it was supposed to be, was empty. A meeting of vegetarians was next door in the Fatty Arbuckle Room, and all the other conference rooms were locked. The channeler was still in the ballroom. "Come!" she commanded when I opened the door. "Understanding awaits!" I went upstairs to bed.

I had forgotten to call Darlene. She would have left for Denver already, but I called her answering machine and told it the room number in case she picked up her messages. In the morning I would have to tell the front desk to give her a key. I went to bed.

I didn't sleep well. The air conditioner went off during the night, which meant I didn't have to steam my suit when I got up the next morning. I got dressed and went downstairs. The programming started at nine with Abey Fields's Wonderful World workshop in the Mary Pickford Room, a breakfast buffet in the ballroom, and a slide presentation on "Delayed Choice Experiments" in Cecil B. DeMille A on the mezzanine level.

The breakfast buffet sounded wonderful, even though it always turns out to be urn coffee and donuts. I hadn't had anything but an ice-cream cone since noon the day before, but if David was around, he would be somewhere close to the food, and I wanted to steer clear of him. Last night it had been Grauman's Chinese. Today I was likely to end up at Knotts' Berry Farm. I wasn't going to let that happen, even if he was charming.

It was pitch-dark inside Cecil B. DeMille A. Even the slide on the screen up front appeared to be black. "As you can see," Dr. Lvov said, "the laser pulse is already in motion before the experimenter sets up the wave or particle detector." He clicked to the next slide, which was dark gray. "We used a Mach-Zender interferometer with two mirrors and a particle detector. For the first series of tries we allowed the experimenter to decide which apparatus he would use by whatever method he wished. For the second series we used that most primitive of randomizers—"

He clicked again, to a white slide with black polka dots that gave off enough light for me to be able to spot an empty chair on the aisle ten rows up. I hurried to get to it before the slide changed, and sat down.

"—a pair of dice. Alley's experiments had shown us that when the particle detector was in place, the light was detected as a particle, and when the wave detector was in place, the light showed wavelike behavior, no matter when the choice of apparatus was made."

"Hi," David said. "You've missed five black slides, two gray ones, and a white with black polka dots."

"Shh," I said.

"In our two series, we hoped to ascertain whether the consciousness of the decision affected the outcome." Dr. Lvov clicked to another black slide. "As you can see, the graph shows no effective difference between the tries in which the experimenter chose the detection apparatus and those in which the apparatus was randomly chosen."

"You want to go get some breakfast?" David whispered.

"I already ate," I whispered back, and waited for my stomach to growl and give me away. It did.

"There's a great place down near Hollywood and Vine that has the waffles Katharine Hepburn made for Spencer Tracy in *Woman of the Year*."

"Shh," I said.

"And after breakfast we could go to Frederick's of Hollywood and see the bra museum."

"Will you please be quiet? I can't hear."

"Or see," he said, but he subsided more or less for the remaining ninety-two black, gray, and polka-dotted slides.

Dr. Lvov turned on the lights and blinked smilingly at the audience. "Consciousness had no discernible effect on the results of the experiment. As one of my lab assistants put it, 'The little devil knows what you're going to do before you know it yourself.' "

This was apparently supposed to be a joke, but I didn't think it was very funny. I opened my program and tried to find something to go to that David wouldn't be caught dead at.

"Are you two going to breakfast?" Dr. Thibodeaux asked.

"Yes," David said.

"No," I said.

"Dr. Hotard and I wished to eat somewhere that is *vraiment* Hollywood."

"David knows just the place," I said. "He's been telling me about this great place where they have the grapefruit James Cagney shoved in Mae Clark's face in *Public Enemy*."

Dr. Hotard hurried up, carrying a camera and four guidebooks. "And then perhaps you would show us Grauman's Chinese Theatre," he asked David.

"Of course he will," I said. "I'm sorry I can't go with you, but I promised Dr. Verikovsky I'd be at his lecture on Boolean logic. And after Grauman's Chinese, David can take you to the bra museum at Frederick's of Hollywood."

"And the Brown Derby?" Thibodeaux asked. "I have heard it is shaped like a *chapeau*."

They dragged him off. I watched till they were safely out of the lobby and then ducked upstairs and into Dr Whedbee's lecture on information theory. Dr. Whedbee wasn't there.

"He went to find an overhead projector," Dr. Takumi said. She had half a donut on a paper plate in one hand and a styrofoam cup in the other.

"Did you get that at the breakfast brunch?" I asked.

"Yes. It was the last one. And they ran out of coffee right after I got there. You weren't in Abey Fields's thing, were you?" She set the coffee cup down and took a bite of the donut.

"No," I said, wondering if I should try to take her by surprise or just wrestle the donut away from her.

"You didn't miss anything. He raved the whole time about how we should have had the meeting in Racine." She popped the last piece of donut into her mouth. "Have you seen David yet?"

Friday, 9–10 A.M. "The Eureka Experiment: A Slide Presentation." J. Lvov, Eureka College. Descriptions, results, and conclusions of Lvov's delayed conscious/randomed choice experiments. Cecil B. DeMille A.

Dr. Whedbee eventually came in carrying an overhead projector, the cord trailing behind him. He plugged it in. The light didn't go on.

"Here," Dr. Takumi said, handing me her plate and cup. "I have one of these at Caltech. It needs its fractal-basin boundaries adjusted." She whacked the side of the projector.

There weren't even any crumbs left of the donut. There was about a millimeter of coffee in the bottom of the cup. I was about to stoop to new depths when she hit it again. The light came on. "I learned that in the chaos seminar last night," she said, grabbing the cup away from me and draining it. "You should have been there. The Clara Bow Room was packed."

"I believe I'm ready to begin," Dr. Whedbee said. Dr. Takumi and I sat down. "Information is the transmission of meaning," Dr. Whedbee said. He wrote "meaning" or possible "information" on the screen with a green Magic Marker. "When information is randomized, meaning cannot be transmitted, and we have a state of entropy." He wrote it under "meaning" with a red Magic Marker. His handwriting appeared to be completely illegible.

"States of entropy vary from low entropy, such as the mild static on your car radio, to high entropy, a state of complete disorder, of randomness and confusion, in which no information at all is being communicated."

Oh, my God, I thought. I forgot to tell the hotel about Darlene. The next time Dr. Whedbee bent over to inscribe hieroglyphics on the screen, I sneaked out and went down to the desk, hoping Tiffany hadn't come on duty yet. She had.

"May I help you?" she asked.

"I'm in room six-sixty-three," I said. "I'm sharing a room with Dr. Darlene Mendoza. She's coming in this morning, and she'll be needing a key."

"For what?" Tiffany said.

"To get into the room. I may be in one of the lectures when she gets here."

"Why doesn't she have a key?"

"Because she isn't here yet."

"I thought you said she was sharing a room with you."

"She *will* be sharing a room with me. Room six-sixty-three. Her name is Darlene Mendoza."

"And your name?" she asked, hands poised over the computer.

"Ruth Baringer."

"We don't show a reservation for you."

We have made impressive advances in quantum physics in the ninety years since Planck's constant, but they have by and large been advances in technology, not theory. We can make advances in theory only when we have a model we can visualize.

Excerpt from Dr. Gedanken's keynote address

I high-entropied with Tiffany for a while on the subjects of my not having a reservation and the air-conditioning and then switched back suddenly to the problem of Darlene's key, in the hope of catching her off guard. It worked about as well as Alley's delayed-choice experiments.

In the middle of my attempting to explain that Darlene was not the air-conditioning repairman, Abey Fields came up.

"Have you seen Dr. Gedanken?"

I shook my head.

"I was sure he'd come to my Wonderful World workshop, but he didn't, and the hotel says they can't find his reservation," he said, scanning the lobby. "I found out what his new project is, incidentally, and I'd be perfect for it. He's going to find a paradigm for quantum theory. Is that him?" he said, pointing at an elderly man getting in the elevator.

"I think that's Dr. Whedbee," I said, but he had already sprinted across the lobby to the elevator.

He nearly made it. The elevator slid to a close just as he got there. He pushed the elevator button several times to make the door open again, and when that didn't work, tried to readjust its fractal-basin boundaries. I turned back to the desk.

"May I help you?" Tiffany said.

"You may," I said. "My roommate, Darlene Mendoza, will be arriving some time this morning. She's a producer. She's here to cast the female lead in a new movie starring Robert Redford and Harrison Ford. When she gets here, give her her key. And fix the air-conditioning."

"Yes, ma'am," she said.

The Josephson junction is designed so that electrons must obtain additional energy to surmount the energy barrier. It was found, however, that some electrons simply tunnel, as Heinz Pagel put it, "right through the wall."

From "The Wonderful World of Quantum Physics,"
A. Fields, UNW

• • •

Abey had stopped banging on the elevator button and was trying to pry the elevator doors apart. I went out the side door and up to Hollywood Boulevard. David's restaurant was near Hollywood and Vine. I turned the other direction, toward Grauman's Chinese, and ducked into the first restaurant I saw.

"I'm Stephanie," the waitress said. "How many are there in your party?"

There was no one remotely in my vicinity. "Are you an actress-slash-model?" I asked her.

"Yes," she said. "I'm working here part-time to pay for my holistic hairstyling lessons."

"There's one of me," I said, holding up my forefinger to make it perfectly clear. "I want a table away from the window."

She led me to a table in front of the window, handed me a menu the size of the macrocosm, and put another one down across from me. "Our breakfast specials today are papaya stuffed with salmonberries and nasturtium/radicchio salad with a balsamic vinaigrette. I'll take your order when your other party arrives."

I stood the extra menu up so it hid me from the window, opened the other one, and read the breakfast entrees. They all seemed to have cilantro or lemongrass in their names. I wondered if "radicchio" could possibly be Californian for "donut."

"Hi," David said, grabbing the standing-up menu and sitting down. "The sea-urchin pâté looks good."

I was actually glad to see him. "How did you get here?" I asked.

"Tunneling," he said. "What exactly is extra-virgin olive oil?"

"I wanted a donut," I said pitifully.

He took my menu away from me, laid it on the table, and stood up. "There's a great place next door that's got the donut Clark Gable taught Claudette Colbert how to dunk in *It Happened One Night.*"

The great place was probably out in Long Beach someplace, but I was too weak with hunger to resist him. I stood up. Stephanie hurried over.

"Will there be anything else?" she asked.

"We're leaving," David said.

"Okay, then," she said, tearing a check off her pad and slapping it down on the table. "I hope you enjoyed your breakfast."

Finding such a paradigm is difficult, if not impossible. Due to Planck's constant the world we see is largely dominated by Newtonian mechanics. Particles are particles, waves are waves, and objects do not suddenly vanish through walls and reappear on the other side. It is only on the subatomic level that quantum effects dominate.

Excerpt from Dr. Gedanken's keynote address

The restaurant was next door to Grauman's Chinese, which made me a little nervous, but it had eggs and bacon and toast and orange juice and coffee. And donuts.

"I thought you were having breakfast with Dr. Thibodeaux and Dr. Hotard," I said, dunking one in my coffee. "What happened to them?"

"They went to Forest Lawn. Dr. Hotard wanted to see the church where Ronald Reagan got married."

"He got married at Forest Lawn?"

He took a bite of my donut. "In the Wee Kirk of the Heather. Did you know Forest Lawn's got the World's Largest Oil Painting Incorporating a Religious Theme?"

"So why didn't you go with them?"

"And miss the movie?" He grabbed both my hands

across the table. "There's a matinee at two o'clock. Come with me."

I could feel things starting to collapse. "I have to get back," I said, trying to disentangle my hands. "There's a panel on the EPR paradox at two o'clock."

"There's another showing at five. And one at eight."

"Dr. Gedanken's giving the keynote address at eight."

"You know what the problem is?" he said, still holding on to my hands. "The problem is, it isn't really Grauman's Chinese Theatre, it's Mann's, so Sid isn't even around to ask. Like, why do some pairs like Joanne Woodward and Paul Newman share the same square and other pairs don't? Like Ginger Rogers and Fred Astaire?"

"You know what the problem is?" I said, wrenching my hands free. "The problem is you don't take anything seriously. This is a conference, but you don't care anything about the programming or hearing Dr. Gedanken speak or trying to understand quantum theory!" I fumbled in my purse for some money for the check.

"I thought that was what we were talking about," David said, sounding surprised. "The problem is, where do these lion statues that guard the door fit in? And what about all those empty spaces?"

Friday, 2–3 P.M. *Panel Discussion on the EPR Paradox.* I. Takumi, moderator, R. Iverson, L. S. Ping. A discussion of the latest research on singlet-state correlations, including nonlocal influences, the Calcutta proposal, and passion. Keystone Kops Room.

I went up to my room as soon as I got back to the Rialto to see if Darlene was there yet. She wasn't, and when I tried to call the desk, the phone wouldn't work. I went back down to the registration desk. There was no one there. I waited fifteen minutes and then went into the panel on the EPR paradox.

"The Einstein-Podolsky-Rosen paradox cannot be reconciled with quantum theory," Dr. Takumi was saying. "I don't care what the experiments seem to indicate. Two electrons at opposite ends of the universe can't affect each other simultaneously without destroying the entire theory of the space-time continuum."

She was right. Even if it was possible to find a model of quantum theory, what about the EPR paradox? If an experimenter measured one of a pair of electrons that had originally collided, it changed the cross-correlation of the other instantaneously, even if the electrons were light-years apart. It was as if they were eternally linked by that one collision, sharing the same square forever, even if they were on opposite sides of the universe.

"If the electrons *communicated* instantaneously, I'd agree with you," Dr. Iverson said, "but they don't, they simply influence each other. Dr. Shimony defined this influence in his paper on passion, and my experiment clearly—"

I thought of David leaning over me between the best pictures of 1944 and 1945, saying, "I think we know as much about quantum theory as we do about May Robson from her footprints."

"You can't explain it away by inventing new terms," Dr. Takumi said.

"I completely disagree," Dr. Ping said. "Passion at a distance is not just an invented term. It's a demonstrated phenomenon."

It certainly is, I thought, thinking about David taking the macrocosmic menu out of the window and saying, "The sea-urchin pâté looks good." It didn't matter where the electron went after the collision. Even if it went in the opposite direction from Hollywood and Vine, even if it stood a menu in the window to hide it, the other electron would still come and rescue it from the radicchio and buy it a donut.

"A demonstrated phenomenon!" Dr. Takumi said. "Ha!" She banged her moderator's gavel for emphasis.

"Are you saying passion doesn't exist?" Dr. Ping said, getting very red in the face.

"I'm saying one measly experiment is hardly a demonstrated phenomenon."

"One measly experiment! I spent five years on this project!" Dr. Iverson said, shaking his fist at her. "I'll show you passion at a distance!"

"Try it, and I'll adjust your fractal-basin boundaries!" Dr. Takumi said, and hit him over the head with the gavel.

Yet finding a paradigm is not impossible. Newtonian physics is not a machine. It simply shares some of the attributes of a machine. We must find a model somewhere in the visible world that shares the often bizarre attributes of quantum physics. Such a model, unlikely as it sounds, surely exists somewhere, and it is up to us to find it.

Excerpt from Dr. Gedanken's keynote address

I went up to my room before the police came. Darlene still wasn't there, and the phone and air-conditioning still weren't working. I was really beginning to get worried. I walked up to Grauman's Chinese to find David, but he wasn't there. Dr. Whedbee and Dr. Sleeth were behind the Academy Award winners folding screen.

"You haven't seen David, have you?" I asked.

Dr. Whedbee removed his hand from Norma Shearer's cheek.

"He left," Dr. Sleeth said, disentangling herself from the Best Movie of 1929–30.

"He said he was going out to Forest Lawn," Dr. Whedbee said, trying to smooth down his bushy white hair.

"Have you seen Dr. Mendoza? She was supposed to get in this morning."

They hadn't seen her, and neither had Drs. Hotard and Thibodeaux, who stopped me in the lobby and showed me a postcard of Aimee Semple McPherson's tomb. Tiffany had gone off duty. Natalie couldn't find my reservation. I went back up to the room to wait, thinking Darlene might call.

The air conditioning still wasn't fixed. I fanned myself with a Hollywood brochure and then opened it up and read it. There was a map of the courtyard of Grauman's Chinese on the back cover. Deborah Kerr and Yul Brynner didn't have a square together either, and Katharine Hepburn and Spencer Tracy weren't even on the map. She made him waffles in *Woman of the Year,* and they hadn't even given them a square. I wondered if Tiffany the model-slash-actress had been in charge of assigning the cement. I could see her looking blankly at Spencer Tracy and saying, "I don't show a reservation for you."

What exactly was a model-slash-actress? Did it mean she was a model *or* an actress or a model *and* an actress? She certainly wasn't a hotel clerk. Maybe electrons were the Tiffanys of the microcosm, and that explained their wave-slash-particle duality. Maybe they weren't really electrons at all. Maybe they were just working part-time at being electrons to pay for their singlet-state lessons.

Darlene still hadn't called by seven o'clock. I stopped fanning myself and tried to open a window. It wouldn't budge. The problem was, nobody knew anything about quantum theory. All we had to go on were a few colliding electrons that nobody could see and that couldn't be measured properly because of the Heisenberg uncertainty principle. And there was chaos to consider, and entropy, and all those empty spaces. We didn't even know who May Robson was.

At seven-thirty the phone rang. It was Darlene.

"What happened?" I said. "Where are you?"

"At the Beverly Wilshire."

"In Beverly Hills?"

"Yes. It's a long story. When I got to the Rialto, the hotel clerk, I think her name was Tiffany, told me you weren't there. She said they were booked solid with some science thing and had had to send the overflow to other hotels. She said you were at the Beverly Wilshire in room ten-twenty-seven. How's David?"

"Impossible," I said. "He's spent the whole conference looking at Deanna Durbin's footprints at Grauman's Chinese Theatre and trying to talk me into going to the movies."

"And are you going?"

"I can't. Dr. Gedanken's giving the keynote address in half an hour."

"He is?" Darlene said, sounding surprised. "Just a minute." There was a silence, and then she came back on and said, "I think you should go to the movies. David's one of the last two charming men in the universe."

"But he doesn't take quantum theory seriously. Dr. Gedanken is hiring a research team to design a paradigm, and David keeps talking about the beacon on top of the Capitol Records building."

"You know, he may be onto something there. I mean, seriousness was all right for Newtonian physics, but maybe quantum theory needs a different approach. Sid says—"

"Sid?"

"This guy who's taking me to the movies tonight. It's a long story. Tiffany gave me the wrong room number, and I walked in on this guy in his underwear. He's a quantum physicist. He was supposed to be staying at the Rialto, but Tiffany couldn't find his reservation."

The major implication of wave/particle duality is that an electron has no precise location. It exists in a su-

perposition of probable locations. Only when the experimenter observes the electron does it "collapse" into a location.

The Wonderful World of Quantum Physics,
A. Fields, UNW

Forest Lawn closed at five o'clock. I looked it up in the Hollywood brochure after Darlene hung up. There was no telling where he might have gone: the Brown Derby or the La Brea Tar Pits or some great place near Hollywood and Vine that had the alfalfa sprouts John Hurt ate right before his chest exploded in *Alien*.

At least I knew where Dr. Gedanken was. I changed my clothes and got into the elevator, thinking about wave/particle duality and fractals and high-entropy states and delayed-choice experiments. The problem was, where could you find a paradigm that would make it possible to visualize quantum theory when you had to include Josephson junctions and passion and all those empty spaces? It wasn't possible. You had to have more to work with than a few footprints and the impression of Betty Grable's leg.

The elevator door opened, and Abey Fields pounced on me. "I've been looking all over for you," he said. "You haven't seen Dr. Gedanken, have you?"

"Isn't he in the ballroom?"

"No," he said. "He's already fifteen minutes late, and nobody's seen him. You have to sign this," he said, shoving a clipboard at me.

"What is it?"

"It's a petition." He grabbed it back from me. " 'We the undersigned demand that annual meetings of the International Congress of Quantum Physicists henceforth be held in appropriate locations.' Like Racine," he added, shoving the clipboard at me again. "*Unlike* Hollywood."

Hollywood.

"Are you aware it took the average ICQP delegate two hours and thirty-six minutes to check in? They even sent some of the delegates to a hotel in Glendale."

"And Beverly Hills," I said absently. Hollywood. Bra museums and the Marx Brothers and gangs that would kill you if you wore red or blue and Tiffany/Stephanie and the World's Largest Oil Painting Incorporating a Religious Theme.

"Beverly Hills," Abey muttered, pulling an automatic pencil out of his pocket protector and writing a note to himself. "I'm presenting the petition during Dr. Gedanken's speech. Well, go on, sign it," he said, handing me the pencil. "Unless you want the annual meeting to be here at the Rialto next year."

I handed the clipboard back to him. "I think from now on the annual meeting might be here every year," I said, and took off running for Grauman's Chinese.

When we have the paradigm, one that embraces both the logical and the nonsensical aspects of quantum theory, we will be able to look past the colliding electrons and the mathematics and see the microcosm in all its astonishing beauty.

Excerpt from Dr. Gedanken's keynote address

"I want a ticket to *Benji IX*," I told the girl at the box office. Her name tag said, "Welcome to Hollywood. My name is Kimberly."

"Which theater?" she said.

"Grauman's Chinese," I said, thinking, This is no time for a high-entropy state.

"Which theater?"

I looked up at the marquee. *Benji IX* was showing in all three theaters, the huge main theater and the two smaller ones on either side. "They're doing audience-reaction surveys," Kimberly said. "Each theater has a different ending."

"Which one's in the main theater?"

"I don't know. I just work here part-time to pay for my organic breathing lessons."

"Do you have any dice?" I asked, and then realized I was going about this all wrong. This was quantum theory, not Newtonian. It didn't matter which theater I chose or which seat I sat down in. This was a delayed-choice experiment, and David was already in flight.

"The one with the happy ending," I said.

"Center theater," she said.

I walked past the stone lions and into the lobby. Rhonda Fleming and some Chinese wax figures were sitting inside a glass case next to the door to the restrooms. There was a huge painted screen behind the concessions stand. I bought a box of Raisinets, a tub of popcorn, and a box of jujubes and went inside the theater.

It was bigger than I had imagined. Rows and rows of empty red chairs curved between the huge pillars and up to the red curtains where the screen must be. The walls were covered with intricate drawings. I stood there, holding my jujubes and Raisinets and popcorn, staring at the chandelier overhead. It was an elaborate gold sunburst surrounded by silver dragons. I had never imagined it was anything like this.

The lights went down, and the red curtains opened, revealing an inner curtain like a veil across the screen. I went down the dark aisle and sat in one of the seats. "Hi," I said, and handed the Raisinets to David.

"Where have you been?" he said. "The movie's about to start."

"I know," I said. I leaned across him and handed Darlene her popcorn and Dr. Gedanken his jujubes. "I was working on the paradigm for quantum theory."

"And?" Dr. Gedanken said, opening jujubes.

"And you're both wrong," I said. "It isn't Grauman's Chinese. It isn't movies either, Dr. Gedanken."

"Sid," Dr. Gedanken said. "If we're all going to be on the same research team, I think we should use first names."

"If it isn't Grauman's Chinese or the movies, what is it?" Darlene asked, eating popcorn.

"It's Hollywood."

"Hollywood," Dr. Gedanken said thoughtfully.

"Hollywood," I said. "Stars in the sidewalk and buildings that look like stacks of records and hats, and radicchio and audience surveys and bra museums. And the movies. And Grauman's Chinese."

"And the Rialto," David said.

"Especially the Rialto."

"And the ICQP," Dr. Gedanken said.

I thought about Dr. Lvov's black and gray slides and the disappearing chaos seminar and Dr. Whedbee writing "meaning" or possibly "information" on the overhead projector. "And the ICQP," I said.

"Did Dr. Takumi really hit Dr. Iverson over the head with a gavel?" Darlene asked.

"Shh," David said. "I think the movie's starting." He took hold of my hand. Darlene settled back with her popcorn, and Dr. Gedanken put his feet up on the chair in front of him. The inner curtain opened, and the screen lit up.

About the Author

CONNIE WILLIS has received five Nebula Awards and two Hugo Awards for her short fiction, and the John W. Campbell Award for her first novel, *Lincoln's Dreams*. Her first short-story collection, *Fire Watch*, was a *New York Times* Notable Book, and her latest novel, *Doomsday Book*, just won the Nebula Award. Ms. Willis lives in Greeley, Colorado, with her family.